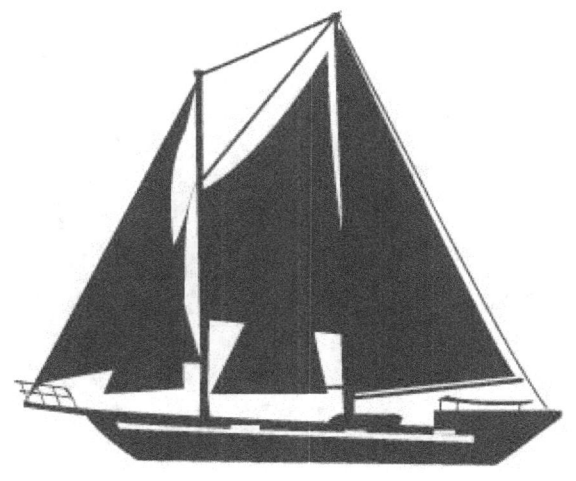

Other titles by this author
Bequia Mystery Series
Dead Reckoning
Deadeye
Deadlight

Science Fiction
Geborah's Seed

Map of the Eastern Caribbean and The Grenadines

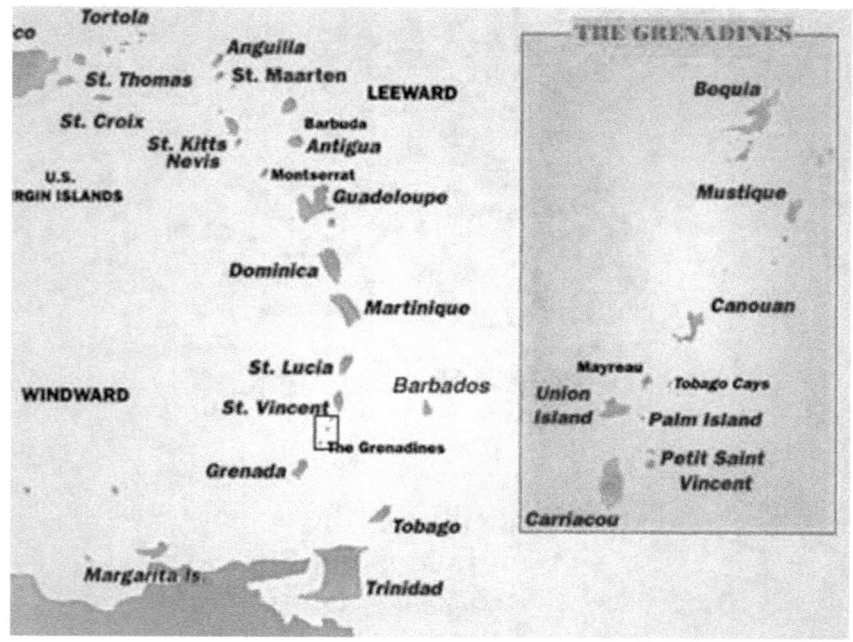

Bequia Map

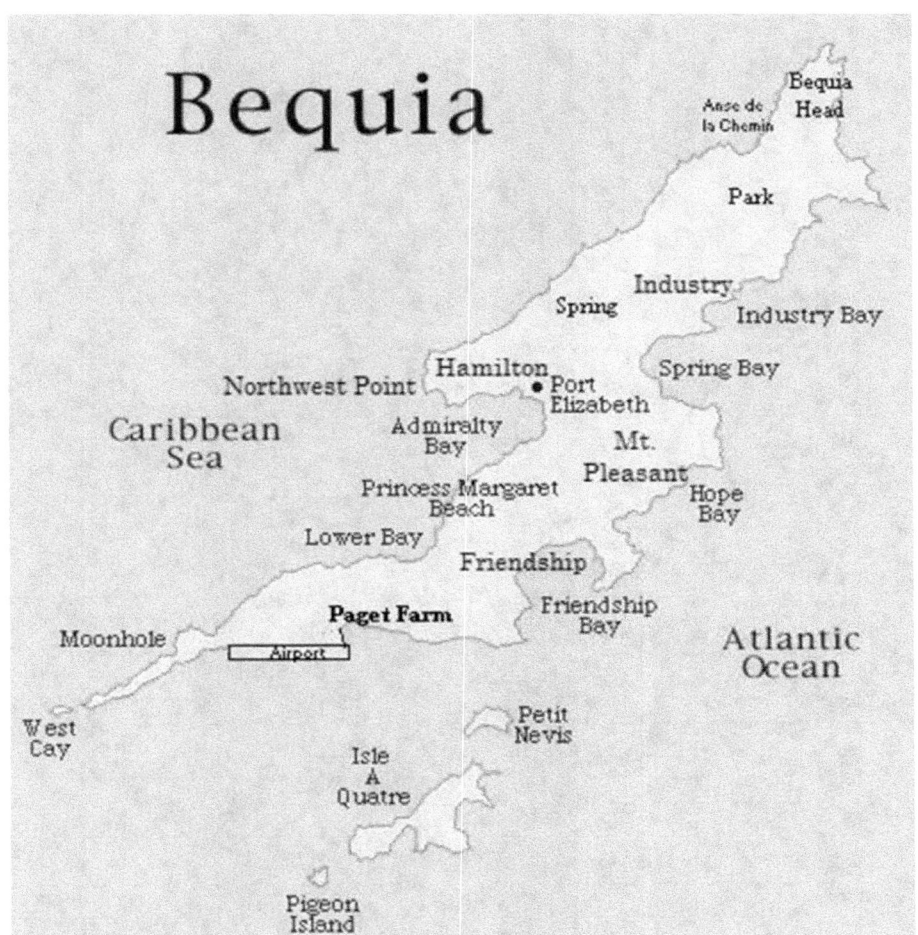

St. Vincent Map

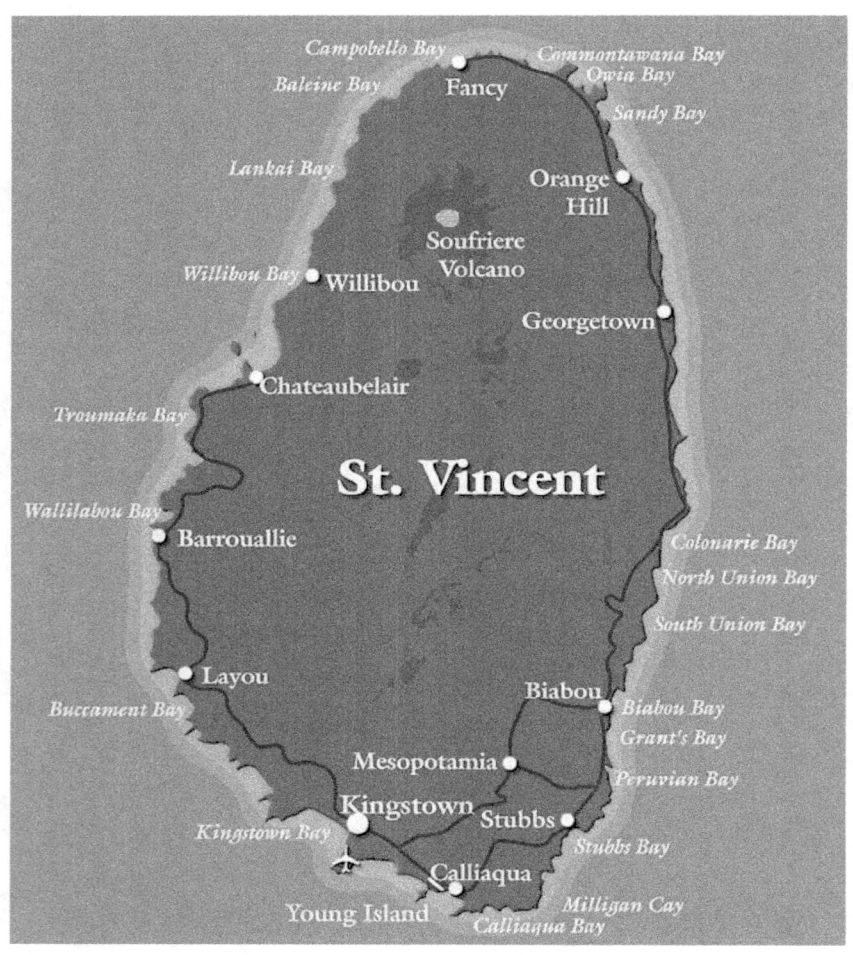

Deadlight

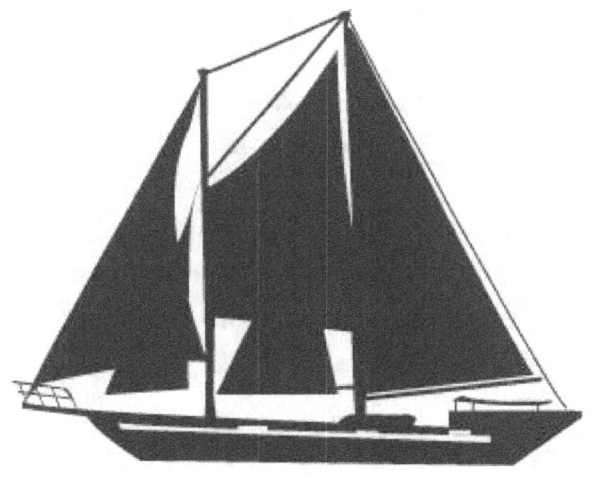

A Bequia Mystery

Michael W Smart

Copyright © 2012 by Michael W. Smart
First published 2014
Available in print ISBN: 978-0-9914008-6-7
Availabe in ebook ISBN: 978-0-9914008-7-4

Cover Illustration Copyright © 2013 by Michael Smart
Cover design by: Denise Kim Wy
http://www.coveratelier.com)
Editing by: Amanda Hough, Progressivedits
http://www.progressivedits.com
Author photograph by: Camilla Sjodin
(www.sjodinphotography.com)

Published by Michael W Smart at CreateSpace

This one is for mom, known affectionately as Smo, and to her many friends as 'Cissy'.

Deadlight:
A strong metal shutter or plate fitted over a ship's porthole or cabin window in stormy weather or a heavy glass window set in the deck or hull of a ship.

CHAPTER 1

I awoke to the cackling cries of roosters my mind clear and refreshed, The phantom ache of my wounds no longer a waking presence.

The fresh fruity scent of a brand new day greeted my short trudge up the steep road from Friendship Bay. The sky held the promise of a bright cloudless day, the last lingering lentils of puffy white fading, as the cerulean blue sky paled beneath the rising sun.

The day also promised another mind-numbing medley of meetings. The meetings my tedious daily routine since the recent scandals and their aftermath. I'd soon be immersed in the dread I'd fallen asleep to. No longer a nebulous worry, it'd coalesced into solid form, whole and substantial. And as dangerous as a cobra poised to strike.

And I'd soon be unemployed. My second retirement. The first had occurred twelve years earlier, prior to relocating to the Grenadines from Florida. Unlike the first retirement, this one promised to be acrimonious, accompanied by a foreboding sense of a job left unfinished.

I feared for the future of the Royal St. Vincent and the Grenadines Police Force. Questioned if I'd achieved any real impact, contributed to a lasting difference. And beyond that, I feared for the future of these islands I now called home.

St. Vincent and the Grenadines remained under siege, though the public remained unaware of it. We'd barely dodged the last bullet, aimed at a takeover and control of the Island Nation by a foreign entity. But we hadn't escaped unscathed.

The Attorney General had been forced to resign, and soon after Prime Minister DeFretas followed, the only viable option to prevent a complete collapse of the government. Arturo Bacchus, number two in the party leadership, had assumed the office of Prime Minister until an early general election could be called. The party held a scant one-seat majority in parliament, and the opposition appeared poised to win a landslide at the polls. I'd be out of a job sooner than I'd expected.

The threat, although exposed, remained. A foreign Bogeyman, Superintendent Jolene Johanssen's description for the nameless, faceless enemy, was still out there. Still possessing designs on St. Vincent and the Grenadines. We'd uncovered his operation, and his possible motive, given St. Vincent's strategic geographic location. But not who.

At the main road I flagged a dollar van heading into Port Elizabeth. Drowsy smiles and "Mawnin Commisshunah" greeted me as I hopped into the back, one buttock on the edge of the wood seat. The van overloaded as usual to meet the first early morning ferry to Kingstown. The van's passengers packed into the back, each hairpin turn squeezing the crush of bodies together.

Normally I'd have police transport, including a Coast Guard Cutter for the trip across to St. Vincent. Normally I returned home only on weekends, living at my rental residence in Kingstown during the week to avoid a daily commute. But sometimes I needed to get away. Needed the solace of my own space, the respite of personal time; the reason I'd returned home to Bequia the night before.

The van unloaded its passengers on the road facing the crowded, bustling wharf. Passengers and vehicles swarmed around a red and white ferry tied alongside, like bees around a hive. Cars, vans, small trucks, and motor bikes, mounted its stern ramp lowered onto the dock.

Gazing out across the tranquil harbor, brightening as the sun peeked above Bequia's highland, I glimpsed the Coast Guard Vessel "Chatham Bay," a twenty-four foot fiberglass Boston Whaler normally based on St. Vincent, accompanied by the sixteen-foot skiff, SVG 12, based in Bequia. They headed toward the dry dock at the Hamilton Marina, the rigid bottom inflatable Whaler towing a small fishing boat.

Returning to the van, I asked the driver to drop me in Hamilton instead. The road through the harbor passed the spot where I'd been found, shot and dying, a little over a year before. I'd crawled through the littered yard between the marina and supermarket to get to the road, my lifeblood flowing from three bullet wounds. An involuntary constriction squeezed my chest, and my pulse quickened, as the van drove past the spot.

A year and a half later, I still have no memory of the events immediately following being shot. Or how I'd made it to the road.

At the Hamilton Marina dock, I encountered an unexpected surprise. Superintendent Jolene Johanssen and two CID detectives disembarked from the Boston Whaler. Disheveled and preoccupied, she nevertheless projected a striking presence among the men on the dock. Tall, gorgeous in a natural, earthy manner, brilliant and determined, she evoked an intense familial pride. The kind I felt for my own daughter. In many ways I treated her like a daughter.

"An early morning I see," I said in greeting.

"Morning Chief." She and her contingent of police and Coast Guard personnel stamped to attention and saluted, Jolene's less formal than her colleagues.

"As you were," I said to the gathered group. "What's this?" My question directed at her.

"Some fishermen spotted that fishing boat washed up on Petit Nevis. They went to check it out and found a body on board. Dead at least two days. I summoned the Coast Guard and Detectives Cato and DeSilva. We processed the scene. I had the Coast Guard tow the boat in for further processing and called Calliaqua for a cutter to transport the body"

"Any identification?"

"No ID on him," she said. "Decomp is pronounced, and sea birds have been at the remains. Not a pretty sight Chief. Just this in his pocket."

She held up a clear plastic evidence bag containing a few coins, some paper currency, and an odd shaped bronze medallion the size of a silver dollar.

The breath rushed from my body, like I'd been punched in the gut. My senses reeled. My knees turned weak and spongy. A vertiginous wooziness clouded my vision.

"Chief. You OK?" Jolene gripped my arm. Her voice reached me as though from a great distance. My eyes refocused on her face.

"You look like you've just seen a ghost or something."

"I need to see the body," I said.

Concern filled the hazel eyes staring back at me, and etched delicate lines across her mocha toned brow. The arm she'd placed around mine attempted to hold me back, or maybe hold me up. I moved toward the covered bundle lying in the Boston Whaler.

Her eyes, and the eyes of the detail, followed my movements as I knelt next to the body. I turned back a corner of the canvas tarp covering it. I stared down at the bloated, unrecognizable face. I lifted a side of the tarp, revealing the corpse's right arm and hand.

"Will someone please hand me a pair of gloves."

I didn't see who the outstretched hand holding the blue nitrite gloves belonged to. My gaze fixed on the corpse before me. I lifted the corpse's right hand. A ring embedded in the blackened swollen flesh of his fourth finger bore the same design as the medallion. The dizzying sensation returned, not due to the sight of the lifeless, decomposing body. I'd seen many, too many, and worse, in a long law enforcement career. But the body lying beneath the tarp had been one of my own.

I'd lost colleagues before too. Felled in the line of duty. A hard thing to witness. A terrible burden to bear. Especially when your decisions and orders had placed them in harm's way.

I needed a plausible excuse for my initial reaction. I needed to resume a professional, detached demeanor. No other person knew of this constable's existence. I needed it to remain so for a little while longer.

On the dock I drew Jolene aside. Her earlier concern dissipating, replaced by a knowing curiosity. She knew me too well, and possessed a keen perceptiveness. Another of her remarkable traits.

"I want you in charge of this case," I said. The sharp edge in my voice only increased her curiosity.

"Inform the Coast Guard vessel coming for the body I'll ride over with them. But I'll be back home tonight. Let's meet at my place around eight. I'll want as much on this case as you can put together by then. So you need to get a move on."

I perceived the questions forming, many of them, but turned away before she had a chance to voice them. Not the time or place.

"Oh," I said turning back to face her. "Bring Gage."

CHAPTER 2

I waited in the marina dining room for the Coast Guard Cutter to arrive, nursing a cup of steaming coffee, pondering my own litany of questions. I'd wait for Jolene's report before speculating about the constable's death. But two things I needed to do immediately.

I used a pay phone at the marina for the first. I placed a call to the Vincentian newspaper, requesting a change to a classified ad I ran periodically in the Business Opportunities section. The ad to appear in the following day's edition.

Next, I used my cell phone to call the Pathology Department at Milton Cato Hospital in Kingstown. When Doctor Eileen Gash, a Peace Corps pathologist, answered the call, I informed her of the body heading her way.

"Highest priority Doc. Any resources you need," I told her. "I need answers on this one ASAP. And Doc, for now your findings are for Superintendent Johanssen's and my eyes and ears only. If that's a problem tell me now."

"No problem Commissioner," she said without hesitation.

"Thanks doc. You'll probably be hearing from Jolene soon."

The body had been transferred to a zippered black body bag and placed aboard the forty-foot patrol boat CGV Hairoun. I waited until they were ready to cast off before boarding. Jolene had waited on the dock to see me off. The stern expression on my face discouraged her questions.

"You have work to do Superintendent," I said, controlling a pang of guilt at my abrupt dismissal and departure.

A stony silence accompanied the trip from Bequia. Usually I'd discuss coast guard matters with the officers and crew. Informal, up close and personal. Not this trip. A morgue van met the cutter at the Kingstown wharf. I waited and observed the body's transfer from cutter to van before striding purposefully toward the first waiting taxi.

"Mawnin' Commisshunah," the driver greeted me. "Drap you at de stachun?"

"Not just yet. Need to make a stop at SVG Bank first."

The driver settled into his seat, started the car and dropped the steering column mounted gearshift into first. We departed the crowded and bustling wharf, driving along Bay Street. The street equally congested as a crush of pedestrians and vehicles headed to and from the wharfs and the Port Customs building.

Traffic crawled, amid a chorus of blaring horns. The driver jockeyed back and forth, occupying any empty space enabling him to move a few yards farther along.

"So what you t'ink goin' happen Commisshunah. I mean all dese investigashuns and t'ing?" Curious eyes inspected mine in his rearview mirror while he spoke.

I met his gaze in the mirror. "Honestly I don't know. Just have to see what comes out and where things lead. And that's all I can say about it."

I didn't need a reminder of the political chaos enveloping the country. Nor add to the rampant gossip and speculation. My days immersed in it. And now, I had a more immediate problem requiring my attention and focus.

"Well sum peeple need go a prison fe dese crimes," he remarked.

"As soon as you can let's get off this street," I said.

He squeezed his vehicle into a tight space to make a right turn onto South River Road. Traffic moved easier. A left onto Halifax Street and traffic flowed even easier on the broad main thoroughfare. We crossed Hillsboro, travelled along the main market for another block before making a left onto Bedford Street. The Bank of St. Vincent and the Grenadines appeared on the right, opposite the market.

I paid the fare, thanked the driver, and exited the taxi, no longer needing it. A half block walk to Bay Street, another block along Bay Street to Hillsboro, and I'd be at the Kingstown Central Police Station.

I walked past the bank to a small hole-in-the-wall eatery farther up the block. I found what I needed. A stack of Vincentian newspapers. I picked up a copy and retraced my steps to the bank.

The St. Vincent and Grenadine Bank was a new entity, created from the remnants of the National Bank of St. Vincent and the Grenadines. The predecessor bank had been the target of numerous frauds perpetrated by the unknown group attempting to gain control of St.Vincent and the Grenadines. It'd also been on the verge of collapse, due to the government using it as a personal piggy bank and almost defaulting on extensive loans owed to the bank.

The bank had been acquired by Eastern Caribbean Financial, a financial services group headquartered in Saint Lucia. After the revelations uncovering the frauds, all prospective buyers had been extensively vetted by the Eastern Caribbean Central Bank, which regulates all domestic commercial banks in St. Vincent and the Grenadines. And by the FBI, and Scotland Yard's Special Branch, sniffing for the slightest scent of a connection to the companies and persons who'd perpetrated the frauds. The scandal had contributed to the downfall of St. Vincent's Attorney General, and Prime Minister.

I entered the bank, the newspaper tucked under my left arm. I strode across the tiled floor toward the teller counter against the far wall, glancing at desks on my left occupied by the bank's management staff. A petite woman, straightened shoulder length black hair, wearing a navy blue skirt suit, briefly caught my eye. I joined the end of the line to wait my turn for a teller. At the window, I completed a funds transfer from a U.S. bank to my account at the SVG Bank. Precisely two thousand six hundred and twelve U.S. dollars.

I'd completed my second immediate task, necessitated by my constable's death.

CHAPTER 3

It'd been my standard practice since the scandals broke to meet first thing each morning with Deputy Commissioner Huggins. Followed by a meeting with Assistant Superintendent Taylor, head of the Public Information and Complaints Department. Occasionally these meetings had to be pushed back when other matters required my immediate attention. Like this dreadful morning. I'd called my office during the crossing from Bequia to have my secretary push back the meetings.

I rushed into the outer office an hour and a half behind schedule. I stopped at Cecilia's desk.

"See if the Deputy Commissioner and AS Taylor is available Cissy. Let them know I'm here."

No-nonsense perceptive eyes examined me. Maternal instincts in overdrive.

"You should look rested from going home last night. Instead you look more haggard than ever," She said with motherly authority.

No use arguing, prevaricating, or pretending. Sixty-two years old, widowed for almost twenty years, she'd never remarried, and raised two sons on her own. And she read me as well as Jolene.

I escaped into my office, physically, mentally, emotionally drained. The day only just winding up and far from over. I eased into the leather recliner behind my desk. I needed to compose my thoughts, and myself. If Jolene and Cecilia noticed it so clearly, so might others. I doubted the men I'd see all day would. Jolene and Cecilia on the other hand had grown especially attuned to my moods.

I bore the weight of my fifty-nine years, and the approaching big six o milestone, and the crushing burden of my office. Especially given the threat we faced. It was still out there. Still headed our way. I spent each waking hour waiting for the other shoe to drop.

My intercom buzzed. "The Deputy Commissioner," Cecilia announced.

"Send him in," I said.

Master of her domain, she ushered him in. No one gained access to me without first passing her. An impossible task if you landed on her wrong side. Or if she thought I needed protecting. Cecelia closed the door behind Deputy Commissioner Huggins after showing him in.

He wore regulation day uniform, grey slacks and jacket with shoulder epaulets and collar insignia. White shirt and black tie. He carried his uniform cap under his left arm U.S. Navy style. His silver-tipped swagger stick tucked under his right arm. Despite my time in the job, I still hadn't grown accustomed to the swagger stick part of the uniform. Didn't for the life of me understand why the tradition persisted.

Tall, slim build, he wore a no-nonsense expression on a clean shaved dark brown face. Lively and intelligent eyes, behind thick, black framed glasses, examined me as he waited for me to speak first.

"Take a seat Reggie," I said, motioning toward a sitting area on the far side of the office. Comfortable stuffed armchairs surrounded a low mahogany topped coffee table. Shaded table lamps sat on two side tables next to the closest and farthest armchairs. He laid his uniform cap and stick on the polished mahogany surface. Waited for me to sit before sitting himself.

"Ev'ryting' okay Commisshunah? You seem a likkle worse for weah.

God. Not you too.

"What do we have today Reggie?" I said instead.

"Fortunately nuttin' new to add fuel to de situashun," he said. Before the scandals had broken, I'd briefed Huggins on the firestorm headed our way. Including the particulars surrounding the murders of Arnold Greene, aka Charles Mansfield, and Jackson Taylor. Huggins among a few in a tight circle who were aware of the full extent of the conspiracy. I'd tasked him with monitoring the ensuing fallout, keeping a close watch on political groups and activities, which might exacerbate the situation or pose a threat to public safety.

"De various inquiries are proceedin'," he said, pushing his glasses back from where they'd slipped on the flat bridge of his nose. "De Commishun of inquiry into de National Bank, and de Commishun of inquiry into Clair Hall and Union Island. No unusual repohts regardin' de Commisshunahs or witnesses. And so far, no disturbances at de hearings. De streets are relatively quiet. People puttin' dey minds to Vincy Mas," he said, referring to the annual Carnival celebrations scheduled to commence in three weeks.

Carnival, a huge deal on St. Vincent and the Grenadines. The festivities included street parties and costume street parades. Calypso, Soca, and steel pan performances and competitions. A Miss SVG and Miss Carnival beauty pageants. Two weeks of Mardi gras style partying, culminating in nationwide street parties on J'Ouvert morning, 'Jewveh' as pronounced in the local vernacular. A huge strain on my force's resources.

"How're manpower and scheduling preparations going?"

"Very good Sir," he said. "As usual we expect some absenteeism since many members of de force also take part in costume bands and competitions. But we hope to compensate for dat."

"Good Reggie. And like you say the distraction is a big help right now with the elections only two months after Carnival."

"Yes Commisshunah. But we still seein' an increase in serious offenses. Especially firearm related assaults and violence. Guess it could be worse though. Vincy Mas will divert some of de public's anger and upset. Right now is mostly de politicians still carrying on at de rallies, and letters and commentary in de newspapers and de radio. One side chargin' government cover up and callin' for more inquiries. De other side claimin' dey de ones cleanin' up de mess. And we gettin' an increase in complaints against police constables. Another two taken to court on criminal offenses yesterday. One for indecent language and assault. De other for indecent language and woundin' wid a knife. AS Taylor can give you details on dose."

"What about Mitchell and his cronies?" I asked, referring to the threat on my flank from Superintendent of Police Nigel Mitchell. The current crisis and anticipated change of governing party provided a perfect opportunity for his mischief, aimed at placing himself in the top job following my departure.

"Stayin' undah de radar, mekin' noise quietly, if you know what I mean. He tryin' to tie you to Prime Minister DeFretas and de scandals. He preachin' de same old story, de force need to forget all dis mamby-pamby modernization and get back to pilin' on, his favorite phrase."

I'd been pondering how to protect that flank, under the radar. Nothing overt. Protecting myself not important. The priority rather, protecting the force, and the gains we'd made over the past eight years. For now, I'd continue to maintain a close watch on him.

"Thank you Nigel. Anything else?"

"De Guide is complete," Huggins said, saving the best for last. The news lifted my spirits. At least a little. My reaction produced a satisfied smile across his dark chocolate face.

"When can I see a copy," I asked, returning his smile.

"It at de printer now. You'll have a copy by tomorrow mornin'."

We'd been working on the project almost a year. The Guide, the preferred term in Vincentian parlance, was in fact a comprehensive manual for the Royal St. Vincent and the Grenadines Police Force. The first of its kind in the history of the force. The product of consultations among other Eastern Caribbean Police Forces, Scotland Yard, the U.S., and our regional security partners.

The manual covered best practices, procedures, and laws. It contained sections on recruitment and training, community policing, investigative techniques and practices, particularly concerning major crimes, organized crime, and narco trafficking. It outlined how to best present cases for prosecution, including evidence handling, and preliminary inquiry and trial testimony. It incorporated recent changes to St. Vincent's criminal code. And it included sections on citizens' rights, complaints against police, effective media relations, and public information and transparency.

My legacy.

"Best news I've had all day Reggie. Thanks. I guess that's all for now," I said, rather than the formal 'dismissed'.

He exited the office, immediately replaced by Assistant Superintendent Taylor who'd been waiting in the outer office.

No respite. But my mood had brightened. I motioned Taylor to the chair Huggins had vacated.

"Before we get started Vince, DC Huggins just told me the Guide is complete and at the printers. You need to come up with a presentation strategy. Press conference, whatever."

"I'll get on it Sir," he said, maintaining his habit of speaking non-patois English in my presence.

"Just remember whatever you come up with must maintain our neutrality. The timing sucks, and in the current atmosphere we can't afford to appear partisan, as if we're bolstering one party against the other. We can't allow a document as significant as this, or the force for that matter, to become a political football."

"Understood sir."

"Good. Now, anything waiting to blindside me when I meet the usual lineup of ministers today?"

"Nothing sir," he said smiling.

"What about these two constables the DC mentioned?"

"A constable Roland Harris of Layou district," he said, reading from a file he carried. "Got into a verbal altercation with another constable, Daniel Peters, at a ULP meeting. Harris used indecent language in referring to Peters, and the altercation escalated to blows, in front of witnesses. Harris also caused property damage to the building. Both have been suspended from duty, and Harris was brought before the court."

"The second incident involved constable Desmond Smalls of Arnos Vale and a civilian, James Geddes, in an incident outside the Huffles Ranch night club. The constable ended up stabbing Mr. Geddes in the back with a fishing knife. Mr. Geddes is in hospital, expected to recover. Constable Smalls was relieved of duty and brought before the court on charges of assault with intent to harm, wounding, and possession of an offensive weapon."

"Christ Almighty."

"Sir, these incidents are growing in frequency. And they will continue to. People are choosing up sides."

"I know. We have to do something proactively, but I'm not sure we can stem the tide in the current atmosphere. I was just discussing with DC Huggins the hope Vincy Mas might provide a needed distraction."

"Could be sir."

"In the meantime we can't appear to show coddling or leniency to any delinquent officers."

"Understood sir."

"Thanks Vince," I said, rising from my chair. I escorted him to the door.

I stuck my head out, captured Cecilia's gaze.

"Ready for the daily circus now," I said. Her mouth curled in a mirthless smile.

Tedious, monotonous meetings occupied the remainder of my official day. Some in my office. Some at theirs. Some ministers preferred the appearance of having summoned me. Including a few opposition members of parliament, who fully expected to be in the ruling majority following the election. As the afternoon wore on, I glanced frequently at my watch. I had an important rendezvous to keep.

At six pm precisely, I entered a strand of trees between the cemetery and gardens of St. Paul's Anglican Church, four miles outside Kingstown. I moved deeper into the tree line, climbing a small hill offering a view of the Parish Hall and Rectory. She stood at the top of the rise, arms folded, waiting.

She turned as I approached. A welcoming smile parted wide full lips. The smile reflected in lively dark eyes peering from a round brown face. She hadn't changed out of the business suit I'd seen her wearing earlier that morning.

"Commisshunah," she said.

I leaned forward, planting a welcoming kiss on her smooth cheek.

"Good to see you Elana, despite the circumstances."

A frown furrowed the smooth dark skin of her brow, thin eyebrows arched upward.

"I was suhprised to see you too dis mornin'. Got de message. What circumstances?"

I knew she'd receive my message after observing the newspaper signal. As an account administrator at the bank, she routinely checked daily transactions. One of the reasons I'd infiltrated her there. The numbers in the amount I'd transferred held the message. First number the place. Last three digits the time. Old school spy craft. Something Gage might appreciate. In fact, he'd inspired my particular methods of communicating with my undercover officers.

"Remember when I first selected and recruited you, I told you there were others. But none of you would know who the others were?"

"I remembah," She said. "We wouldn't know each odder except for dis," raising her right hand. On the fourth finger she wore a ring, its design exactly like the medallion and ring found on the body. She had a medallion too, probably worn on a chain around her neck. Their undercover badges.

"This morning we found the body of one of your colleagues," I said, as gently as possible, without equivocation or circumvention of the harsh truth.

A sharp intake of breath. Her frown deepened. The nostrils of her broad nose flared.

"What happen?"

"Don't know yet. Just started looking into it. Don't know what it means yet either. But I wanted to warn all of you."

"How much concern for me?"

"Enough to take precautions and be careful. Not enough to jeopardize your cover. Not until I know more."

"Who was he....or she?"

"Can't tell you that right now. But after I finish the investigation I'll tell you and the others, and the family."

We both fell silent. Side by side, we gazed out through the trees concealing us from view.

"One other thing Elana," I said, breaking the silence. She turned to face me.

"I'm not sure how much longer we can maintain this arrangement. You're aware of everything going on. Elections in a couple of months. I have to begin making preparations to bring you guys in."

"What you t'ink will happen?"

"Not sure. Depends on who the next Commissioner is. But I intend to make sure you're all in secure positions before I leave."

"T'anks Commisshunah. What will be will be. Not even sure I'll stay in de poliss aftah you leave."

"Well, think about it. I'll need people like you to carry on the good fight."

A smile replaced her frown.

CHAPTER 4

Refreshing being home, in my own space. The cares of the world, at least of St. Vincent and the Grenadine, weighed upon me. Here they seemed bearable.

A cool evening breeze wafted through open window shutters, gently brushing my skin. The soaring sound of Miles Davis's trumpet filled the room, accompanied by the booming bass of surf crashing along the beach. The house, set back from Friendship Bay behind a wall of tall coconut trees, provided peace and solitude. Its simple, comfortable furnishings suited my taste and needs.

I loved this place. These islands. These people. Had from the first day I'd set foot on Bequia fifteen years before, deciding it'd be the place where I'd retire. Bequia had that effect on people, weaving a magical homey spell.

I sat on the stone verandah, bare feet atop the porch rail, nursing a glass of Jack Daniels on the rocks. I soaked in the warm tropical evening, contemplating a future which didn't include leaving these islands.

"Anybody home?" Jolene's voice, the greeting shouted from the back of the house, which faced the road.

"Out front," I yelled in reply.

They appeared from the side verandah together.

"You're looking much better than when I saw you this morning," Jolene said, planting a tender kiss on my cheek.

She had a happy glow about her, in her countenance, in her startling hazel eyes, now dark green in the diffused lamp light.

"I feel better," I said. "Not that my day helped any. But being home, here, seems to wash it all away".

She scrutinized me. Her eyes piercing and perceptive. Searching for truth in mine. She worried over me like a mother hen sometimes. And I over her. Since the day we'd first met, I'd taken her under my tutelage. She'd seemed so alone, and lonely. Given to brooding. Something deep within haunting her, and driving her at the same time. She'd throw herself into her work, tackling each assignment I handed her with single-minded determination. She'd had no social life, and I'd despaired of her chances for love and happiness given the meager pickings of worthy men around St. Vincent and the Grenadines. I'd often wished, though it'd mean a great loss to me, she'd consider returning to the States, or home to Canada.

Then Gage had appeared in the islands. Mysterious, enigmatic, and magnetic. My worry increased.

Dangerous, my immediate impression the first time I'd set eyes on him. Apparent in his vigilant eyes, the set of his jaw, his fluid movements. But disciplined, controlled, harnessed. Younger than me by only three years, another cause of my worry for Jolene, but more solidly built, with a broad chest, wide shoulders, and a physique molded by hard conditioning and use. Some kind of soldier for sure. The kind who fought in the shadows, I'd learn later.

I'd recognized it before Jolene did. Despite the denials, the deliberate distancing, I'd observed the subtle signs of her falling for him. I'd been concerned for her. A fatherly instinct kicked in to protect her. As I would for my own daughter. I'd watched helplessly, an enormous ache in my heart, but not wanting to interfere, as she struggled with her emotions, and a growing attachment to him amid her doubts of a sustainable relationship.

She had eventually worked through it, and they'd been together the past four years. She was happy. Happier than I'd ever seen her.

I considered Gage a friend. A close trusted friend. Yet I still knew little about him. Mostly educated guesses based on long conversations we'd had in the air, or at sea, as our friendship matured. I guessed he'd been some sort of operative in another life. Fancy way of saying spy, and assassin. A shooter in his vernacular. A rogue at some point, I surmised. Hunted, a price on his head and a target on his back. Couldn't say for sure which. Maybe all of the above, at one time or the other. But my one certainty, he was one of the good guys. And I trusted him with my life.

"How you doing?" I said, turning from Jolene to face him, gathering him in a short embrace. Envious at the hardness of his arms and shoulders. Even working out regularly, I'd never again achieve a body like that. Time, gravity, and a sedentary job had taken its toll.

"Can't complain," he said in his soft monotone.

"I'm sure you can't," I smiled. "Not while living the leisured life of Riley. Guess I'll be joining you in retirement soon. What can I get you guys?"

"Beer will do me," Jolene said.

"The usual," Gage said.

As I headed into the house I said, "Make yourselves comfortable, then we'll get down to business."

When I returned carrying the drinks, they sat side by side in a wicker love seat on the verandah, gazing over the tops of coconut trees at white caps rolling across Friendship Bay. The sweet citrus scent of orange and grapefruit trees populating the yard perfumed the night air.

"Ok JJ. Everything you've got," I said, lowering my frame into a wicker armchair facing them.

"Why you so riled up about this Mike?" she asked instead. "This morning you looked like you were about to pass out."

"In a bit JJ. First, I need to know everything you've got so far. And I don't want to hear you've got nothing."

"Oh I've got something all right. Murder."

"Confirmed?"

"Eileen completed the autopsy. Said you called her just before I did, by the way. Told her this case was a priority, to use whatever resources she needed." Her gaze fixed on me, probing, questioning. Her brows raised in curiosity. Indicating by my silence I had no intention of responding, she continued.

"Two gunshot wounds to the back. One bisected the aorta, the other ripped through his heart. He bled out internally. We couldn't tell when we examined the body at the scene because of the state of the body. The entry wounds were difficult to spot and there were no exit wounds. And there wasn't much blood. Death was probably immediate, and it didn't occur in the boat."

"Mike, you okay?" she sprang forward in her seat, leaning toward me. Her hands reached out to steady me, as if to keep me from falling, even though I remained seated in the wicker armchair.

"What the hell Mike? It's like this morning all over again."

"I'm okay," I managed. "Continue."

"I'm not sure I should."

"I need you to JJ," I demanded, more forcefully than I'd intended. In a gentler tone I said, "I'll be all right. And I'll explain in a moment."

Following a quick glance at Gage, she leaned back in the love seat. Gage's eyes watchful. His expression impassive, impossible to read.

"So we have a murder victim," Jolene continued, her voice hesitant, still unsure. "But no ID yet. Eileen wasn't able to get any usable prints, so she took a dental impression and DNA samples. But she'll need something to compare them to."

"Time of death?" I asked.

"Eileen puts it at around four days. The Coast Guard boys and I put together a chart of wind and weather conditions for that time frame. Factor in tides and currents, and we figured a drift pattern from south or southeast. Canuoan or Mustique. I have CID canvassing down there to see if anyone with a fishing boat like his is missing."

"No need," I said. "His name is Derrick Whittaker."

"So you did know him?" Jolene leaned forward again, concern reappearing in her eyes.

"Quite well in fact," I said. "He's an undercover cop."

"What?" She sat bolt upright.

"An undercover cop," I repeated. "One of three working under deep cover, known only to me."

"I don't understand." The exquisite features of her face registered shock and disbelief. Exhaling a melancholy sigh, I leaned forward, faced her, and explained.

"Last year right after the Ramirez affair I initiated a project. I recruited two young men and a woman from applicants for the police force, before their acceptance and entrance to the academy. I sent them to the States for specialized training in anti-crime and undercover work. Different cities. They don't know each other. But they each carry an identifying medallion and ring, like the ones found on the body. They're like badges. That's how I knew this morning he was one of mine."

Two pairs of eyes stared at me. Jolene's a mixture of astonishment and renewed concern, now aware of my attachment to the victim. Gage's inscrutable as usual, revealing nothing.

I smiled in Gage's direction. "We communicated old school. Messages in classified ads, coded emails, dead drops. That kind of thing." A slight nod his only acknowledgement.

"But why the secrecy, the cloak and dagger?" Jolene asked.

"Under the circumstances no one on the force he could trust with that kind of operation," Gage said, speaking for the first time.

"This wasn't the usual buy and bust operation JJ," I said, my explanation directed at her. Gage implicitly understanding the circumstances. His kind of world. Secrecy his default setting.

"And you know how difficult it is to be undercover on these islands. Everybody knows everybody. People know who's been recruited or graduated from the training academy.

Anyone we use undercover is blown after a few busts and has to be reassigned. I selected these three because they had no close immediate or extended families on the islands. Most of their relatives had moved abroad. They used their real first names in case they ran across people who knew them. Last name a cover ID. Any family they still have living here, and those abroad, knew nothing about their real occupation. Now one of them is dead. I need to find out what got him killed, find his killer, and determine whether the other two are compromised. And I need to do it fast."

"Can you tell us what he was working on?" Gage asked.

"He'd infiltrated a smuggling operation in the southern Grenadines. Mostly local fishermen moving merchandise offloaded at sea from freighters and private yachts. Most of them independent, not organized. But his information filled big gaps in our knowledge of smuggling down there. Drugs, guns, money, goods, even people.

"And you've been acting on that intelligence without compromising your source," Gage said, more a statement than a question.

"Yes," I said, facing him. The tiniest hint of a smile at the corners of his mouth. The slight nod repeated.

"Anything in his latest reports to indicate he might've been compromised, anything he might've been tracking that could've gotten him killed?" he asked.

"Nothing. His last few reports were routine intelligence. Who, when, where."

Gage caught the infinitesimal hesitation in my voice. The slight drift of my thoughts as I spoke.

"But?" he said.

Jolene had been observing our interchange with keen interest and without interruption. Her beer bottle on the stone floor next to the chair, all but forgotten.

"As I said, I initiated this operation at the end of the Ramirez thing. Partly because of our conversation that night sailing back from St. Lucia. To protect my flanks while we shored up the force. And partly because of JJ's so called bogeyman, who we now know is all too real. Anyway, I infiltrated all three into positions where I could accomplish the first, and perhaps have early warning on the second."

"What about the other two?" Gage asked.

"They're my responsibility. I'll take care of that end. But I'm going to need your help. Both of you. And you can't do that if you're in the dark," I said, shifting my gaze to each of them. "You're the only people I can trust with this." Another almost imperceptible acknowledgement from Gage.

"I have a woman undercover at the SVG Bank," I said. "Any movement of money in or out of the bank that might have bogeyman's fingerprints on it I'll know about immediately. The other is in with a gang operating on the windward side of St. Vincent. Marijuana for guns. He's already identified three Rapid Response Officers who provide protection and support for the gang."

"Impressive Mike," Gage said, his understated tone having an opposite effect, conveying a huge compliment. And it carried greater weight and meaning coming from him.

"What do you need us to do?" Jolene asked, breaking her long silence.

"JJ, I need you on this case full time. I need it solved, and fast. Gage, I need to borrow Wherever for a night, maybe two."

"Sure. Whenever you want. I'll be ready."

"No. I mean I need to take Wherever myself. Me and JJ."

"Not if it's for what I think it is, and entails the kind of danger you think it might. I'm coming with you. You'll need a secure perimeter for your meet."

That he'd already figured out my intention didn't surprise me. He possessed an astute strategic mind, and an uncanny ability for reading people, getting inside their heads, including mine sometimes. The steely expression in his perceptive brown eyes signaled he considered the matter closed.

"Okay then. The meet is set for Saturday night, ten pm, in Troumaka Bay. There's an old abandoned building off the beach we use. If we can't meet we try again the following night, same time. The message I sent him had an emergency code word, so if we can't make either meeting for some reason, he's to break contact with the gang, go to ground, and wait for further instructions."

"Speaking of our bogeyman," I said in an untidy segue, "either of you have anything new on that front? Don't mind telling you I'm on pins and needles waiting for the other shoe to drop."

"Getting closer," Gage said. "My guy's been able to build a pretty accurate picture of the corporate structure, but the principle is well hidden. A few promising leads turned out to be dead ends. My guess is deliberate misdirection. This guy seriously does not want anyone discovering his identity."

"Same here," Jolene said when Gage finished speaking. "According to the latest from Agent Forde, the FBI hasn't been able to pierce the veil, though they've flagged and are monitoring a number of offshore bank accounts associated with the various corporations."

"They don't have access to the same information as my guy," Gage said.

"Whaddo you mean?" I asked.

"We still have the Director," he said, his nonchalant statement belying the enormous implications of his words.

"You're still holding prisoner a man you kidnapped months ago?"

"The correct term is rendition," he said, unconcerned.

"I don't care what the hell you call it," I said, an unexpected indignation in my voice. "Putting aside the legality, it's indecent."

A horrible thought struck me. "Gage. Your guys aren't..."

"Doesn't work like that," he interrupted, a cold, hard stare pinning me. "He's treated well and no one's laid a hand on him. There're more effective ways to get him talking. Though I could care less what happens to him. He meant to hurt Jo. Then kill her."

His unblinking gaze held mine. A cold, dangerous deadliness in the pale brown eyes. I glanced at Jolene, who'd retrieved her beer, swallowing a long swig, displaying no discernable reaction to Gage's statement.

"But it's been months," I insisted. "Hasn't he been reported missing? Isn't anyone looking for him?"

"Not as far as we can tell. Could be he's considered expendable. Or making any effort to find him might expose whoever's behind him. Or his information isn't that valuable. In fact the sense I'm getting of whoever's behind all this, is someone who's a master of misdirection."

"Why do you think that?"

"The dead ends. This 'Director' guy is spilling what he knows. He isn't aware as far as we can tell that some of his information leads to dead ends. Same with the paper trail. It's not coincidence. It's deliberate. I'm also starting to think getting our hands on Taylor's material and exposing the scandals was another deliberate misdirection."

I didn't follow his reasoning. Taylor's material had proved genuine. The evidence damming. It'd brought down a Prime Minister, and created turmoil and uncertainty in the country. But I didn't discount Gage's instincts either.

"What're you saying Gage?"

"We know his end game, create enough chaos and confusion while he quietly moves in and takes control. No matter what moves we made, we'd be in check. Exposing everything Taylor uncovered played right into Bogeyman's plans, creating exactly the chaos and confusion he wanted. Which makes your undercover operation such a brilliant move Mike. He couldn't have anticipated that. But now, with the murder of your undercover..."

"You believe the murder is connected to our Bogeyman?"

"I believe the timing isn't a coincidence. It may be the fingerprint you've been looking for. The other shoe dropping. Jo, you said there were no exit wounds. Did Eileen recover the bullets?"

"Fragments. Not enough for ballistic tests."

"Hollow points," Gage and I said at the same time.

Which provided greater weight to Gage's reasoning. The implication hit me like a pile driver to the stomach.

CHAPTER 5

Wherever completed the passage in three hours. Much of the time motoring in St Vincent's lee. But the journey had buoyed my spirits. Wherever effortlessly plowed the rolling swells in the strait between Bequia and St. Vincent, her graceful motion soothing. Fresh sea air bathed my lungs. By the time we lay St. Vincent, the coast's sheltered calm matched my own, my shore-side woes dispelled by the endless blue sea to leeward, and the spectacular hues painted by the setting sun. I wanted to point her bow at that apricot sky and just keep on sailing.

We approached Troumaka Bay, small, secluded, shrouded in darkness. Not as popular among transiting yachtsmen as other bays along the coast, like Buccament Bay and its resort to our south. Or Wallilabou Bay where they'd filmed the Pirates of the Caribbean movies.

A thin sliver of moon peeked above St. Vincent's peaks, providing no unwanted light in the bay. Wherever glided in under diesel power, her sails furled and battened to her booms. Her deck and running lights blacked out.

Typical of bays along St. Vincent's leeward coast, Troumaka shoaled almost at the shoreline. Gage dropped anchor in deep water, half a football field length from the beach. An onshore breeze carried the sound out to sea.

Wherever secured, Jolene and I waited in the salon while Gage changed in the aft cabin.

"Can I get you something Mike? Coffee?"

"Thanks JJ. Coffee would be great."

She moved aft, busying herself in the galley. At home, I noticed, not for the first time. My initial apprehension regarding her relationship with Gage had long since disappeared. Transformed into a satisfying appreciation of the beneficial effects the relationship held for them, individually, and as a couple. Who'd have thought? The obvious obstacles, difference in their ages, and their backgrounds, had proved irrelevant non-factors. The happiest I'd seen her in a long time. At ease, fulfilled, able to be completely herself. And she'd somehow managed to soothe the savage beast, grounding him in a peaceful domesticity he'd probably never experienced at any time in his life.

When Gage entered the salon, his menacing past sprang immediately to mind. He wore all black. Black slacks, and a long sleeved black turtleneck, his head covered by a black cotton baklava cap. Perched on his forehead, an optical device resembling diving goggles. On his right thigh, in a sheath specially designed into the pants, a black handled combat knife. If armed beyond the knife I couldn't tell.

I glanced reflexively at Jolene. She stood nonchalantly at the galley pouring a cup of coffee, an amused grin on her face.

"Dressed for a fun night on the town I see?" she said.

Fun. When had she started thinking a get up like that signified fun? Too much time spent around him I gathered.

She probably knew him better than anyone did. Things in his past I still didn't know. And during their trip to New York, she'd briefly encountered the world he used to inhabit, up close and personal. Almost getting killed in the process.

I'd seen him similarly dressed on one other occasion. Had considered it unnecessary and perhaps a bit of overkill. But his cautionary paranoia had saved my life. It afforded him the benefit of the doubt.

"I'll need the medallion," he said approaching the settee.

I handed it to him.

"You two stay below. Keep the blackout curtains drawn and the hatch closed while you wait for your contact."

Jolene handed me a steaming mug of coffee before following him forward to the forecastle hatch.

"Think all that's really necessary?" I asked when she reentered the salon.

"Never hurts to be prepared," she said. I recognized a Gagism.

"You're both more alike than you might care to admit," she said, perceptive green eyes holding me in a steady gaze. "Accounts for how quickly you two bonded. I never quite understood that until I got to know him too."

I smiled. "I'd rather you kept your psychoanalysis to yourself," I said.

We waited. Interspersed by conversation and impatient glances at my watch. Waiting never one of my strong suits, despite its annoying requirement in my line of work.

We both heard the soft bump against the hull. Jolene dowsed the salon lights and moved into position at the bottom of the companionway, her service Glock held in a two fisted grip pointed at the cabin sole. From the dinette, I covered the hatch opening using my own service weapon.

Soft footsteps sounded on the deck overhead, approaching the hatch, followed by a light knock on the hatch cover.

"Commissioner Daniels?" A whispered shout.

"Sammy?" I called back

"Yes sir."

"Open the hatch and come on down. Watch your step. It'll be dark. And close the hatch behind you."

"Yes sir," the voice repeated. The overhead hatch slid open, revealing a small black square dotted by stars. The hatch doors swung open. A dark silhouette erased the view through the open hatch. No light entered from outside. None inside to spill out.

The hatch reclosed, I snapped on a cabin light above the dinette. A figure stood crouched halfway down the companionway steps, his back to the cabin. His first sight Jolene, standing to the companionway's right, her weapon leveled on him.

"Superintendent," his voiced registering his surprise.

"Good to see you Sammy," I said.

He peered over his right shoulder, spotted me. A smile replaced the bewildered, concerned expression on his dark face.

"And you Commissioner," he said.

At the bottom of the companionway he turned fully into the room. Tall, thin and lanky, but well muscled and fit, like a running back. He too dressed for the night, in well-worn dark jeans and a black short-sleeved tee shirt.

"Superintendent," I said, addressing Jolene. "Constable Keston Samuel."

"Nice to meet you Constable Samuel," she said, tucking the Glock into the waistband of her jeans at the small of her back.

"Ma'am," a slight nod, acknowledging her greeting.

"Relieved to see you made it," I said.

"Me too," he said. "Almost had a heart attack at de meeting place. One minute I waiting for you, de next a voice right up behind me. Never even hear nor see him. Like a duppy." Having trained in the U.S, Sammy spoke West Indian accented American, patois, or a mixture of both.

I grinned at his description. "No ghost I assure you. But some have called him that."

"So I'm thinking I dead, when a arm come over me shoulder and him holding de medallion. Commissioner, I think dat de first breath I draw since I hear him voice. He tell me go to de beach and take de dinghy. Row out to de schooner. What going on commissioner?"

"Lots to talk about Sammy," I said motioning him to the settee. "Can I get you anything? Coffee, tea. A beer maybe?"

"De coffee smells good. Maybe a cup of dat please."

He eyed Jolene as she moved toward the galley. His gaze shifted back to me as we sat. Concern and curiosity in the dark eyes peering out beneath a thick prominent brow, his thin eyebrows almost invisible.

I switched on a lamp next to the settee. Its dim light cast the smooth dark face, broad nose, and thick lips in sharp relief. His hair matted in short dreadlocks. Jolene returned carrying two mugs of steaming aromatic coffee. She handed him a mug. A fresh one for me.

"First of all Sammy," I said, holding his gaze. "I had to read the Superintendent in on our operation. She's the only one on the force I trust, and right now, she's investigating a homicide. One of you."

Constable Samuel fell back against the settee as though punched in the chest. His nostrils flared. Thin wavy lines creased his smooth brow. His deep-set eyes held a pained expression.

"I'm sorry Sammy," I said, understanding his shock. The same shock I'd experienced at the sight of Whittaker's body.

"None of us know de others," he stammered. "But still..."

"I know," I said.

"And you certain?" his voice almost a plea.

"The remains were too far gone for facial identification. But he had the medallion on him, and was wearing the ring," I said, indicating the ring he too wore on his right ring finger. He absently touched it, turning it with his thumb.

"First thing I wanted to do was warn you and the other undercover."

He looked up as I said that. "So one more besides me leave?"

"Yes. There were three of you to begin with."

"What him name? De one get killed?"

"Can't tell you that right now, but soon. I can't even tell his family yet. You'll probably hear about it soon, from the news or something. All anyone knows officially right now is the body hasn't been identified. A John Doe."

"When dis happen?" he asked, the mug of coffee forgotten on the low coffee table.

"His body was found two days ago, in a fishing boat washed up on Petit Nevis off Bequia. The autopsy indicated he'd been killed four days before we found him. Sometime between Saturday and Sunday night."

Samuel merely nodded. "So what now?"

"The Superintendent here is investigating this full time. We won't stop until we find who did this. We need a full debrief from you, just in case something you know, or heard, might turn out to be useful."

"You think it might be connected to de gang?" he asked, concern rising in his voice as he considered the implication.

"Can't see how. But I'm not leaving any rock stone unturned," I said, using a local colloquialism for emphasis. "Any and every bit of information might hold something useful. And the other thing I need to know, where are you right this minute in your operation? We may have to close it down sooner than expected. You know what's going on. I'll probably be replaced regardless of which party wins the election. I need to conclude the current operations and bring you guys in before that happens."

Samuel focused on the coffee mug. He lifted it to his mouth in a hand disproportionally large for his body type. He swallowed large sips of the hot brew. While I waited, I sipped my own.

"Nothing going on right now," he said, setting down the mug. "Nothing in planning either. Is like everybody waiting. Waiting to see what going happen. And some of de gangs joining together, like I've been reporting. Affiliating wid other gangs. Thing is Commissioner, if you're going raid dem, de gangs like a army now. A well-armed army. Dey have heavy automatic weapons. And dey not selling dem. Dey stockpiling."

"Not good news," I said, contemplating what it might all mean. I turned to Jolene.

"For the past few months Constable Samuel's reports have indicated a consistent pattern of these gangs arming up. For what, we can't tell. They don't seem to be gearing up to take each other on. As Sammy said they seem instead to be banding together. With elections nearing that could be a powder keg."

"You think this might be political?" she said.

"Happened before on St. Vincent. Not to mention everywhere else in the Caribbean. And right now, with people distrusting their institutions, and tempers flaring, anything might set this off. They might be waiting to take advantage of the situation. Or to ignite the situation."

Her gaze held mine, a subtle expression in her light green eyes. A silent acknowledgement of thoughts aligning in accord. Her bogeyman.

"How do you intend to shut them down?" she asked, without telegraphing her suspicions to Constable Samuel.

"Been giving that a lot of thought. Not sure yet. But the longer we wait the worst the scenarios become. Thanks to Sammy, we know where they are, where they operate. But like he said, a full on raid could turn into a blood bath. And a move like that will require coordination, using large contingents of the force, practically guaranteeing a leak."

I turned to face Samuel. "I'm going to need your input on this Sammy. I'm thinking it's probably time to pull you out and have you work this with me from headquarters."

"Whatever you think best Commissioner. But I might still be able to see de best angle from de inside."

"What else can you tell us?"

"Well, I was thinking about what you said jus' now. Last weekend Natty, de guy running de gang ma'am," he said parenthetically to Jolene. "He say he have a meeting wid someone. Wouldn't say who de person is. When he get back he have a load of cash. I mean a whole heap a money commissioner. Had to carry in a bag. Fresh twenty and fifty dollar U.S. bills. Wouldn't say where he get it. Just dat his contact give it to him. But Commissioner, I don't know any of his contacts who deal in dat kind of cash. Anyhow dis happen about de same time as de murder. Why I thought of it."

"Who are his contacts outside the gang?"

"Not sure. Usually he goes to meetings like dat on his own. But I've heard him talk about a politician work for opposition leader Ballantyne. And of course de dirty cops on de Rapid Response Unit."

"Okay," I said. "Run it down for us Sammy. Everything, even what you've already reported to me."

The meeting lasted another hour. Sammy did most of the talking. Jolene and I listened, our focus intense and attentive. Occasionally one of us interrupted Sammy with a question. We combed over the Rapid Response Unit officers in detail. Names, stations, homes, families. Any indication of others involved, including their superiors.

"You have your cell phone on you?" I asked when we finished. "Let me have it."

He pulled it from a jeans pocket. I handed it to Jolene.

"You remember how to do it?"

"No worries," she said, heading toward the nav station. She sat and removed the back of the phone, pulling components and attaching a cable from a laptop on the nav table.

"She's making a little modification to your phone Sammy," I explained. "We're going to encrypt it and program it with a two special numbers. Call the first number and you'll reach me anywhere, anytime. The second will reach the Superintendent. I have to move quickly on this Sammy, and I'll be pulling you out. All this will be over soon."

"Thanks Commissioner," he said.

"All done here," Jolene said, approaching from the Nav area.

Sammy rose to leave. Jolene stood in front of him, handed him the phone and extended her hand.

"Constable Samuel," she said. "An honor to meet you. I admire and commend your courage."

"Thanks ma'am," he said, a wide appreciative smile on his face.

"You stay safe, you heah," she said in patois.

"Yes ma'am. Commissioner, what about your man on de beach?"

Jolene smiled. Couldn't help myself either.

"Don't worry about him Sammy. You probably won't meet him again, or see him. But he'll be watching you, making sure no one else is watching you, or following you from the beach. You take care. I'll be in touch."

Thirty minutes later Gage returned as silently as he'd departed. He changed into faded jeans and an army green tee shirt before joining Jolene and me in the salon. Jolene and I alternated turns relating the salient points of the meeting, and Constable Samuel's briefing.

We talked late into the night. Way past my usual week-night bedtime. But being the weekend, I didn't have to be up early in the morning for the office. And yet, my internal clock pushed me toward sleep. Coffee didn't help.

Gage had switched to rum and Coke. I thought of switching to something alcoholic myself, but it'd probably produce greater drowsiness. My thinking process already sluggish, my thoughts colliding randomly, purposelessly, careening off on unproductive tangents.

"Guys, I need to turn in. I need to sleep on all this and come up with a plan. Any plans for the weekend Gage?"

"Nothing can't keep."

I smiled. Leaned over to plant a goodnight peck on Jolene's cheek, and rose from the settee, heading toward the guest cabins.

"See you guys in the morning," I tossed over my shoulder.

CHAPTER 6

My internal clock woke me to the rising sun. As usual. I rolled off the bunk, stretched the kinks from my cramped joints, and stumbled to the forward head, thinking I'd be the only one up so early. But the rich scent of fresh brewed coffee permeated Wherever's interior.

A pale grey sky, turning from black to blue, greeted me topside. The island's peaks shrouded in chalky mist. The lush green-brown landscape emerged from the dark. To the west, the bay's rippling cobalt surface merged into an indigo sea.

Jolene was already on deck, forward, between the foremast and staysail stay. She'd disconnected the staysail boom sheets and hoisted the boom out of the way. Wearing only a black cotton sports bra, and cut-off sweat pants, she performed a series of stretching and warm up exercises.

She noticed me entering the cockpit, paused her routine, and beamed a warm welcoming smile in my direction.

"Morning. Sleep well?"

"Like a baby," I said. "Out like a light the moment my head hit the pillow."

"Good. How're you feeling?"

"Other than the usual aches and pains, pretty good, refreshed," I said, inhaling a deep breath of salty sea air.

"Can I get you anything?"

"Found the coffee," I said, holding the mug of fresh black coffee I'd carried into Wherever's cockpit. "Don't let me interrupt. Get back to your workout."

"Oh, this isn't the workout," She said chuckling. I'm just warming up for Aquaman there," shifting her gaze to a spot in the bay. "That's when the real workout begins."

She padded aft to the cockpit, but my attention focused on the swimmer, heading in from the mouth of the bay. Still a good hundred yards away, making straight for Wherever, the strokes strong, even, rhythmic. The swimmer cleaved the blue water, scarcely leaving a ripple.

"He likes to start right after a swim," Jolene said from somewhere behind me. When I turned to face her, she'd donned a sparring helmet and half weight sparring gloves.

Gage emerged over the aft rail. Seawater sluiced off his broad shoulders and chest, forming a puddle at his feet. I attempt to work out regularly, as my schedule allows. Partly to slow the effects of time, and partly to maintain a certain fitness level. Not field level fit. In the past twenty-five years my forays from behind a desk into the field entailed supervision and command.

Nothing close to the fitness exhibited by Gage. Only three years younger than me, he somehow retained the physique and musculature of a man half his age. The lean mean fighting machine he used to be, hinting at the restrained power I'd perceived the first time we'd met. Mottled spots, and thin jagged lines, marred the sun darkened brown of his torso, arms and legs. Observing them produced a dull phantom ache at the locations of my own bullet scars.

"Morning buddy. How you feeling?" His greeting boisterous and cheerful. He stepped into the cockpit and grabbed a towel hanging on the spoked wheel. Not waiting for an answer, he turned to Jolene. "You ready sweetness?"

"Just waiting on you."

"Then let's get to it."

They both flashed me amused grins and headed forward. Jolene carried a padded chest protector she picked up from the cockpit. Gage donned a pair of sparring gloves as he walked by her side.

I'd known Gage going on six years. Jolene much longer. I'd watch them become a couple. In the past six years, I'd spent more time in their company than anyone else's. But this was a first for me. I watched in fascinating curiosity as they squared off against each other on the foredeck.

Gage attacked, while Jolene defended. Blow followed blow in a whirlwind of fists, forearms, elbows and feet. Swift and furious, like the real thing. Jolene grunted into each counterattack, her ponytailed hair swinging from side to side, as she parried and blocked attacks raining in from Gage.

He twisted and turned to take her counterpunches and kicks on the fleshy parts of his forearms, upper arms, and thighs. As quick as Jolene moved, none of her blows penetrated his defenses.

They moved around the small foredeck space, close in, toe to toe, as it would be in a close quarter hand-to-hand fight. Jolene demonstrated astonishing speed and skill. A side of her I'd never known.

They grappled next. Gage caught her in arm locks, a chokehold. Jolene broke them and caught him in holds of her own. A wristlock and rapid leg sweep sent Gage onto the deck.

Jolene locked her thighs around his waist, a chokehold around his neck. Gage broke free using a rapid maneuver I didn't follow. They regained their feet to grapple again.

When it ended, they fell into each other's arms, sweat glistened bodies pressed together. Café-au-lait against dark cocoa. I glanced away, momentarily embarrassed, as thought witnessing an intimate sexual moment.

Gage's voice recaptured my attention.

"No more than three. Try for one."

Jolene nodded. Pony tail bobbing. She removed her sparring gloves. Gage donned the padded chest protector they'd left lying on the deck. He attached a padded throat protector around his neck, held by Velcro straps.

This time when Gage attacked Jolene parried and moved in. Three swift blows, grunting the count as she delivered them. One, a straight-arm heel of her hand strike to Gage's solar plexus. Two, a head lock and twist as she stepped back and fell to one knee, taking Gage down, face up and prone before her. Three, a closed fist strike to his throat.

They reset. Gage fired a straight right-handed punch to Jolene's face. She slipped to the side, allowing it to pass over her left shoulder. Gage's left already coming at her from the other direction. Her right arm parried the blow. Her left elbow swung into the padded collar protecting Gage's throat.

"One," she grunted.

Gage stepped back, dropping his arms.

"That would definitely do it," he said, smiling at her.

They fell into another embrace, retrieved their gear from the deck and headed aft to the cockpit. Both noticed the stunned expression on my face. Broad, satisfied grins on theirs.

"Gage has been teaching me hand to hand," Jolene said.

"No shit."

She laughed.

"Remind me never to piss you off," I said. "How long you two been doing this?"

"Almost a year," she said. "But more regularly and more advanced since New York,"

"Impressive," I told her.

"Never can be too prepared," she said, glancing at Gage. "I'm heading for the shower. You guys hungry? I know you must be," she said to Gage, planting a kiss on his cheek before heading down the hatch.

Alone alongside Gage in the cockpit I said, "That was...interesting," the only word I could conjure at short notice to express a discomforting ambivalence.

I eyed him speculatively. He returned my stare, his hard brown eyes expressionless. The source of my unease uncertain. The exact nature of the emotion welling up inside me also uncertain. An irrational paternal protective instinct maybe. This man a killer. Teaching Jolene how to kill.

"She's good," I said instead, a surge of familial pride mingled with the other as yet unidentified emotion.

"You should see her shoot," he said.

"Shoot?"

"Her off hand is still a little weak, but she's getting there."

"Gage..." I began, hesitant, the disquieting emotion rising again. I squashed it before it found voice in words. None of my business. It troubled me just the same.

"I need to ask you a favor," I said instead.

"Ask," he said, characteristically succinct.

"It's a pretty tall favor to ask."

"If it has anything to do with this situation I'm already involved," he said, eyes pinning me in his stare.

"I need surveillance on three guys. RRU members. They're dirty. I've wanted to clean up that unit for a long time. This may be my chance. I haven't figured out how to watch all of them yet. Maybe pull my undercovers off their current assignment. No one else I can trust at the moment."

"No need," he said. "I'll give each subject a day. Should be enough time to spot the weak link. Then I concentrate on that one. Put enough pressure on the weak link and we can break him. Maybe turn him against the others. Leave your people in place Mike. At least for now. Which reminds me, is your operative at the bank checking for large cash deposits? Some of these guys may be just dumb enough to put their dirty cash in the bank."

"I'm thinking the same thing. And yes she is."

"Have a plan in mind yet?" he asked.

"The beginnings of one. Couldn't think clearly last night, but it's starting to come together. This shit makes me feel so tired all the time, Gage. The kind sleep doesn't help, you know?" I said, lapsing into a familiar unburdening. The only person in my life, best friend if truth were told, with whom I could share such sentiments. "Think I'm feeling my age."

"I know the feeling buddy," he said. "One other thing is bugging me though."

My eyes gazed into his expectantly.

"If I were running Bogeyman's operation I'd want to penetrate the Government, present and future, and the police force. You have to assume they've already done that."

"I thought we'd pretty much exposed that part of his operation?"

"Just what he wanted you to expose. He still needs eyes and ears in the power structure, and a covert means of manipulating the levers of power."

"What're you saying Gage?"

"I'm saying your instincts so far have been correct. Be careful who you talk to and read in. There're probably more moles in the woodwork we don't know about yet."

Jolene popped through the hatch before I'd fully digested the threat implied by Gage's statement. She carried a tray of eggs, toast, sliced melon and coffee. She wore cut off jeans and a navy blue tee shirt. Her damp hair hung in wild gold streaked curls on either side of her creamy, freshly scrubbed face, as radiant as varnished teak in the brightening sunlight.

The sun had climbed above the peaks, turning the sky pale blue and heating up the day, heralding the blisteringly hot, dry season months ahead. Summertime in the States.

Gage consumed a few bites of eggs and fruit, and downed another cup of coffee before announcing, "My turn for the shower." He disappeared through the hatch.

I contemplated Jolene, her gaze staring out to sea. Slanting sunlight shifted the colors of her exceptional eyes, green to amber, and a light shade of golden brown.

"That was some workout," I said, giving voice to my unresolved emotion.

She turned to stare at me, perhaps catching the hint of disapproval in my tone.

"But..." she said, her eyes mesmerizingly green.

"I'm wondering to what end."

"Well dad, I'm not planning on running off to become an international assassin or anything."

"Sarcasm too," I said.

She laughed. A soft chuckle like the whisper of surf upon the beach, accompanied by a sympathetic softening in her eyes, as though aware of the precise nature of my discomfort.

"I enjoy it is all. Besides the skills, the confidence of knowing I can handle myself in a fight, I enjoy the exercise. The physicality of it. It's exhilarating. Like running."

"Or sex from the looks of it."

"Mike," she admonished in a soft breath, emphasized by a playful punch on my upper arm.

"And the shooting?" I asked.

"Gage tell you about that?" a slight lift of delicate brown eyebrows.

"He mentioned it in passing."

"You should see him shoot," she said. "He's Zen-like. Like he can direct the rounds with his mind. Never misses. With either hand. Even with his eyes closed. Sometimes he'll put something on the target to make a sound. Close his eyes, target the sound."

"I'm not sure that make me feel any better."

She repeated the chuckling sound. "For me it's like when I learned to fly. Acquiring the skill is the thrill. Mastering it. And I never had an appreciation of the psychological aspects before. The mental conditioning required to shoot the way he does. Not something they teach you in police firearms training. It's fascinating."

The lines of her glamorous face formed into a gentle, reassuring smile, designed to put my mind at ease.

"Speaking of psychology, given any thought to what you might do next? If you don't stick with the force that is."

"Not really," she said, brushing a delicate hand, deadly too as I'd witnessed, through the tangled curls of gold brown hair. "I don't want any distractions during this case."

"There's a future there for you," I said. "If you want it."

"I'm aware. Not sure I want it though. And I feel like at the end of the day, we've accomplished what we both set out to do."

I no longer detected the plaintive wistfulness usually present when she spoke of the police force. Neither in her voice nor her manner.

"Seems to me you've finally made peace with something. Something having to do with why you joined in the first place?" my intonation forming a question.

The open, reassuring smile again. Acknowledgement of a deep dark motivation I'd often perceived. Gage too. Of which she never spoke. Any mention of it produced a cold glint in her eyes, and a tightening set of her jaw.

"Let's just say transforming the force as you did coincided with my interests. I'm satisfied."

"Are you ever going to tell me what that interest is, or was?" My gaze held hers, searching her eyes.

"Why do you need to know?" Green-amber eyes questioning.

"I worry about you," I said.

"I know," she said, leaning across, a light kiss on my cheek. "Thanks. But I'm really fine. Anyway, what about you?" she continued. "What are your plans after this? And what if you're asked to stay on?"

"No chance of that," I said. "And I feel it's time to move on anyway. Like you said, we fought the good fight and accomplished what needed to get done. I'm proud of your part in that."

"But we still have one job left to do," she said.

"Yeah. And failure is not an option, or everything we've accomplished might vanish."

CHAPTER 7

Monday morning and back in the office, invigorated by the leisured weekend spent in the company of dear friends aboard Wherever. Having nowhere pressing any of us needed to be, we'd elected to remain in the tranquil bay, relaxing, swimming, afternoon napping, chatting. Most importantly, planning.

"Morning Commissioner," Cecilia greeted. Already at her desk. Always there before my arrival.

"Top of the morning to you too Cissy," I greeted her back.

Dark dilated pupils measured me. Her expression softened. Thin, penciled eyebrows arched upward on her forehead. The corners of her usually severe mouth curled upward in a rare smile.

"Good to see you finally got some rest."

"I did happen to have a restful, restorative weekend Cissy, thank you. And today I feel great."

"Well enjoy it while you can," she said with sardonic resignation. "I'm sure it won't last."

"Oh thanks so much for that," I said, passing into my inner office, fully aware her words would prove correct.

The first order of business involved pulling the personnel files of the three dirty RRU officers. To be safe, I mixed them randomly among a dozen other personnel files I accessed. When I had the information I needed, I emailed the particulars to Gage over his secure server.

Cecilia ushered the next order of business through my office door. Deputy Commissioner Huggins, his uniform crisply pressed as always. He approached my desk, his daily briefing file tucked under his left arm. I'd need to brief him on everything soon. But not yet. I still needed more information. Still needed to line up all my ducks in row. And Gage's warning gnawed at the back of my brain.

I particularly wanted to discuss his plans for the future. Huggins was next in line and the logical choice for the Commissioner's chair. Unless the new Prime Minister bumped someone above him, or brought someone in from outside the force. I'd heard a rumor Huggins planned to retire, and another rumor he'd begun a quiet lobby on his own behalf.

"Whaddo we have today?" I said, tabling those thoughts for the time being.

He settled into one of the two chairs facing my desk.

"Status Quo, t'ank goodness. Quiet weekend. De usual incidents. Harassment of election workers handing out leaflets and hanging posters. Some stone throwing incidents. Some minor assaults and two stabbings. Both parties held rallies over de weekend, de ULP in Stubbs, Biabou and Georgetown, NDP in Calliaqua and Layou. No incidents of significant violence at any of de rallies."

"Good news, Reggie. Your strategy for keeping the lid on this pressure cooker seems to be working. Keep at it. Heavy police presence at each event. Just the regular constabulary, right? No special units?"

"Correct Commisshunah. De special units held in reserve if we need dem."

"Carry on then," I said, terminating the meeting.

Assistant Superintendent Taylor next, also carrying a briefing file.

"Whaddayougat Vince?"

"An increase in complaints about constables being prejudiced when taking statements from victims of political harassment. Depending on which party the victim supports, and which the particular constable supports.

"Dammit," I said. "And not much we can do if no offense is committed."

"Correct Sir. The constables haven't committed any offense, but they're ignoring complaints. Or giving more attention to one person's statement over another, depending on party affiliation."

"How're you handling the complaints?"

"For now just compiling the complaints, the names of the constables involved, and supervisors, whether they had knowledge or took any action. I've pulled some of the more serious complaints for further inquiry."

"Good. Anything else?"

He eyed a copy of the guide sitting on my desk.

"Some preliminary thoughts on rolling out the Guide, Commissioner. I think the upcoming ceremony for new police officers graduating the training academy on Barbados might be the perfect opportunity. In fact, we have a class of constables completing RSS training at the same time. We might combine the two ceremonies. The Prime Minister must attend of course, but so will the Governor General, and we might also invite some other dignitaries, from Barbados, maybe some RSS countries too. No one can say an event like that is political."

"Vince you just made my day," I said leaping from my chair in unrestrained enthusiasm, a broad smile spreading across my face. "Get me a list of Regional Security System members you think should be represented. I'll make the calls personally. And I know one embassy official on Barbados I'm definitely going to invite," I said, hoping he didn't see the expectant gleam in my eyes.

"Prepare a press release about the event, that the Guide will be announced there. Include details about the Guide. What it contains, how it came about, blah blah blah. And let's meet back here with Huggins at four o'clock. We should have details on the arrangements and attendees for you by then."

"Yes, Commissioner," he said. He gathered his file and departed.

By day's end I still had a spring in my step, and an unburdened soul. Cecilia's prediction as yet unfulfilled, despite a handful of tedious unproductive meetings with preposterous pedantic government officials. None of it deflated the satisfactory results of numerous phone calls successfully arranging the graduation ceremonies for the coming Friday. One invitation in particular.

At home in my rental house in Montrose, I'd dismissed the household staff for the evening before checking in with Gage and Jolene. Gage already had the first subject under surveillance. The officer had departed his home in street clothes following his shift, and headed to a local drinking hole.

Gage indicated he'd continue his surveillance until the subject returned home for the night.

Jolene's people had been canvassing the southern Grenadines since discovery of the body. Equipped with a name, they'd been able to identify people who knew Whittaker, and commenced constructing a time line of his movements. They'd encountered some stonewalling, not unexpected given most of Whittaker's acquaintances were smugglers, who believed he'd been one too.

By midweek Cecilia's prediction on its way to proving true. I returned home to Bequia reeling and exhausted. But anticipation of the coming weekend, and a special visitor, buoyed my spirits.

I'd returned to Bequia hoping for a chance to casually run into Sanford Wallace, known to everyone on the island as Solly. An architect and building contractor by trade, Solly moonlighted as the local equivalent of a fixer. A pseudo private-eye, possessing no official standing or office, or claim to being any such thing. Nothing nefarious, at least to my knowledge. But people often sought his help in matters where they thought the police had been no help. Or where they didn't want the police involved. He had a reputation for assisting the police in recovering stolen property, and identifying individuals responsible for the crimes. And he maintained an extensive network of contacts in and out of government, and among the criminal element. His information often proved as good, or better, than any police informant, who were universally known and therefore useless anyway.

On Wednesday evenings Solly might be found at De Reef in Lower Bay, having beers with friends, or 'liming' the local girls. Entering De Reef I spotted him sitting on a wood stool at the end of the polished pine bar. No one around him. Deep in conversation with the young, attractive bartender.

Mid-week, and off-season, only a smattering of locals occupied the large open-air room used for dining, dancing, and gaming. The room walled on three sides, one side open to the evening breeze, a view of Lower Bay, and the surf rolling on and off the long crescent shaped shoreline. Two couples dined at separate tables close to the low brick wall overlooking the beach. Close to the entrance, four local fishermen engaged in a rousing game of dominoes. The bar lined the far end of the room, the kitchen behind it, from where the succulent odor of chicken, fish, and conch scented the air. Sultry country tunes emanated at low volume from hidden speakers.

I sat on the stool next to Solly. I recognized the young woman behind the bar as Delma, a cousin of De Reef's owners, and one of numerous family members who helped to staff and run the establishment.

"Evening Delma," I greeted her. "A Heineken please, and put the rest of Solly's drinks on my tab."

"Oh Oh. Shoa you want do dat," Solly said, turning to face me. "I might be heah a long time."

Cool, light grey eyes stared out from a tawny complexioned face, darkened by a lifetime exposure to the tropical sun. He had the light complexion of his ancestors, Wallaces who'd emigrated from England back in the eighteen seventies, and the dark, tightly curled hair of the African and Carib forebears with whom they'd intermarried.

"No problem," I said.

A sly smile creased his face. "So what can I do fa de Commisshunah of Poliss? he said.

"How about a little walk?"

"Sweetheart bring annoder cold Hairoon," he said to Delma, finishing the last swallow from the bottle in front of him.

When she placed the fresh opened beer on the bar, he lifted it and swung off the stool, heading for the concrete ramp leading from the bar onto the sand. I grabbed my Heineken and followed.

A warm tropical breeze greeted us on the beach. A crescent moon, more than a sliver, but less than half, hung low in the western sky. The Bay unlit and dark, its gentle rolling swells invisible until they neared the shore, crashing foamy white upon the sand.

"So what's up Commisshunah?" Soft powdery sand crunched beneath our feet. Solly barefoot. I should have removed my shoes. I'd have to deal with the sand collecting in them later.

"Just looking for some information. I know you have your ear to the ground in a lot of places."

"Like what kind of informachun?"

"What are you hearing about the election?"

A long pull of his beer. "Aye sah," he sighed heavily.

"Doesn't look good for de NDP," he said in accented English, dropping the Patois, Solly among many educated Vincentians who spoke proper English when it suited them, depending on the circumstances.

"De split in de assembly right now is eight to seven. ULP look like they will hold the seats they have, and maybe pick up another five. It'll give them a clear majority. De Green Party not expected to get anything."

"That bad?"

"Look so."

I drank from my beer, gazing out at the dark sea, pondering the implications of his news. My gaze lingered on the dark empty space in the bay where Wherever usually floated on her mooring. I lifted my gaze toward the highland silhouetted against the dark night and the star sprinkled sky. Jolene's house sat nestled on that hillside, but the surrounding trees hid any light peeking from it.

"Say you're right." I'm certain he was, Solly attuned to the pulse of the electorate better than anyone on St. Vincent and the Grenadines. "You hear anything about who might be in the Cabinet?"

"A few names floating around. Nothing for sure yet though. But I can make a good guess about who might get portfolios. Anyway your concern is de Security Ministry right? And you know de prime minister holds that portfolio. Going be Junior Ballantyne for sure."

"Any word on his thinking for Commissioner?"

"Nothing. Most of the talk coming from de police ranks. Dat blowhard Mitchell pushing for himself. DC Huggins is in line too. Beginning to make some quiet inquiries. I'd like to see him get the job, but I also hear talk about him retiring. And for what it's worth Commisshunah," turning to hold me in his grey-eyed stare. "I support what you've done with the force dese last years. Dey needed it bad. And long overdue. Especially with the sort of crime they have to deal with nowadays. You done a hellava job Commisshunah. Lots of people will be sorry to see you leave, me included."

We turned and headed back toward De Reef, strolling beyond the surf's finger like tendrils flicking across the sand.

"Thanks for that Solly," I said. "Job's not done yet though."

"I know. Still a few rotten mangos to pick from de barrel."

"I plan to get to them before I leave. You have some names for me maybe?"

"Won't do you any good," he said, displaying the type of discretion people sought him for. Also probably a selfish motivation to not burn his sources. "You probably already know some a dem anyway. But with nothing to charge dem with what good de names going do you? So what you going do after? Go back to the States?"

"For a long visit maybe. Catch up with friends and family. But Bequia is home now. Maybe I'll write my memoir," I said in jest.

"Ha." A half laugh in the single word. "Da'll be a piece of work."

He held me in his gaze again. "Anyt'ing you can tell me about de fisherman murder?"

"Continuing investigation Solly," I said, deflecting his question. "Anything you can tell me?"

"Word is him was mixed up with smuggling."

I smiled. "One of the things we're looking into," I said.

I accompanied him back to the bar. I hadn't eaten since breakfast, figured since I was at De Reef anyway I might as well. I ordered a plate of curried chicken and rice and peas. I ate at the bar. Solly declined food, watching me eat as he consumed more beer, and our conversation turned to local goings on, politics, crime, the upcoming Carnival, life in the Grenadines. Inconsequential but fascinating. Solly at times obtusely fishing for any useful information.

Preparing to leave, I paid my bill and said, "Good talking to you Solly."

His gaze fixed on the shelves of liquor bottles behind the bar, he said, "Dere's a woman, name Sonya Johnson. Works at the Port Customs House in Kingstown. You might want to have a conversation wid she Commisshunah."

"Who is this woman and why might I want to have a conversation with her?"

His gaze remained focused behind the bar.

"You won't know dat till you talk to her. But you know dat saying about a woman scorned." He turned to face me. The corners of his eyes and mouth wrinkled in a mischievous smile, an amused twinkle in the clear grey eyes.

"Night Commisshunah," he said.

CHAPTER 8

The sun blazed bright and hot in the afternoon sky, its searing heat reflected by the black airport tarmac, making the surrounding air even more stifling. Standing in the shade beneath the terminal's overhang partially alleviated the overbearing heat. The seaside location of the E.T. Joshua airport also helped. An offshore breeze, bearing the heavy scent of kerosene-laden fuel burnt by turboprop engines, provided a smidgen of relief.

I stared across to the far end of the ramp, past the blue terminal building, focusing on the white, gold trimmed twin engine Piper Seneca parked in front of the airport's fire station. I'd flown it from Bequia earlier in the morning, anticipating I'd need it for another flight later tomorrow evening.

The Leeward Islands Air Transport flight from Barbados had landed moments before. Randall Gibbons, a permanent secretary at St. Vincent's foreign ministry stood next to me, nervously fidgeting, hopping from foot to foot, constantly dabbing his dark chubby face with a pocket handkerchief. In the oppressive heat, perspitation poured copiously from his portly frame, creating a slick ramp on the flattened bridge of his nose, along which the thick framed glasses he wore continuously slide down.

We watched and waited as the De Havilland Twin Otter in white, blue, orange, and yellow striped LIAT livery, taxied to the ramp.

The person we'd been waiting to meet, Melanie Barnes, the Political Economic and Security Official at the U.S. embassy in Barbados, disembarked among the last of the passengers. She strode purposefully toward the terminal in a tailored light grey pants suit. A silk maroon shirt, open at the collar, revealed a short strand of small white pearls adorning her neck. She carried a briefcase type handbag on a long strap over her left shoulder, and a garment bag folded over her right arm. Her gait graceful but authoritative in black closed toe low heeled pumps.

Permanent Secretary Gibbons moved toward the line of disembarking passengers heading for the terminal building. His gait labored, he waved his arms to attract her attention. Noticing him, Melanie Barnes veered from the line, heading toward us.

"Welcome to St. Vincent and the Grenadines ma'am," Gibbons greeted her.

"So nice to see you again, Mr. Gibbons, her voice soft and provocatively husky.

""Allow me to introduce Commissioner of Police Michael Daniels," Gibbons said, indicating me. "Unfortunately I will not be riding back to town with you. I'm meeting another flight, arriving from St. Lucia in thirty minutes. My office has been shuttling between Kingstown and de apoht all day," he explained with a nervous smile, the ever present handkerchief dabbing his slick forehead. "However the Commissioner is here to escort you. Will you be staying at de embassy residence?" he asked, referring to a home in Old Montrose leased by the U.S. Embassy.

"I'm well acquainted with Commissioner Daniels," she said, the gaze of her wide set, dark brown eyes under short curled lashes, meeting mine. An alluring lift at their corners hinted at Asian genes somewhere in her ancestry. As did her straight sleek black hair. Her full lips, straight nose slightly broader at the nostrils, and mustard complexion indicated some other mixtures. Lightly glossed lips parted in an enchanting smile, producing dimples in her smooth cheeks, and drawing attention to the generous mouth, elegant cheekbones, and firm rounded chin.

"We've worked together on a number of regional security issues," she explained to Gibbons.

"Yes," he said, ignoring me, and the fact she hadn't answered his question. Instead, he pulled a typed sheet from a folder he carried.

"I've prepared a schedule and itinerary of events surrounding de ceremony," he said, pushing the sheet toward her. "A reception and dinner at government house dis evening. Then de ceremony itself tomorrow afternoon. De Commissioner's office has made arrangements for transpo'tation to all events."

Her eyes, lively and inquisitive, met mine again. "So kind of you Commissioner," she said.

I grabbed the typed sheet Gibbons still held toward her.

"Do you have any luggage to collect?" He asked.

"No. Just this," she said, raising her right arm to indicate the suit bag. As she did I slipped the bag off her arm onto mine.

"Den is dere anything further I can assist you with ma'am?"

"Not at this time Mr. Gibbons. Thank you so much for everything," she said, her dazzling smile charming him.

"My pleasure. Den if you'll excuse me, I'll be seeing you dis evening."

When he departed for the Terminal, I escorted Consul Barnes to a waiting Mitsubishi sedan. I settled in the back seat next to her.

The sedan's air-conditioned interior provided welcomed relief from the scorching heat. During the drive from Arnos Vale, through Kingstown's congested streets, to the Montrose area three miles north and west of Kingstown, we engaged in small talk and the upcoming graduation ceremony. She represented the United States in many of the regional security initiatives and forums aimed at combating drug trafficking and money laundering. Her office monitored U.S. monetary and training assistance to individual island police forces and regional security programs. As we spoke, the corporal at the wheel cast frequent furtive glances at his back seat passengers through the rear view mirror.

He departed the Leeward Highway, turning onto a one lane climbing secondary road bordered on both sides by woodland. He turned off the secondary road, negotiating a steep curving driveway leading to a two story, four-bedroom colonial style house. The house, its white washed exterior bright under the afternoon sun, sat in the center of sloping manicured lawns, surrounded by two acres of woods and trees. Less than a quarter mile from the Prime Minister's official residence. Less than a half mile from mine.

"Wait in the car for me," I instructed the driven before he'd opened his door. I'll see the Consul gets settled and be right out."

I threw the garment bag over my left arm, walked around the vehicle to open the door for her. Together we walked up stone steps leading to a wrap around verandah on two sides of the house. A sturdy wood door stood under an arched entrance. She produced a key from her bag and opened the front door.

I closed the door behind me. Placed her garment back across the back of a nearby chair. She turned, facing me. Her face, her mouth, rose to meet mine.

The world stopped.

Soft, sensual, yielding lips. Her shoulder bag slipped to the floor. I wrapped my arms around her. Felt hers circling my waist, palms flat against my back, pressing me against her, our tongues meeting, tasting, demanding.

I savored the delicious warmth of her mouth, the heat of her touch, the subtle scent of her, the brush of her silky hair on my cheek. A stiffness rose at my crotch, a throbbing ache straining against constraining clothing, accompanied by a desire burning a hole at the center of my being.

"Hi," I said, breaking the lock of our lips.

"Hi," she whispered back.

"I've been dying to do that since the moment you stepped off the plane," I said.

"I miss the way you hug," she said, burying her head against my chest.

Our lips touched again, sweet softness, less demanding. My eyes soaked in the contours of her oval face, the dark brown eyes, warm and sympathetic one moment, determined and authoritative the next. And her smooth forehead, partially covered by cropped bangs.

"Can we fast forward," she whispered. "Skip right past the reception."

I laughed. "If only wishing made it so," I said. "The important thing is you're here. I'll just have to take a couple of cold showers until tonight. Actually, I still have to work on my speech for tomorrow, which is the same as taking a cold shower."

She laughed, a soft, throaty chuckle.

"The housekeepers?" I asked.

"Won't be back until I leave tomorrow. And you?"

"I volunteered myself as your personal chauffer and escort."

"How gallant of you Commissioner."

I returned her smile. "I'll pick you up at seven."

"Can't wait," she said, touching her lips to mine.

At seven thirty precisely, Melanie Barnes and I entered the reception room of Government House, the official residence and office of Governor General Sir Christopher Brathwaite. The room buzzed with the mingled conversations and sporadic laughter of two dozen or more voices, high-ranking police officials, our counterparts from Caribbean Community and Organization of Eastern Caribbean States, cabinet ministers, wives, and assorted other guests.

In a far corner a small combo of guitars and steel drums played traditional calypso music. Servers in traditional Vincentian garb passed among the crowd carrying trays of drinks and hors d'oeuvres. A mixture of colognes and perfumes scented the air.

After first greeting the Governor General and his wife, and Prime Minister Bacchus and his wife as protocol demanded, I reluctantly released Melanie to her obligatory round of mingling, while I did the same. I met and greeted my counterparts from other CARICOM and OECS countries. I'd worked closely with them over the years, developing methods, protocols, and joint regional training for our police and security forces. We shared common problems regarding crime, training, and resources. Particularly an increase in violent crime, narco trafficking, and money laundering.

Many of those methods, protocols, and training programs, had been incorporated into the new manual. And many, if not all countries in the region, had already created, or were in the process of creating manuals of their own. All endorsed by influential CARICOM and OECS partners like Jamaica, Trinidad and Tobago, Barbados, the UK, and the United States, one reason for my confidence the manual wouldn't be shelved to gather dust by a new regime. And we'd already been looking beyond the just completed manual to another, aimed at police management, the middle and upper ranks, where training in advanced police management methods and techniques were sorely lacking. As I mingled among them, I thanked them for their support and acceptance of my invitation.

The dinner hour approaching, I went in search of Melanie, spotting her in conversation with the British High Commissioner to the OECS. Her rose-colored cocktail dress perfectly complimented her complexion and jet black hair. Not to mention her figure. The V neckline created by the dress's wrapped bodice accented her bosom. The satiny material rose over her shoulders, leaving her toned upper arms bare. Its gathered fabric circled her middle like a cummerbund, delineating her slim waist, the flair of her hips, the curve of her buttocks, before falling in tapered folds to just below her knees.

Taking it off the only thought in my head.

She noticed my approach and graciously excused herself from the High Commissioner's admiring attention. I steered her toward the dining room, out of range of any prying ears.

"Since I have no intention of discussing shop when we're alone later, this might be the best time to ask if you've heard anything new regarding our little international situation."

My euphemistic understatement elicited a smile.

"The only new development is the CIA's interest. They've begun monitoring the situation. For the time being they seem content to let the FBI take the lead. But Langley doesn't always read my office into their operations in the region. So who knows."

She glanced discretely around our immediate vicinity, ensuring we weren't being paid any undue attention. I wondered whether due to our conversation, or the other thing.

We'd met two years before at a security conference, after she'd been posted to the U.S. Embassy in Barbados, and assigned as liaison to the Regional Security System. Being new on the block, she'd met often with Police Commissioners across the region, and was a frequent guest at meetings of the Association of Caribbean Commissioners of Police.

We'd formed a friendship, based on shared interests, the fact I'm American, and my self- appointed role as cultural guide, providing her a Caribbean perspective and experience.

Friendship blossomed into romance. But small islands being what they are, and given her position at the embassy, we both agreed to keep the relationship discreet.

"Anyway," she continued, "The last thing the U.S. needs is a failed state, or a narco state in their backyard. Hench the CIA interest."

The call to dinner interrupted any further conversation of the topic. But her information, its implications for a particular friend of mine, worried me.

We survived dinner, and another brief round of after dinner mingling, before managing a discreet escape. At the embassy house, we retired directly to the upstairs master bedroom, the mosquito netting already tucked around the double bed by whoever had prepared the house for her arrival. Melanie headed for the bathroom while I stood at the foot of the bed undressing, laying my suit jacket carefully across the divan.

The toilet flushed, followed by the sound of water running from the sink faucet, and the brushing of teeth.

"How's the speech coming," she said, her words muffled.

"Haven't found the right tone yet," I said. "I want to hit the mark with the least amount of words possible. Speaking in public isn't in my comfort zone. And there'll be enough long winded people speaking tomorrow. I don't intend to be one of them. How about you?"

"I had my remarks prepared before I left. Fortunately I have a public relations officer for that sort of thing," a teasing inflection in her voice. The sound of running water ceased. I slipped under the net to wait for her in bed.

She stepped into the room, wearing a sheer white teddy, which left little to the imagination. She flipped on the window AC unit and approached the bed. She lifted the teddy above her head, revealing a body belying her fifty-two years, or the birth of two children. One of those women possessing Lena Horne type genes, who looked forty when they were fifty, and fifty when they were sixty. No drooping or sagging, except for her breasts, though there, the meager sag gave their soft, rounded size and shape a pleasant supple appeal.

Not a taut stomach, but flat, smoothly flowing into a mounded pubis covered by a triangle of straight, dark, silky strands of hair. She dropped the teddy over the bedside lampshade, diming its light further. The immediate area around the bed illuminated as if by candlelight. She lifted the mosquito net and slid next to me beneath the top sheet.

Moist lips met mine. Her breath minty fresh. Our tongues met, probing, tasting, flicking in teasing little circles around each other. Her mouth moved lower, to my chest, taking a nipple between her teeth, nipping gently, running her tongue across it. A hot, flaring flood of desire surged through me like lava flowing from a volcano. Blood rushed to my extremities. To the sensitive tissues of my lips, my skin, my groin.

Her hand caressed my chest. Brushed across my stomach. Reached lower. Her fingers curled around my rigid erection, grasping it, stroking it. She threw a leg across my lower body. Rose to straddle me. Dark vivacious eyes stared into mine as she guided my erection toward the soft slippery opening between her thighs. Slipped it inside. Warm, moist, and titillating. A long breathy sigh escaped her lips as she slid down its length, burying it deep inside her. Pressed against its hilt, a throaty groan replaced the sigh.I fought for restraint, fearing I'd already lost to the swelling impulse to burst inside her.

She favored this position, already working her way to an inevitable climax. Her hips swayed and swiveled, rocking back and forth as she performed an erotic dance on top of me, my pelvis thrusting as she moved. Eyes closed, mouth ajar, her gasping breaths exploded against my face, her rhythm building to a feverish intensity. Her swinging hair and breasts brushed my cheeks, my eyes, my nose.

I captured a gyrating breast in my hand. Soft and smooth. Drew the nipple to my mouth. Licked it. Sucked on it. Nipped it between my teeth. The small brown nub hardened. I blew gently on it. Heard her responsive groan.

I enclosed the breast in my mouth. Suckled it. Then the other. The free breast slapped my face as she rode me in unrestrained abandon, her intensity building. Her groans reached a higher pitch, forming my name, repeated over and over as the tension built inside her. Her thrusting developed a mind of its own, a rhythm of its own, a runaway dynamo pumping, writhing, uncontrollable. Her breath ragged, catching on disjointed, inchoate words. Crying out my name as vaginal muscles spasmed and squeezed, demolishing my restraint.

My pent up sexual desire exploded in her like a burst dam. A strangled cry escaped my lips as the breath rushed from my lungs. A groan from deep within her accompanied the convulsive rippling of her arms and thighs.

She collapsed on top of me, shivering, breathing heavily, slowly descending from the ecstatic peak she'd been transported to. And wonder of wonders, I retained a measure of rigidity. It'd been four months since our last time together, the accumulated desire damned behind the waiting, ready for a long fulsome release.

A familiar stirring rose again in my groin. I rolled her over, on top of her, still joined to her, embedded within her. My mouth explored her face, her nose, cheeks, and lips, the sides of her neck, the curve of her throat, enveloping a nipple, sucking, switching to the other. The stirring in my groin more intense, my tumescence hardening inside her, squeezed by snug, moist walls, a tightness contradicting she'd ever given birth. Twice.

She wrapped her legs around me, her heels pressing my buttocks downward. Her hips and pelvis arched upward, thrusting to meet my own. I stared down at her closed eyes, at the perfectly proportioned nose, nostrils flaring with each inhalation. At the parted lips emitting low throaty moans. At the flushed skin, and undulating breasts, rippling like swells on a creamy white ocean.

I spread her legs wide, my hands pressed against her thighs, just below her knees, bouncing her on the springy mattress in rhythm to my rapidly increasing thrusts, propelled by an intensifying tightening in my loins. An excruciatingly long way off, but steadily approaching, with each bounce, each thrust. Faster and faster. Closer. Closer.

The room disappeared and awareness dissolved. The intensifying ache my entire universe. In danger of fading if I slackened the pace. My hips a thrusting piston, driving into her fast and hard. Her pelvis bounced beneath me, against me. My entire being fixed on one purpose, reaching the top of the approaching pinacle.

Muscles straining, rivers of sweat on my chest, nerve endings raw, blood screaming in my ears. My heart on the verge of busting. Her muscles clenched, contracting around me like a fist. The exquisite friction transported me the final distance, pushing me over the brink, unleashing an explosion in my brain, and an equisite pulsing release.

Raw, primitive sounds penetrated my returning awareness. A mingling of two voices, hers, and mine, calling out in gasping breaths. Our bodies wet, sweat covered and glistening. Her interior muscles clenched, squeezing my hypersensitive glans, producing a jolt of energy along its shaft, into my groin, through my pelvis and along my spine, culminating in tingling aftershocks at the base of my brain.

Her body quivered beneath me, fingernails embedded in my sides. My full weight collapsed on top of her. She wrapped her arms around me, pulling me down onto her with even greater force.

"Jesus Christ Mike!" she moaned, her voice next to my ear.

I lay in her arms, our sweat mingling as time drifted by.

When I rolled off to her side, our breathing had returned to normal. Our bodies hot to the touch. The heat we'd generated overwhelming the small air-conditioner. Disheveled bed linen crumpled beneath us.

I sat up, found the corner of the rumpled top sheet and covered our lower halves. Reaching outside the netting, I retrieved the flimsy teddy and doused the lamp. My hand sought hers in the darkness, grasped it, held it to my mouth. I pressed my lips gently against it.

We lay next to each other, spent, until blissful sleep claimed us both.

CHAPTER 9

Cecilia glanced up from her desk when I entered the outer office, her eyes wide in a startled expression.

"You're humming," she said.

"What's that?"

"You're humming."

"And what's so wrong with that?"

A smile softened the austere lines of her face. Thin, penciled eyebrows rose on her broad brown forehead.

"You never hum," she said.

I switched to whistling and passed into my inner office. When I turned to sit, she stood directly behind me, a mug of coffee in her hand, her sharp stare inquisitive. She placed the mug on my desk.

"And you seldom bring me coffee," I said, eyeing the mug.

Wearing the same sly smile she said, "Humming and whistling. Are you going to tell me who she is?"

"Leave me alone woman," I said, not unkindly. "I have work to do. And so do you.

Her usual severe expression replaced the smile. "Be like that," she said, turning to leave.

"You can get your own coffee from now on."

"I already do," I threw at her departing back.

I had no scheduled meetings for the day except the usual briefings by Huggins and Taylor. After dispensing with them, I strode to the large arched window overlooking Bay Street, absently observing the traffic and pedestrians moving along the busy thoroughfare. My mind focused on the speech I had to deliver in the afternoon.

Turning toward my desk I paused, surveying the office, a representation of the last eight years of my life, and the culmination of a career in law enforcement. In the corner sat a glass topped, chrome legged curved desk I'd finally bought and shipped from the States, replacing the bulky metal monstrosity I'd inherited. A fitting metaphor for the police force I'd also inherited.

Behind the desk a credenza, framed photographs of my son and daughter at either end, like bookends. Toward the center of the credenza a police band scanner, among mementoes and artifacts collected over the past eight years as Commissioner of Police. On the adjacent wall hung a framed portrait of the first Police Commissioner following St. Vincent's independence in 1979. A severe white face, possessing a bushy handlebar mustache, stared out from the black and white photograph. Next to it the obligatory portrait of Her Majesty the Queen.

On the opposite side of the room a sitting area, and against the wall, a floor to ceiling bookcase. Books, journals, and periodicals on the subject of law enforcement lined the shelves. And more mementoes.

A door next to the bookshelves led into my conference room, one end of a long rectangular conference table visible through the open door. The table surrounded by cushioned straight backed-chairs. Another door at the near end of the conference room provided access from the outer office.

Sighing, I decided I wasn't going to miss this office, and headed to my desk. The intercom buzzed as I reached my padded black leather swivel reclining armchair, another personal purchase.

"Superintendent Johanssen on the line for you," Cecilia announced when I picked up.

"JJ," I greeted her cheerily, leaning the chair back, my humming, whistling disposition still in full force.

"Morning Chief," she said. "Think maybe we caught a break in the case."

I sprang forward in the chair, returning it to its upright position.

"Tell me."

"We identified a fisherman buddy of Whittaker. Also a smuggler. They were seen together the night before Whittaker was killed. Now he's disappeared. But we may know where to find him."

"He a suspect?"

"From everything I've been able to learn about him I don't think so. But he may know something, and I'm interested in why he's hiding all of a sudden."

"Where do you think he is?"

"My information is he has relatives on Grenada and he may try to make a run there today."

"Awright. What do you need?"

"A Coast Guard fast interceptor."

"I'll call the Commander and arrange it. When and where?"

"I'm on Canuoan now. I'll use their Boston Whaler to rendezvous with the interceptor as soon as it can get here."

"Think you'll still be able to make the ceremony this afternoon."

"Not sure Mike. I'd hate to miss it, but have to see how this goes."

"That's the priority. Keep me appraised. And JJ, be careful."

"Always. Talk to you later," she said, ending the call.

I placed the call to Lieutenant Commander David Pompey, the Coast Guard commander, explaining the situation. After hanging up, I leaned back in the chair, pondering Jolene's new development, when my cell phone rang. A satellite prefix and index number. Gage.

"Any progress," I said.

"I've found our man," the calm baritone said through the earpiece.

"No shit."

"Yes shit. We need to meet. I know you have that thing this afternoon, so any time before then is fine."

"Let's say noon. We can meet somewhere for lunch."

"No lunch. Meet me on Glen Road, at the switchback above the Adventist Church."

"Okay. See you there. Noon," I said.

He disconnected.

I had two hours before the meet. Two hours to work on my still incomplete speech. I carried in my head the things I wanted to say. Still in bullet points form. But focusing proved useless. My thoughts ran instead to the phone calls from Gage and Jolene.

At the appointed time, I waited in an unmarked Toyota RAV4 on the side of Glen Road. A sprawling area of densely packed low-income homes. The complete opposite of Montrose. Many of the homes mere rudimentary wood structures. Sheets of galvanized tin served as roofs, and fences, separating dusty dirt yards.

A moderate amount of vehicular traffic swept past, Glen Road a main thoroughfare connecting Calliaqua, Arnos Vale, and Villa. Foot traffic too, people who didn't own cars, or couldn't afford the dollar vans. Stout women carried heavy bundles on their head. Children in rag tag thread bare clothing and school uniforms passed on either side of the road, and men headed to and from nearby farms.

I had no idea from which direction Gage might appear. I checked the road ahead. Glanced frequently at the rear view and side mirrors to check behind. No sign of him. I wondered if he'd been delayed somehow. Passersby checked the vehicle with vacant glances, continuing on their way. A man approached from the rear, on the driver's side. Like the others, non-descript, head bowed, focused on the road. Another laborer, dressed in yard clothes, which had seen better days.

I shifted my gaze ahead, checking the faces of people heading toward the vehicle. Still no sign of Gage. Glanced to the side mirror. More pedestrians farther back heading my way. Where'd the other man go? I wondered

The passenger side door opened.

My chest constricted. My heart froze. The breath caught in my throat. What the fuck...?

I spun in the seat, an indignant rebuke at the ready, or to defend myself. Brown eyes as hard and cold as a glacier stared back at me.

"Jesus Christ Gage! You almost gave me a heart attack."

"You need to be more careful," he said. His only greeting.

"I was being careful. Like it matters with a ghost like you."

"Never did like that nickname," he said calmly. "Drive."

I started the SUV, threw it in gear. "Where to?"

"Anywhere. Doesn't matter. Down toward the church will do."

After I turned off the main road, Gage handed me a folded sheet of paper.

"That's the guy you want," he said. "Constable Devon Weekes. Lives over by Brighton. Works out of the Calliaqua Station. He's on duty there now. Tight with the Coast Guard boys at the base. Do a lot of drinking together. Probably how he gathers info on their assignments and deployments."

I'd studied the personnel files long enough to have their faces burned into my memory. But I still unfolded the sheet between hands holding the steering wheel. I briefly glanced at the photo and particulars I'd emailed to Gage earlier.

"Kid has a serious gambling and drug problem." Gage said. "Pilfers stuff to raise cash. He also sells weed. The others don't trust him. Definitely bad blood there we can exploit. I have photographs and I also tossed his place. Idiot keeps a lot of incriminating stuff around. If you pick him up at home you'll find more evidence than you'll need. But I want to soften him some before you do that."

"What the hell does that mean?"

"I've already planted a seed the gang doesn't trust him and is pressuring his buddies to dump him, or worse. I need a little more time to let it take root. And I'm going to dry up his supply. Make it look like the gang is cutting him loose and his buddies are coming to get him."

"How'd you manage to get all this in just a few days?" I asked, approaching the church grounds.

"I buy his weed."

"Okay. Say I go along with this, how much time do you need?"

"By this weekend you'll be able to play him like a piano."

We'd reached the church. In its dirt parking lot I U-turned, heading in the direction we came.

"Where to now?"

"Drop me off back on Glen Road."

"Hey Gage. Is there any particular reason the CIA would want to come after you?" I asked.

"I can think of a few," he said, the heat of his stare burning the side of my neck. Forthright as always. But also succinct. Taciturn. Never revealing more than he wanted.

I glanced at him before returning my attention to the narrow winding road.

"I happen to know the CIA is monitoring our situation here."

He didn't ask how I knew. "Monitoring?" he said.

"Doesn't appear to be much more than that for now. But can't know for sure," I said.

"They have eyes and ears in the political and business community," he said with nonchalant certainty. A statement which both surprised and disturbed me. "No one on the ground as far as I know. But I'll fine tune my radar anyway. Thanks for the heads up."

We'd reached the main road. I turned left, heading in the direction of Calliaqua.

"Got your speech ready?" he asked, a sly smile creasing his mouth, accustomed to my penchant for procrastinating whenever I had to give a speech.

"Working on it," I smiled back at him, aware of time slipping by, and running out.

CHAPTER 10

The Old Montrose Police Station outside Kingstown possessed the space and facilities suitable for the ceremony. Including a parade ground, upon which rows of folding chairs had been arranged, facing a raised reviewing stand.

The reviewing stand, covered to shield the dignitaries from the sun's harsh glare and heat, held a single row of folding chairs. A mahogany dais bearing the RSVPF coat of arms stood at the front. At the front corners, the national flag of St. Vincent and the Grenadines, and the Royal St. Vincent and the Grenadines Police Force banner, fluttered in the hot breeze. Next to the reviewing stand, the Police band played a medley of martial music.

Vincy time in full sway. The Prime Minister had not yet arrived, and the crowd milling around on the parade ground showed no sign of taking their seats. The event already twenty minutes behind schedule. The visiting dignitaries, already in their seats, waited in the stifling heat. I'd delivered Melanie to her seat before settling into my own, three away from her.

At twenty seven minutes past the scheduled time Superintendent of Police Byron, commander of the Southern Division, strode across the platform, stepped to the microphone and called for everyone to take their seats. The chairs on the parade ground slowly filled.

A line of ranking police officials occupied the front row. Deputy Commissioner Huggins, Superintendents Randolph Chambers of Recruiting, Training and Personnel, Mitchell of CID, and Basil Hughes of RSS. All in crisp dress greys, wearing braided uniform hats, their swagger sticks held across their laps.

Next to Hughes, Assistant Superintendents Bernard Rogers of the Major Crimes Unit, Keith Manley of the Special Services Unit, and Colin Browne of the Rapid Response Unit. Also in the front row, Lieutenant Commander David Pompey, Coast Guard commander, in naval dress whites, navy type insignia on his jacket and rank stripes on the sleeves.

Seated next to Pompey, to my surprise, Superintendent Johanssen, Commander of the Grenadine Division. Cool and confident, her smart grey uniform tailored to fit her tall shapely figure, her hair pulled back and tied in a tight bun in the back, just below the rim of her uniform hat. Assistant Superintendent Taylor sat to her right, and in the last three front row seats, the Permanent Secretaries of the Ministry of Security, the Ministry of Justice, and Cecilia.

Prime Minister Bacchus arrived, passing along the row of seats on the reviewing stand shaking hands, smiling and greeting the assembled dignitaries before finally assuming his seat.

Superintendent Byron stepped to the microphone again.

"Governor, honorable Prime Minister, distinguished guests, comrades, graduates, family and friends. It is wid great honor dat I welcome you heah today, to congratulate dese graduates. Let us proceed now wid de singing of de anthem."

He stepped back from the microphone. The assembled crowd and dignitaries stood in a rustle of scraping metal chairs. The police band struck up the anthem, and a discordant chorus of high, low, and off key voices sang the national anthem, hands crossed over their hearts.

Following the anthem, Byron introduced Police Constable Stephanie Blake to lead the opening prayer.

Constable Blake crossed the platform, her regulation day uniform crisply pressed and resplendent in the bright sunlight. White tunic and broad black patent leather belt, Knee length black skirt, white stripe down the sides, and uniform cap, a white crown instead of black. The black peak polished to a mirror like shine.

Following the benediction, the band played a march. On cue marchers appeared from behind a building at the rear of the parade ground. Two columns, in straight lines, representing the various units of the police force, led by a burly constable wearing a blue sash around his waist and carrying a sword, its polished metal flashing in the sun.

They marched toward the reviewing stand in lockstep, stiff straightened arms swinging forward and back in the British manner. Approaching the reviewing stand the constable shouted a command, and swung the sword upright to his face, the brass hilt in front of his chin. His head snapped to the left to face the reviewing stand.

The marchers turned their heads in unison to face the reviewing stand as they filed past, right arm raised and bent in a rigid salute. The first to pass the reviewing stand regular constabulary, clad in white tunics and black belts, black trousers, a single white stripe down the sides, and white crowned peak caps. The women in black skirts. A contingent of Tourism Police next, wearing white London Bobby style custodial helmets. A silver spike atop the helmet glinted in the sun.

Followed by Port Police, and the Fire Service. Rapid Response Unit officers dressed in dark blue uniforms and black combat boots filed past. And the Coast Guard contingent, in light blue shirts and navy blue pants, the officers in dress whites. Behind them Regional Security System police, dressed in green, red cravats around their necks, and red tams on their heads. They carried parade rifles at shoulder arms as they marched.

Finally, a single line of marchers whose leader ordered a halt in front of the reviewing stand. The graduates. The newly minted Police Constables in constabulary uniform. The RSS graduates in green camouflage fatigues and combat boots. At the given order, they stood at ease.

The speeches next.

God. These poor people in this heat. In this sun.

The Governor General spoke first, limiting his remarks to welcoming the visiting dignitaries on behalf of her Majesty, and congratulating the graduates.

Blessedly and thankfully short.

Next up to the podium the British High Commissioner. He congratulated the graduates and spoke of the remarkable progress in law enforcement and security he'd witnessed around the region during his time as High Commissioner. He congratulated the RSVGPF on its achievements, and spoke of the continuing need for improvement and regional cooperation. In closing, he pledged the continued support of Her Majesty and the United Kingdom.

Again, thankfully short.

Melanie spoke next. Her remarks echoed those of the High Commissioner. I wondered if they used the same speechwriter. She cited the Caribbean Basin and Security Initiative as the foundation for a continuing partnership between the United States and the Caribbean, aimed at ensuring sustainable, durable solutions for common security.

My turn.

Stepping to the lectern, a familiar dreaded fluttering awoke in the pit of my stomach. My breathing quickened. The first beads of sweat rose on my forehead and upper lip, having nothing to do with the heat. I gazed out at the expectant faces, found the one or two to hold my focus, including Jolene's. I paused, slowed my breathing, and dove in.

"Governor, honorable Prime Minister, distinguished guests, colleagues, honored graduates, and proud families and friends. In many police forces around the United States, and indeed around the world, the words protect and serve are an anthem, a motto, an objective to aspire to. You, who have graduated from the Regional Police Training Center on Barbados, and you, who have completed the Regional Security System training program, have answered the call to protect, and to serve, your community, your country, and your neighbors in the Caribbean community."

I paused a beat, focusing on each group in turn. The graduates stood proudly in brand new pressed uniforms, defying the heat. I glanced at the index cards on the lectern, placed my hands on its raised sides and forged ahead.

"You have chosen an honorable calling. But know it will not be an easy one. During your careers in law enforcement, you will encounter gratitude, appreciation, admiration, and also derision and hostility. You'll encounter every hue and shade of the human condition. Innocence, tragedy, graciousness, violence, resentment, and just plain mean. You're only human yourself, and may be tempted to lash out, to abuse your authority and trust, to look the other way. Those tests will define your character, as men and women, and as law enforcement professionals."

Another pause. The beads of sweat on my brow and across my upper lip turned to a stream. But I'd hit my stride, confident in my pacing and delivery to get through to the end. I wiped my forehead and mouth with a handkerchief, the blistering heat providing an appropriate excuse.

"We your leaders, we as a community, and we as a country, must encourage and support that level of professionalism. We must provide the tools to ensure you are better equipped and able to protect and serve. And so it is my great privilege to announce the completion of the first comprehensive Guide to be used by the Royal St. Vincent and the Grenadines Police Force."

Unexpected applause threw me off my stride. Jolene and the front row of police brass clapped loudly and enthusiastically. All except Mitchell and Browne. Jolene caught my gaze, flashing a wide smile and a thumbs-up sign. I regrouped while waiting for the applause to subside.

"I must thank my distinguished colleagues here at home, and from around the region, some of whom are with us here today," I said, turning from the lectern to face and acknowledge the officials seated behind me. Surprised again by their renewed applause.

"I must also thank Her Majesty's Government, and the Government of the United States, whose assistance and support made this achievement possible."

More applause behind me.

"This Guide is not a static document. It must have the capacity to change, to evolve, as times and circumstances change. It is a guide, a roadmap, a tool, for creating a professional police force capable of meeting the demanding challenges ahead. To better prepare you to protect and serve the life, property, rights, and dignity of all residents of St. Vincent and the Grenadines, and our neighbors in the region. Congratulations to you all, and God bless you all."

Jolene sprang to her feet, clapping excitedly. Huggins followed her. More followed, standing and applauding. I turned to find everyone on the platform on their feet, palms slapping together in enthusiastic applause, a beaming smile on Melanie's face. She winked at me. Christ almighty.

I resumed my seat, the applauding crowd waiting for me to sit before taking theirs. Prime Minister Bacchus the next and final speaker.

Not a pleased expression as he rose and stepped to the dais. Not known for his rhetoric or eloquence, I'd unintentionally provided a difficult act to follow. His disposition upon taking the lectern didn't help his speech. Though I doubt anything could. Expectedly long winded, and rambling, he delivered his remarks in a dull monotone. He alluded to statements made in the press, and on radio, and by computer bloggers, not giving the institutions of government a chance to work. He switched to the dangers of organized crime, and the obligation of the police force to meet and defeat those dangers.

Unable to forego a political opportunity, he cited a litany of operations undertaken during his party's rule to combat organized crime, drug trafficking and corruption. Apparently no one had advised him this only served to draw attention to the scandals plaguing his party and the country.

He turned next to rogue police officers who in his words, "do no service to their oath or their uniform". Who would rather "connive" with unscrupulous public servants and businessmen. But he was sure none of the graduates in front of him will become a rogue officer.

He circled back to organized crime, making references to money laundering, conflating it and gang activity connected to guns and drugs. He concluded by appealing to all "right thinking persons," to keep the neighborhood safe.

A polite but restrained response from the audience. The applause tepid. The universal expression akin to bewilderment, and thank God it was over.

Superintendent Byron approached the Prime Minister, bent to whisper something in his ear. The PM nodded, and they departed the reviewing stand together to stand in front of the graduates. Byron produced a clipboard and hand held microphone on a long cable from beneath the platform.

He proceeded to call the names of the graduates. As he called each name, the individual marched smartly to the front, stamped to attention, and offered a stiff salute. After the PM shook their hand, each graduate saluted again, performed a sharp about face, and marched back to the line, stamping to a halt before executing another about face.

A few graduates received certificates and awards for accomplishments during training. A female RSS graduate, standing head and shoulders above the Prime Minister, received an award for best marksmanship in her class.

"Ahhhh ten shun" Commanded Superintendent Byron. In unison the line stamped to stiff attention. Byron led the new constables in reciting the police oath.

At the conclusion, Byron shouted, "Dissss missed"

The line saluted, executed a sharp about face, and broke ranks.

The police band played. This time lively popular music. The crowd dispersed into small groups. The graduates surrounded by knots of family and friends. Police brass gathered in little cliques.

Jolene found me off to the side of the reviewing stand in conversation with Huggins and Taylor. They departed after mutual congratulations.

"Congratulations Mike," Jolene said, a warm, proud smile on her gleaming face. "Helluva nice speech."

"Sometime I surprise even myself," I said.

"You say that, and you hem and haw until the last minute whenever you have to give a speech. But I've never known you to not pull it off. Just like you did today."

"Your being in the audience may've helped. Surprised you made it. How'd your thing go?"

"Peters is in custody in the Bequia jail. We intercepted him between Union and Carriacou before he'd made it into Grenadian waters. I had time for a preliminary interrogation. Showed him some of my cards. Figured I'd let him stew for a while. I'll get back to him during the weekend."

"I emailed you everything I have on him from Whittaker's intelligence. Should give you a few more cards to play in your interrogation."

Melanie's approach interrupted any further discussion of the case. Her eyes locked on Jolene in an appraising gaze.

"Excellent speech Commissioner," she said, shifting her gaze to me. "Poignantly short and inspiring."

"Thank you Consul Barnes," I said, suddenly overcome by a discomforting awkwardness.

She turned to face Jolene again. "And you of course must be Superintendent Johanssen," she said, before I had the chance to introduce them, offering her hand. They shook.

"It's a pleasure to finally meet you," Melanie said. "I've heard so very much about you. The excellent work you're doing here," she added quickly.

"Thank you Consul Barnes," Jolene replied politely.

"Oh please," Melanie scoffed, "It's Melanie."

"Your Commissioner has kindly offered to fly me back to Barbados," Melanie told her. The women smiled at each other, eyes locked in continuing mutual appraisal, producing a subtle change in demeanor. A silent communication and understanding I wasn't privy to.

"The Superintendent is a pilot too," I interjected quickly, in a feeble and failed attempt to stem my inexplicable discomfort.

"I believe you've mentioned that," Melanie said, eyes still glued to Jolene's. Jolene's smile coyishly brighter.

"Well, if you'll please excuse me. I have to catch a ride back to Bequia," Jolene said. "And it's really been a pleasure meeting you," shaking Melanie's hand again, a meaningful emphasis on 'pleasure meeting you'.

"Commissioner," she said, her gaze meeting mine, a mischievous twinkle in the amber-green irises of hers. "You'll call me when you're back on Bequia?"

"Lovely woman," Melanie said, her gaze following Jolene's departure across the parade ground.

"She knows, doesn't she?"

"Of course she does. She's not only very perceptive, she's very close to you. Our little secret's safe with her though," Melanie said, smiling. "Anyway did I mention how devastatingly dashing you look in that uniform," her smile transforming into a teasing grin. "I believe it's the first time I've seen you in your dress greys, full regalia, swagger stick and all. Very British. Very sexy," she said, eyebrows raised provocatively.

"Hate that damn thing," I muttered under my breath.

She laughed.

Dusk by the time we arrived at E.T. Joshua airport, the sun below the horizon, and the western sky painted in lingering shades of scarlet and orange. Dark by the time we reached the sky, the dim horizon behind us, Barbados a thirty minute flight east through a clear, star filled sky. The sea, a dark undulating mass nine thousand feet below. In the distance, Barbados appeared as a tiny oval galaxy of twinkling lights in the center of a dark void.

The Seneca's twin Continentals droned steadily, their monotonous regularity comforting. Melanie and I sat in quiet, relaxed companionship in the cockpit, our faces lit by the dim red and amber glow of the panel.

"It's so peaceful up here," Melanie remarked. "The perspective just isn't the same when you're sitting in the back surrounding by a bunch of passengers."

"The feeling never gets old" I told her.

"You sound like my Daniel. Or he sounds like you. You two have a lot in common. About the only thing he seemed to have inherited from his father is a love of the military. Being a Navy pilot just far enough from his father's footsteps."

"And how's Justin," I asked, referring to her younger son, a State Department lawyer.

"Chafing. His love is the international side of law. But State is a huge slow moving bureaucracy."

"Well he's smart. And having you as his mother he's got some juice. He just needs to be patient. It'll happen."

"Patience has never been one of his virtues. And he won't have anything to do with even the appearance of maternal nepotism. Wants to make it on his own. Doesn't stop me from having a few well placed friends keep an eye on him though. How about yours?"

"Terrific," I said, during a visual scan of the panel. "June is swamped in the workload of her residency. Ungodly hours. But enjoying it. Jared is enjoying life and work. Remember being their age?" I asked smiling. "Just starting out. Your whole life ahead of you."

The circle of lights grew steadily in the windshield. Fifteen minutes out, I trimmed for a gentle five hundred foot per minute descent.

"Coincidence or by design your roommate is away for the weekend?" I asked.

"Does it matter? As long as we have the place to ourselves."

"Just wouldn't want you thinking of me as a foregone conclusion," I teased. "What if I hadn't been free this weekend?"

"When it comes to our infrequent booty calls we're both foregone conclusions. And you are free this weekend?" Spoken as a question.

"Barring some national emergency, I'm all yours."

Grantley Adams International airport on Barbados's southern coast emerged from the clutter of surrounding lights. I set up for the approach and landing.

After securing the Seneca and clearing Immigration, a perfunctory process given Melanie's diplomatic status and my police status, we grabbed a taxi outside the general aviation terminal.

During the ride I remembered neither of us had eaten since lunch. "You hungry?" I asked. "Maybe we should stop on the way."

"There's food at the house," she said. "Enough to nosh on anyway. Whatever else we need we can pick up tomorrow. Anyway food isn't what I'm hungry for," she said, a loaded smile aimed at me, eyebrows alluringly raised, eyelids lowered, the tip of her tongue peeking out between parted lips.

Melanie and a senior consular affairs officer shared a beach house just off Highway 7 in Oistin Bay, on Barbados's southern coast. The only senior single women in the embassy, the arrangement benefited them both. The house sat a hundred yards from the water, on a small tree shaded lot, Neighbors to the left and right. Close, but far enough removed to offer privacy.

Melanie switched on interior lights as we passed through the sliding French doors of the deck overlooking the beach. She draped her garment bag over the back of a settee in the sitting room. I dropped my small overnight bag on the floor.

In the kitchen she opened the refrigerator and produced a chilled bottle of red wine. From an overhead cabinet she retrieved two wine glasses, the crystal clinking as she held the stems between her fingers.

"You hungry?" she said, decanting the wine, handing me one of the glasses.

"Not really," I said,

"Good." She set her glass down on the kitchen counter, hiked her skirt above her thighs and sat back on the kitchen table, her legs open, inviting.

Whether it'd been my mentioning during our getting acquainted phase of my ex's unimaginative and non-spontaneous approach to sex, or a natural proclivity to experiment and surprise, Melanie repeatedly proved the exact opposite of my ex.

Her hand reached behind my neck to pull my mouth down on hers. Her free hand worked at my belt buckle and the zipper of my pants.

Our tongues probed and explored. Waves of pleasure and anticipation rippled through both of us. Her hand reached inside my opened pants, through the front opening of my boxers, grasping me, massaging, stroking, freeing my erection.

I almost dropped my wine glass. I groped around for a safe place to set it down

"I want you. I want you now," she breathed in my ear, opening her legs wider, pulling me toward her. Surrendering herself.

My mouth, lips, tongue, roamed her face. One hand pushed her flat on the kitchen table. A gentle suck at the sensitive spot of her neck elicited a soft moan. My fingers grasped the waistband of her black lace underwear, pulling it from her crotch. The elastic material stretched across her parted thighs.

An animalistic groan escaped her lips when I entered her. Soft, slippery friction as I pushed in and withdrew in a slow, tantalizing rhythm, our pleasure mounting, transporting us to that ecstatic sexual high.

I lifted her legs. Laid each leg across a shoulder, the position facilitating my thrusting penetration. She writhed beneath me. Cried out my name as I plunged deeper and faster. She gasped. Tremors rippled her body. Her inner muscles clenched my shaft buried inside her. My pelvis hard against her swollen clitoris. Her orgasm spurred my own. The hot shock of it forced the breath from my lungs, my groan mingling with her cries.

Her eyes opened. She smiled up at me. "Delicious," she said.

Our session in the kitchen turned out to be only the opening round of a carnal weekend, interspersed by brief interruptions for food, sleep, and light inconsequential conversation. We utilized every room and surface in the house. We used the bedroom only once, when she woke me in the morning, the moist heat of her mouth pulling me from sleep. I grew hard and thich from her licking and sucking, the up and down friction of her lips and tongue triggering a spurting eruption in her mouth.

We rutted like teenagers. But with the acquired knowledge and experience we didn't have as teenagers. Our generation had precipitated the sexual revolution. The era of free love. Playboy and Hustler. Gloria Steinhem and Deep Throat. Yet it'd still taken many of us another three decades to acquire the hang of it.

Late Saturday afternoon we lay sunning on the deck. She lay face down on a sturdy padded chaise. The waist high brick wall surrounding the sun porch shielding us from errant eyes passing along the beach. I rubbed lotion on her bare, naked back. I ran a finger lightly along her spine, inducing a shiver.

Reaching her bare bottom, I massaged the soft yielding flesh of her buttocks. Ran my hand down the split between her cheeks. My fingers threaded a path through the fine strands of hair. Found and parted the curled lips between her legs. Another shiver ran through her as my fingers rubbed and probed inside. The satiny texture produced a familiar stirring in my groin.

God. I could stay hard all day for this woman.

She shivered again, arching her bottom as my fingers stimulated the moist lips and sensitive nub, my thumb resting against the puckered hole just above. I pressed the tip of my thumb into the sphinctered enclosure. She gasped.

"Sorry," I said, removing my thumb.

"No. It's okay. Just wasn't expecting it. Keep doing it."

I pressed my thumb in again, farther the second time. She moaned. The sound primal, guttural. My erection rigid hard, perpendicular to my body, unable to contain my desire aroused by her continuous moaning, by her writhing hips, arching upward.

I spread her thighs. Her legs dangled on either side of the chaise. I cupped her cheeks in my hands, pressed my erection against her slippery opening and entered her from behind.

Oh sweet Jesus. The tight sensation amplified by my position behind and above her. She gasped. Breath hissed through clenched teeth. She moved against me as I pushed deeper. We worked together to establish a rhythm. Her breathing changed from closed mouth hissing to open mouth grunting. She arched her rear to meet my thrusts, pushing back against me, heightening the friction, rushing me to the brink.

I reached around her hip. Found the moist and hardened nub. Massaged it. Her voice penetrated my awareness, crying out my name amid pleasurable grunts. I concentrated on my hand and fingers, stimulating her as I pushed back and forth in her, my thighs slapping against her soft jiggling gluteus.

I sensed the gathering in my loins, the anticipatory tightening, an instant before a shuddering eruption shook me, summoning her own orgasmic release. Beneath me, a familiar quivering rippled through her, and against my skin.

God, I thought, as I sank against her, and kissed the back of her neck.

CHAPTER 11

I arrived home late Sunday Afternoon literally drained, but emotionally euphoric. A forlorn ache in the pit of my stomach signaled I was already missing her. But that absence probably provided the spice and passion in our relationship, ingredients which might wane over time, and too much closeness.

I'd informed Jolene of my return. She said she'd be over to brief me on her interrogation. I had a cold beer open and waiting when she arrived. I clinked my glass of Jack Daniels against her bottle, while those stunning and perceptive amber-green eyes scrutinized me.

"Relaxing weekend?" she asked, her smile sly. Damn well aware of how I'd spent the weekend.

I returned her smile. My sexually saturated disposition imperturbable.

"Wonderful," I said.

"Why'd you never tell me about her Mike? Why the big secret? And all this time I'm worrying about you."

"A gentleman doesn't kiss and tell," I said. "Especially to someone who's like a daughter."

"Who else knows? Gage? Your kids?"

"No one else knows. And I guess now that you do Gage will too."

"Not if you don't want me to tell him."

"Doesn't matter. And if there's anyone can keep a secret it's that close mouthed sonnabitch."

"No kidding," she chortled. "He's been gone on St. Vincent all week. He calls me every night, but I can't get a goddamned thing out of him.

"He's doing a little job for me," I said. "Tracking those rogue RRU guys. He's gotten close to one of them, and we're getting ready to make an arrest."

"Oh," she said, thin delicate lines furrowed her brow, quickly shrugged off.

"Anyway Dad," her facetious and playful nature ever close to the surface, "I like her. June and Jared will too. You guys make a nice couple." Her curious inquisitive eyes peered into mine. "Is it serious?"

"Been seeing each other a couple of years. It's monogamous. But we've never talked about where it might be heading. Or a future together. For right now it is what it is and we both enjoy the time we spend together."

"Yeah I bet you do. Going by that Cheshire grin fixed on your face and the gleam in your eyes."

"See. That's exactly why I don't talk about it."

"Well I like it. Good for you Mike," raising her bottle in salute.

We'd been standing in the kitchen. I motioned her to the living room, a step lower than the kitchen area. A warm but soothing breeze wafted through the open shutters, billowing the window curtains on the windward side of the room, flattening them against the open windows on the other.

I settled into the comfortable armchair, Jolene perched on the corner of the couch closest to the chair.

"What's the latest?" I said.

"Not sure what it all means yet. Apparently this man, Gregory Peters, took a job to deliver something from Mustique to St. Vincent, and was supposed to bring back a package from St. Vincent. That day he had engine problems with his boat. He arranged for his friend, Whittaker, to do the job, for a small consideration to Phillips of course. Anyway, when he heard it was Whittaker's body we found, he started thinking maybe the same was supposed to happen to him. That the person who'd offered him the job in the first place might come looking for him. He got scared. Went into hiding, and then tried to make a run for Grenada."

"Any idea what the packages were?" I asked.

"Said he was never told. And since he didn't do the job he never saw them."

"What about the person who hired him for the job?"

"That's the weird part. He says the man who hired him was on a Venezuelan freighter he met up with out at sea one night. The man wasn't Venezuelan, and had an American accent, not Spanish."

"And the person he was supposed to meet on Mustique?"

"Says he doesn't know. He was supposed to go ashore in Obsidian Bay. Someone was supposed to meet him there."

"Doesn't give us much at all," I said.

"I know. But I believe him. One, he's seems too scared to lie. But also I don't read him as lying or holding back."

"And now you're stuck."

"Exactly. I can't just go around questioning everyone on Mustique. If the killer's there he'll know we're looking as soon as I start asking questions. Then there're the visitors. They'll require delicate handling."

"Well before you do anything let's take a look at who's there. It's off season. May not be too many visitors. Go through the immigration records and see who's staying on the island. Who arrived just prior to and during the time Whittaker was killed. Should be a short list. And maybe you start with Basil. Don't let him see you're focusing on Mustique, and tell him to keep his mouth shut."

"Yeah. I've been thinking Basil might be a place to start. Trying to figure how to approach him."

"Make it look like a routine canvas of the Grenadines. If he's seen or heard anything that might help with the inquiry. Anyone new on the island. That sort of thing. You know how to work him."

She smiled, glanced at my empty glass and asked, "Refill?"

"Please," I said, handing her the glass. She stood, plucked her empty bottle from the coffee table and headed toward the kitchen.

From the kitchen she said, "When will Gage be done with your little errand?"

"By tonight probably. Should be hearing from him soon in fact. Hopefully we can wrap it up by tomorrow and you can have him back." Still drenched in the afterglow of my sexually creative weekend, I wondered about their sex life. I quickly banished the thought and the mental picture from my head. Don't even go there, I admonished myself.

Gage called later in the evening, after Jolene had departed to meet a friend for dinner at the Frangipani.

"He's primed and ready," Gage said. "When do you want to do this?"

"Tomorrow night," I said. "I'd thought of taking him before moving on the others. But no way to keep a lid on arresting an RRU constable. When he doesn't report for work there'll be questions. The station will probably send someone to his house. And if his cronies go into hiding it'll just prolong this and make it more difficult."

"Sounds right," he said. "When do you want to meet?"

"First thing in the morning. You name the time and place."

"How about breakfast at the Beachcomber."

"See you there," I said, disconnecting.

I called Sammy next, using the secure phone I'd provided him. I gave him a heads up on the impending arrest. I informed him he'd completed his assignment and I'd be bringing him in. I arranged a rendezvous to pick him up in the morning.

Before I turned in for the night, Melanie called.

"Wanted to catch you before you went to bed," she said, a wistfulness in her voice distance and cellular service couldn't disguise. "Could hardly walk all afternoon," she said. I imagined her smiling. "Been waddling around like when I was pregnant."

The word produced a sharp pinch in my chest. A quickening of my breath. We'd ceased using contraception some months before. When she'd thought she'd been experiencing perimenopausal symptoms. She still experienced periods, though irregularly. And she still lubricated easily and well for a woman her age, I often thought. And she possessed those slow aging genes.

A bit late for either of us to begin parenting again.

"Just wanted to say goodnight," she said, the wistful tone resurfacing.

"I'm glad you called," I said.

"Night then," she said. "I miss you."

"Miss you too. Sleep tight."

She disconnected. We'd never spoken the 'L' word, but I recognized the depth of my emotional connection to her. Beyond just sex. And small gestures like her phone call might mean she felt the same way too.

Arriving in Kingstown early the following morning, I headed directly to Villa, southwest of Kingstown. I used a taxi rather than police transport. I stepped onto the outdoor dining deck of the Beachcomber Hotel, the air sea salt fresh, a remnant of the overnight cool in the air. Dew lingered on the leaves and flowers, not yet evaporated by the sun commencing its climb in the eastern sky.

Gage waited at a table by the railing, nursing a cup of steaming aromatic coffee. The deck overlooked villa beach, the tranquil blue water of Indian Bay, and the Young Island resort. The high priced resort just awakening. The bay, usually crowded in season with transient yachts, currently empty, except for Wherever bobbing contentedly on her anchor.

At my approach Gage motioned to the waitress. The only occupants of the dining area, she'd been waiting for him to order. We ordered a breakfast of eggs, sausage, fruit and toast. And more coffee.

"You're looking chipper," he said after the waitress departed.

I eyed him suspiciously. "You talk to JJ?" I asked more defensively than I'd intended.

His brown eyes narrowed in a questioning stare. "Just want to be sure you're on your game," he said. "This guy is only the first domino in a network you're attempting to dismantle. You've got the other two, maybe more you haven't identified yet, and at least two gangs. Not to mention our other little situation. You have a plan?"

"Yeah. It works for bringing Sammy in too."

"The target's gonna be skittish," he said, using a term for the suspect I found discomforting, but appreciated from his perspective.

"I've got him pretty well wound," he continued. "He's paranoid enough to do something stupid and unpredictable. And there're weapons in the house. You and your people need to be careful."

He smiled. His eyes turned inward, conjuring memories. He zoned out momentarily, a peculiar habit I'd grown used to.

"What?" I asked.

"Ironic," he said, returning from wherever his reminiscing had transported him. "Usually I'm the one in your shoes. Receiving intelligence, acting on it. For a long time I never questioned where it came from. Until it almost got me killed. And I didn't like what I found when I looked behind the curtain. Now here I am providing you with intel, and you're the one going out to act on it."

"At least I know and trust my source."

"Speaking of which," he said, producing a large brown manila envelope concealed beneath a cloth table napkin on his lap. He slid it toward me. "That's everything you need. How're you going to explain where you got your intelligence?"

"Part of my Sammy strategy." I said.

The arrival of breakfast interrupted our conversation. After the waitress departed we continued the discussion between bites and sips of coffee.

"Still think a late night raid is the way to go?" I asked.

"If you want to take him at home," he said. "Usually gets home around ten pm. Sometimes he goes out again. But I've got him wanting to stick close to home. But like I said, he may do something unpredictable. I'll keep tabs on him during the day. Give you enough warning if anything changes. You'll find a layout of his place in there," nodding at the envelope. "Place is a dump. And he's not too bright about hiding incriminating evidence. Also there's a shipment supposed to be going out tonight. Particulars are in there."

"Where you gonna be when this goes down?"

"I'll be around," he said simply.

CHAPTER 12

The taxi I'd boarded outside the Beachcomber pulled up to the designated corner in front of a jerk chicken and roti shop. Within moments, Keston Samuel walked out of the shop, dressed in the garb of his undercover persona, a stretched and faded blue tee shirt, the collar frayed, and threadbare blue jeans, an old rip over the right knee. Worn down hi-top sneakers without socks on his feet, the laces missing. His short spiky dreadlocks, unkempt. He slid onto the rear passenger seat next to me. We rode in silence to the station.

Curious, perplexed glances followed us as we strode briskly through the old halls to my office. We didn't stop. We spoke to no one.

In my outer office Cecilia gaped in undisguised disapproval at the scruffy person accompanying me. I'd called earlier to inform her I'd be in late and to cancel my morning briefings. Although DC Huggins should hold himself available.

"Morning Cissy," I greeted as my guest and I strode across the room without pausing.

"Commissioner? Commissioner?" She sprang out of her seat as if to defend me from the slovenly intruder, who'd somehow made it all the way into her sanctum. Her stern visage and disapproving glare targeted on him.

At my door I turned. She stood in the middle of the room, fists on her hips, and a dumbfounded expression on her austere face. Its severity amplified by the small tuft of grey rising from the right side of her hairline, her hair cut short and close to her scalp male style.

"Absolutely no calls. And absolutely no one comes through this door," I said, before disappearing inside behind Samuel.

Closing the door behind me, I leaned my back against it and smiled. The entire melodrama somehow amusing.

"Have a seat Sammy," I said indicating the sitting area. I sat at my desk, disposed of a few phone calls, before removing two thick files from a locked desk drawer and rejoining Constable Samuel.

"First of all Sammy, congratulations. Well done son. Well done. We're preparing to roll up your gang, and the rogue RRU constables. The raids go down tonight. Later we'll go over the operation with DC Huggins and the others. But before we get to that there're a few things I need to go over with you."

"Yes sir," he said, his steady stare, his entire demeanor, attentive.

"First off I need to ask you to do something. I'm hoping you'll agree, but I'll completely understand if it makes you uncomfortable."

Furrowed lines creased the smooth forehead. Thin eyebrows above thick brow ridges arched upward. I slid the envelope Gage had given me toward him.

"That contains intelligence on the rogue RRU constables. Surveillance photographs etcetera, etcetera. For reasons I cannot divulge, I have to protect the source of this intelligence. I'm asking you to claim you're the source."

A broad smile crossed his face. He nodded, "No problem Commissioner. I understand de situation."

"Good. Then study those until you know them forwards and backwards. There're notations on the back." I picked up one of the files I'd laid on the table.

"This is all the intelligence you've provided over the past few months. We'll use it to plan tonight's raids. This file is for your eyes only. It never leaves your sight, you understand. And you hand it back to me personally when you're done with it."

"Understood sir," he nodded again.

"Okay. Take those into the conference room and begin familiarizing yourselves with that," I said pointing to the envelope. "I'm going to call in Huggins and the others who'll head up the task force."

I left him in the conference room, exiting through the door to the outer office and Cecilia's desk, closing it behind me. Vestiges of her earlier vexation remained, mostly replaced by a demanding curiosity in her inquisitive stare.

"It's alright Cissy," I reassured her. "Constable Samuel and I needed to meet unexpectedly this morning."

"Constable?" Her mouth agape in disbelief.

"For your ears only," I said. "For now."

She nodded. Still unsure whether to believe it or not.

"I need to see Deputy Commissioner Huggins, Commander Pompey, Superintendent Hughes, and Assistant

Superintendents Phillips, Rogers, and Manley as soon as they can get here."

Raised eyebrows and a knitted brow her only reaction. But the inquiring eyes betrayed her increased curiosity.

"Right away sir," she said.

"Show them into the conference room when they arrive."

Except for Commander Pompey, all the commanders' offices were located in the Central Police Station building. Yet twenty minutes passed before they arrived. And they arrived together. Knowing Cecilia, she'd probably corralled them in the outer office until they'd all gathered. She ushered them into the conference room as a group, her curious gaze riveted on Constable Samuel, before retreating and closing the door behind her.

When the police officials entered the conference room, Samuel leapt to his feet as if springs had uncoiled in his chair. He stood at rigid attention and saluted the six men who stared at him in open-mouthed astonishment.

"At ease Constable," I said. Sammy immediately shifted to parade rest, his hands clasped behind his back.

"Gentlemen," I said. "Please," indicating seats surrounding the conference table. Sammy remained standing while they settled into seats around the table.

"Allow me to introduce Constable Keston Samuel," I said. Their gazes shifted uncertainly between Sammy, me, and each other. I motioned Sammy to sit.

"For the past five months Constable Samuel has been working undercover in a gang of weapons and drug smugglers. His identity known only to me. Not even his family knows he is a police constable." I allowed my statement to sink in. All eyes now intently focused on me.

I pushed the file I'd set down before me toward the center of the table.

"Constable Samuel's personnel file and record," I said. "He was recruited prior to acceptance into the police force and inducted privately. He received his basic and undercover training in the United States. Constable Samuel is an outstanding officer, with an exemplary record, who has just completed a very difficult and highly dangerous assignment. An operation we are about to bring to a close."

DC Huggins reached for the file, scanning through it as I spoke.

I retrieved the intelligence file I'd handed Samuel earlier. Opening it, I placed five by seven photographs of a dozen individuals on the table before them, laying them down like playing cards, commenting as I laid each photograph on the table.

"Clifton Barry, aka Natty. Gang leader," I said, reciting names, aliases, associations and offences as I laid each photograph on the table. "Guns, marijuana, cocaine smuggling. We have it all, thanks to Constable Samuel."

"And this," I said, lifting the manila envelope in front of Samuel and laying down photographs as before.

"Devon Weekes and Trevor Peters, out of the Calliaqua Station. Sergeant Clifford Ashton out of the Georgetown Station. All Rapid Response Unit and all dirty. They provide protection and support to Natty's gang. Devon Weekes is also a marijuana distributor."

Five pairs of eyes fixed on the photographs spread across the table, astonished expressions on the assembled faces.

"We're going to take them all down, gentlemen. Tonight."

Five heads raised in unison. All eyes refocused on me.

"Tonight Commisshunah?" Superintendent Hughes the first to regain his voice.

"Commisshunah," Huggins the next to speak. "You talking multiple raids dat need planning and coordination."

"I'm aware. But the timing is dictated by the need for operational security. Intelligence indicates a shipment of marijuana going out tonight from a cove between North Union Bay and Cedars Bay. These three RRU constables will be there. Actually only two. We're going to arrest one of them just prior to interdicting the shipment. You'll all drop anything you're working on at the moment and focus on this. Use whatever resources you need. Constable Samuel here is available to flesh out details and advise on the plan. Set up in here. Bring your people here. I want to see completed plans by sixteen hundred hours. Completed arrangements and assignments by nineteen hundred. Final preparation and staging by twenty one hundred. According to the intelligence, the shipment is supposed to load at midnight. The raids will commence simultaneously at twenty three hundred hours. And gentlemen, needless to say, nothing we say and plan here is to be discussed beyond this office. That is a direct order. Am I absolutely clear?"

I fixed my stare on each of them in turn. Waited for their acknowledgment before shifting my stare to the next. I trusted them all. Had handpicked and promoted each of them to their present positions over the past year. Yet Gage's cautionary words echoed in my ears. An act of betrayal by any one of them would be personally devastating.

"Select people you can trust, at least for the planning stages. The others don't need to know their objectives beforehand. The task force will include your Major Crimes people Bernie, your narcotics unit Leroy, Hughie your RSS people, the Special Service Unit and the Coast Guard. I haven't included the Rapid Response Unit for obvious reasons."

It couldn't be lost on any of them the only units not represented at the table were the Rapid Response Unit and CID. The RRU had been created specifically to target drug and firearms offences, but had become a thorn in my ass. A politically connected commander, trigger happy officers, and a string of abuse complaints from the public.

"That's all for now guys," I said, wrapping up the meeting. "Thank you. Dismissed."

Chairs scraped on the wood floor as they stood from the table, already bouncing ideas back and forth between themselves, nodding at Constable Samuel as they turned to exit the room.

"Reggie, a moment" I called, as they queued for the door.

"Ambitious plan Commisshunah," Reggie said softly after the others had departed. "Sure you don't want to take more time?"

"Can't be helped. The longer we wait the more chance of word leaking out. And there're a couple of other reasons for not delaying. One is I want to leave you guys a clean barrel after I'm gone from this office. There's not much time left. It'll be up to you and the others to keep the fruit from spoiling and rotting after that. The other is what I really want to talk with you about."

His eyebrows arched upward a fraction behind the black frames of his spectacles.

"Having to do wid him I presume," nodding in Samuel's direction.

"Yes." I said.

Huggins stepped toward the conference table, approaching Samuel who'd remained standing after the ranking officers departed. Huggins held out his hand. While the traditionalists in the force emphasized the rigid hierarchical structure, an intransigent relic of the British class system, I'd always encouraged a bit less formality in the chain of command. Especially among people who'd earned my respect and trust. It pleased me to observe it rubbing off on others.

Samuel shook the offered hand.

"A pleajah to meet you Constable," Huggins said. "Rema'kable what you've accomplished."

"Just doing de job sir," Samuel replied.

"Reggie you are among a handful of people on St. Vincent, the only one on the force, who knows the full extent of the threat we uncovered with the murders of Alfred Greene and Jackson Taylor. One of the reasons I recruited Samuel and kept it to myself."

"I understand Commisshunah."

"There're two more. Or were."

Those facile eyebrows danced upward again. His dark pupils fixed on mine.

"One still in place. I won't bring in that constable until we can see an end to this thing. The other was the fisherman murdered in the Grenadines. The case Superintendent Johanssen is investigating."

"What?" his eyes opening wide. His glasses slipped on his flat nose. Lines of bewilderment and disbelief formed on his dark brown face.

"So sorry to hear dat sir. You know yet what happen?"

"Not yet," I said.

"So sorry," he repeated, his face a mask of pain and grief for someone he didn't even know. "You knew dis person?" he asked Samuel.

"No sir. None of de Commissioner's undercovers knew each other."

Huggins merely nodded.

"Anyway Reggie, we need to formally bring Constable Samuel in. Without any fanfare. And as of today I'm promoting him to Sergeant. With his training and experience Major Crimes or RRS might be the best place."

"I agree Commisshunah."

"As for the other undercover, we'll have to figure it out too when the time comes. But it'll have to be before a new Commissioner is appointed. For this country's and this force's sake, I hope that'll be you Reggie."

It'd been the first time I'd openly endorsed his appointment. A pained expression, perhaps embarrassment, spread across his face.

"I have to be honest and tell you there is one other I also have in mind. But if you get the nod you'll have my full support," I told him.

"Thank you Commisshunah. Thank you," he repeated, accompanied by a slight bow of his head and an uneasiness I attributed to his self-effacing modesty. I grasped and shook his hand before he turned for the door.

For the remainder of the day I worked in my office, quietly observing the frenzied activity in the conference room. People entered and departed, contributing some new piece to two large dry erase boards set up on easels, covered in photographs and maps. Cecelia the traffic cop, kept the procession moving, and barred any unauthorized persons from entering the conference room or lingering in the outer office. Word of something going in the Commissioner's office spread through the building.

Occasionally a head popped through the door to my office; a question, a point to be clarified, or an idea needing approval. My input minimal as the planning proceeded.

After one particular question regarding backup I entered the conference room to emphasize a point to everyone in attendance.

"It's entirely possible," I said to the roomful of attentive eyes, "That in the ruckus some civilian will make a report to the police. Notify all police stations in the affected areas a joint police task force will be conducting an operation in their area, at the specified time, without giving specifics regarding intended targets." Channeling Gage? I thought.

"Emphasize that plain clothes policemen are involved, and no response to reports of disturbances must be taken. If backup is needed a specific request will be made by the units involved."

Nodding and "Yes sirs" from around the room.

At seventeen thirty hours Cecilia, who I assumed had left for the day, entered my office carrying a tray of food from a take-out place on Bay Street.

"I totally forget about food," I said, the strong aroma of the rotis and fries she laid before me eliciting a growl from my stomach.

"I know you did, what with all the running around going on around here today."

"Thanks," I said,

"Now eat," she commanded in a mother's voice. "You need to keep your strength up."

"Thanks Cissy," I said again. "You can go on home. We're done for the day."

"I leave when you leave," she said, an emphatic finality in her voice inviting no argument. She headed toward her desk, and I smiled at her retreating back as I settled to eat at my desk.

At nineteen hundred hours, the task force commanders and Samuel reconvened. We repaired to the conference room for the briefing. Assistant Superintendent Rogers tidied and organized the dry erase boards while Huggins assembled notes.

"Twelve raids in total Commisshunah," Huggins began, "commencing at twenty tree hundred hours. Six private homes, four drinking establishments and two farms. De objectives scattered across a wide geographic area, but mostly on de windward coast."

He stood and approached one of the easels. "De farms are heah and heah," he said, using a collapsible pointer to indicate a forested inland area west of O'Briens, unpopulated. The other in the hills northeast of Charlotte. All rugged terrain, with dense foliage and hidden footpaths.

Christ! I hadn't seen it before.

"Commisshunah..." he hesitated.

"I see the problem," I interrupted. "Suggestions?"

Relief on the faces gathered around the table.

"Dese two objectives we assigned to RSS and SSU. De RSS have the training for dis type of terrain, and SSU is tasked with marijuana eradication." He nodded in Superintendent Hughes direction. Hughes replaced Huggins at the easel.

"We suggest staging de squads heah and heah," Hughes said, using the pointer to indicate positions on aerial photographs pinned to a second easel. The images appeared recent. As in taken today. I couldn't help being impressed.

"We create a cordon while de odder raids are takin' place. And we detain anyone tryin' to go in or out until we ascertain what business dey have being dere. Den we raid de objectives at first light. Constable Samuel pinpointed de arms caches as being heah and heah. And de marijuana fields heah and heah," he said tapping the images. "Cyan see anyt'ing from de photos. Samuel says dey use camouflage. He also say de gang members not always dere at de same time. Maybe tree or foh most time. So if de others get scoop up in de raids we can catch dem all. And my men won't have many to contend wid at de farms."

"Sounds good. Approved" I said. "Sammy you have any thoughts on the kind of resistance the squads might meet? What with all the weapons up there."

"The guns are hidden Commissioner. All de boys carry guns. Some have automatic weapons. But as I told de Superintendent, there'll be no more than three or four of them at de most. If we isolate them from the cache we only have to deal with what they'll be carrying."

I nodded. "And our guys Hughie? I assume the standard equipment."

"Correct Commisshunah." Automatic assault rifles and side arms."

"Body armor?"

"De standard issue," Huggins said. "And not enough for everyone. We'll distribute dem accordin' to de hazard."

I nodded. Hughes and Huggins switched places again.

"De four drinking establishments," Huggins said, "one in Georgetown, one in Mesopotamia, one in Biabou, and one in Calliaqua. And de six private residences, two in Georgetown, one in Biabou, one in Stubbs, one in Brighton and one in Mesopotamia. Dose assigned to Major Crimes supplemented with RSS and SSU."

He paused. From where he stood, and I sat, he had to look down at me, through the spectacles and along his broad flat nose.

"As wid de RRU we haven't included de CID in de task force, even though a lot of de CID are good trustworthy men," his eyes conveying a message we both understood. Better to keep Mitchell out of this for the time being.

"Objective identification?" I asked, glancing first at Huggins, then at Hughes.

"Verified and confirmed sir," Hughes said.

"And civilians in the residences, other than our suspects?"

"Four of de residences," Hughes said.

"You know what that means?" I said, staring at each in turn.

"Yes Commisshunah," Hughes said. "Specific instructions have been made. And photos of all suspects will be distributed to the men prior to de raids."

"I want this to be a clean victory for the force," I said, again pinning each pair of eyes in the room for emphasis. "Not have it blow up in our faces because of some trigger happy constable."

"Yes Commisshunah," they said in unison.

Turning to Huggins I asked, "What about the shipment?"

"De Coast Guard will handle dat," he said, nodding at Coast Guard Commander Pompey.

Lieutenant Commander Pompey, his dark beefy face and clear brown eyes projecting a competent confidence, picked up his side of the briefing.

"I'll have two vessels in de area. De Cutter MacIntosh and a fast pursuit rigid hull inflatable, which can also operate inshore. The coast dere is treacherous, wid large swells comin' ashore. And very rocky. Dere is only dat small cove dey can land. Whoever bringin' in de boat must know it better than dey own backside."

Smiles and chuckles around the table.

"I also have a shore party supplemented wid RSS officers. We wait for de shipment to arrive. Hopefully we also get de vessel dey offloadin' to."

"Why not wait for the vessel to go ashore first?" I asked.

"Don't want to risk my people going in there sir. Especially at night. If de vessel arrives same time as de load, we can take both from shore while de RHIB blockage de bay. Or we can intercept it outside de bay."

I nodded. "Your operation David. Whatever you think is best without exposing your people to unnecessary risk. Warrants?" I asked next.

"I met wid de Director of Public Prosecutions dis after-noon," Huggins said. "All necessary warrants have been prepared."

"What about processing?"

"All de prisoners will be processed and charged at local stations den transported to the de Kingstown prison. All collected evidence will be processed at de scene and brought to evidence storage at Old Montrose Station. By morning de Public Prosecutor's office will begin processing de prisoners for appearances before a magistrate."

"Good," I said.

The briefing progressed as I ticked off my mental checklist of items. Communications, weapons, transportation, medical backup, and police backup under the guidelines I'd established earlier. Finally contingencies.

At nineteen fifty hours, we prepared to adjourn, final preparation and staging to commence in just over an hour. Rogers and Phillips would coordinate from one of two mobile police stations. Hughes and Manley from the other mobile police station close to the farms. Pompey from his command center at Calliaqua.

"One final thing," I said. "Reggie, I want you coordinating at central communications."

"Commisshunah? We'd assumed you'd have dat post sir."

"I'll be in the field," I said. "For reasons I can't explain right now the suspect Weekes is a linchpin in this operation. His arrest and interrogation is critical to providing incriminating evidence against the others. I want to handle that situation personally."

"Understood Commisshunah," he said, but I noticed the quick glances and curious expressions exchanged across the room. Following the astounding revelations of the morning, they were undoubtedly wondering what other secrets their Commissioner had up his sleeve.

CHAPTER 13

At eleven pm, the tiny neighborhood southeast of Brighton, bordered by parallel dirt roads, was quiet and still. The small fragile houses shuttered and dark. Their occupants in bed.

A three-quarter moon rose in the eastern sky, providing the sole illumination in the area which had no streetlights. It's soft, pale glow, created deep shadows among the close packed houses and scattered trees.

I stood next to the parked unmarked RAV4 as Detective Corporals Curtis Baynes and Noel Raimie of Major Crimes donned bulky outdated protective vests. Being able to afford my own gear, I wore a close fitting Bianchi Protech tactical vest.

The Detective Corporals approached the small flimsy wood-planked house, crossing the dirt yard before splitting up. Baynes moved toward the front and Raimie headed for the rear. On the count, Baynes kicked in the front door. I assumed Raimie did the same at the rear.

All hell broke loose.

Sounds of a struggle from the interior. Breaking noises and furniture smashing. The dull pop, pop, pop of gunfire, accompanied by bright flashes behind the grimy uncurtained windows. The sound of breaking glass. Cursing under my breath, I rushed toward the house. I needed this guy alive, but not at the expense of injury to my men.

Baynes retreated through the smashed front door. Noticed me sprinting toward the house, service Glock up and taking aim.

"He running," Commisshunah, Baynes yelled. Noel after him from de back. We okay," before rushing off to my left.

Turning in that direction I noticed a figure sprinting through the dirt yard, Raimie following, but keeping well back, zigzagging to find available cover. The fleeing suspect fired random unaimed pot shots over his shoulder. The gunshots echoed in the still night, and off the walls of homes squashed together. The noise awakened neighborhood dogs and chickens, their loud barking and panicked squawking contributing to the ruckus, threatening to wake the entire neighborhood.

I ran after the three men, instinctively joining the foot pursuit, thought better of it, and headed back to the SUV. I kept the fleeing suspect in sight as he pelted headlong through neighboring yards, headed toward the main road. If he reached and crossed the main road, he'd have a dense growth of trees in which to take cover and hide. I fired up the SUV and maneuvered to cut him off.

He turned right between two houses. Headed toward me now, and a strand of trees on the corner. I lost visual contact as he ran between the trees, heading in the direction of a commercial building off the main road.

I arrived before him, exited the SUV, and ran to the corner of the building. I peered around the side. Quickly pulled my head back. He continued running in my direction, his heavy breathing, the sound of his running feet, moving closer. Closer. Almost upon me. Holding the Glock in my right fist, I timed his arrival.

He reached the corner at full speed. I swung my left arm out. It caught him at the top of his torso just below his neck, in a clothesline tackle. His legs raced out from under him. His head snapped forward, and he went down with the sound of a coconut hitting the ground from a great height. His weapon flew from his grip. He lay stunned and incapacitated, the wind knocked out of him. I stepped over him holding the Glock in a two fisted grip aimed at his chest.

A voice behind me set my heart racing and pounding in my chest. I hadn't seen or heard him.

"Nice move. And you let the youngsters do the running."

"Goddammit Gage. One of these days you're gonna really give me a heart attack." Gage glanced in the direction of running feet.

"How'd you know which way he'd run?" I asked.

Gage smiled. "Always bring your quarry to you?" He disappeared as stealthily as he'd appeared, before the pursuing officers reached me, and the semi-conscious Weekes.

Baynes and Raimie arrived in a swirl of dust, their breathing heavy but unlabored. The benefit of youth and conditioning. Baynes bent to retrieve Weekes's weapon from the dirt. A forty-five colt semi automatic. Certainly not police issue. Raimie knelt next to the prone suspect, rolled him onto his stomach, tugged both arms behind his back and applied plastic flex cuffs.

"You guys okay?" I asked.

"We good Commisshunah," they answered in turn.

"What happened?"

"Him come at me de minit we break in de door," Baynes said. "Must not been sleepin'. And I smell weed in de house. He throwin' anyt'ing him could find at me. Den he must find de gun, cause him start shootin'. Just wild, no aimin' nor anyt'ing. Him dash a chair through de window and jump through it. Tek off runnin'."

"Get him in the truck," I ordered. "We'll drive back to the house. Start searching it. Baynes call the local Station. Get some constables up here to secure the scene."

"Yes Commisshunah," he said, while his partner stood Weekes up. Still stunned and groggy, it required both men to get the suspect upright and on his feet. They dragged him to the SUV and dumped him onto the back seat.

Weekes regained a semblance of lucidity by the time we returned to the house. Although in the form of incoherent weeping about not killing him.

"Dohn kill me! Lard dohn kill me! Please I dohn done nuttin'. Dohn kill me." His agonized face streaked by tears.

After dispatching Baynes and Raimie to search the house I climbed into the back seat next to the wailing Weekes.

"Stop you bawlin' mahn," I yelled in a rare use of patois. "Nobady here fe kill you."

To no avail.

I slapped him across the face with an open palm. The blow stunned him into abrupt silence. Eyes set deep beneath prominent brow ridges narrowed. The brows drew together forming deep frown lines between his eyebrows and across his forehead. The corners of his mouth turned down, and thick lips pushed upward toward his broad nostrils in a menacing snare.

He turned to face me.

Dull wet eyes widened in surprise. "Commisshunah Daniels?" His eyes darted side to side as he conjured his story.

"T'ank God is you Commisshunah. Some mahn break in de house jus' now. I t'ink dey come fe kill me. I have fe jump out de window."

"Save it Devon. I know exactly who wants to kill you and why. You are under arrest for a whole list of serious offenses. And I know we'll find evidence in your house. The only thing gonna save you from life in Her Majesty's prison, or getting killed by your pals, is if you cooperate and tell me everything I want to know."

My words silenced him as effectively as the slap. His facial features rearranged themselves again, aligning naturally into the sneering frown captured in photographs of him. Apparently his normal expression.

"Be that way then. I'll just put you right back out on the street where everyone will know you cooperated with us. Right now, we're arresting your pals Peters and Ashton. And we're raiding that shipment at Cedar Bay. Now who could tell us all that but you. When dat gang ketch you, you dead," I finished, lapsing back into patois for emphasis.

His eyes widened. The frown deepened. Ugly son of a bitch, I thought.

An older model blue and white, yellow stripped Toyota Tacoma, blue rooftop light bar flashing, pulled in behind the RAV4. Two uniformed constables emerged from the truck at the same time I exited the SUV.

They stamped to attention and saluted upon recognizing me.

"At ease," I said. "Corporal, Constable. You two will be posted here until further notice to secure this house after the

detectives and I leave. For right now Corporal begin canvassing the neighborhood in that direction," I said, pointing in the
direction Weekes had taken off running.

"Make sure no one in any of those homes is hurt. And
get statements of anything they may have heard or seen."

"Yessah," he said, moving off in the direction I'd indicated.

"Constable, you remain here and watch the prisoner.
You are not to make contact or speak with him. Is that understood?"

"Yessah," he said.

"Carry on," I said, leaving him and moving toward the
house.

Gage had been correct. Weekes's home a dump. Even
before the overturned and smashed furniture, and the busted
window in the rear wall of the cramped living room. Un-
painted wood walls, a single couch and armchair, both
threadbare, their fabric ripped and stained. The linoleum floor
peeling, and littered by weeks of old trash.

It pained me a police constable lived in such conditions.
But I rationalized this particular constable had squandered his
income on gambling and ganja.

Baynes and Raimie had almost completed their evidence processing and collecting. Two bulging pillowcases
contained approximately ten kilograms of marijuana packed
in bricks. In an old cardboard box, Raimie had deposited a
stash of illegal weapons, including two thirty eight caliber
revolvers, three semi automatic handguns, and ammunition.
Another box contained letters and notes written on lined
pages ripped from a school exercise book. Other bits and

pieces of paper they deemed relevant, including crumpled receipts, also filled the box.

We returned to the RAV4 after Baynes had erected evidence tape over the doors and smashed window of the house.

"You guys take the prisoner to Central Police Station," I instructed them. "He's to be kept in strict segregation. No contact with anyone. That includes prisoners and police. I'll begin questioning him when I get back."

"Whey you going be Commisshunah?" Baynes asked.

"Drop me at the Calliaqua base on your way."

At the end of a narrow road winding down to Fisherman's Wharf, now the Coast Guard Wharf, an Able Seaman stood sentry duty at the entrance to the Calliaqua Coast Guard base. He stamped to attention and saluted when he checked the vehicle and recognized me. I returned the salute.

At the main building, a Leading Seaman alerted by the sentry met me at the entrance and escorted me inside. Lieutenant Commander David Pompey waited for me in the command center.

"Ten chun!"

The men and women in the command center rose and stood at attention, their arms held in stiff salutes.

"As you were," I said, returning the salute before grasping Pompey's strong hand. A big bulk of a man, he had a linebacker's build, beefy and muscular in the chest, arms, and thighs. "How's it going?" I said. "I noticed the Mulzac wasn't at the dock."

"Correct sir. She's on patrol in support of de operation. I also have de RHIB on station, and de shore party in place. Right now we jus' waitin'. Also we pickin' up an echo standin' off to de east. She was makin' passage from de south, but been slowin' over de past hour as she get close to St. Vincent."

"Can you make out the type of vessel?"

"Some type of freighter sir. Cyan be more specific dan dat. We get a lot of surface clutter and sometimes false echoes dependin' on de seas."

"Okay. If I could use your office David. I need to check in with the other units."

"Certainly Sir. Right dis way."

I remembered the location of his office, but he escorted me anyway. David Pompey had been another of my hand-picked promotions. A dedicated professional, he embraced not only the Coast Guard's security role, but also the cultural and educational role it provided for the nation's youth. A career of service they might aspire to, in an environment which offered them very few career opportunities.

He'd welcomed and supported Jolene's push for enlisting and promoting more women. Had developed youth programs which introduced equal numbers of boys and girls to the Coast Guard. And he'd designed and instituted training programs, beyond the off island training provided by other countries and the U.S. Coast Guard, designed to improve competence and proficiency in the local marine environment.

After I'd settled behind his desk, he turned to leave.

"May I get you anyt'ing Commisshunah?"

"Maybe some coffee, thank you. And please call me the moment anything happens."

"Yes sir," he said, retreating from the office.

I called Huggins in the Police Command Center.

"How're things going Reggie?"

"Everyting going to plan Commisshunah. All de raids completed successfully wid no casualties or injuries. We have close to a dozen people in custody, and collectin' evidence from de various places."

"Good news Reggie," I said, breathing a sigh of relief. "Constable Weekes is being transported to Central Police Station. He's to be kept in strict segregation until I finish questioning him."

"Understood Sir."

"I'm at Calliaqua now, just waiting for that raid to begin." As I said it, an Able Seaman knocked on the door.

"Hang on a sec Reggie."

I motioned the seaman in. He entered carrying a steaming mug of coffee.

"Thank you seaman," I said, taking the hot mug and placing it on the Commander's desk.

"De Commander says he have word a truck just arrive by de beach Sir," he said.

"Thank you seaman," I said again. "I'll be right there."

He saluted, which I acknowledged by a wave of my hand in the vicinity of my brow. He executed an about face and exited the office.

"Okay Reggie. Looks like things might be starting on the beach. I'll get back to you later."

CHAPTER 14

Lieutenant Commander Pompey stood by a large table in the middle of the command center. Wide set intense eyes stared down at the table's flat surface, covered by a magnified chart of St. Vincent's windward coastline. Concentration etched on his dark features, his thin arching eyebrows drawn together. A stubby finger absently stroked the small moustache above his thick upper lip.

A female seaman wearing a slim headset, padded earphones and a boom microphone, positioned domino-sized rectangular blocks representing Coast Guard vessels and radar targets around the map.

Behind the Commander, against the wall, a long counter spanned the length of the room, divided into work stations. Male and female seamen and petty officers sat at the various stations.

Two petty officers wearing headsets and boom microphones sat at adjoining communications stations. An array of radio equipment, Marine VHFs, UHF, single sideband, shortwave, citizens' band and police band, mounted on the wall before them. Three other petty officers, two male, one female, sat before active radar screens. One radar scanned the Leeward coast. The other two, recently installed Advanced Coastal Surveillance Radar Systems, scanned the windward Coast.

At the meteorological station, a nineteen-inch computer screen displayed satellite feeds of regional weather, and a weather facsimile printer spewed out hard copies of weather conditions and forecasts. A senior petty officer manned a computer equipped supervisory station at one end of the counter.

Pompey glanced up as I approached the table.

"We have confirmation Commisshunah. Two vehicles jus' drove down to the beach. And we spotted a twenty six foot whale boat headin' toward de beach. De RHIB movin' into position to intercept dem now," he said, pointing to blocks on the map.

He turned at the call from the senior petty officer, who'd left his station to stand behind the communications stations.

"Contact wid de whale boat sah," he said. "Also contact pon de beach."

"Put dem up on de speaker," Pompey said.

"Aye."

One of the communications petty officers toggled a switch on his panel. Sound filled the room from overhead speakers.

"Calliaqua base, oh tree, preparin' to intercept now," amid ambient background engine noises and shouted orders through a megaphone.

"Roger oh tree."

"Calliaqua base, beach one, five subjects in custody, and one truck wid a load of ganja seized."

The sound of heavy automatic weapons fire filled the command center.

All heads in the room swiveled toward the overhead speakers. Some of my coffee spilled from the mug onto the floor. Anxious expressions on everyone's faces. Most of all Pompey, whose normally calm features transformed into an angry frown.

"Oh tree, Calliaqua base. Oh tree, you copy."

"Calliaqua base, oh tree. Tree subjects in custody. Wahnin' shots fired. Repeat wahnin' shots only. No casualties. Automatic weapons found on de boat."

"Copy oh tree." A collective sigh swept the room. I swallowed a sip of the strong coffee.

"What's the position of that freighter?" I asked Pompey.

His attention returned to the table. The thick, pursed lips relaxed, and the frown lines between his brows and across his broad forehead smoothed. The dark brown eyes softened.

"Here," he said pointing to a block on the chart.

"Good. Vincentian territorial waters. And this is the Mulzac standing off here? And MacIntoch here?" I asked pointing to two blocks on the table, one of them designated SVG 01. "How long to intercept the freighter."

"Six minutes for Mulzac sir."

Nodding, I gave the order. "Intercept that freighter. Escort it to the base."

"Aye sir," Pompey said, relaying the order to the Chief Petty Officer.

"Great job David." Turning to the room I said, "Excellent job everyone. Thank you. Please pass that on to the crews and the shore detail, will you Commander."

"Yes sir."

"Now I need your office for a few more minutes and if you could arrange for someone to drive me into Kingstown."

"No problem sir," a satisfied smile on his broad beaming face.

When I had Huggins on the phone again I said, "You heard?"

"Yes Commisshunah," he said, a mixture of relief and exhilaration evident in his voice. "A complete success all round."

"Did we get Peters and Ashton?"

"Yessir. Identities confirmed."

"Excellent. I'm heading back to the station now. See you when I get there."

Two am by the time Reggie and I retired to my office, following updates from the field and my personal congratulations to the men and women of the task force.

"Quite a night Commisshunah," Huggins said, an uncharacteristic broad smile on his face, lifting his prominent cheekbones, and putting a sparkle in his tired eyes."

While I shared his enthusiasm, a bone-tired weariness dampened my response. Undoubtedly it'd been a huge success for the force. A veritable coup. But we still had a great deal to do. It'd be all over the news in a few hours. We had to prepare for that, and coordinate our statements with the Public Prosecutor's office.

Not to mention the attendant political firestorm in an already heated election environment. Each side spinning the events to their own advantage. I didn't give a fuck. My main concern focused on shielding the force from devolving into a political football caught in the middle.

My other concern, the interrogations. Assembling and collating the information from so many subjects into coherent intelligence, and ensuring timely distribution of the information to appropriate departments and units.

"We need a plan for questioning all the subjects," I said to Reggie.

"I was tinkin' dat too Commisshunah. Over a dozen prisoners, we need a central person to coordinate de questionin' and bring ev'ryting into one place."

A smile spread across my face. "And that's why you belong in this chair," I said.

His gaze steadied on mine. His embarrassed reluctance to speak on the subject, especially to the person who held the office in question, evident in his uncomfortable shifting in the armchair facing my desk.

"I heard a rumor you're thinking of retiring?" I said.

"Might be Commisshunah," he said. "Not sure I could work for a different Commisshunah anyway."

"The force needs men like you leading it," I said.

"De force will be fine sir. Don't t'ink I don't see what you been doin' de past year," his informality simultaneously surprising and gratifying. "You put good people in place sir. And now you can fix de RRU. Dat only leave Superintendent Mitchell. "

I smiled again. I hadn't discussed my agenda with him any more than I'd discussed the undercover operation. That he'd perceived my intentions a testament to his acumen for the top job.

"Working on that," I said. His eyebrows rose behind the spectacles.

"So about the prisoners," I said, deflecting his curiosity and returning the conversation to our immediate problem.

"Yessir."

"I'm thinking of putting Sergeant Samuel in charge of coordinating the interrogations. He's already familiar with the territory and knows the type of information we need."

"Yessir," he repeated. "I can put together a team from Major Crimes for him."

"Good. Let's get that going in the morning." I glanced at my watch. "Still a few hours until daylight. Why don't you get some sleep. We'll meet back here at oh nine hundred."

"Begging the Commisshunah's pardon sir, but some of de task force still in de field. I'll wait for them to get back."

"Very well Reggie," my appreciative smile returning yet again. "If you need me I'll be questioning Weekes."

"Very good sir."

I returned to my office at oh eight fifty hours relatively refreshed, following a one-hour nap, a cold shower, and a change of clothes.

Cecilia already at her desk, undisguised suspicion in her appraising gaze.

"You know Commissioner, people your age get bags under dey eyes from lack of sleep."

"I don't have bags under my eyes," I shot back. "I specifically checked."

"Affects eyesight too," she said.

"Please see if Assistant Superintendent Taylor is available," I said, escaping into my office, surrender the wisest course of action.

At nine a.m. sharp she ushered Huggins into the office.

"Show AS Taylor in as soon as he arrives," I said before she closed the door.

Reggie settled into the same seat he'd occupied a few hours before. Both of us in the same positions as though the intervening hours had never occurred. He carried a stack of folders, which he placed in his lap. His uniform pressed and sharply creased. He'd found time to change, and I wondered if he'd had a chance to sleep. I scrutinized his smooth defined features, unable to tell. He appeared as fresh as when he'd reported for duty twenty four-hours before. Only his eyes betrayed his fatigue.

"De preliminary reports," he said, reaching forward and placing the stack of files on my desk.

"You've already been through them I presume."

"Yes sir."

"Can you capsularize all this for Taylor? He'll be here shortly for a briefing."

"Already done sir. Dat top file. I can brief him for you Commisshunah."

"Thanks Reggie. Appreciate that," I said, picking the folder from the top of the file. I leaned back. Perused the printed sheets in the file. A statement regarding information developed on a marijuana shipment. The gangs and other individuals involved, avoiding specific identification of sources and no mention of Keston Samuel. The units comprising the task force, the locations raided and the individuals arrested. Including the seizure of approximately 400 kilograms of marijuana from the various locations, ten acres of planted marijuana, a hundred and fifty firearms, and a Venezuelan registered Freighter.

A knock on the door signaled Taylor's arrival. Cecilia opened the door and led him in. He stood at attention and saluted.

"At ease Vince. Any inquiries from the press yet?"

"They're just now beginning to get around to us Commissioner. They're hearing bits and pieces from de public and local police stations. But they haven't put it together as one operation yet."

"Here's a synopsis of last night's operation," I said, handing him the file. Put it together in press release form. DC Huggins will brief you on the details."

"Yes Commissioner."

Another knock at the door. Cecilia's face, hairless eyebrows raised in pleasant surprise, a smile of delightful approval stretching her lips.

"Sergeant Samuel to see you," she announced.

"Show him in," I said.

Samuel stepped past her beaming face. The reason for her expression evident the moment he entered the office. He'd undergone a transformation. The knotted hair shorn off, leaving a neatly groomed layer close to his scalp. The face scrubbed clean. A crisply pressed sand colored Guayabera shirt worn over police grey slacks. Black loafers replaced the sneakers.

"At ease Sammy," I said in response to his salute. "Yesterday she was ready to throw you out. Today she wants to adopt you," I said smiling.

"Yes sir," he said, a wide grin on his face.

"Vince why don't you get acquainted with the file in the conference room. The DC will join you momentarily. I just need a few minutes."

"Sammy, we've got an assignment for you," I said, including Huggins in the decision. "We're setting up a team to question the prisoners. We want you to head up the team."

"Yes Commissioner."

"I've picked three experienced men from Major Crimes for your team Sergeant," Huggins said.

When did he find time to do that? I wondered. And the reports. He'd have had to wait for the teams raiding the farms. Had he never left the station this entire time?

"You'll make the prisoner assignments for each officer, and receive de reports. We want to centralize and coordinate all de infomation from de prisoners."

"Good idea sir," Samuel nodded.

"And you'll be in charge of distributing de infomation to de relevant departments and units. You'll probably have interaction wid de Director of Public Prosecutions too."

"Yes sir."

"You have a desk yet?" Huggins asked him.

"No sir. I reported straight here when I came in."

"Come wid me. I'll get you set up. Den I'll have your team report to you."

"Very good sir."

"Wid your permission Commissioner?" Huggins said.

"Carry on Reggie. Thank you." I said.

Turning to Samuel I said. "Here are my notes and a statement from Weekes, the RRU officer," handing him a file sitting apart from Reggie's stack on my desk. "Let me know if you think of any follow up questions we need to ask him. And I need that file back Sammy."

"Yes Commissioner."

"Carry on,"

Huggins ducked into the conference room. A quick exchange between him and Taylor before he exited the office, Samuel in tow.

Shown the overwhelming amount of evidence against him, including Gage's photographs, his mouth dropping open in stunned disbelief when he'd seen them, Devon Weekes had decided to talk. For close to two hours.

He recounted his earliest introduction to Trevor Peters and Clifford Ashton, the other rogue RRU officers. His need for money, which they provided, first as loans. Until he'd been in so deep he began helping in their extracurricular activities to repay his debt. They'd introduced him to Natty's gang. He needed the money and it provided a personal supply of ganja; Natty gained another distributor on the street. Weekes swore he didn't know of any other rogue officers in the unit. But he thought Sergeant Ashton sometimes received orders from someone else. He didn't know who.

Rocking in my recliner I pondered my interrogation of Weekes. Gage had peformed a number on him, shaking the foundations of his world, convincing him he'd been marked for a bullet in the back of the head.

My thoughts turned to Gage. The personification of the cliché 'an enigma wrapped in a paradox', or however the damn phrase went. And to Jolene, who I hadn't conferred with regarding the investigation since seeing her on Sunday.

I glanced at the stack of files sitting on my desk. I pondered the enormity of what we'd accomplished. None of it filled the empty void deep in my gut. All I wanted at that moment was to share the victory in the comforting arms of a woman who was a hundred miles away.

CHAPTER 15

Gage remained on St. Vincent until the operation wrapped up. He planned to return to Bequia the afternoon following the raids. I asked for a lift, rather than using my usual Coast Guard transport, or the ferry.

Truth be told I needed Wherever's soothing comfort, and Gage's. Only Tuesday, my week just beginning, but I desired the relief of home, and a face-to-face update from Jolene. The sail, though short, would hopefully lift my spirits and improve my disposition. The sea and the sky had never failed me.

Handling Wherever's rig, the chore I'd insisted on while Gage manned the helm, occupied and focused my mind. And provided much needed manual exercise. I'd been too preoccupied since the discovery of Constable Whittaker's body to work out. My arms, shoulders, and back ached by the time I'd hoisted and trimmed Wherever's sails.

We broad reached out of Indian Bay, maintaining a westerly heading to lay us abeam Kingstown harbor before turning south for Bequia. Entering the channel between St. Vincent and Bequia, the swells rose in height and frequency, pitching and rolling Wherever as they curled beneath her. The sea on her quarter, she had a tendency to gripe, wanting to swing her stern down and turn her head toward the wind, disobeying her helm and rudder. But Gage knew her through and through, easing her helm as she bucked and started her swing, using her momentum to ease her back on course.

I tended her sheets, trimming her sails to each shift of wind produced by Villa's headland to starboard, Young Island to port, and as Gage eased her farther off St. Vincent's southern coast.

Abeam Kingstown Harbor Gage jibed her. Wherever's booms swung across to the starboard side amid the horrendous crack and slap of flogging sails. He steadied her on a southerly heading. I trimmed her sails for a beam reach, the swells no longer on her quarter, but coming at her port side, lifting her as they rolled beneath her hull, foaming white on the opposite side as she slid down their backsides into the troughs. Wherever sailed easier on the new heading, rising and falling on each passing swell.

"I gather everything went according to plan," Gage said when I'd settled in the cockpit.

"Like a charm. A complete success. Rolled up the entire shebang. Even seized a freighter waiting offshore for the pickup. Though no one will admit to that. Causing a major diplomatic headache for Bacchus and the Foreign Ministry. Coast Guard's still searching it at Calliaqua. But I don't want to think about any of that right now. I need to clear my head and this is exactly what the doctor ordered."

"I'd think you'd be ecstatic."

"I am. Can't you tell?" Screwing my face into a faux smile.

"Coulda fooled me."

"I'm just tired Gage. Like all the time. Bone weary tired. And it seems to get worse the closer I get to the finish line."

"Know the feeling buddy. Always gets that way towards the end of an op. The endgame is the toughest most dangerous time. At least mentally. Requiring you to maintain total focus when all you want to do is curl up into a little ball. Relax for one second the whole thing might blow up in your face. But it'll be over soon. Then you can relax and reflect."

I studied the confident face, the natural determined set of his jaw, the discerning eyes. His words curiously comforting.

"I guess," I said. "I just need some time at home to recharge. We'll get into it later when JJ updates me on her investigation."

"Jo mentioned something about a special friend," he said, his tone neutral, not curious or playful or teasing. Wasn't his style. And knowing him, more than idle interest beneath the simple statement.

"Yeah. I guess that's part of it too. I miss her. First time I've felt like this since we've been together. All the other times we'd get together, enjoy each other for the night, the weekend, however long, then we'd go about our business until the next time. Now I can't get her out of my head."

"Probably all part and parcel of the same thing. Big life change coming up. Even though it's what you want, there's bound to be some anxiety too."

"You know, most of the time I think you're rubbing off too much on JJ. Now I see some of her is rubbing off on you too. Thank you for that insight Dr. Gage."

He smiled. But the concern remained in his eyes.

"Am I right though?"

"What if you are?"

"You're not at the finish line yet," he said.

"I'm aware."

"Whatever you need Mike. Never hesitate to ask." He turned his attention to Wherever.

Gage had not corrected for her leeway, allowing the sea to push Wherever westward until he could bear up on a direct course past Bequia's North point into Lower Bay.

"Let's bring her up," he said, waiting on me to move into position at the sheets.

When I nodded ready, he turned the wheel a few spokes to port. Wherever answered her helm, swinging her thrusting bowsprit windward, until Gage steadied her on a close reach. I hauled on the sheets. First the jib, and staysail, followed by the foresail and finally the main. They bellied into taut graceful curves, transferring their energy to the hull.

Wherever responded to the new surge of power, heeled onto her side, and raced ahead. Entirely delighted by this point of sail, she put her head down, shouldering aside the swells in bursts of white spray. She forged ahead with the gracefulness of a living creature born to the sea.

The rush exhilarating. Wind on my face, the sweet swish of her passage through the water reverberated through the bare soles of my feet. The whistling of her rigging rang in my ears.

The icing on the cake, as though especially ordered for the occasion, the sun setting as we crossed the mouth of Admiralty Bay. The western horizon a mesmerizing, soothing swatch of scarlet and magenta, amber and gold.

I shortened sail as Wherever glided across the tranquil bay, uncrowded at this time of year. The bay's sole occupants a handful of cruising yachts calling Bequia home.

Wherever approached her mooring in Lower Bay under mainsail alone. Gage pointed her into the wind and let the main sheet fly. Wherever crept toward the white fiberglass float. I snagged it with the boathook, hauled the leader aboard until the mooring line appeared. I led it through the starboard hawser and dropped the loop over Wherever's Sampson post as twilight cloaked the bay.

"How about dinner at De Reef before you head home?" Gage asked.

"Thought you'd want to see JJ the minute you got ashore," I said.

"I will. If she's not busy she can join us for dinner."

"I am starved," I conceded. "Haven't eaten much since our breakfast yesterday morning. Just a bite at my desk Cissy brought me."

"Then it's settled."

We secured and tidied Wherever, coiling and hanging her lines, tying and covering her sails, dressing her deck, before motoring ashore in the dinghy.

As we entered the restaurant from the beach, Solly swiveled on his barstool to greet us. His presence there on a Tuesday evening surprised me. But De Reef being one of his favored watering holes, and Delma his latest female interest, maybe not so surprising.

"Commisshunah. Captin' Gage," he greeted us, his light grey eyes scrutinizing Gage as they normally did whenever the two met. Still attempting to figure Gage out. Though whatever thoughts and speculations Solly held regarding Gage, he kept to himself.

"Solly," Gage said in return, his voice neutral.

"Commisshunah heah hit de ball for a six. Or as you guys would say, a home run. Congratulations."

"Thanks Solly," I said.

"What you have in the kitchen tonight?" I heard Gage ask Delma as Solly continued pumping me for information.

"So a clean sweep Commisshunah?"

"Still some tidying up to do," I said, extending his metaphor.

Jolene entered from the front, striding across the large open room. Her gaze locked on Gage like a targeting laser.

Gage moved from the bar to meet her. They met in the middle of the room. No frenzied throwing themselves at each other. Rather a slow, lingering, welcoming embrace. Her arms circled his shoulders, his around her waist. They kissed. A simple welcome.

I joined them. Jolene planted a welcoming kiss on my cheek. Her eyes appraised me, discerning the dull weariness in mine.

"Everything Okay, Mike?" she asked, concern evident in her voice, and the piercing perceptive eyes.

"Just tired," I said.

"No shop talk for the evening," Gage said, his eyes communicating a silent message to hers.

We slid onto chairs at a table close to the wall, overlooking the beach. Gage relayed the evening's kitchen menu and signaled Delma. We ordered. A jerk chicken dinner including rice and peas, and sweet plantains for me. Gage chose broiled Bonita, also including rice and peas, plantains and boiled bananas. Jolene ordered a green salad. We all opted for soft drinks, bitter lemon for Jolene, lemonades for Gage and me.

Our dinner conversation remained light and inconsequential. Jolene picked from Gage's plate to supplement her salad. I even managed to laugh during the conversation, their congenial company always affable, relaxing, and restorative.

Later we bid each other goodnight. Gage and Jolene walked along the beach under a full moon, in the direction of Jolene's house. His arm around her shoulder, hers around his waist. Before turning in for the night I called Melanie.

"Just wanted to say hi," I said when she answered.

"Well hi," she said.

In the short silence following she said, "Mike? Everything all right?"

"Just tired," I said. "And I miss you."

She heard the longing, the yearning in my voice.

"Mike you know..."

"I know. I know," I said. "Guess I just needed to talk to you. Hear your voice." And so we talked. For another hour. The sound of her voice soothing, comforting; conveying her close, but incapable of alleviating the ache of her absence.

We said our goodnights, the L word on the tip of my tongue. Its utterance stifled by a reality separating us by more than absence. Her life was embedded in the States. Mine here. Her career in the State Department might send her anywhere in the world, at a moment's notice. Would she, could she, give that up? I had no ties save a sentimental one holding me on Bequia. Would I give it up to follow her? Would either of us want that?

Those thoughts rattled around my brain, until merciful sleep claimed me.

CHAPTER 16

Crowing roosters and my internal clock dredged my conscious mind from the depths of a sound sleep. Before I'd fallen asleep, I'd decided not to go into the office in the morning. But I didn't sleep in. I leapt from the bed, donned a pair of bathing trunks and flip-flops, and headed for the beach.

I waded through the seaweed dense shallows until the bay turned deep enough to immerse my entire body. I plunged beneath the surface, the temperature bracingly cold, the briny sea water smooth against my skin. I swam parallel to the shoreline, toward the Friendship Bay Hotel, acting on a spontaneous decision to order breakfast there. Though not part of their regular service, as a favor to me they often delivered meals to my house down the beach. A favor for which I tipped extremely well.

After ordering, I walked back along the beach, gazing toward the southern Grenadines, irregular shaped mounds rising from the sea. Rocky, uninhabited Battawia and Baliceaux islands the closest. Mustique's low-lying silhouette visible in the distance. Canouan a fainter silhouette father south. The normally enthralling view now spoiled. I'd never gaze at them again without remembering one of my men had been brutally murdered on one of them.

I retrieved my flip-flops and headed through the thick wall of coconut trees to my house. The house sat on a rise behind the beach and trees, providing a view of the Bay and the southern Grenadines. I discarded the sand filled flip-flops on the front verandah, slapped my feet free of sand on a beach towel, and headed for a cold shower.

Washed, shampooed, refreshed, I stepped naked to the bathroom mirror. I ran my hand along my jaw and across my chin. The texture of fine grain sandpaper. Contemplated whether to shave. Decided I would. Though I didn't plan going to the office, I did have work to do. I intended reading through the initial reports of the raids. Shaving and dressing for work, created the impression of my not merely playing hooky.

I checked the face reflected in the mirror for Cissy's bags under the eyes. She'd been correct dammit. Even if just a slight puffiness, barely discernable. The reflection staring back at me familiar, but also changed. The features less sharply chiseled than I remembered, softer, the lines deeper. The hair along the temples greyer. The hair itself thinner, exposing more of the forehead, the sides receding farther than at the front, forming two shallow coves on either side of my forehead, a peninsular of hair in the middle.

The body still trim but not as firm. A slight sagging in the chest and around the middle. The beginnings of love handles around the waist. Round mottled spots just below the right shoulder and armpit. Remnants of wounds, which had almost ended my life. The gunshots themselves erased by my memory. The phantom pain an occasional recurrence.

By the time I'd finished dressing and set the coffee maker brewing, I heard a knock at the front door. Opening it revealed a slender young teenage girl in hotel uniform bearing a covered tray. The smell of fresh bacon overpowered the other scents.

"Mawhnin' Commissshunah," she said in a soft, high-pitched voice.

"Morning," I said, stepping aside to allow her in. "Just set it on the table," I said, ushering her inside.

She laid the tray on the table and turned to leave.

"You not goin' in to Kingstown today Commisshunah?"

"Working at home today," I said.

"Den if you need lunch or dinnah too jus' call. Not too many guests in de hotel now."

"I will," I said, reaching in my trouser pocket for the twenty dollar EC bill I'd put there for the occasion.

"Thank you," I said, handing her the bill and escorting her to the door.

"T'ank you Commisshunah," she squeaked, doe-like eyes widening at the generous tip. "Have a good day Commisshunah."

"You too," I said, watching the sturdy slim legs below the swishing hem of her uniform frock carry her across the yard.

At eight thirty am, sated by a breakfast of eggs, bacon, hash brown potatoes, sliced paw paw and coffee, I called the office.

"Commissioner's office," Cecilia announced in her deep authoritative voice.

"Morning Cissy."

"Morning Commissioner. I take it you'll be delayed getting to the office."

"Actually I won't be in today Cissy. Have you seen Deputy Commissioner Huggins this morning?"

Silence.

"Cissy?"

"Is everything all right Commissioner?"

"Everything is fine Cissy. I prefer to work at home on Bequia today where I won't be disturbed or interrupted."

"In that case I do believe I saw the DC downstairs when I arrived."

"Good. Please refer anything requiring immediate attention to him. And don't call me unless the building's on fire. And even then..."

"Understood Commissioner. You get some rest. God knows you can use it."

"Thanks Cissy. I'll see you tomorrow."

I called Huggins next.

"Reggie," I said when his secretary connected us. "I'm going to work from Bequia today. Any further developments?"

"Nothing except for de various units finishing up de final reports. And Taylor is fielding numerous calls from de press."

"He can handle that for today. If he thinks we need to do a press conference, we can schedule one for later in the week. But I don't want this turning into a self-congratulatory circus.

"Yes Commisshunah," he said.

"Also ask the unit commanders to hold off submitting their final reports. I'll read the preliminaries this morning. I may have some notes for them to follow up on."

"Very good sir."

"Anything else?" I asked.

"De interrogations team ready to start dis morning. Samuel has assigned prisoners to de team members and dey should be leaving for de prison just now."

"Ok. You can cover for me today Reggie. The PM and cabinet will be huffing and puffing all day wanting to see me."

"I'll tek care of it Commisshunah." I visualized his smile over the phone.

"Thanks Reggie. I'll call if I need anything."

After we'd disconnected I gathered the files I'd brought home, a legal pad, a pen, and headed to the verandah. The sun's silvery disk hung in a pale azurine sky, the temperature rising as it gained altitude. The roof overhanging the verandah provided comfortable shade. I half sat, half lay lengthwise on the cushioned wicker loveseat, the pile of folders on my belly. I lifted the top file, opened it, commenced reading to the rhythmic accompaniment of surf booming along the beach.

Close to lunchtime when I completed my reading. My handwritten notes filled half a dozen legal pad pages. I decided to see if Jolene might be free for lunch. The midday sun bright and hot. The water staved landscape a dull, parched green. The leaves on the trees a thirsty brown. Dollar vans slowed to offer me a ride. I declined, preferring the walk, enjoying the leisurely trek into Port Elizabeth, despite the scorching heat.

I hadn't called the Bequia station beforehand. My unexpected appearance might cause alarm, as in a surprise inspection, or someone's head on the chopping block. Not my deliberate intent. Nor did I expect to find anything untoward at the station. Jolene ran a tight ship. Living on Bequia I'd occasionally drop in unexpectedly, something the station should be accustomed to by now.

I entered through the main entrance off the harbor road, opposite the ferry wharf and tourist information center. The first person to notice me a uniformed corporal staffing the front desk. She stamped to attention, shouting "Ten....shun!" loud enough for the other constables to hear, her arm raised in a stiff salute. The constables in the room, after a momentary confusion, followed suit.

"As you were everyone," I said returning the salute. "Afternoon Corporal Blake," I greeted her.

Despite her evident consternation, she smiled. "Wasn't expectin' you Commisshunah," she said.

"Working from home today Rowena," using her first name in an attempt to forestall the formality and ease the tension.

"Would the Superintendent be available?" I asked.

"Yes sir. In she office. I'll jus' ring up and let she know you heah to see her."

"Don't trouble yourself Corporal. I'll just run on up to her office."

"Yes sir," she said.

Friendly, smiling faces greeted me as I passed through the small duty staff to the staircase at the back of the station. One or two even broke protocol to offer a muted "congratulations sah," as I passed, aware I didn't care much for standing on ceremony and rigid formality. Neither did their Superintendent.

"Thank you. Thank you," I responded as I passed. "You guys keep up the good work. I'm proud of you," I said, heading up the staircase.

Jolene's office door stood ajar and I heard voices from inside the office. I knocked on the door, pushed it open farther and waited.

Station Sergeant Dennis Lucenti, short, stocky, paunchy, wire framed glasses halfway down his straight nose, his dark brown eyes peering over them, reacted automatically.

"Ten.....shun!" stiffening to attention and saluting.

"Chief" Jolene exclaimed, springing upright from her chair, surprise eclipsing formality.

"As you were Sergeant," I said. "I just dropped by to see if the Superintendent might be free for lunch. Carry on. I'll wait downstairs until you're done."

"We were just finishing up," Jolene said. Turning her attention to Lucenti she said, "You'll have those progress reports to me by the end of the week?"

"Yes ma'am." Turning to me he said, "De Suprintendent and me just mentionin' your success Commisshunah," a wide smile on his light olive brown face. "Congratulations sir."

"Thank you Dennis," I said.

Pausing next to me on his way out he said, "And I have a likle somet'ing for you Commisshunah. Some Cuban Cohibas I get from a fren' workin' at Argyle."

I wasn't the cigar aficionado, or as habitual a cigar smoker as Dennis. But he knew I enjoyed a good cigar on occasion. Though we seldom socialized, the occasional off-duty run in at a local bar or restaurant, or some island event, provided the opportunity to enjoy a primo cigar together. And to pick each other's brain regarding the job. He'd make certain I received a small package to enjoy at my leisure, whenever a new supply of choice cigars arrived. A pleasure I indulged during times of relaxed solitude on my verandah, accompanied by a glass of Jack Daniels or Amaretto, sultry jazz oozing from the CD player.

Jolene and I sat at an outdoor dining table at the Frangipani, steps away from the sea lapping along the beach. The table shaded from the harsh midday sun by a large circular umbrella. Jolene ordered a fresh tuna sandwich and bitter lemon. I ordered a chicken roti wrap and limeade.

"Taking the day off?" she asked.

"At least from the office. I've been reading the initial reports of the raids. Needed a little space before facing all the blowhards wanting a piece of me. How's your investigation going?"

Our lunch order arrived. Jolene bit into her sandwich, chewed, and swallowed before answering.

"The kid gloves approach is frustrating and getting us nowhere. Our canvassing hasn't produced any leads since Gregory Peters. I've traced Whittaker's movements up until the afternoon he went to Mustique. After that nothing. No one saw him after that. I believe it's where he was killed."

"Anything useful from Basil?"

"Just confirmation of what we already know."

"What about the guests? Anything from the immigration records?"

"Only three guests staying on the island during our time frame. A couple, William and Helen Greer. He's a high priced Washington attorney. They left this past weekend. The other is a Mister James Dougan. Rented the Les Jolies Eaux Villa for the entire month."

I whistled. The villa she referred to sat on a private peninsula overlooking Mustique's southern coast. It'd been designed for Princess Margaret as her vacation retreat, and rented for close to twenty grand per week.

"Basil and others we've talked to says Mister Dougan brought his personal security and household staff, so the household totals five in all."

"Not unusual for the type of guests Mustique gets."

"I know," she said, swallowing a mouthful of her bitter lemon.

"What do you know about this Mister Dougan?" I asked.

"His immigration papers just lists financier. I bypassed the liaison office in Barbados and asked Special Agent Forde for a background check on both the Greers and Dougan."

"How's Forde doing?"

"Fully recovered," she said, wiping her mouth on a red cloth napkin and swallowing the last of her bitter lemon. "He's back at work even though the FBI gave him more time off."

"Close call for both of you," I said.

"I also asked Gage to have his guy run background checks too," she said, deflecting my reference to her almost getting killed in New York. "Cross reference it against information they have the FBI might not."

"What's your next move?"

"Dunno Mike. We need a break in this case. The trail's already cold and getting colder every day."

"But you've narrowed your focus to Mustique?"

"Yes. But we have no leads and no suspects."

CHAPTER 17

The swells between Bequia and St. Vincent were higher than usual, and fast moving, fed by a foreboding grey mass to the east. The day dark and dreary. The rising sun hidden behind a thick overcast. A veil of rain showers hung between the darkened sky and gunmetal sea.

The tropical depression steered a path east of the Grenadines, desperately in need of its moisture. It'd drench St. Vincent instead, the island's mountainous topography providing rain-inducing updrafts.

The heavy ferry heaved and rolled across the channel. The odor of regurgitated stomach contents and diesel fuel permeated the shipboard air. Accompanied by the sounds of retching and heaving, inducing seasickness in more passengers, like an insidious infection.

The ferry battled a roiled sea hindering its race to stay ahead of the approaching squalls. An occasional bright flash lit the grey darkness, followed by the rolling rumble of thunder borne on the wind. The first rainsquall hit as the ferry approached the Grenadine Wharf.

Still raining when I arrived at Central Police Station. The downpours intermittent, but each squall followed close on the heels of the other. Pedestrians making their way around

Kingstown stole an advantage between each break, running along wet streets to the find shelter before the next deluge.

Only mildly soaked, I entered my outer office. Cecilia sat at her desk. When I reached my desk in the inner office she stood behind me, holding out a bath towel.

Where in the world had she found that in the seconds it'd taken to pass her desk and reach my office?

"Do you need a change of clothes Commissioner?"

"No. Thank you Cissy," I said, accepting the towel and running it across my head and arms.

"Wouldn't want you catching cold on top of everything else," she said, the contours of her face concerned and determined.

"I'm fine Cissy. What do you have for me?"

"DC Huggins and AC Taylor wished to be notified when you arrived. And the Governor General's office called yesterday for you," her penciled eyebrows rising in curiosity.

"Tell Huggins and Taylor I'm available and please get the Governor General's office on the line for me."

I wondered, but already guessed, the probable reason for the Governor General's call. A personal face-to-face briefing on the raids. Huggins and Taylor arrived together.

"What have you got for me today gentlemen?" I said, standing in front of my desk, my buttocks leaning lightly against the glass edge.

"Everybody talkin' bout de raids Commisshunah" Huggins began. "And dey also preoccupied wid preparations for Vincy Mas. Seems politics push to de back burner for now."

"And the press Vince?"

"They're satisfied with the press release for now sir."

"Thank goodness our press isn't like the sharks in the States."

"Yes sir," Taylor acknowledged, a grin creasing his face.

"Speaking of sharks, what about the political reaction?"

"Dat you will know better dan me sir," Huggins said. "I did field a lot of calls yesterday. Looking for you sir."

"Thanks for that Reggie."

"And Superintendent Mitchell isn't too happy."

"I'll bet he isn't. If that's all gentlemen, dismissed."

They'd both remained standing since entering the office. Their heels came together in attention. Taylor saluted. They both turned and headed for the door.

Huggins lagged behind, turning to me after Taylor had exited. "How de investigation into de murder of your man going Commissioner?"

"Slow. Superintendent Johanssen believes he was killed on Mustique. But so far no suspects."

His eyebrows drew together. Pinched nostrils and a downward curve of his mouth formed a pained frown. I wondered again at the depth of his emotional response for someone he didn't know. Maybe it'd been the circumstances, the cold-blooded nature of the crime. And the fact the victim had been a police constable. Or maybe his reaction was some sort of empathetic response to me.

The intercom buzzed as I settled into my comfortable recliner. Cecilia inquired if I'd be available for afternoon tea at the Governor General's residence. I instructed her to make the appointment. Saying no to the Governor General tantamount to saying no to the Queen. You didn't without good reason. Even then...

Since the raids, my usual morning meetings now included a daily briefing by Sergeant Samuel. He arrived an hour after Huggins and Taylor departed.

Cecilia ushered him into my office. Her beaming smile whenever in his presence conveyed the fond approval in which she now held the sergeant. Samuel played into it. His own smile whenever he arrived at my office aimed at charming her. Samuel stood at attention. His right arm raised in a salute.

"Morning Sammy. At ease," I greeted him, motioning him over to the sitting area.

"What do you have so far?" I asked, settling into the armchair facing him.

"Continuing to collate de interrogations Commissioner. Some of de prisoners talking freely, others not so much. I've put together a report for de Public Prosecutor, but he can't say for sure when dey'll be brought before a magistrate."

"The usual problem or something on our end?" I asked.

"De usual sir. Only three official magistrates, and even though de registrar of de high court and de presiding judge of family court have been serving as magistrates, de court still have up to a six month backlog."

"Gives us more time to continue building the cases."

"Yes sir. Though de cases already strong. Not only de prisoners incriminating each other, but de interrogations led to evidence de prosecutor can use in court. Won't even need their testimony in some of de cases."

"I've been going over the reports on the Rapid Response Unit in particular," I said. "I haven't seen any indications of Superintendent Browne being involved in the illegal activities."

"No sir. But more than sufficient for administrative leave due to irresponsible conduct, dereliction, violation of police policy, and other offenses sir. More than enough evidence provided by statements from de rogue officers, and interviews with others in de unit."

"And you're certain there's nothing else?"

"Yes sir. Indications are someone else was giving de orders. From the bits and pieces of de prisoner's statements, I think is somebody outside de force. Somebody in government. Superintendent Browne just facilitated de whole thing by looking de other way."

Gage's words sprang to the front of my thoughts. 'I'd want to penetrate the Government, and the police force. You have to assume they've already done that'. Raising the question, was this old fashioned run of the mill official corruption, or part of Bogeyman's operation? Maybe both. Corrupt politicians and police officials made ideal targets for manipulation.

"Any idea who this person is?" I asked.

"No sir. Seems none of de guys ever met or seen him. But is somebody with influence."

"The priority is identifying this person Sammy," I said.

"Understand sir." His intelligent eager eyes indicated a mind already at work on the problem.

"Anything else?"

"Not at de moment Commissioner."

I rose from the chair, the meeting concluded. "Damn fine work Sammy," I said, rather than the formal 'dismissed'. I walked him to the door.

No sooner settled into my recliner again, ruminating on Sammy's information, when Cecilia buzzed.

"Superintendent Mitchell would like a word."

I hesitated. A meeting I didn't particularly relish. And one I'd not yet prepared for. But I couldn't turn him away. I needed to appease him until I had enough to strike.

"Send him in," I said.

Mitchell's belligerent expression and manner upon entering my office signaled appeasement an unlikely option. He strode purposefully toward my desk, his puffed chest aggressively leading the way. Wide set eyes stared at me, his contempt undisguised. The charcoal dark pupils surrounded by bloodshot sclera, like fiery tendrils leaking from the furnace of his anger. He managed a facsimile of attention, and a tepid salute.

"Commisshunah," he said, breaking protocol by not waiting for me to speak first. His voice barely controlled, the fleshy jowls of his cheeks quivering in suppressed rage. "I have to protest in de strongest terms you deliberately leavin' my division out of dese raids"

"On what grounds?" I said. My voice calm, even.

"I wuz not informed of de operation. And my division wuz deliberately excluded."

"The CID was not needed for the operation," I said. "The Special Services Unit is tasked with marijuana interdiction. The major crimes squad with gang activity. In fact the only unit deliberately excluded was the Rapid Response Unit, because three officers in the unit were known to be collaborating with the gang."

"So you sayin' de CID same as de RRU. Cyan be trusted."

"I said nothing of the kind Superintendent."

"Den you sayin' is me you cyan trust."

"I didn't say that either."

"You cyan just exclude a 'hole division of poliss like dat..."

"You forget your place Superintendent." I said, standing to meet his stare, irritation rising in my voice. "You may have ambitions to occupy this office, but I am currently sitting in this chair and while I do, you, your division, and every member of this police force are subject to my orders."

My outburst silenced him. But not for long. His adams apple bobbed in his neck in a visible effort to control his anger.

"As you say but..."

"Dismissed," I interrupted him.

"I wuzn't finished wid..."

"Dismissed Superintendent," I repeated, barking the command, my patience exhausted, not merely by his presence and this disagreeable encounter, but the accumulated aggravation of the past five months.

Anger flashed in the red-rimmed eyes glaring at me. I held his stare. A contest he'd never win.

He turned abruptly, headed for the door. He flung it open, exiting without a salute. I didn't give a damn, more annoyed at myself for allowing him to burrow under my skin. The exchange hadn't altered our relationship or our mutual dislike of each other. His antagonistic resentment had been there from the moment I'd stepped into the job. It'd still be there even after my departure. The police force no longer the cliquey boys club through whose ranks he'd risen. But such confrontations were premature, and didn't serve my purpose to have him dismissed from the force permanently.

Cecilia filled the doorway, her stern visage appraising me. The tiniest upward curl of her mouth indicated satisfaction at what she'd overheard. She reached for the door to close it.

"What time is tea at Government House?" I asked before she retreated.

"Four o'clock Commissioner."

"Thanks. I have a lunch appointment. I'll be out of the office for the next hour or so. When I get back I need to see Assistant Superintendent Colin Browne and Superintendent Chambers."

"Yes Commissioner," she said, closing the door softly behind her.

My lunch appointment had nothing to do with food or eating. Rather a response to an email I'd received that morning prior to departing Bequia. The email account had been created a year earlier using a fictitious name, address, and profile.

The fast moving storm had passed, leaving in its wake drenched streets and overflowing roadside gutters, colloquially referred to as 'Kingstown Rivers'. Shafts of sunlight pierced a clearing sky smeared by wispy clouds, resembling a mare's tail ruffled by a breeze.

I decided to walk. It'd provide an opportunity to check for a tail. I didn't expect to find one. No reason for anyone to be shadowing me. Since I'd initiated my undercover operation, I hadn't sensed or spotted a tail, or observed anyone paying undue notice to my activities. But it did no harm to be careful. Channeling Gage again.

I turned into Kingstown's main market. Unusually deserted, even for a Wednesday, when you'd expect at least a handful of vendors occupying stalls, boutiques and makeshift stands along the narrow lane. But the morning's rain showers had kept the vendors indoors, and out of town. Except for a few Rastafarians, pushing homebuilt wheelbarrow carts loaded with fruit and produce.

Fridays and Saturdays were the market's busiest days. Every available square inch occupied by a crush of hucksters and vendors from all across the island, displaying and hawking a bewildering variety of fruits, vegetables, and produce. The colors vibrant and inviting, the scents exotic and intoxicating, the clamor off-putting and exhilarating.

I exited the market on Bedford Street. Crossed Bedford, and continued along Lower Long Lane. I turned into a narrow alley wide enough to accommodate a single subcompact car. Trash bearing 'Kingstown Rivers' flowed along shallow gutters on either side. The alley opened onto a small parking area behind the buildings fronting Bedford Street.

I located the blue Madza Demio, parked among three other vehicles next to a makeshift fence of corrugated zinc sheets separating the lot from the adjacent property. Each sheet painted a different color.

No one had observed me enter the alley. No one in the tiny lot.

I approached the Madza sandwiched between two other vehicles. I checked the alley again. I opened the Mazda's gas filler door and unscrewed the fuel cap. A small flat rectangular cylinder lay in the closed filler neck. I plucked it out, substituting an identical cylinder from my pocket. I replaced the fuel cap, closed the filler door, and exited the lot.

I returned to my office an hour later, ostensively following my luncheon appointment. I sat at my desk and booted my laptop. I retrieved the cylinder from my pocket and pried open a concealed lid. I turned the cylinder upside down, allowing a small thumb drive to slide into my palm. I plugged the thumb drive into a USB slot of the laptop.

An autorun file opened on the laptop screen requesting a login password. I typed it in. A word document file replaced the login screen.

Your inquiry regarding Sonya Johnson. 31 years old (DOB: 28/2/1980); resides Murray's Village Road, Murray's Village, with mother Louise Johnson and two children Ashton O'Keefe 10 years old, and Denise Phillips 6 years old. Current whereabouts of fathers unknown. Employed as Customs Inspector, Port Customs House Kingstown. Subject spends most evenings after work at Agricultural warehouse on Bypass Road constructing costumes for a Carnival street band in which she is a member. No known current romantic association. Last known to be mistress of Superintendent of Police Nigel Mitchell.

The sentence leapt from the screen like a flash of lightening. A smile crept across my face as I pictured Solly sitting at De Reef, his parting smile mysterious and mischievous. Much of the information in Elana's summary confirmed what I'd already learned from Sonya Johnson's personnel file. But Elana had been following Sonya over the past five days, providing details on her personal habits, associates, and the explosive item regarding her connection to Superintendent Mitchell.

The intercom buzzed. "The Commissioner of Police of St. Lucia on the line for you," Cecilia announced.

Word had spread around the region. Gordon Patrick of St. Lucia the first of many congratulatory calls I'd receive during the afternoon.

Melanie called too, offering the U.S.'s official congratulations. The conversation carefully circumspect. I read between the lines, following her lead. She promised to call again soon.

And the meeting I most anticipated. "Assistant Superintendent Browne to see you," Cecilia announced.

She escorted him through the office door, as usual. A subtle informed glance in my direction as she quietly closed the door behind Assistant Superintendent Colin Browne. I seldom discussed operational or administrative police matters with Cecilia. I didn't have to. Cecilia was intimately aware of everything taking place in my office. She screened my calls, set my appointments, typed my reports. And ran the office with the efficiency of an air traffic controller, offering unsolicited and usually astute advice in her characteristically acerbic manner. She'd been aware of the precise nature of my meeting with AS Browne.

He stepped toward my desk, stood at attention, and saluted. His uniform hung loose and ill fitting on his tall thin frame. Its slovenly appearance indicative of a lack of professional pride in its wearer. His gaze roamed around the office, avoiding mine.

I prolonged his discomfort. I waited before standing before him and returning his salute. His wandering gaze finally settled on my face. Small, round, dark squinty eyes, set wide in a long thin black face, stared into mine. Their expression blithe unconcerned anticipation. I did not order him at ease, or offer him a seat. Instead, I retrieved a file from my desk, opened it, my movements slow and deliberate.

"This file contains the results of interrogations of three rogue officers from your unit Superintendent. And a report on the unit based on those interrogations and interviews with other members of the unit."

I lifted my gaze from the file to his face. Deep lines delineating thin sunken cheeks ran from flat wide nostrils, to the corners of thick lips. The downturned corners of his mouth fixed in a permanent frown, a characterizing feature of the entire bunch of malcontents, it suddenly occurred to me.

"This report demonstrates conclusively that you are unfit to command the Rapid Response Unit. Or any police unit for that matter."

His reaction a jump in his prominent adams apple.

"I am not responsible for de unlawful actions of rogue offices..." he began.

"Yes you are," I said, interrupting him. "The ultimate responsibility for the men and what occurs in the unit is yours. You are their Commander. But apart from that I have evidence of gross incompetence and mismanagement within the unit, and with the public. Not to mention misappropriation and misuse of police property, including assignment of police vehicles for non-official, even political purposes, in direct violation of police policy. All authorized and signed out by you," I said, allowing the accusation to penetrate.

His shaved head leaned side to side as he nervously shifted his weight from foot to foot. The small, furtive eyes, no longer focused on me, shifting constantly, while his adams apple hopscotched in the thin narrow neck.

"These are serious charges which can no longer be overlooked. The rogue behavior in your unit is a direct consequence of your leadership, or rather lack of leadership. And because of their criminal actions, your cronies on the force and in government can no longer protect you."

I paused. Waited. My words fortified by the fierce unyielding stare I drilled into the shifting target of his eyes.

"Effective immediately you are relieved of command of the Rapid Response Unit. You are also placed on administrative leave pending the outcome of further investigation, which may result in criminal charges."

His thick lips parted, mouth hanging slightly agape. The expression of blithe unconcern disappeared from the small eyes. They grew larger as the full import struck him. I believe he fully expected to be reprimanded, maybe even removed from the unit. But being dismissed from the force, or charged before a court, had never occurred to him.

I lifted the telephone handset and buzzed Cecilia.

"Assistant Superintendent Browne will be right out. Please have my aide ensure he remains there until I've spoken with Superintendent Chambers," I said, adding salt to the wound.

"And please send in the Superintendent."

I replaced the handset. "Dismissed," I said.

CHAPTER 18

A quick detour to my house in Montrose for a freshen up, and change into uniform, before heading out to Government House. I seldom wore the grey day uniform, preferring short-sleeved dress shirts and a tie. But the afternoon tea appointment constituted an official summons by the representative of St. Vincent's head of state, who remained Her Majesty the Queen. A queer state of affairs, reflecting St. Vincent and the Grenadines status as a member of the British Commonwealth. A status the Government not surprisingly wished to change. Its effort to do so recently rejected by the population in a referendum.

Standing before the bedroom's full-length mirror, I inspected my attire. Slacks crisply pressed and creased. Tunic jacket neatly fitted and properly buttoned. Shoulder epaulets, rank insignia, and collar insignia correctly affixed and straight. Black corded braid over the left shoulder, passed under the epaulet, the bottom loop under the left armpit extending precisely to the left breast pocket.

I lifted the black uniform cap from the dresser table and placed it on my head. Polished Police coat of arms pinned to the front of the crown. The cap's black peak below the white braid polished to a mirror like finish. And last, the anachronistic silver tipped swagger stick tucked under my left arm.

An assistant dressed in a dark suit met me in the reception hall inside the main entrance to Government House, the Governor General's official residence and office.

"Dis way Commissioner," he said. "Sir Brathwaite is expecting you."

He led me through the reception room to an outdoor table on the stone verandah. The verandah overlooked manicured lawns and flowerbeds, part of the grounds of St. Vincent's botanic gardens. The variety of contrasting colors vibrant in the bright sunlight. A white China tea service, delicate china teacups turned down in saucers, sat in the middle of a table covered by a red linen tablecloth. Next to the tea service a silver tray, covered by a linen cloth.

The assistant pulled out a chair from the table, holding it for me to sit. "I'll inform Sir Brathwaite you've arrived Commissioner. He'll be out directly," he said, before heading through curtained double doors.

Sir Christopher Brathwaite stepped onto the verandah. Tall. Elegant. His distinguished features accentuated by a shock of white hair, bushy white eyebrows, white chevron moustache spanning the width of his mouth, and a tuff of white hair under his lower lip. The white of his head and facial hair a vivid contrast against his dark brown complexion. He strode toward the table dressed in an immaculately tailored navy blue suit, white shirt, and red patterned silk tie.

He extended his hand as I stood to meet him, tugging at the hem of my uniform tunic to straighten it.

"Commissioner," he greeted in a soft, melodious voice. "So good of you to come."

"Sir Christopher," I said, taking the offered hand. "My pleasure sir."

Of course I'd been obliged to accept his invitation. The equivalent of a royal summons by the Queen. As Governor General, he possessed limited constitutional powers in the day-to-day governance of the country. Required to act only on the 'advice' of the elected Prime Minister. But as the Queen's representative, his official duties included swearing in the elected Prime Minister, Deputy Prime Minister, and Attorney General. Adjourning, dissolving, and commencing new sessions of Parliament. Appointing Senators and cabinet ministers upon the 'advice' of the Prime Minister, validating acts passed by Parliament before they could become law, and receiving and entertaining official and diplomatic visitors. Technically a Member of Parliament, by protocol he attended only when invited. But he had to be kept informed of all matters occurring in the Parliament.

He'd been the liaison between the FBI, Scotland Yard, and me, regarding the conspiracy uncovered during the Jackson Taylor murder investigation. He'd conveyed the explosive information to a specially called session of Parliament.

"First and foremost allow me to personally congratulate you on the recent arrests," he said, taking the chair opposite me, unbuttoning and opening the suit jacket. "Please, sit Commissioner," he said, noticing I'd remained standing.

As though observing from hiding, a demure young woman in a prim uniform stepped onto the verandah as soon as we'd both settled into our seats. She carried a china teapot matching the set on the table. She set it down, removing the linen cover to reveal a matching cream carafe, sugar bowl, and a platter of pastries, scones and Vincentian sweet cakes.

"If you'd prefer coffee, Commissioner..."

"No sir. Tea will be fine thank you."

"I think you'll find this blend every much as strong as a good cup of coffee," he said as the girl poured a dark steaming liquid into our cups. Its fruity scent distinct. One I recognized.

"A Darjeeling black tea. One of my favorites," Sir Brathwaite said, pouring a dollop of cream into his cup followed by a half a teaspoon of brown cane sugar.

"I'm familiar with it sir," I said, grateful for a tea I recognized, and in fact liked. I preferred it dark and heavy like my coffee, forgoing the cream but stirring in two heaping teaspoons of sugar to cut the astringent tannin taste.

We both drank small exploratory sips until the girl departed the verandah. Placing his cup in the saucer on the table, Sir Brathwaite said, "Tell me about these raids and arrests Commissioner."

As concisely as possible, I outlined the intelligence and details of the raids and arrests, without mentioning my undercover operation or Gage's involvement. Far more detail than had been reported in the press, including details regarding ensuing prosecutions and disciplinary actions in the police force.

"Do you see any connection to our other situation?" he asked.

The heart of the matter. As I'd expected.

"Not at this point sir. But it doesn't mean there isn't one."

"You've seen the reports I've forwarded to you from the FBI and Special Branch. Not much progress I'm afraid. And

I'm not entirely sure either agency is telling us all they know. What are you hearing from your private sources?"

"Private sources sir?"

A smile stretched the white bordered lips of his dark brown face. A twinkle in the intelligent caramel eyes. He passed a hand over the red tie as though brushing it free of cookie crumbs.

"Come now Commissioner. You and Superintendent Johanssen have solved two remarkable cases in the past year, and developed extraordinary information which exposed this conspiracy. The FBI continues to sing your praises. I assume you have contacts from your days in Florida law enforcement."

If he only knew, I thought.

"Some sir," I said. "But they're not of much use in this situation. However we do know an FBI agent who worked closely with Superintendent Johanssen on the Taylor and Greene cases. They have a working quid pro quo relationship. Unfortunately he isn't telling us anything different from his bosses."

"And you trust this agent?"

"I have no reason to doubt his information sir."

"I've heard through private channels the CIA is taking an interest," he said.

"I've heard the same sir," I said, eliciting a subtle raised white eyebrow.

"Wouldn't do to have those cowboys running around in our yard Commissioner."

"I agree sir."

We'd finished our tea, but hadn't touched any of the treats decorously displayed on the platter. Sir Fredericks refreshed our cups and offered the tray of sweet cakes, insisting I join him as he bit into one of the cup cake sized confections.

"I also wish to thank you for your service to my country Commissioner."

"It's my adopted country too sir."

He smiled. "You've achieved remarkable results in the police force. I'll be sorry to see you go. If it were up to me, you'd remain as Commissioner of Police no matter the outcome of these elections. But as you know I make appointments solely on the advice of the Prime Minister."

I appreciate the sentiment sir," I said. "But I believe the force is beyond the point of turning back to the old ways. And I also believe I'll be leaving it in good hands."

"Good to hear Commissioner."

I spent another hour in his company, departing Government House a bit after six pm. Back at my house in Montrose I unceremoniously ditched the uniform, changing into comfortable street wear. I ate a light supper and dismissed the staff for the evening.

At ten pm I sat in the Toyota Liberty Jeep I leased for my personal use. I'd parked on Bypass Road, across the street from an Agricultural Department warehouse. The area quiet and dimly lit by a single street light. At fifteen minutes past ten Sonya Johnson exited the building in the company of two other women. I exited the Jeep and approached from the opposite side of the road.

"Miss Johnson," I called, startling the little group. "I wonder if I might have a word."

"Commisshunah?" Dat you Commisshunah Daniels," her eyes squinting in the dim light, providing just enough illumination for her to recognize me.

"Yes ma'am," I said. "I just need a quick word if you don't mind."

"Commisshunah I have fe get home. I gettin' a ride from me fren' heah."

"I can give you a lift home. It's no bother and we can talk on the way."

"Talk 'bout what?"

"It's kind of a sensitive matter. And it is important," I said, eyeing her two friends who were giggling like schoolgirls, while casting coquettish glances in my direction.

"Well seein' is you. Okay."

Her friends continued to giggle and eye me as Sonya bid them goodnight. We crossed the road together to the parked jeep. No doubt, stories would circulate in their circle of acquaintances the next day. But it couldn't be helped.

I pulled into the empty road, a stark contrast to Kingstown's congested daytime traffic. I passed easily along the dimly lit, unencumbered road, connecting onto James Street.

"So must be Nigel you wan' talk 'bout," she said as we headed away from town.

"Why would you think that?" I said, glancing at her. She turned to face me, world-weary eyes just shy of a combat soldier's thousand-yard stare fixed on me. Eyes accustomed to sorrow, disappointment, and not enough joy. But sensible eyes, in a hardy face. A homely, earthy kind of pretty, with a broad mouth and generous lips.

"Why else you wan' talk to me? And is 'bout time somebody start lookin' at what dat man doin'."

"Why do you say that?"

"Him not a good man. And him is poliss. A woman bea-ter. Him try dat wid me an me tell him go way."

"How'd you come to be with him in the first place?"

She sucked in air between clenched teeth, producing the peculiar sucking sound Vincentians made to display annoyance or impatience.

"Don't mek any difference. But when he wuz wid me him also tek up wid two more women besides me. I tell him no sah. Me havin' none a dat. Dat wuz 'bout tree months ago."

She fell silent, gazing out at the dark landscape and lit buildings as James Street turned into Murray Road.

"He don't like you at all Commisshunah," she said. "Al-ways complainin' 'bout you dis and you dat."

"What else can you tell me about him?"

"Like what?"

"Who his associates are? What he does in his free time?"

""He spend a lot a time wid him politician fren'. De two a dem drinkin' and clubbin'. And a poliss fren' too. I tink him wid de black shirts," she said, using the public's derogatory term for the Rapid Response Unit.

"Who's this politician friend?" I asked.

"Name Glen Mackee. Glenford. He de ULP member from South Windward constituency. Dem come up in primary and grammar school togeder. All tree a dem. Tick as teeves. Probably what dem doin' too. Teevin'. Cause dem always have plenty cash money. One of de reasons I wuz wid Nigel. He carry me nice places. Fancy parties and such.

"So why'd you leave him?"

"Like I tell you. He tek up wid dose odder woman. And he beat dem too. But you cyan mek no complaint to de poliss.

Dey just tek his side. Nobody cyan bring him to court and charge him. Den he ask me to pass some t'ings thru' customs widout inspection. No sah. Me nah get mixed up in dem illegal stuff and go a prison. Me tell him so. Tell him me out a dis and he must leave me alone."

I turned onto Murray's Village Road, climbing the heights above Kingstown. The brightly lit wharfs of the harbor appeared in the distance.

"Two Sundays past he come to me house," she continued. "He bring me a present and show me a whole heap a money. U.S. money. Say him want get back wid me.

"Two Sundays ago? Did he say who he was meeting that night?"

"Glenford. He say dey jus' get paid fe some business and dey goin' celebrate. Wanted me to come. Jus' ovah heah Commisshunah," she said, as we drove into Murray's Village, pointing to a modest brick home set behind trees in a small yard.

"So what you goin' do 'bout Nigel?" She asked.

"Well you probably won't have to worry about him bothering you again. And you made the right decision Sonya. Otherwise you'd probably be going down with him. Maybe even to prison as you said. Also it's probably best if you keep this conversation just between us."

She nodded. Reached for the door handle. "Me have nuttin' more fe do wid dat man," she said, opening the passenger door and sliding from the seat. After closing the door she bent to eye me in a parting glance.

"Thank you Sonya," I said, holding eye contact.

Her lips parted in a wan, cheerless smile.

I drove through Kingstown. Not headed home, instead back to my office, my mind alive. A wave of anticipatory excitement grew inside me. But tempered by experience. I'd had promising leads turn into dead ends before. Sonya had mentioned seeing Mitchell carrying lots of cash, American currency, two Sundays before. It stirred a memory of something Samuels had said during our meeting in Troumaka Bay.

I switched on the overhead fluorescent lights and desk lamp in my office. I unlocked the desk's file drawer, searching though it until I located the relevant files. I dropped them on the desk. From another drawer I retrieved a yellow legal pad, grabbed a pen, and settled into my comfortable recliner.

I recalled my conversation with Samuel. He'd seen Natty the gang leader carrying a bag of cash, some of it crisp, bank fresh U.S. currency. I drew a circle at the bottom of the pad. In the circle I wrote 'Natty', 'cash', and the date. I rummaged through the files for the reports on Natty's interrogation. Found it. I leaned back in my chair and commenced reading.

After reading the report, I drew a second circle just above Natty's, and a short straight line connecting both circles. Along the line I wrote, 'received cash from'. In the new circle I wrote, 'Sgt. Clifford Ashton'. I pulled the file on Ashton's interrogation and settled back to read.

Finished reading, I dropped the file on my desk and wrote in Ashton's circle 'cash from Glenford' and the date. According to Ashton the payment had been for private security work, and he identified Glenford only as a friend, without providing a name.

I drew a third circle above Ashton's. Along the line connecting those circles I wrote 'paid cash to' and in the new circle wrote 'Glenford Mackee'. Next to Mackee's circle I drew another circle, and another short straight line connecting the circles as I'd done the others. Along this line I wrote, 'paid cash to', and in the circle I wrote 'Supt. Nigel Mitchell', and the date.

Setting the legal pad aside I rummaged through the files now spread across my desk for the reports on Devon Weekes, and Trevor Peters, and the RRU review on Assistant Superintendent Colin Browne.

I tackled the Browne review first, looking specifically at dates when police vehicles had been improperly used for non-police business. I found the entry I'd been hoping for, an unmarked vehicle authorized by Browne and signed out by Trevor Peters.

According to Peters' interrogation, he'd driven the vehicle to a location in Stubbs, where a man Peters did not recognize placed a backpack in the vehicle, giving Peters instructions to deliver the backpack to Sergeant Ashton in Georgetown. I noted it in the Ashton and Mackee circles, placing a question make next to the Mackee notation. In parenthesis, I wrote a reminder to obtain a description of the backpack man from Peters. I had no doubt it'd match Glenford Mackee.

I studied the diagram I'd created. Struck by two things. Glenford Mackee was now a significant person of interest in the investigation. Secondly, the dates matched the Sunday Whittaker had been killed. Nothing I'd read indicated a definitive connection. But neither did I consider it mere coincidence.

My cell phone rang. The time displayed on the screen a shock. I'd immersed myself in the project, completely oblivious to time's passage. I glanced at my watch, an automatic and uselessly redundant exercise. The watch and phone agreed. The numbers displayed on the screen indicated a satellite connection.

I expected Jolene's or Gage's voice when I answered. Surprised and elated to hear Melanie's instead.

"Wanted to catch you before bedtime," she said.

"Believe it or not I'm at the office."

"What the hell're you doing there this time of night?"

"Connecting some dots. Lost track of time. And so glad to hear your voice."

"Told you when we spoke I'd call later. I used the special number you gave me. I assume it's a sat connection. Does that mean your phone's secure?"

"On my end it is. A bug on your phone would pick up the conversation but the number is untraceable."

"Couldn't say much when I called earlier."

"I gathered. What's going on?"

"Your little operation lit a fire under the CIA boys here. Still just signals traffic, but a lot more of it."

"They plan on taking any action?"

"Difficult to say. Right now they aren't seeing a connection to the other matter. But the conventional wisdom is your force is ripe for penetration. Probably already compromised."

"I'm working under a similar assumption. Wouldn't want to dissuade them of the notion if it keeps them looking. But putting people on the ground over here will just complicate things."

"Agreed. Any way I can help you over here?"

"Run interference and keep me posted."

"Oh is that all," an unmistakable levity in her voice. "That could be construed as treason you know."

"A bit melodramatic I think. I'm merely discussing security concerns in your official capacity."

"How've you been?" she segued, her voice lower, more personal and intimate.

"Missing you," I said.

"Miss you too. But I have a surprise for you."

"Oh yeah, what's that?" I said, aware of a playful smile spreading across my face.

"Your Governor General has requested an appointment. I'll probably be over there sometime next week."

The smile grew to a wide excited grin.

"He's following the situation closely," I said. "Believes the folks at Scotland Yard and the FBI are holding back information. I had my audience with him today at afternoon tea."

Her pleasant chuckle reached me through the phone.

"So I probably won't get any work done while I'm waiting with bated breath," I said.

"Or you could work like crazy clearing your desk so there'll be no distractions."

"I like your plan better."

She laughed again. "I'll call you with my schedule. Sleep tight. See you soon."

"You too," I said. "Night."

I stared at the phone for several moments after she'd disconnected. The project wiped from my mind. Replaced by only thoughts of her.

I tidied my desk. Gathered the files and replaced them in the desk drawer. Staring down at the yellow pad I intended to take home, I picked up the pen and drew a final circle above Glenford Mackee's. In it I placed a question mark. And a notation.

'Where did Mackee get the money?'

CHAPTER 19

First thing upon arriving at my office in the morning, I asked Cecilia to have Sergeant Samuel report to me.

He arrived fifteen minutes later, dressed casually in plain clothes, dark khaki cargo slacks, and a loose fitting white Guayabera shirt.

"At ease Sammy. Good morning."

"Morning Commissioner."

"I take it Trevor Peters is being held at the Kingstown prison?"

"Yes sir."

"Have him transported over here immediately," I said. "I need to ask him a few questions."

Eyebrows rose on his thick brow, a curious gaze in his deep-set alert eyes.

"I'll tell you about it later," I said. "Right now just get him over here. That'll be all for now."

"Yes sir," he said, saluting and exiting the office.

Back at my desk, I buzzed Cecilia.

"Please step in a moment Cissy."

She arrived holding a pen and notebook, anticipating dictation.

"Have a seat Cissy," I said, indicating the chair facing my desk. "I have a special request to ask you." I said.

Her thinly painted eyebrows arched, and the familiar curious expression lit her eyes. She waited.

"I want you to put together a profile on Gilford Mackee for me. Do you know who that is?"

"Yes sir. He represents the South Windward constituency in Parliament."

"That's the one. Any information you're able to gather, discreetly," I said, emphasizing the last word.

"Understood Commissioner." As our relationship had developed and my faith and trust in her grew over the years, I'd often entrusted such special projects to her. For her part, she returned that faith and trust in unquestioned devotion and discretion.

"When do you need this Commissioner?"

"Whatever you can put together by the end of the day. Thanks Cissy," I said as she rose to leave.

I called Jolene's secure cell phone from my cell phone. Gage had supplied the encrypted satellite accessible phones during his search for the person who'd shot me. Who'd damn near killed me.

"Hey JJ," I greeted her. "Need a favor."

"Name it Chief."

"Need you to track down Solly. I need everything he knows about a Gilford Mackee, ULP Parliamentary representative from South Windward. You can tell him it's me asking. Buy him lunch."

"I'll get on it. By the way, is Gage running another little errand for you?"

"No. Why?"

"He and Rodney left this morning with Wherever. Said he had charter."

"A charter? The only time he has so called charters is when he's up to some damn thing. But it isn't anything I asked him to do."

"Well he's as tight lipped as ever about it. Said he expects to be back by tomorrow afternoon. Anyway, I'll see what I can get from Solly. Have it for you by the end of the day."

"Anything new on your end."

"Nothing. I expected Gage to have something by now but I guess I'll have to wait until he gets back."

"I may have something on this end," I said. "We'll get together when I'm home tomorrow evening."

Trevor Peters sat on an unfinished raw wood stool in the dank, dinghy, holding cell. The harsh suffering of a bygone century imbued in its cold colonial stone walls. The cell smelled of stale sweat, urine, and fear.

He stood. Turned to face me and the constable opening the wrought iron cell door. His black oblong face morose, the dark eyes dejected, the left eye swollen and bloodshot. The injured eye, an unhealed laceration on his thick swollen upper lip, and an ugly purple bruise around the damaged left eye, indicated a recent fight. A common hazard for ex constables incarcerated in Her Majesty's prison.

I asked the constable attending the jail to leave us alone. I waited until he'd exited and locked the heavy oak door at the end of the hall of cells, before stepping into Peters' cell. His good eye warily appraised me. I stood facing him, back straight, in an open stance, legs slightly apart, my arms at my sides. Authoritative but non-aggressive.

"It's only going to get worse," I said, using a sympathetic tone. "But maybe there's a way out for you."

He remained silent. His eyes attempted to hold my stare, instead shifting downward. The downturned corners of his mouth, and crow's feet between the curved eyebrows, set in a permanent scowl. A characteristic I'd come to expect.

"You help me and you also help yourself," I said.

"I don't have no help fe you, and I don't need none from you," He said, breaking his silence.

"You're a corrupt dirty officer Peters, and we have sufficient evidence to send you to prison. The only question is for how long and what kind of prison."

He lifted his gaze, meeting my unwavering stare for the first time. The lifeline I'd suggested registered, taking hold in the despondent eyes.

I didn't give it time to ruminate. "You told the constables who questioned you that you drove an unmarked police vehicle to Stubbs two Sundays ago, where a man placed a backpack in the vehicle, and told you to deliver it to Sergeant Ashton in Georgetown. Is that correct?"

He hesitated. Still thinking through the offer. Resistant, but also desperate for a possible port in his personal storm.

"Dat correct," he said, the voice docile, almost a whisper.

"And you said you didn't know the man who put the backpack in the vehicle?"

"He look familiar. I t'ink I see him somewhey befoh. But I don't remembah, and I don't know him." His voice, his entire demeanor, indicated compliant surrender.

"Can you describe him?"

His gaze met mine again. A brief hint of defiance, as he mentally appraised his bargaining position, concluding we didn't know who this person was. He hadn't been caught up in our raids. Peters' dark eyes stared into mine while he calculated his price.

"You should know this man is a person of interest in a murder investigation. You want to add obstruction of a police inquiry, and accessory to murder, to the charges against you. That one is a hanging offense."

"What you talkin'! Me no kill nobody. Me no kill nobody!" he repeated, his manner agitated, fear a new element in his eyes.

"That may be, but you were one of the people who saw this man on the night of the murder. Let me ask you this," I said, paying close attention to his body language. "Did you look in the backpack?"

The segue surprised him. As I'd intended.

"Me nevah open de bag," he answered quickly.

I observed him carefully for the signs. The tilt of his head, the movement of his eyes, frequency of blinking, the placement of his hands. His confusion and nervousness apparent, but no telltale signs of lying. Yet the swiftness of his answer, the downward shift of his eyes to the right as though recalling an emotion, the slight nervous twitch at his throat, indicated more there than he'd revealed.

"But you wanted to? Was tempted to? I prodded.

"Yes."

"Why didn't you?"

"Me 'fraid fe open it."

He didn't know about the money.

"Describe the man," I said pivoting back to my earlier question.

No hesitation this time. His mind had switched gears to focus on the backpack, and the threat of a murder charge, added a new factor in his calculation.

"Tall. Maybe six foot. Slim. Maybe a hundred an fifty pounds or so," his police training kicking in. "Slim face. Lots a grey in him hair. And a moustache."

"Tell me if you see the man in any of these pictures," I said, opening a file I'd held tucked under my arm during the questioning. Earlier I'd prepared a photo lineup using pass-port-sized photos taped to the inside of the file. A dozen in all. Among them a photograph of Glenford Mackee.

The policies and procedures regarding photos lineups as practiced in the States didn't apply in St. Vincent. But I followed them anyway, providing an array of photographs similar in features to my subject. Not for the sake of prosecution. I wanted a clean, positive identification.

Peters picked Mackee's photo without hesitation.

"Dat's him," he said, pointing to Mackee's photograph.

"You're positive?" I asked.

"Dat de man leve de backpack in de truck," he said.

I'd obtained the information I needed. I turned, exited the cell, and called for the constable.

"What 'bout me?" he called to my departing back.

"What about you," I said without turning.

Entering the outer office Cecilia handed me a stack of phone messages. She caught the inquiring glint in my eye. She nodded.

"By the end of the day Commissioner," she said. "And DC Huggins and AC Taylor have been waiting for you to return."

"Tell them I'll see them now if they're available," I said.

In my office, I collapsed into my desk chair and leaned back, reclining it all the way, my ankles crossed atop one corner of the desk. Mackee's involvement confirmed. I'd found the bagman, but I didn't have him yet. How to accomplish that? I wondered.

The light tapping on my door fifteen minutes later interrupted my ruminations. I hadn't reached any conclusions, my mind a foggy blank. Running in circles. The door opened to reveal Cecilia ushering in Deputy Commissioner Huggins.

"Morning Reggie," I said, rising from my chair and crossing the room to greet him, indicating the sitting area.

"I was told you were questioning a prisoner Commis-shunah," he said, eyebrows raised behind the spectacles, the eyes inquisitive.

"Yes. I'd been going over the interrogation reports and just needed to confirm some details," I said evasively, not ready to disclose the picture I'd been piecing together.

"What do we have today?" I asked before he might pursue the matter further.

I paid scant attention to the briefing. My mind continued to work the other problem. And nothing he said set off any alarm bells.

"Thanks Reggie," I said when he'd finished, having barely heard him.

"Oh by the way," I said, halting him by the door. "Arrange to have Trevor Peters put in segregation, like we did with Devon Weekes."

Again, the curious lift of eyebrows. "Yes sir," he said. I turned to my desk without further explanation.

Taylor arrived fifteen minutes later. As with Huggins, my preoccupied mind only half listened to his briefing, sifting his words for anything significant requiring my full attention. When something he said planted the seed of an idea.

"What was that Vince?" I said.

"I was saying the Vincentian is looking to do follow up articles on the story. They've been waiting for the Public Prosecutor so they can report on the court appearances and charges. But so far only one or two have been taken before a magistrate."

"What do you suggest?"

"Well we can't speak for the Public Prosecutor or the court. But maybe if we gave them something further on the investigations."

"Let me think about it and get back to you. That'll be all Vince. Thanks," I said, ending the meeting by rising from the chair.

Lunchtime. I needed to think. The seed had germinated and taken root. But I needed to think it all the way through. Remaining in the office would be a hindrance. I needed to get out. Do something. Anything. Allow my mind room to free associate, minus the mundane interruptions, or even the anticipation of interruption.

I buzzed Cecilia. Asked her to have my driver ready a vehicle.

"Where can I reach you?" she asked.

"You won't. I'll only be gone an hour," I assured her.

From my desk drawer I grabbed the yellow legal pad with the chart I'd sketched the night before.

"Take me to the Botanic Gardens," I instructed the driver, before settling into the back seat of my usual unmarked RAV4.

The passing scenery as he navigated the route out of Kingstown held no interest for me. I turned the legal pad to provide a landscape size page. I drew a small box in the upper left corner, labeled it, and from there created a flow chart of actions, outcomes and logical conclusion.

My plan.

Each box contained a sub box of variables, unknown factors, and contingencies. By the time the driver arrived at the Gardens, I'd completed the plan.

"Where to Sir," the corporal asked.

"Pull up to the Visitor's Center. I'll walk from there."

The Gardens, founded in 1765, represented an historic landmark of national, regional, and global significance, in which Vincentians expressed great pride. One of the most visited sites on the island, its twenty acres of rare plants and trees, its picturesque landscaping, and its storied history, attracted visiting tourists, while providing an idyllic retreat and wedding venue for local Vincentians.

I walked along a concrete footpath, aimlessly, surrounded by tropical plants and trees in a verdant variety of green, accented by the reds, yellows, oranges, and purples among the bewildering array of flowering plants.

I breathed a mixture of exotic tropical scents, coconut, breadfruit, frangipani, while pondering the elements of my plan. It entailed a measure of deception, unfortunately including the local press. I assuaged my conscience by rationalizing an argument could be made for opening a new line of investigation, albeit one having no basis in fact. At least none to which I was aware. Didn't mean it might not exist. The only decision remaining, whether or not to put the plan into effect.

Sweeping through the outer office following my visit to the Gardens, I paused at Cecilia's desk. She'd just returned from lunch herself.

"Cissy, I need AS Taylor and Sergeant Samuel in my office as soon as they can get here."

She recognized the buoyant vitality of my mood. Something about to happen. Without acknowledging, she plucked the handset of her desk phone from its cradle to track down the officers.

She buzzed ten minutes later. "AS Taylor, Commissioner."

"Show him in."

I bounded from my chair as the office door opened, meeting Taylor across the room, ushering him to the sitting area.

"Vince, about that idea you had earlier regarding a follow up story for the press. I may have something for you."

"Very good sir."

"When do you need to get the story in to make tomorrow's paper?"

"For something like this I believe they'll hold the space."

"Good. Then I want you to get out a press statement to all media. You ready to write?"

When he had pen and notepad ready, I outlined the statement.

"Among the evidence collected during the raids was a lot of cash, as you know, and as they've already reported. Some of it bank fresh U.S. currency. You can repeat the details on amounts and denominations if you need to. Anyway, these being new bills we found they had sequential serial numbers. We're circulating a list of these numbers to banks and businesses around Kingstown, requesting they report any transactions involving new bills close to those serial numbers, allowing us to establish and follow the money trail, and perhaps identify other persons involved in the corruption."

"Got it Commissioner," he said, studying the notes he'd written. "I'll notify the press a statement is forthcoming. I'll have a draft ready for you within an hour."

"Great," I said, springing from the seat, my enthusiasm still at full throttle.

I escorted him to the door. Noticed Samuel waiting in the outer office.

"Sammy. Please come in," I said, a parting pat on Taylor's shoulder as he departed.

Closing the door behind Sergeant Samuel and waving aside the formality I said. "Sammy, I have a special assignment for you. Have a seat."

After outlining the assignment and ushering Samuel to the door, I had one more piece to put in place. I sat at my desk and opened my laptop. I typed furiously for a few moments, back spacing frequently to correct typos. Done, I studied the message carefully for correct coding, and sent the email. I opened a new document and typed a set of instructions. I inserted the encrypted thumb drive into the USB slot and downloaded the document to the drive.

At three p.m, I departed the office again, exiting the station compound at the back, facing Lower Long Lane. I strolled along the narrow lane bordered by store fronts and boutiques on either side. I approached the new Kingstown library.

Quiet, studious youngsters in school uniform occupied the reading and periodical sections off the main entrance. I headed toward the reference section. Deserted and silent, except for the hum of overhead fans.

In the last aisle, I turned to a bookshelf against the wall, midway down the aisle. Third shelf from the top, last book in the row on the right. I pulled the heavy volume from the shelf, prying at a knot in the wood planking in the wall behind the shelves. The knot came away, revealing a hole through the wood.

A six-inch length of heavy fishing line had been secured to the back of the knot, , a small S hook attached at the end. I fitted the hook through a hole in the canister concealing the thumb drive, fed it into the recess until it dropped free behind the wall. I replaced the wood knot and the book.

The message to Elana, the final piece of the plan.

CHAPTER 20

I remained on St. Vincent over the weekend. Something I seldom did, but waiting while the plan stewed, not my strong suit. The plan evoked a restlessness, setting me on edge, while I waited for it to spook Mackee, as intended, and whoever stood in the circle above him. Maybe Mitchell too. I wanted to be close if anything broke suddenly in the case. Jolene had nothing new beyond the information I'd requested. Gage still down island on his so-called charter. I occupied myself reading and rereading the news article in the Vincentian. The two main broadcast television stations repeated the items during their news segments. I'd also brought home paperwork from the office to occupy my restless mind. But my thoughts focused only on the report Cecilia had prepared, and the one emailed by Jolene.

Glenford Emanuel Mackee; 50 years old; non practicing Anglican; Divorced; Single. Four adult children and two ex-wives who'd all moved abroad to the U.S. He'd completed preparatory and grammar schools, completed O and A level examinations, and studied agriculture at the University of the West Indies. Elected as the ULP Parliamentary Representative for the South Windward constituency for ten years, having won reelection during the last election cycle. An anomaly, according to Solly, since Mackee's popularity had waned precipitously after his first term. But he'd been reelected due to financial largess in his constituency during the run up to elections, and jobs on his banana plantation. A pattern Solly claimed was being repeated in the upcoming election. And much more money, in Solly's estimation, than could be accounted for from his agricultural business. Especially given the severely depressed banana prices on the world market, and the devastation to the island's banana crops during the recent hurricane. Mackee owned and operated a large banana plantation in the foothills north of Charlotte, passed down through generations of his family. A portion of which it turns out, bordered the area used by the gang to cultivate their marijuana crop. Following the destructive hurricane, relief money had poured into St. Vincent, much of it distributed with lax oversight. And much of it unaccounted for. Mackee was also an Advisor to the Ministry of Agriculture, Rural Transformation, Forestry, Fisheries, and Industry. According to Solly a ministry portfolio he'd be in line for when the ULP became the ruling party. His known associates according to Cecelia, included a list of women with whom he'd conducted short lived affairs, his mother, who still lived in a one room house in a rustic rural area outside Charlotte, and of course his political and police buddies, including Sergeant Ashton and Superintendent Nigel Mitchell. The three had grown up and attended school together.

The long torturous weekend, endured on pins and needles, passed without incident.

In my office on Monday following the uneventful weekend, I continued to contemplate Mr. Glenford Mackee, the bagman. The waiting had already exacted an erosive toll on my patience. I'd been contemplating how to spend the lunch hour without going insane when a brisk knock sounded on my door. It opened to reveal Cecilia. Her penciled eyebrows lifted high on her lined forehead, eyes wide, shock engraved on her ashen face. The severe mouth agape in disbelief.

"There's been a shooting," she announced, her usually authoritative voice quavering.

My heart froze in my chest. The expression on her face indicated someone we knew. My mind immediately envisioned Sammy or Elana.

"Who?" the single word barely audible, constricted in my throat.

"Glenford Mackee. Sergeant Samuel is on the line for you."

She remained in the open doorway as I snatched the handset from its cradle, a plea in the watery eyes staring unwaveringly at me. Guilt amid the shock. Probably wondering if she'd somehow been responsible for Mackee's death. She'd spent the Friday before researching and gathering information on Mackee. An assignment I'd given her. She'd prepared a report on him. Now he was dead.

"Sammy?" I said into the phone, motioning Cecilia into the office. I indicated the chair in front of my desk. She passed her hands along the back of her skirt, smoothing it as she sat.

I replaced the telephone receiver following my conversation. My gaze rested on Cecilia, her face a landscape of soul-searching agony. She stared at the floor, her hands clasped firmly in her lap.

"Cissy, I assigned you the project on Mackee because he is a person of interest in the ongoing corruption investigation, and possibly a murder." I said.

Her gaze rose to meet mine. The lines across her face rearranged themselves into a determined scowl as my words registered.

"Murder?" she whispered.

"Yes. And it's probably why he was killed" I said, attempting to further reassure her, assuage her guilt. Mine would require much more.

"The assignment I gave you played no part in his death," I said, aware I couldn't say the same for the part I'd played. "I need you to call my driver, inform him I'll be right down. If DC Huggins is in the building, have him meet me downstairs. Or at the scene. And find Assistant Superintendent Bernard Rogers. Have him meet us at the scene. Can you handle all that?"

"Yes Commissioner," composing herself, her stern voice resurfacing, mocking me, as though I'd committed an offence by questioning her ability to perform her job.

Huggins waited for me next to a police liveried Toyota Rav4, the rear door open and waiting. The corporal driving pealed out of the station courtyard into Bay Street traffic, blue roof light bar flashing, siren squealing and bleeping to clear the way.

"What do you know?" I asked Huggins as the vehicle raced through Kingstown, turning onto James Street, and Sally Springs Road, to connect to the main road leading to Arnos Vale and the Windward Highway.

"Victim is Glenford Mackee, ULP representative from South Windward. We been expectin' some kind of political violence like dis. Dis goin' to be a sensitive case, 'specially now. Goin' need delicate handling."

"This may have nothing to do with politics Reggie," I said, turning toward him, holding his gaze. "But you're correct about the political firestorm. What you need to know now, Glenford Mackee was the bagman who passed cash to the marijuana gang and the rogue RRU officers."

His eyelids opened wide. Eyebrows rose above the thick frames of his spectacles. His dark eyes stared into mine, his facial expression one of stunned disbelief.

"I confirmed it yesterday," I assured him. "The reason I'd been questioning Peters. He identified Mackee as the person who gave him a backpack and instructions to deliver it to Sergeant Ashton. The backpack contained money which Ashton distributed to the gang and the rogue officers."

Huggins remained speechless. His mouth agape as I explained Mackee's role.

"Some of that cash also reached Superintendent Mitchell," I said.

I'd supposed he'd couldn't be further shocked following my revelation regarding Mackee. Proved incorrect by his stunned reaction to my naming Mitchell.

"My God Commisshunah! What de hell goin' on heah?"

"That's why I'm assigning the case to Major Crime." I informed him.

"Yes Commisshunah."

"Something else Reggie. I deliberately planted the statement about the money serial numbers," I said, holding his stare. The shocks piling up on him. "I was having Mackee and Mitchell followed, hoping they'd lead us to others involved in the conspiracy and to the rest of the cash."

"I wondered 'bout dat. Didn't see any mention in de interrogation reports 'bout serial numbers on de bills. Though it's logical to t'ink it might be so."

"My thought exactly. Which is why I have the Financial Intelligence Unit looking into it. We might get lucky."

"So how dis happen if he was under poliss su'veilance?"

"We'll soon find out."

"Who?" Huggins asked.

"Sergeant Samuel."

The police RAV4 sped along St. Vincent's Windward Highway, it's warbling and yelping siren clearing any traffic it encountered. We flashed by the excavated construction sites at Argyle for St. Vincent's new international airport. The Highway wound along a rocky, white capped, black sand coastline, the air salty fresh, and misted by sea spray.

We raced through rural villages bearing political posters plastered on roadside signs and buildings. Slogans spray-painted on walls and village streets, 'NDP a better way;' 'Vote ULP;' 'Vote NDP;' 'Miss SVG and Miss Carnival July 6th;' 'Ragga Soca June 29th;' 'Vincy Mas,' politics and Carnival competing for wall space and attention.

Fifteen minutes after departing Kingstown the driver slowed. He turned inland, navigating narrow streets into the populated center of Biabou. He turned onto a side street partially blocked by a police vehicle, its roofbar flashing blue.

A uniformed constable stood by the vehicle, directing traffic away from the street. Another stood on the corner shooing away gawking pedestrians. The first constable waved the RAV4 through. We entered a narrow street lined on both sides by hole-in-the-wall shops and offices, a Real Estate office, a bank branch, a shoe store, restaurants, a Levis clothing shop. The street further constricted by parked vehicles along both sides.

Halfway along the block another police vehicle sat in the middle of the street, blocking further progress. Visible beyond the cruiser, yellow crime scene tape had been stretched across the street, and more constables held a crowd of pedestrians at bay.

Huggins and I existed the RAV4, approaching the scene together. We ducked under the yellow tape. At the other end of the block, more tape had been stretched across the street; more curious pedestrians being corralled by a harried constable.

A knot of uniformed police crowded around a small four-door vehicle parked in front of a non-descript storefront, ULP posters pasted to the walls. Sergeant Samuel among the group. He noticed our approach, said something in a whisper to the others. The gathered constables turned as one, standing at attention and saluting.

"As you were," I said, approaching the vehicle, a teal 2009 Subaru Imprezza. Its body paint faded by the tropical sun, the right hand driver's side facing the street. The gathered constables parted, allowing me and Huggins clear access to the vehicle.

A body in the driver's seat, torso slumped across onto the passenger side. Blood pools on the upholstery and floor. Spatters on the lining of the driver and passenger doors. More spatters on the headliner, dashboard, and windshield. Blood everywhere.

Spider web cracks emanated from a central hole on the driver's side windshield. The rear passenger window behind the driver, and the rear windshield, both shattered. Diamond like glass shards lay spread across the backseat. A hole in the driver's door panel just below the glass.

Visible bullet holes on the body. One in the center of Mackee's chest. Probably the one through the windshield. Another toward the side of the chest. One in the right side of the neck. Another in the side of his head. Large holes, as from thirty-eight or forty-five caliber rounds.

I left Huggins still peering into the Subaru's interior, while I pulled Samuel aside, out of earshot of the other constables.

"So what happened? Just the events here. I'll get your full report later."

"I followed him to dat building," he said, indicating the ULP decorated storefront. A two-story building like all the others on the street.

"I followed him inside. He went up to de second floor. Closed offices off a hallway. He went into one of de offices wid a ULP sign on de door. I came back outside to wait. Not wanting him to come out of de office and maybe spot me in de hallway. I was standing right over there." He pointed toward the end of the block where we'd entered the street.

"He comes out of the building about ten minutes later, heads to de car. Then a blue Mitsubishi minivan pulls out from that spot there," pointing to an empty space between a white Toyota Nadia, and a fluorescent blue Suzuki Sidekick parked against the curb.

"Next thing I hear shots fired from de van. I count eight shots. I ran over to de car and see Mackee lying in it shot. Dead by de time I reached him."

"You get a plate number on the Van?"

208 Michael W Smart

"Yes sir. Already call in the plate, and color make and model of de van."

"You see who was in the van."

"Couldn't see Commisshunah. De van was moving dat way, away from me. All I saw was a hand out the window, black, holding de weapon, and heard de shots."

"What's been going on here?"

"Nothing. Been waiting for de crime scene detectives. But I made sure de scene was secured."

"Good work Sammy. Okay. Organize that group of constables standing around the vehicle doing nothing. Canvas all the businesses on the street. Especially the shops close to where the van was parked. See if anyone saw and can describe the driver. And those people behind the tape. Anyone who might've witnessed the shooting. You personally take the people in the office Mackee visited. Find out what he was doing there."

"Yes sir," he said turning away to his task.

As he did, a squealing siren approached the far end of the block. Superintendent Mitchell leapt from the Toyota Corolla before it'd fully stopped.

"Reggie," I called. I signaled him to follow me as I steered an interception course for Mitchell bullying his way through the spectators behind the tape. We reached him as he ducked under the tape at the crime scene's periphery.

"Superintendent, you do not want to be here," I said, halting him.

He leveled an angry glare at me. The red rimmed eyes ready to shoot lightning bolts at any moment.

"Dat man is a fren' of mine Commisshunah. I not goin' have you..."

"That's exactly why Superintendent. I'm aware he's your friend. There's no need for you to see and remember him like that," I said, summoning as much sympathy as I could muster.

His glaring eyes softened. Anger replaced by suspicion.

"We have this under control Superintendent. Since you were his friend if there is any family you want to notify, you can take care of that."

Still suspicious, but the huffed out chest deflating. His aggressive manner dissipated, replaced by genuine grief.

"T'ank you Commisshunah," he managed.

"Take care of what you need to for your friend. We got this," I said, subtly crowding him back toward the tape, away from the crime scene.

"Any of my detectives here yet?" he asked.

"Not yet. They're on the way. They know what to do when they get here. You go do what you have to for your friend."

Maybe the shock, or the grief, had short-circuited his normally bellicose nature. He acquiesced without argument, stepping back under the tape, heading for the police car he'd arrived in.

"Dat was kind of you Commisshunah," Huggins said.

"Anything to keep him away from the scene and out of our hair Reggie."

"And de other thing?"

"I'll deal with that later. This wasn't the time or place."

CID and Major Crime detectives arrived. As did AS Bernard Rogers. And news vans from SVG Broadcasting, and TBN Channel Four. Huggins accompanied the detectives to the vehicle while I pulled Rogers aside.

"Bernie, I'm assigning Major Crime as lead on this investigation. The victim is a political figure. Don't have to tell you what that means. Work with the CID, but this is your case."

"Yes Commisshunah."

I stood off to the side, out of the way, observing the detectives processing the crime scene. Having nothing to occupy me, a wave of guilt bubbled up inside me. Unlike Cecilia, I had no doubt I'd precipitated Mackee's death. In all the scenarios I'd postulated while developing my plan, I hadn't seen this one coming. The manner in which it'd blindsided me unnerving. The audacity of it.

A drive-by assassination in broad daylight. Like Huggins, most people would assume it'd been politically motivated. What had Mackee known requiring him to be silenced in such a manner? I wondered. The threat of following the money? Who would it lead to?

Which reminded me. I fished my cell phone from my trouser pocket, dialed a number, bouncing the call from a satellite to the local cell service. At least my end secure. I checked the vicinity around me, ensuring no one in earshot.

"Were you able to accommodate the funds transfer I inquired about?" I asked when the other end answered.

"I believe I have a positive answer for you sir," Elana's voice on the other end. "We will be able to facilitate the funds transfer from de location you specified."

"Thank you. You've been very accommodating. I'd want to complete the transaction as early as possible this afternoon."

"I can make de arrangements within de hour if dat will be suitable."

"Most suitable. And thank you again for your assistance."

"You're welcome sir, and thank you for using our bank. We appreciate your business."

The call disconnected. I noticed Huggins approaching, a plastic evidence bag in his hand.

"Found the victim's cellular phone on the body Commisshunah," he said, holding the evidence bag toward me.

"I want the records of that phone by the time we get back to the station."

"Right away Commisshunah," reaching for his cell phone and retracing his steps.

I checked my watch. One o'clock, the buildings facing east already casting shadows on the north-south oriented street. The roar of pounding surf echoed from the nearby coastline. Huggins approached a second time.

"We jus' 'bout done heah Commisshunah. Finish takin' de photographs, processin' de vehicle and de victim. We recovered eight forty-five caliber shell casings. And looks like four bullets in de victim, tree we pull out of the car body, and one unaccounted for. Jus' waitin' now for de ambulance to come recover de body."

"Have them transport it to the morgue at Milton Cato. I want Dr. Gash to perform the autopsy."

"Yes sir. And de canvas? I heard Sergeant Samuel detailing de men."

"Brief Bernie and turn it over to him. Have his detectives collect the statements and handle the follow up interviews. When you're done here we can head back to the station."

"Yes sir."

On the drive into Kingstown I instructed the corporal to drop me four blocks from the library.

"I just have a quick stop Reggie," I explained to Huggins. "Meet you back at the station."

CHAPTER 21

Television and Radio already carried the news of Mackee's murder by the time I returned to the office. Cecilia handed me a stack of phone messages as I passed her desk. All from government ministers, including the opposition leader.

The onset of the anticipated firestorm. But nothing compared to what would follow once they took to the airwaves and party rallies. I spent the next hour returning their calls, appeasing the Prime Minister, opposition leader, and irate members of Parliament and the cabinet. Calls from the press I referred to Taylor's office. At this point, we weren't making any statements beyond the particulars already reported.

The phone calls out of the way, I set about rescheduling the remainder of my day. Mackee's murder cleared everything else off my agenda. I needed to see Sergeant Samuel, Assistant Superintendent Bernie Rogers, Assistant Superintendent Taylor, and Assistant Superintendent Angela McKinley from the Financial Intelligence Unit.

Ambivalence regarding Superintendent Mitchell. Especially after I'd read Elana's report and the accompanying scanned documents. The trap I'd set for Mackee had snagged Mitchell too. The results of a search at a location Elana had provided uncovered incriminating evidence. But a confrontation on the day of his friend's gruesome murder, crooked as both of them were, felt uncomfortably inappropriate.

Huggins stopped in to drop off the records from Mackee's cell phone. There'd been a flurry of calls soon after the evening news had broadcast the serial number story. And another flurry that morning, mere hours before he'd been killed. The numbers called repeatedly. The serial number ruse had scared him. And he'd scared someone higher up the food chain. But still no trace of the money.

Huggins had run down the most frequently called numbers. One number belonged to the cell phone account of Superintendent Mitchell. The other a cell phone account belonging to an Elon Fredericks.

A new player on the board, I mused.

Taylor arrived next, bearing a draft of the official police statement. Adequate. Minus the investigative details we weren't ready to share publicly. I signed off on it. The acquiescent local media would accept it. The politicians and their partisan mouthpieces, especially in the opposition party, would be screaming cover up by morning.

Superintendent Mitchell himself removed the decision from my hands. He arrived of his own volition coincidently, or perhaps providentially, after I'd received the results of the police search. The eyes once again angry and fiery red. His loose jowls quivered in self-righteous indignation. I wondered at the state of his blood pressure. The perpetually red bloodshot eyes perhaps portending a stroke in his future.

"What de meanin' assignin' dis case to Major Crime. Dis is a CID case plain and simple. And you jus' always tryin' to spite me 'cause I don't like you, and you don't like me."

"In the first place Superintendent," I said, my voice deliberately calm, "I don't have to explain to you how I allocate the resources of this force. And second, you're correct, this is about personal feelings. Yours. You're emotionally invested in this case because the victim was a close friend. It disqualifies you from participating in the investigation,"

"Even if I not personally involved is still a case fe de CID," he argued.

"I disagree. This was an assassination of a political figure in broad daylight. Do you have any idea what happens next? You want to put yourself in front of that?"

It momentarily silenced him. His blood shot eyes shifted left and right as thoughts raced through his mind. He hadn't considered the implications. In his myopic shortsightedness the case, the CID, political repercussions, didn't matter. This was between him and me. A perceived challenge he couldn't simply let go.

"Still an all..." he persisted.

"Then there's the matter of illegal cash you received from Sergeant Ashton three Sundays ago." I interrupted. "Of which a thousand dollars U.S. has just been recovered from a boat you own in Blue Lagoon. It makes you a suspect in the ongoing police corruption investigation. And in Mackee's murder. He placed several phone calls to you last night and this morning. The two of you met last night. That makes you a suspect, or at the very least a material witness, in his murder."

His mouth clamped shut like crocodile jaws. Red streaked eyes bulged, staring, the usual condescending animosity replaced by a ferocious desperation, like a trapped animal. And a hint of defeat.

"Effective immediately you are on Administrative leave Superintendent, pending the outcome of inquiries into these matters. You're dismissed."

I'd remained calm throughout the meeting. My breathing controlled. I hadn't allowed him under my skin. I had the upper hand. I finally had the ammunition. Yet the exhaled sigh of relief as he departed my office, indicative of the enormous effort maintaining control had required. The sigh also a release from an accumulated burden being shed. I'd wrested control of the Rapid Response Unit following months of frustrated effort. And now I'd permanently rid the force of Mitchell.

Sergeant Samuel arrived twenty minutes after Mitchell's departure. Almost four o'clock when I glanced at my watch. Usually I'd be wrapping up for the day. But there were still more people to see. Samuel wore a weary frown. He'd had a full day. And witnessed a man being killed. There'd be similar days in his future. And worse, I thought sympathetically. Hazards of our trade. Hazards we'd willingly signed up for.

"Let's hear it Sammy," I said, leading him to the sitting area. More comfortable and informal than sitting at the desk. "From the top. From when you picked him up Friday night."

He reached for a small spiral notebook in the left breast pocket of his shirt. Flipped the pages.

"I found him at his home Friday evening about supper time. Then about eight p.m, he come out rushing from de house. You really spooked him Commissioner. He drove through de streets like a crazy man. He went to a residence on Corbie Lane in Stubbs Village, where he met a woman name of..." He flipped to the back of the notebook. "Name Kwanna Quashie. Appears to be a girlfriend."

He flipped back to the front of the notebook, "Then he drive all de way to Cane Garden to a large house on Harbor Hill Road. A man answered de door. Wouldn't let Mackee in. They stood on de porch arguing. I was too far away to hear what dey arguing about. But de two of dem really vex."

"Did you find out who lives there?" I asked.

He flipped to the back of the notebook again. "A Mr. Elon Fredericks."

Our new player. Interesting, I thought.

"Can you describe this man?" I asked.

"Only vaguely Commisshunah. I was far off. But there was a porch light where dey was standing. He was tall, stout build, but not de fat kind. Like an American football player. Dark complexion. Darker than Mackee. Dat's all I could get from a distance."

"Then what?"

"Well Mackee really vex when he left de house. He went straight home. Stayed in de rest of de night. And most of Saturday and Sunday, going out just to get someting to eat, and staying close to de house. Den Sunday evening he drove to Calliaqua, to de diners delicious restaurant and bar, where he met up wid Superintendent Mitchell."

Where Elana had followed Mitchell, I recalled. She and Samuel in such close proximity, on the same job, unaware of each other.

I noticed a shy, playful smile creasing the corners of Samuel's mouth.

"What?" I said.

He shook his head. As though to dislodge the thought producing his smile.

"Dey was drinking till around half past midnight. Den Mackee drove back home. Until around seven dis morning when he leave de house. De first place he went was his banana depot in Charlotte, where they process de bananas for shipping. He was there for about two hours. After dat he went to a branch office of de St. Vincent Cooperative Bank in Charlotte, and de local office of de Banana Growers Association. After dat he drove to Biabou and went to de ULP office, where he was killed. Looks like he was tending to business all morning sir."

"And no indication of the money," I asked, more a statement than a question.

"No sir. But Commisshunah, he may have hidden it well in de first place, and wasn't so much concerned about anybody finding it, but worrying dat what he spent before now might trace back to him."

The buzzing intercom interrupted us. Cecilia informed me DC Huggins and AS Rogers were waiting in the outer office.

"Give me a minute Cissy," I said into the phone.

Returning to Samuel I said, "I want you to find out everything you can about this Elon Fredericks. For my eyes and ears only."

"Yessir."

"Okay Sammy. Good job. On your way out tell Cecilia to send in Huggins and Rogers."

He stood, not at formal stiff attention, the salute less rigid but respectful. The mysterious smile reappeared briefly before he departed.

Deputy Commissioner Huggins and Assistant Superintendent Rogers waited for me to sit before settling into the comfortable armchairs.

"What do you have so far Bernie?"

"As you know Commisshunah we processed de crime scene, collectin' evidence includin' several forty-five caliber shell casings. One bullet still unaccounted for. May have been a stray missin' de victim and de vehicle. I have men lookin' to find it. De vehicle was transported to New Montrose Station for furder processin'. And de body transported to de Milton Cato Morgue. De manner and cause of death look obvious, but Dr. Gash who received de body will confirm de details in de autopsy.

"De van," he continued, "Was a nineteen ninety Mitsubishi Vasita Minivan, found a little while ago abandoned outside Richmond Park. It bein' transported to Old Montrose too for processin'. De van belong to a Neil Gregg of Campdem Park, who reported it stolen from de Lime parkin' lot in Villa last night."

"So whoever is behind this knew from last night he needed a vehicle for the hit," I said, primarily to myself. "What time?"

"Sir?"

"What time last night was the minivan stolen?"

"Mr. Gregg say he park it around ten o'clock and was inside de Lime partyin' wid some frens' until about two in de morning. When he come out de vehicle was gone. De canvas come up wid some witnesses who say dey saw the Minivan parked on de street, and some who say dey witnessed de shootin'. But so far de descripshuns dey give us contradictory, or of no use. And de witnesses say dey didn't get a good look at de drivah's face 'cause he wearin' a baseball cap, de brim pull low ovah his face. All we know for sure is a dark skin man in de mid twenties maybe. Dat's all we have for now Commis-shunah."

"Thanks Bernie," I said rising. Both men rose from their seats when I did. "Keep Reggie and me informed. Oh by the way," I said before they turned for the door. "Effective immediately Bernie, I'm promoting you to full Superintendent and putting you in command of the CID."

Both men stared at me in open-mouthed astonishment. Huggins wore a hint of a smile.

"Nigel Mitchell has been placed on administrative leave pending inquiries into his involvement in official corruption and the murder of Glenford Mackee. Submit your candidate to replace you at Major Crime Bernie, but for the purposes of this investigation, you have full use of CID and Major Crime. Major crime still has the lead on this."

"Yes sir," he said, his surprised expression transforming into a satisfied gleam in his dark piercing eyes.

"Congratulations Superintendent," I said, emphasizing the rank and saluting.

"T'ank you Commisshunah." He returned the salute.

"That'll be all," I said.

They turned to leave. "Reggie a moment," I said.

He escorted Rogers to the door, congratulated him, shook his hand and closed the door behind him. He turned to face me. The smile I'd noticed before now a broad congratulatory grin.

I reached into my desk drawer and pulled out the legal pad on which I'd charted the investigation. I passed it to him. He studied the page of circles and labels. Nodding as he did.

"I'm expecting AS McKinley shortly. Want to see if there's any substance to the serial number thing beyond simply a ruse. I want you to hear it too."

"And," I said, reaching for the pad. I plucked a pen from the pen and pencil cup on my desk, wrote a name in the empty circle at the top of the page and handed the pad back to him.

"I believe that is the person at the top of this chart. I also believe he's implicated in Mackee's murder." He stared at the page. His brow above the spectacles furrowed in consternation.

"Dis is just too overwhelming Commisshunah," he said. "Mackee and Mitchell, and now Elon Fredericks, all mixed up in dis." A pained, bereft expression lined his face.

"You know this man?" I asked.

"Yes sir."

"What can you tell me about him?"

"Mr. Fredericks is a local businessman and financier. Has lots of real estate in St. Vincent and de Grenadines. And partnerships wid foreign developers who require someone wid Vincentian nationality due to the Aliens Holding Ordinance. He also advises government on finance and economic planning, Security and Foreign Affairs. Like Jackson Taylor before he was killed."

"How come I don't know him?"

"Not many people do Commisshunah. He keeps a low profile. Not like Jackson Taylor who everybody knew. And he don't spend much time in St. Vincent. Only heah a few weeks out a de year. Rumors he mix up in sellin' Vincentian passports overseas to raise election money. Doin' it for both parties. But mostly is jus' party loyalists in the public sayin' dose tings'. No officials in eider party accuse him of sellin' passports. And anyhow both parties deny any such ting' goin' on."

Cecilia's buzz interrupted us.

"That's probably her now," I said, heading directly for the door instead of the intercom on my desk.

Assistant Superintendent Angela McKinley stood at Cecilia's desk waiting. Both women in quiet conversation. She turned when the door opened.

"Angela," I called, my welcoming smile greeting her.

She returned the smile. Her grey uniform tunic hiking over her ample chest as she raised her right arm to salute.

"As you were. Please. Come in."

She adjusted the tunic, tugging on its hem. The tunic and slacks fitted her petit, sturdy curves as though tailored. Probably recommended by Superintendent Johanssen. Jolene had recognized Angela's talents early on. Had brought Angela to my attention, privately lobbying on her behalf for overseas training and promotion. Though younger than Angela, Jolene had mentored Angela's career on the police force.

"I wanted DC Huggins to hear your report as well," I said, ushering her into my office, motioning them both to the sitting area."

"Sir," she greeted Huggins.

"Superintendent," he acknowledged with a nod.

She waited until Huggins and I were seated before sitting herself.

"What do you have for me Angela? Anything to this serial number scheme?"

"Afraid not Commisshunah. Dat proved to be a dead end. We did a trace to see if all the bills from de various locations might have been part of de same originating batch.

And see if maybe we could get a complete set of de serial numbers for de batch. Instead we discovered something else interesting."

I leaned forward, my curiosity aroused. "Go on."

"De cash trace back to a St. Vincent off shore account, Brightwaters Capital, which received de funds as a wire transfer from a company named Global Initiatives in Bahrain." She paused. Her light brown eyes gazed at me expectantly.

When I said nothing, a blank stare answering her gaze, she continued. "Both entities on de list you ask us to red flag six months ago Commisshunah."

The revelation rocked me back into the armchair. Bogeyman's fingerprint. Connecting everything. Political and police corruption. The murder of Glenford Mackee. Elon Fredericks. And I had no doubt the murder of Constable Derrick Whittaker. But having the connection didn't reveal what to do about it. Or the identity of the invisible Bogeyman.

The astounding revelation continued to occupy my thoughts following Huggins and McKinley's departure. News I needed to get to Gage and Jolene. As if privy to my thoughts, my cell phone rang, Gage's number.

"Got information I need to brief you and Jo on," he said when I answered. "Think you can make it back to Bequia tonight?"

Six p.m. when I glanced at my watch. "No problem. In fact I have information for both of you too. I'll call you when I get to the house."

A little after six thirty my driver pulled into the Calliaqua base. I didn't enter the main building, not wishing to linger, eager to impart my news and hear Gage's. I headed directly to the long wharf stretching into the bay, and the

Coast Guard Cutter SVG Hairoun waiting at the dock, its twin diesels idling. My gaze swept across the rust covered Venezuelan freighter still anchored in the bay. Since its seizure, the Vincentian and Venezuelan governments had been engaged in a running battle of public statements and diplomatic maneuvering. A delicate situation for St. Vincent since cozying up to Venezuelan President Hugo Chavez, who provided St. Vincent refined petroleum products at subsidized prices, invested in development projects like the Argyll Airport, and provided financial assistance and relief funds to St. Vincent's agricultural sector.

Venezuela wanted the ship and its crew back. St. Vincent stalling, seeking an amicable political resolution for the Venezuelan flagged freighter seized in its territorial waters carrying a half a ton of cocaine on board.

Powerful twin diesels pushed the aging forty-foot steel-hulled patrol boat across the Channel at twenty-five miles per hour, trailing a swath of frothy white water in its wake. The usual jarring collision of swells against the bow ameliorated by the sea running on her quarter. The sun's golden disk hung low in the western sky, bathing the horizon in a warm scarlet and amber glow.

A cruise ship lay anchored in Bequia's outer harbor. Probably recently arrived. In the morning it'd disgorge off season passengers onto Bequia's shores, before moving on to its next stop by nightfall.

I noted Wherever's tall distinctly raked masts in the distance, returned to her mooring in Lower Bay. Slinging the long strap of my laptop bag, which doubled as a briefcase, across my shoulder, I hopped a dollar van from the ferry wharf. I disembarked at the top of the hill overlooking Lower

Bay on my right, Friendship Bay on my left. I paused, savoring the view and the cool evening breeze against my skin. The horizon held the vestigial glow of the departed sun. The cruise ship lay in the distance like a floating city, its bright lights illuminating the outer bay. On my left the southern grenadines barely visible as dark mounds rising from the sea, dark silhouettes against the night sky.

A wave of contentment embraced me as I stepped into my yard, greeted by a rich citrus scent, the rustle of coconut branches overhead, and the splash of surf against the beach in Friendship Bay.

Immediately aware of something off upon entering the house. Something not right. A presence unseen. The side table light snapped on, startling me. My chest constricted. My breath froze in my closed gullet. My hand reached for the sidearm holstered on my hip. Halted by semi automatic pistols suddenly appearing in the fists of two men standing just inside the cone of light, flanking me on either side. A third man, older, white hair, the one who'd switched on the lamp, sat on my settee staring up at me. His lips parted, revealing a row of crooked teeth as his mouth stretched into a sly, predatory smile.

CHAPTER 22

Three men in my living room. The older man on my settee in his mid sixties at first glance. White hair receded from a lined forehead. Bushy white eyebrows. His hand fell casually into his lap from the lamp he'd switched on.

The two other men younger. Armed. Their eyes cold and watchful. A nod from the seated older man, and the flanker on his right moved to turn on more lights in the room, illuminating their faces.

I stood frozen. My mind a whirlwind of anxious thoughts. The uppermost, my impending death. Curiously, the thought didn't frighten me. More occupied by the why? And who? My mind assimilated tiny details, the scar above the left flanker's right eye, the small holster bulges beneath the un-tucked shirttails. The older man's artificial bronze tan, and crooked teeth.

He remained seated when he spoke. "Good evening Commissioner Daniels. Welcome home. My apologies for the intrusion." His voice throaty, cultured, smooth, like a lawyer. Accustomed to dissembling. Deception disguised as plati-tudes. Like his apology.

"Who are you and what are you doing in my house?" I said, finding my voice. Still rooted to the spot I'd been in when the lamp first snapped on.

"Who I am is irrelevant," he said. "What I represent however is of primary importance." The smile still in place, but the blue eyes hard, hostile, reflecting a different sentiment altogether.

"As to what I'm doing here. That would be to convince you to cease your current investigations. To leave those matters alone."

"I'm afraid that won't be possible."

"Creating possibilities is my specialty Commissioner. Including possibilities for your future after you're no longer Commissioner of Police."

"I can't be bought," I said.

"Be that as it may, you will not be Commissioner of Police for much longer. And what is about to occur here is inevitable, and will no longer be your official concern. I merely need you to mark time until your much deserved second retirement. A logical and practical choice since you cannot in any case change the course of events."

"And if I refuse you intend to kill me."

"Oh come now, Commissioner," the insincere smile widening, the eyes exuding a reptilian menace. "Killing a high profile figure as yourself would be a mistake. And completely unnecessary. Unlike your man. Might've handled that differently had I known at the time he was one of yours. Then again perhaps not. He was privy to information which needed to be protected. No Commissioner, we wouldn't kill you. However..." he said, leaning forward, pulling an envelope from the inside breast pocket of his navy blue, Piombo double breasted linen blazer. Expensively cut and fitted. Gold buttons adorned the front. Below the jacket he wore a cream colored silk shirt, probably chosen to accent the bronze tan and blue eyes. He emptied the contents of the envelope onto the coffee table, spilling a stack of five by seven photographs.

"Please Commissioner. These are for you. Have a look."

I did as he instructed. Moving for the first time since entering the house. I glanced down at the coffee table. My heart a jackhammer in my chest as I recognized the faces in the photographs. I scooped the stack of photos from the coffee table. Flipped through them one by one. A burning rage welled inside me. My daughter June. At home, at work at the hospital, walking along a city street. The interior of her apartment. Similar images of my son, and my ex-wife, their mother.

"You will notice the time stamp on the images Commissioner," white hair said, the tenor of his voice unchanged. His arrogant narcissistic smile replaced by a contemptuous curve of thin lips, a deadly determination in his sinister blue eyes.

"As we speak I have people watching your family. It'd be a pity if some senseless urban violence should befall them. Unfortunately such things happen all the time. Just pick up a newspaper or turn on the news."

I met his stare. A herculean battle raged inside me to control my fury. Control the burning impulse to wrap my hands around his throat and slowly squeeze the smug life out of him. His eyes correctly read the emotions roiling behind mine.

"I can appreciate the sentiment Commissioner. Which is why you'll do what I require and no harm will come to your family."

"What do you want?" My voice cracked and distant. Unfamiliar to my ears.

"As I mentioned before. For you to cease your current investigations. I will also require all your case files. Everything your investigation has uncovered so far. As well as the names and locations of other undercover operatives working for you."

"Getting all those files isn't possible," I said, stalling. My mind turned to thoughts of a way out, finding none. "The investigation is scattered among six different units and dozens of officers."

"You're the Commissioner of Police. I'm sure you can obtain whatever files you need. You will return to Kingstown tonight. Use the aircraft you keep here on the island if you need to. We'll meet again here at the same time tomorrow evening. And you will have everything I have asked for. Please do not disappoint Commissioner. Or attempt anything foolish. I will know immediately any cellular or land line calls you make off the island to your children or ex-wife. Their lives depend on you following my instructions without deviation."

He rose from the settee, buttoning the double-breasted blazer. The set, self-confident smile in place. Smug. His domination never in question.

"Soon you'll be retired again, we'll have accomplished our goals here, and there'll be no further need for interference from us. Your family will be safe. Until then maybe you can do something about your local electricity grid. Inconvenient not having power for an entire evening."

"We're accustomed to it. We have portable generators," I replied to the absurd incongruity.

"Some sort of mechanical problem with ours I'm afraid. All fixed now though. Until tomorrow evening then Commissioner."

He headed for the door, preceded by the two men who'd stood silently watchful throughout.

CHAPTER 23

I remained in the house only long enough to switch off the lights and lock the front door. I stuffed the photographs into a compartment of the laptop-briefcase bag, which had hung from my shoulder the entire time I'd been in the house.

I climbed the steep Friendship Bay road toward the main road. My mind ran the encounter repeatedly, dissecting it, analyzing it. Still searching for a way out of the dilemia. A futile effort, my thoughts hijacked by the haunting images of my daughter, my son, and their mother.

I couldn't do what the white haired man wanted. Or if I did, I'd need a way of undoing it. And I didn't for a moment trust his word my family wouldn't be harmed even after I'd done as he'd asked. As for my well-being, following my departure from office nothing stood in the way of an arranged accident, or heart attack, or some other fatal incident.

I had one chance. The only hope my family had of escaping this situation alive.

I had no doubt the white haired man was James Dougan, the person renting Les Jolies Eaux on Mustique. Nor any doubt he'd have me followed. Here on Bequia, and on St. Vincent. I didn't bother checking for a tail as I flagged down

and boarded a dollar van headed in the direction of Paget
Farm.

At J.F. Mitchell airport I prepped the Seneca for the
short flight to Kingstown. Dougan's suggestion I fly back to
Kingstown offered an opening he wouldn't be aware of. I
completed my walk around and entered the cockpit. I'd deliberately waited until then to pull out my cell phone, holding it
below the cockpit panel, below the sightlines of anyone watching from outside.

I dialed Gage's sat number, the phone on speaker
mode. Dougan may've been able to monitor signals emanating
from the island's cellular towers. But he wasn't aware of my
phone's satellite capability. Or its secure encryption.

Gage's calm voice elicited a brief wave of relief.

"Gage. No time to explain. I need you to sail to
Kingstown right now," I said hurriedly. "You and JJ. I've got a
problem and you're my only hope."

"What's going on Mike?"

"No time to explain," I repeated. A memory surfaced. A
peculiar item I'd attributed to Gage's overarching paranoia.
Not so silly now I thought, as I recalled the code phrase he'd
insisted I memorize.

"Afraid there's a dead tide rising," I said. "I'm flying the
Seneca to Kingstown now. I'll meet you at the Young Island
dock at eleven tonight," I said, figuring it'd give him sufficient
time to sail to St. Vincent, and for me to figure out how to lose
whoever would be following me.

I disconnected. I engaged the left engine start switch.
The three bladed prop turned. A hesitant sluggish whine, until
it caught. As it did I pushed its fuel mixture control to the full
rich position. The sound turned to a roar as the engine sucked

fuel and air and spun at a steady twelve hundred revolutions per minute. I repeated the procedure on the right engine. Both engines turned smoothly, the sound a satisfying deep-throated drone.

Receiving clearance from the tower I taxied out to the single thirty six hundred foot, east-west runway. The sprinkled lights of Paget Farm on my right. The dark sea held behind a stone seawall on my left. Piloting the Seneca the only thoughts in my mind. Dougan and the danger facing my family tabled for the time being.

Throttles forward we raced along the runway. My feet rode the pedals, aligning the nose along the centerline of the dark pavement, its edges visible in the glow of dim runway lights. The Seneca's single headlight, nestled in the nose gear's opened doors, cast a small cone of light ahead. Wing strobes flashed in the night. At rotation speed, I eased the yolk toward my stomach. The Seneca lifted her nose, gliding effortlessly off the ground, reaching for the night sky.

A ballistic flight. Up and down. Five minutes following takeoff I lined up on approach to E.T Joshua airport on St. Vincent. A slight squeak as the main gear met the pavement. The yolk all the way back, almost to my stomach, bleeding off speed on the short runway. I lowered the nose wheel, continuing to brake using backpressure on the yolk aided by slight steady pressure on the brake pedals. The Seneca slowed to a fast walk. I turned off the runway, taxied to my usual spot at the airport's fire station and shut down the engines.

My thoughts immediately returned to the death threat facing my family. Outside the quiet deserted terminal I selected a taxi driver I recognized. A regular at the airport, probably waiting for the next scheduled flight, the last of the evening. His familiar face prompted an idea.

"Commisshunah you headin' to de stashun or Montrose?" he inquired, eyeing me through the rear view mirror as I settled into the rear seat.

"Montrose Henry. And I'll need another ride later tonight. Here take this," I said, handing him all the cash in my pocket. Two twenty dollar U.S. bills and four twenty dollar EC bills. Close to two hundred dollars in local currency.

"Pick me up on the corner of Garvey and Grant at ten thirty sharp."

"Commisshunah dat right near de house. Why I don't meet you dere?"

"Because I'll be at a friend's house. I'll walk there from my house, and leave from there. And Henry, don't be late."

"No Commisshunah," he said, his eyes widening as he counted the cash I'd handed him.

He dropped me at my rental house in Montrose. Dark and deserted. The domestic staff dismissed for the night, a single uniformed sentry on duty at the front gate. He stamped to attention and saluted when I approached.

"As you were son," I said, returning the salute, observing the youthful face barely rid of its teenage pimples. Junior man on the Old Montrose Station totem pole, he'd drawn the boring overnight post.

At nine p.m, I shut the bedroom light. The house ensconced in darkness. I lay on the bed during the intervening hour, only my thoughts for company. My initial anxiety less consuming, replaced by the thought of action. Action to neutralize the threat. Though I couldn't see how yet. Gage my only hope.

At ten p.m. I headed down the staircase next to the upstairs sitting room. I crossed the first floor main dining room and exited through a side door onto the tiled verandah. I stood against the wall next to the door, acclimating my eyes to the dark, and the yard beyond. I watched for any sign of the young constable. I'd observed him complete a patrol of the yard a half hour before. This side of the house faced away from the road in front of the house on the opposite side. A large lemon tree and tall hedges hid it from view of the main road.

I still hadn't checked for a tail. But assumed Dougan wouldn't have overlooked such a precaution, even holding all the cards with the threat hanging over my head. Or because of it, assuring I didn't step out of line. Someone out there watching, I assumed. Somewhere along the main street, or parked on the adjacent road.

I stepped to the low decorative brick wall surrounding the verandah. I hopped it, landing in the soft grass on the yard side. I moved swiftly to the hedge. I squeezed through a break to the ground level retaining wall separating my yard from my neighbor's on a lower level. I hopped down into the neighbor's yard. I moved along the wall toward the back of the yard. Into the next yard. And the next. Until I reached a footpath running behind the houses. The path exited onto Grant Street. I waited on the corner, shielded behind a strand of trees. Waited and watched. I checked my watch.

Henry pulled up to the corner five minutes early. I waited until ten thirty. I approached from behind, along Grant Street, walking toward Garvey, as though coming from a house along the street.

I slid into the back seat. "Villa Henry. Young Island dock."

"Yes Commisshunah," he said, a broad satisfied grin on his face as he threw the vehicle in gear.

The ride to Villa proceeded in relative silence. Henry frequently attempted to engage in conversation, which I politely discouraged. In the parking lot facing the dock I handed Henry another hundred dollars in U.S. currency. Two hundred and sixty EC at the current exchange rate.

"That's for your services for the rest of the night Henry. And for your silence. Anyone asks you're waiting for a fare from Young Island. I'll be gone a few hours. But you wait here for me."

Jolene met me on the narrow Young Island dock. Discerning eyes scrutinized my face. Across the water, bright lights strung along the resort's pathways illuminated the bay.

"Gage on board?" I asked as she turned toward the tethered dinghy.

"Right here," the soft velvety voice from behind me, startling me.

Should be used to it by now, I thought.

"You used the danger code," he said. "Just checking."

"I'm sure someone's following me. But not here. Thinks I'm fast asleep in Montrose."

Aboard wherever both pairs of eyes continued to study me. Jolene's anxious and apprehensive. Her worried expression marred the elegant features of her face. Gage's unfathomable, impassive, boring deep into my psyche.

"What's going on Mike?" Straight to the point.

"Can I get you something Mike?" Jolene asked, more empathically attuned. "Some coffee maybe."

"Thanks JJ. Something stronger."

Gage waited. His patience immeasurable.

The swallow of neat Jack Daniels sluicing down my throat further calmed my nerves, already somewhat assuaged by their comforting presence. The two people closest to me. Even closer than my children, who I loved more than life itself. And my only hope of keeping them alive.

After another gulp of the whiskey I sat at the dinette and related the day's events. The chart connecting the money trail. The ruse to trap Mackee and Mitchell. Mackee's murder. Identifying Elon Fredericks. The money connections uncovered by Assistant Superintendent McKinley. Dougan and his thugs waiting for me in my house. His demands. And the threat against my family if I didn't do as instructed. I retrieved the photographs from my trouser pocket and laid them on the table.

Jolene's mouth hung agape in horror as I related the encounter, Dougan's threats, and his demands.

"That enfant de chienne bumbo clat," she cursed.

Gage's face set in marble. Inscrutable. He maintained a calm, stony silence. But his eyes, staring at me, through me, as hard and inanimate as ice. A cold, dark, frightening fury I'd never witnessed before.

He reached into his trouser pocket and extracted his cell phone. He dialed. His dead eyes pierced mine as he waited for the other end to answer.

When it did he said, "Black alpha one protocol. Six locations within the next eight hours. Further to follow."

Without explanation, he stood from the dinette and headed to Wherever's navigation station. He retrieved his laptop and returned to the dinette. He sat. Opened the already booted laptop. He tapped a rapid series of keystrokes on the laptop's keyboard. Jolene and I watched in silent expectation.

"Jo, hand me the scanner."

Jolene rose from the dinette. Retrieved a Fujitsu scans-nap portable scanner from the nav station and returned. Gage attached the USB cable to the laptop and scanned three of the photographs. Close up images of my daughter, son and ex-wife.

"Mike," raising his eyes from the laptop. "Home and work addresses of your kids and ex-wife."

He typed as I dictated. The tip-tip-tip of the keys filled the cabin as his fingers played across the keyboard like a maestro at a piano. His task completed, he lifted his gaze from the laptop.

"You're correct Mike. The man who broke into your house and threatened you is James Dougan. Staying at Les Jolies Eaux on Mustique. He runs a private security agency named The Phoenix Group. We ran into them before, in New York," his glance rising to meet Jolene's. "A small private army really. Global operations. And an extensive intelligence network. The Phoenix Group is actually owned by another corporation, traceable to a man named Otto Wilhelm Von Sachsen. Jo's Bogeyman."

"Sacrament!" Jolene the first to respond.

"Actually the Bogeyman is his son, Godfried Wilhelm Von Sachsen."

I stared at Gage in silent amazement. Astounded by his unexpected revelation.

"It's what I've been working on over the weekend. I haven't had the chance to brief either of you yet. My guy finally pierced the veil. With the help of a little additional information I was able to provide. We now have the complete picture. A global empire possessing multiple sources of revenue.

Income greater than most small countries. Including St. Vincent and the Grenadines. And they've done this before. Taken control of small Nation archipelagoes in Asia and the South China Sea.

"They're into transportation, ships, planes, rail, trucking. Arms dealing on an international scale. Drug trafficking. They franchise the production, refining, and distribution. They have extensive real estate holdings around the globe. The conglomerate is run like a small independent nation. And they have the resources and an army to do whatever they want."

"Mon ostie de saint-sacrament de câlice de crises. Bumbo clat." Jolene hissed in a combination of Quebecois and Patois.

"What do you have on this Von whosis? I asked. What are the names again?

The laptop beeped before he had a chance to answer.

"Wait one," he said, turning his attention to the laptop's monitor.

"Okay Mike. There're people heading to your kids. Contact with your daughter in about three hours. Four for your son. Your ex by morning."

"What about the other three locations? You mentioned six locations in the phone call."

His gaze switched from the laptop. Focused on me again. Piercing caramel eyes drilled into my skull. Devoid of emotion. Yet somehow soothing. The empty stare reassuring.

"I..." hesitation halted my words. Unsure this was the proper time or place. His blank stare expectant and not expectant. Waiting. Patient. "I want to ask you something," I finally managed.

"Go ahead," his expression, or more accurately non-expression, unchanged.

Jolene observed the exchange. Her own curiosity aroused.

"Why do they do this?"

"Why does who do what?"

"From what I can tell you've been pretty much a loner. Worked alone. Led a solitary existence probably your entire adult life. Until you arrived here," I said, glancing at Jolene, her amber eyes locked on my face.

"So I've often wondered, how is it with one phone call, you get people to drop whatever they're doing, fly down here to airlift me to a hospital in Miami, protect me around the clock while I'm there, accompany me back to Bequia to continue protecting me, hack into computers digging up all kinds of private and classified information for you, hold and interrogate people for months, and race to separate cities across the States to protect people they don't even know. Who are these people Gage? You obviously trust them. Why do they do what they do for you?"

The brown eyes held steady on mine, unwavering, questioning, but trusting. A decision being weighed. Jolene's gaze shifted to his face.

"They're people I've worked with, or helped out of tight situations. People I've helped get a second chance. A shot at a new life," his soft voice dispassionate, calming, like his eyes.

He paused. His response characteristically uninformative. But more than I'd expected. In a surprising departure, he continued, as if my question had released a choking clog he'd been unable to clear by himself. Not so much an unburdening, as I'd often done during our friendship. Rather a glimpse of himself he seldom shared.

"It took me a long time to escape my former life. Years. Guess I'd been building up to it for a while though. Even if I didn't realize it at the time. I'd been caching away currency, diamonds, IDs, documents, weapons. Different countries, different locations. Didn't understand why at the time. Instinct I guess. I knew a day would come when I'd need an escape hatch. I didn't expect it'd be my own doubts and demons consuming me, driving me toward it. Some of the money I put into real estate in different cities..."

"Like your place in New York. And the ones on the west coast, Miami, Hong Kong?" Jolene said. The first I'd heard of him owning homes around the globe.

He turned to her and smiled, nodding.

"Yeah. Though some of those came later. And some I unloaded after getting out. I almost didn't make it. I was in a really bad place. Lost and adrift and ready to cash it in, until I met her," the sweep of his head and lift of his gaze to the deck above, indicating he referred to Wherever.

"She helped me find my way back. And that's when I realized I'd established an infrastructure allowing me to operate on my own. I could've laid low. Just disappeared. I thought about it. But I'd seen too much, knew too much. Couldn't just sit back and let the monsters run free. So I turned independent."

"You mean like a mercenary?" I asked. A tone of dismay in my voice. Maybe I didn't really want to know this.

"No." A small smile as his gaze met mine. His eyes devoid of deception. Devoid of anything except the memories floating to the fore. "I wasn't for hire. I couldn't work for anyone after what I'd been through." He paused, searching our eyes. Perhaps expecting a negative reaction from either, or both of us. Instead, Jolene gazed upon him in loving tenderness. I nodded in understanding.

"On my own I didn't have to deal with geopolitical or diplomatic bullshit. Wonder who the good guys or bad guys were. Or agonize over the part I played. Gave me a clarity I hadn't known for a long time. Liberating really. Bunch of folks didn't take too kindly to my new independence. Lots of frazzled nerves and hasty trigger fingers whenever I'd make an appearance in one of their theatres. But I managed to help some good people caught in bad situations."

He fell silent. His eyes searched ours again. Jolene leaned forward to kiss his forehead. I shared the sentiment. But instead of a kiss, I reached up to grasp his shoulder in an affectionate squeeze.

"Thanks," I said.

"For what?"

"For everything," I said. "But I still don't understand why you..." The answer hit me before I'd completed the question. The resources, safe houses around the world, money, people. All at his fingertips.

"Holy shit," I said, staring at him in wonder. "You kept it intact didn't you? Your infrastructure? It's a functioning network isn't it?"

His gaze met mine. A curled smile at the corners of his mouth, his only acknowledgment. Jolene's inquiring glance shifted between Gage and me.

"What're you talking about?"

Instead I asked, "How big...?"

"Not very," he interrupted. "Small actually. One other person at the core. Two or three on retainer at any given time. And a handful we can call on for a favor when needed. But with a global reach."

"And how active? You're obviously still a part of it even if you're not active in the field."

"Also not very. Except in situations like this. Mostly it's intelligence gathering. Keeping tabs on a short list of groups and individuals. A few who'd be happier if I stopped breathing. We turn over any useful or actionable information to select friends in the international intelligence community. You two are only the fourth and fifth people who know about this."

"Christ Gage," I said.

Jolene nodded her silent understanding. "Does anyone want anything," she asked. "Coffee I made before heading topside is still fresh. Or another drink Mike?"

"Coffee sounds good JJ. Looks like it'll be a long night. So you were going to tell us about this Von Sachsen," I said, returning to our original topic.

"Not till I'm ready," Jolene said from the galley.

The laptop beeped. The same alert sound it'd made earlier. Gage tapped the keys. Read the contents on the screen.

"Last three locations acquired," he said. "Check. And now for mate," he said as he typed.

"What are the other three locations," I asked again, remembering he hadn't answered me the first time.

"Dougan's family," he said.

"His family? Gage what are you doing?" Rising uncertainty and concern in my voice.

"Turning the tables. I'm going to do to him what he did to you."

"Gage..." I hesitated. "I want nothing more than to have my hands around that man's throat. But his family. They're innocents in all this."

"You don't know that," he said, his voice harsh.

My response on the tip of being verbalized when he said, "But I do. Which is why no harm will come to them? You have my word. But Dougan has to believe the opposite. And you're the one who has to sell it. You up to that Mike?" His eyes regained their earlier dispassionate hardness, searching mine.

"That part isn't a problem," I said.

Gage nodded. "I'm improvising on the fly here. Didn't anticipate them going after you through your family Mike. But it provides us an opportunity we didn't have before."

"What kind of opportunity?"

"To bring Bogeyman here. To us."

"What?" Jolene said from the galley.

"Me too," I said. "Can't wait to hear how you hope to manage that."

Jolene arrived bearing three steaming mugs of coffee. A milk carton under one arm and a sugar bowl balanced in the crook of her elbow.

"So who's this Von Sachsen," she said, placing everything on the dinette.

"The Von Sachsens are old German aristocracy going back to the nineteenth century. Maybe further back. Maybe even German nobility. I wasn't interested in the family genealogy," he said. "At any rate the family was a major industrial force during the early twentieth century, and during the Nazi era. Munitions, chemicals, aircraft parts production. Rumored to be involved in Nazi theft of Jewish holdings during World

War II, and slave labor in their plants. Either of you ever heard of the Red House Report?"

Jolene and I both shook our heads.

"It's a document written at a secret meeting in the Maison Rouge Hotel in Strasbourg in nineteen forty-four, detailing a Nazi plan for post-war recovery, and a return of the Nazi party to power. It involved Germany's leading industrialists, working with top Nazi officials, to rebuild Germany's post war economy by sending money aboard through Switzerland to set up a network of secret front companies outside Germany.

"Otto Wilhelm's father, Ludwig Wilhelm Von Sachsen, was a member of the group. But because of the charges against him regarding theft of Jewish holdings and slave labor, he was tried by the Allies after the fall of Germany and imprisoned. The Von Sachsen companies were seized by the Allies and eventually liquidated. Ludwig died in prison in nineteen forty-eight and his son Otto, twenty one at the time, left Germany."

Gage paused. His gaze passing from me to Jolene. Both of us silent, the coffee forgotten and growing cool before us. Spellbound by the story unfolding in Gage's smooth dulcet tones.

"Otto ostensibly went abroad to work on Red House in place of his father. But he held a bitter animosity not just toward the Allies, but the Germans too, who he felt had betrayed his father. Over the years he appropriated Red House resources for his own ends, eventually creating the empire that exists today. Otto is now eighty-four years old, living in Switzerland. His son, Godfried Wilhelm Von Sachsen, grandson of Ludwig Wilhelm, is fifty-eight. His primary residence and headquarters is in Bahrain."

"How did your guys finally manage to crack the corporate veil and get all this?" I wondered aloud.

"Dougan provided the final pieces of the puzzle," Gage said in a bland voice, as though discussing the weather.

"But how'd you..." snapping my fingers in sudden understanding. "The power outage," I said.

"What power outage?" Jolene asked.

"Dougan mentioned a power outage on Mustique. And they couldn't get the generator running because of some mechanical failure. That was you. That was your so called charter."

"Gage?" Jolene's piercing gaze leveling on him.

"When I received the report on Dougan I figured we'd have to deal with him sooner or later. I went over to recon the villa. But the more I saw the more convinced I became I needed to get inside the villa itself. I managed to get hold of his laptop and cloned the hard drive."

"Like hell you just managed," Jolene said. "Crisse. Hell of a risk my love."

"But it paid off. Once we had the contents of the laptop we were able to fill in the blanks. Including where they keep their accounts. The money is the key. We'll use it not only to get Bogeyman here, but bring down the whole house of cards."

"Yeah, I'd like to get back to that part," I said. "How're you going to get Bogeyman here?"

"Dougan's going to get him here," he said. "Or we kill his family."

The nonchalant statement hit me like a punch, rocking me back in my chair.

"Gage..." I began, only to notice the bastard wink at me.

I released a breath I hadn't been aware I'd been holding. A 'had me going you bastard' smile on my face.

"You have to sell it Mike," he said, returning my smile. "But not only that, when we meet Dougan again tomorrow, and I mean we," he said, his eyes pinning me like an insect in a display case. "He'll find most of his corporate and personal accounts drained. Close to two billion dollars will be gone. He'll be broke. Won't even be able to pay for Les Jolies Eaux."

I whistled.

"Where will all the money go?" Jolene asked, a sly smile on her face. "Your secret widows and orphans fund?"

"His what?" I asked dumbfounded. Though after learning of his network, nothing would surprise me.

"Some," he said, smiling at her, privy to a secret shared only between them. "But most of it will appear as payments to a list of accounts around the globe which will set off alarms at the CIA, MI6, DGSE, BND, Mossad and Interpol among others. By midweek, they'll be tearing apart Phoenix. I'll brief you on everything Mike, including the documentation for the meet tomorrow."

I merely nodded. The enormity of what he'd accomplished staggering. Not a person you wanted for an enemy.

"I'll also give you a list of corporations and other documents we'll use to play Dougan. It'll be like a domino hand when you're holding all the sixes," he said, his smile devious.

Two a.m. when I glanced at my watch. "I better be getting back," I said. "But before I go there's one more thing." I paused. The inconceivable thought sticking in my throat.

"What is it Mike?" Jolene reading me like a favorite book. She leaned toward me. Concern in the clear hazel eyes.

"Something Dougan said. Smug arrogant son of a bitch. He knew Whittaker was undercover. Knows I have another undercover in the field. Only five people besides me have that information. Eliminating you two, Sammy and Elana, the only person he could have learned it from is Deputy Commissioner Huggins."

Jolene's sharp inhalation audible in the enclosed cabin.

"Mon crisse de tabarnac!"

"You were right Gage. And the son of bitch right under my nose all this time. Moments when I still can't believe it. I trusted him. Thought he could be the next Commissioner. Told him so. And all the time. I just want to put my Glock against his head and pull the trigger."

"I wouldn't rush to judgment too quickly Mike," Gage said.

"It's him Gage. It can only be him," I snarled.

"Don't doubt it," he said. "But from everything I've heard you and Jo say about him it doesn't track. More likely your house cleaning swept up any remaining eyes and ears Dougan had on the force. With the investigation closing in on him and whoever he has in the Government, Duggan needed someone else. And fast. Someone close to you. Close to the investigation. No time to cultivate another mole. Huggins may have been coerced. Like you. Seems to be Dougan's MO."

The thought froze the angry epithets swirling in my brain.

"Gage, I hadn't thought of that. It makes sense. The only thing that makes any sense. But if you're correct, what do we do about it?"

"Find a way to have a quiet chat tomorrow if you can. But only after you hear from me regarding your family. Tell him what you know. How Dougan threatened you too. If he's in the same predicament let him know we can help him."

"How're you getting to Montrose? Jolene asked.

"I have a ride waiting," I said. "Probably fast asleep in the car."

"I'll run him to the dock," Gage said to Jolene, kissing her on the lips. "Be right back."

She stepped past him to throw her arms around my shoulders, squeezing tight.

"No worries Mike. He thinks he has you. But you're the one who has him by the balls."

Gage climbed out of the dinghy onto the dock alongside me, holding the painter in his hand.

"Jo's right Mike," he said, "no worries. Listen, the email program you use for my server, there's a hidden encrypted shell program running behind it. A chat window. When I activate it just hit the accept button. That's how we'll communicate from now until we meet Dougan. I'll contact you in the morning with word on your kids and the ex. You get some sleep. Big day tomorrow."

"Easier said than done," I said. "Don't know if I can sleep until I know everyone's safe."

"Well try anyway. I promise you they'll be fine. Night Mike."

"Hey Gage," I called, halting him as he turned to step down into the dinghy."Thanks again."

"No need buddy. Get some sleep," he smiled, alighting into the dinghy. He fired up the outboard and headed across the bay to Wherever.

CHAPTER 24

As expected, Henry was slumped in the driver's seat, fast asleep, his mouth open. His sonorous breathing muted by the vehicle's rolled up windows. I tapped on the glass, startling him awake. Confused by his surroundings, he rubbed sleep from his eyes as he focused in the direction of the tapping sound.

"Commisshunah. You ready?" He rolled down the window.

"Ready to go Henry. Drop me where you picked me up. Not at the house."

"Yes Commisshunah," he said, a satisfied smile on his face. Whether his own fatigue, or the cash he'd received, he didn't question my unusual request. Or anything else concerning the strange evening. He returned me to the corner in Montrose in welcomed silence, my thoughts thousands of miles away during the ride.

I retraced my steps from earlier, along the footpath and through my neighbors' back yards. Along the stone retaining wall to where I'd hopped down earlier. Not so easy getting back up. My aging muscles barely able to haul the rest of my body up onto the wall. Aching arms straining, teeth clenched, I hauled and pushed, my scrabbling feet finding purchase on the stone wall, until I was able to throw my right leg up over the top. I hauled myself into the yard.

Crouched in the hedges I watched for signs of the police sentry. Or anyone else about. I gathered my legs under me and sprinted for the verandah wall. Less effort to climb over. I slipped silently into the house.

I lay on the king sized bed in the master bedroom. Fully dressed except for my shoes. My mind a whirlwind. Unsettled. Much less anxious and worried than before. But now, I had to endure the waiting.

Amazed by Gage's resourcefulness. His calm. His ability to orchestrate a complex operation from half a world away. And the network I'd just learned about, people who'd answer his call. I realized I'd answered my own question. The question I'd asked him earlier. I too would drop everything, and put my life on the line for him if he called.

Gage had found him. Our Bogeyman. A task which had often seemed impossible. A nefarious phantom too well hidden and protected. But Gage had found him.

Morning light streamed through the curtained windows, awakening me. Still dressed. I didn't remember falling asleep. It'd crept up on me, uninvited, somewhere between thoughts of Gage and Deputy Commissioner Huggins. Not the refreshing, rejuvenating kind of sleep. But sufficient to buoy my spirit. My mind more at ease than the night before. Ready to tackle the pivotal day ahead. My family's safety no longer in doubt.

I showered and changed. My housekeeper arrived, inquiring about breakfast. I opted for a quick bite of fruit and coffee before departing for police headquarters.

In my office, I lay the laptop on my desk, booted it up, and opened Gage's email application. A new window immediately popped up in the foreground.

'Morning Mike. News. Waiting your reply.' The message from Jolene.

I typed, 'Just arrived at office. What News?'

I waited. No response to the message. She must not be at the computer it finally occurred to me. I sat at my desk, at a loss for something to do. I'd asked Cecelia to cancel my morning briefings and I wasn't to be disturbed. If things had gone according to Dougan's plan, I'd be busy compiling the materials he wanted. Instead, I pondered Huggins. I needed to avoid him until I heard from Gage. And what if we were wrong? What if Huggins had been dirty all along? My mind unable, or unwilling, to accept the latter scenario. I'd have to wait to resolve that complication too. After I'd received word of my family. As though privy to my thoughts the laptop beeped.

'Family secure,' the message read. 'Gage putting together information for you.'

'Where is he?' I typed.

'Been up all night on computer and phone. Still working on info for meet with Dougan.'

'Okay,' I typed. 'Stand by. Need to speak to Huggins. Will contact you following. Hope Gage is right.'

'Good luck. Standing by,' the screen read.

One down. Two to go, I thought, contemplating where Huggins might be and how to contact him discreetly. Probably unsafe to use the phone in my office, I reasoned. And thinking of it, I decided not to meet him in my office either. A mental note to have my phones and office swept as soon as possible.

Other offices connected to the investigation may also have been compromised, and I included them in my mental note.

I strode from my office, pausing at Cecelia's desk. "Locate DC Huggins for me. I need to see him right away. Have him meet me in former Superintendent Mitchell's office," I said, her curious gaze following me down the hall. I stepped into the vacated office a floor below and closed the door behind me. All vestiges of the former occupant had been removed. I leaned against the desk and faced the door.

Moments later the door opened. Huggins poked his head in, perhaps expecting to find an empty office. His eyes scrutinized me as I beckoned him into the office.

"Close the door Reggie," I said, attempting to keep my anger from my voice and my eyes. I stared hard into his eyes. A man I'd trusted. I controlled my anger, hoping to God Gage had been correct.

He in turn eyed me. A pained expression in his, as though aware of what was coming. Or if we were correct, anguish at the betrayal he'd been coerced into.

"What's going on Reggie," I said. An effort to control my voice. The anger rose unbiden within me.

"Sir? Bout what..."

"I know Reggie," I interrupted him.

He shifted his weight. His eyes shifted downward too. Focused on his shoes. Not the lying indicator, but rather embarrassment. And Shame. The indicator of submissive surrender.

"When I arrived home on Bequia last night men were waiting for me in my house Reggie," I said. "In my fucking house," I yelled, rising anger slipping my control. "He threatened the lives of my children. He murdered a police constable goddammit," undisguised ire in the rising pitch of my voice.

"He had information he could only have obtained from you Reggie," I said in a calmer, lower voice, remembering the thin walls separating the adjoining offices. "So tell me about it."

His head and eyes remained downcast. "I have family too Commisshunah," he said, his voice almost a whimper, the words mumbled. "Two sons and a daughter. De boys live in de States, my daughter in Canada. Married, wid children. My grandchildren Commisshunah," his voice rising as mine had moments before. His head rose too. His gaze met mine. A momentary flash of anger in the dark eyes.

"A man call me and say he will kill dem if I don't do as he tell me. At my house, I find picchas of dem at dey home, at work, at school. De man say he will kill dem all Commisshunah," a mixture of disconsolate contrition, shame, and anger, in his voice. His shoulders slumped. His ragged respiration a silent sobbing.

My anger disappeared like a dissipating mist. I sympathized. I'd been in his shoes mere hours before.

"Your family will be safe Reggie," I said.

Moist red eyes stared into mine. Uncomprehending. Disbelieving. Defeated.

"I already have people protecting my family. I didn't want to believe you could betray the force, this office, me," I said emphasizing the word. "Unless the same threat had been made against you too. I still have friends and contacts in law enforcement in the states Reggie," the prevarication aimed at protecting the real source. "They'll protect your family too.

These people think they have a hold over us, but they don't. And I'm going to take them down."

The lids surrounding his moist eyes widened. Uncertain, but wanting desperately to believe. To hope.

"You should have come to me Reggie. You should have asked for my help before it got to this."

"I was frightened for my family Commisshunah. If dem was to get killed..."

"How long?" I interrupted.

"Not so long," his shame evident again. "Soon aftah de raids and arrests."

Gage had been correct. We'd unknowingly eliminated Dougan's eyes and ears.

"This goes way beyond the arrests Reggie," I said. "The people who threatened our families are connected to the conspiracy to take over St. Vincent and the Grenadines." I paused. No need to elaborate further at this point. He didn't have a need to know. And I couldn't risk anything getting back to Dougan.

"What did he ask you to do?" I said.

"Keep dem updated on de investigations. Den last night dey call me wid instructions to watch you, see what you doin' and who you talkin' to."

"That's all?"

"Yes Commisshunah."

"Okay." I said, searching around the cleared desk for paper and pen. I found them in a right hand drawer. "Write the home addresses, phone numbers and work places of your family," I said handing him the paper and pen.

Uncertainty remained in his eyes as his gaze met mine. He bent to the desk, commensed writing.

"Is why I tinkin' 'bout leaving de police after you gone," he said, still bent over the desk.

"Unfortunately for all of us now you'll have to Reggie. Even after your family is safe, and we're done with this mess. I'm sorry. But there's no way we can just sweep this under the rug."

"Don't matter now. Long as de family safe."

"It'll give you a chance to go spend time with your grandchildren. Get to know and spoil them," I chuckled. A feeble attempt to lift the tension pervading the room.

He finished writing. Straightened from the desk. He hesitantly handed me the sheet of paper.

"You sure 'bout dis Commisshunah," his gaze meeting mine, seeking assurance in my eyes.

"Got word this morning my family is already safe Reggie. Yours will be too," I said. "How're you supposed to report to him about me?" I asked.

"He always call me on de cell. I expect he'll call when dey ready."

"Okay. When he does, you report to him that you've seen me meeting with the principal investigators all day. That I've been requesting the case files. Let's go back to my office. We can discuss the cases, but no mention of this other thing while we're in the office, understand."

"Yes Commisshunah," he said nodding.

In my office I sat at my desk and opened the laptop. When I logged onto the email server the chat window reappeared on the screen. No new messages had been typed since I'd last used it.

I typed, 'Gage correct. Huggins' family also under threat. Information as follows.' I typed the information Huggins had written on the sheet of paper and waited. Huggins sat on one of the armchairs in the sitting area. Silent. His thoughts probably as troubled as mine had been earlier. The laptop beeped, attracting his attention, before he returned to brooding.

'On it. Good about the DC. Preparing to sail back to Bequia. Gage wants to get there before you. Sweep the house. Figures he'll need a couple of hours to brief you before the meet.'

'Will do.' I typed.

An icon at the top of the chat window changed, indicating the current user had logged out. I closed the application on the laptop and leaned back in my chair. More hours of nothing to do but wait. But it had to appear as though I were following my instructions.

"Reggie," I said, rising from behind my desk. "Let's pick up the briefing later. You'll have to excuse me. Some files downstairs I need to get."

We departed the office together. In the hallway I pulled him aside.

"My contacts are already on the way to secure your family," I told him. "When the man calls you tell him what I told you before. What else did he ask you to do?"

"Nuttin' Commisshunah. Jus' observe your activities until you leave."

"Well go find something to keep yourself busy. I'll do the same. Come back to my office around two o'clock."

When Huggins retuned to my office at two thirty, I'd received word from Jolene. Huggins' family had been secured. Gage had already been at my house for an hour. Both he and Jolene were setting up for my return to Bequia. I escorted

Huggins to the hallway and reported the news. The enormous relief in his posture, his breathing, his worry filled eyes, and effusive thanks gratified me. His career finished. But his family was safe.

"Don't try to contact your family until tomorrow," I cautioned him. "These people are monitoring our cell phones. And you can't tell your family anything about the danger they were in. They don't need to know. And Reggie, nothing that's happened need go beyond you and me. Understand?"

He nodded.

"You'll retire for personal reasons. Full honors. You'll leave in good standing with the force, and with me," I said, offering him my hand.

He shook my hand. "You goin' get dese people Commisshunah?"

"You can take that to the bank Reggie," I said.

CHAPTER 25

I hesitated as I faced the front door to my house in Friendship Bay. Hesitated to push the key into the lock. I'd performed the same routine activity the evening before. Only to find...

The memory produced a constriction in my throat. A delay in my step. But this time Gage waited inside when I pushed the door open. His tall frame sprawled on the living room settee, half-closed eyes focused on the doorway. A compact weapon, a Heckler and Koch nine millimeter from its appearance, stubby round suppressor attached, lay haphazardly on his stomach.

"How'd you know it was me?" I asked, assuming he wouldn't have remained in such a relaxed position if it'd been anyone other than me, or Jolene.

"Footsteps," he said. "And your scent."

"You shitting me?"

"No shitting. How do you suppose a blind person knows who's in a room. How you doing?"

"Better than the last time I walked into this house. How about you? JJ said you'd been up all night."

"Caught some winks on the sail back. And some here too. Place is clean by the way."

He rose to a sitting position. The silenced H and K placed on the coffee table before him.

"Ready to get started?"

About to answer, his buzzing cell phone interrupted me. He held up a silencing finger while he read the texted message on the display.

"Jo's made your Bequia tail," he said, thumbs tapping out a return text. He's set up on the hill. Good sightlines of the house."

He waited for a response to his text, nodding when he received it. He rose from the settee to show me the phone's display.

"Recognize this guy?"

An image of a male Caucasian on the screen, high forehead, wide spaced eyes downturned at the outer corners. A scar over the right brow.

"One of the men with Dougan last night." I said.

Gage merely nodded.

"Let's get started on this." I said. "Can't wait to get this evening over and done with."

"Patience Mike," Gage said, his voice calm, confident, encouraging, like a coach prepping his star player for the big game. "You're going to need it. What you have to accomplish tonight will require a ton of it. Dougan's been neutralized. This is now a classic psyche op to flip him. The ultimate goal is to bring Von Sachsen to us."

"Always bring your target to you. I've heard you say it many times."

"Good," he smiled. "You're learning."

"Since you're going to be here why can't you do this instead of me?" I asked.

"For the psychological impact," he said. "Where were you standing last night? And where was Dougan sitting?"

I indicated the positions.

"Okay. You're going to be sitting exactly where he was. And don't let him get any farther into the room than you did."

He walked over to a table against the wall I often used as a desk when working at home. He picked up a stack of file folders lying on it.

"Here," he said, sitting on the settee, motioning me to join him. "I stacked the files in the order you'll use them. First," opening the top file containing eight by ten photos of men I didn't know, handing them to me one at a time.

"These are the guys tasked to your kids and ex. All Phoenix. A couple of them too hard headed to make the smart play," he said, flipping me an image of a corpse, red stains on the shirtfront, blank lifeless eyes staring into oblivion.

"He was there to kill your daughter," Gage emphasized, perceiving my uncomfortable reaction. "And this one to kill your son," handing me the photo of another corpse. "My guys didn't take chances where your kids were concerned. Not when lives were at stake. Especially theirs."

"This guy," he said, handing me a photo of a man sprawled on a floor, wrists and ankles flex cuffed, "Was assigned to your ex. Wanted by Interpol, who just happened to find him dumped on their doorstep a few hours ago."

Gage replaced the photographs. He opened the second file. Images of two young women, twenty four and twenty seven years old I'd estimate. And an older woman, short platinum blond hair, in her mid-fifties. Images similar to the ones Dougan had shown me of my family. On the street, at work, at home in their apartments.

"Dougan's family. This is where you have to sell it Mike. I understand this makes you queasy, but we need to rattle that bastard to his bones. While you're showing him the file he'll receive three phone calls. Just to seal the deal. Don't let the calls unnerve you. Let them tear him apart instead. My guys have their instructions and understand the game. No harm will come to his family."

"I know you've said that. But still, it's a fine line my friend. Already two dead."

"Not really."

"Maybe you've crossed it so many times you don't see it anymore."

"No. The lines are just different is all. You've spent your career protecting your city, your community, operating within the parameters of the law. Not crossing that line. Now that you're protecting an entire nation, not to mention your family, from people who believe they're above laws, you still looking at the same line?" His hard, penetrating brown eyes searched mine.

"And it's four," he said.

"Four what?"

"Four dead. Beginning with your man Whittaker, and the bag man Mackee." He said.

I nodded. Ceding the point. "What if he calls our bluff?"

"As I said, this is a psy op Mike. We need him so rattled even if he might think it's a bluff, he won't be able to take the risk. By the time he leaves he needs to know his game is over, and he's now playing ours."

Gage opened the third file in the stack. "Dougan's personal and corporate accounts."

And so it went. File after file, until we reached the last file in the stack. Gage's operation targeting Dougan shook me, providing an appreciation of how it'd devastate Dougan. I couldn't afford to allow the sentiment to take root. I banished it from my thoughts. Focused instead on who Dougan was. What he represented. And what might have transpired if I didn't have a Gage on my side.

"You got all this," Gage said, patting the stack of files.

"Yeah, I'm good," I said.

"Okay. Go through it again, or leave it. Whichever gets you psyched. I'm gonna catch a few more winks."

He headed into the front guest room, the bed visible through the open door across the hallway from where I sat. He placed the silenced weapon on the nightstand. He lay on the bed. Sank into a deep sleep moments later.

Gage's cell phone buzzed. Six fifteen by my watch. I retrieved it from the coffee table where he'd left it. I tapped the message icon. A text. 'Speedboat heading toward Friendship from Mustique. ETA twenty minutes. Tail guy on the move.'

I wondered where Gage had positioned Jolene. Somewhere providing a view of both my house and the open water between Bequia and Mustique. Maybe an empty rental house up on the hill. I turned toward the guest bedroom, ready to rise from the settee and wake him. Gage already awake and standing in the arched opening between the hallway and living room. I hadn't heard him awaken, or rise from the bed. Hadn't heard his approach. The man a fucking ghost.

"Showtime?" he said.

"About half an hour," I said, handing him the cell phone. "Man's punctual, I'll give him that."

The cell phone buzzed again thirty minutes later. Gage read the message.

"They're on the way," he said.

We set the scene. The same lights as the night before switched on. I sat in the exact position as Dougan had. Gage stood a little off to my left, hands clasped in a leisurely, unthreatening manner in front of his body.

Footsteps on the verandah. Light, like a whisper. A second set louder, the footfalls heavier. The knob on the front door turned. The door opened. Scarface entered first. Spotted Gage. Small sinister eyes widened in suspicion. Unsure of his next move, needing instructions from his boss, but concluding Gage posed no threat.

Dougan entered next. Commanding and self-important. At ease, like he fucking owned my house. The other man entered behind him, moving to cover Dougan and his partner when he spotted Gage.

Dougan's eyes appraised Gage. A slow, deliberate sweep from head to toe, as through visually undressing a woman. The conceited, self-assured smile settled into place.

"Commissioner? I don't recall any mention of a third party being invited to this meeting."

"He's here at my invitation," I said.

"Be that as it may, I'm afraid I must ask this gentleman to leave us while we conduct our business."

"That isn't up to you," I said.

The tiniest slip of the smile. His eyelids narrowed. My inexplicable defiance an annoyance he'd swat like a buzzing fly. And make me pay dearly for it later.

"Gentlemen, please escort this person outside," he said. His smile unwavering, but the eyes flashing undisguised malevolence.

I'd often pondered Gage's lethality. The many ways he knew to incapacitate, maim. Or kill. The thoughts occurred whenever I tried to imagine his past. They'd resurfaced when I'd met the two friends he'd enlisted to protect me. Hard eyes, like his. Deadly volcanoes lurking beneath a tranquil cultured surface. And again when I'd witnessed his workout with Jolene. Yet no amount of imagining prepared me for the reality. He moved in a blur, uncoiling like a tightly wound spring from his unthreatening, deferential-like posture. His speed and agility difficult for the eye to follow. The two men moving toward him had no chance.

As the first man reached for him, Gage blithely brushed the arm aside and landed a powerful closed fist blow to the side of the man's neck, just below the ear. The man crumpled like an air-filled doll deflating, minus the sound.

The second man's hand whipped beneath the untucked shirt tail. A semi-automatic gripped in his emerging fist. Gage stepped toward him. Captured the gunman's wrist in his right hand as it cleared the shirt tail, allowing its momentum to swing the gun arm straight as intended. Gage pivoted while he wrapped his left arm like a boa constrictor around the man's captured arm, applying downward pressure at the wrist, upward pressure at the elbow. The gunman's fist flew open. The weapon slid from his hand. A metallic clack as it landed on the hard ceramic tile floor. Accompanied by the popping sound of muscles and tendons rending as Gage applied more pressure. A louder pop as Gage dislocated the man's elbow.

The anguished howl immediately silenced by Gage's unwinding left arm flat across the gunman's throat, circling his neck, bending him backward at the waist. My gut clenched as I realized the position allowed Gage to easily snap the man's neck, and I fully expected to hear the crack of cervical vertebrae. Instead Gage's left knee rammed into the man's back, striking with dreadful force in the vicinity of his kidney. He slid from Gage's grasp to the floor.

Less than five seconds. Only two blows. One to each man. A fist and a knee. Both men lay motionless at Gage's feet. No brawler mess. Not a stick of furniture disturbed. Holy Christ Gage. If age had slowed and dulled his edge, I couldn't imagine what he'd been like twenty years earlier.

Dougan stood rooted to the spot in dumbfounded silence. The smug smile finally wiped from his face. His eyes fixed on Gage, who returned his stare. Gage's eyes as empty as a black hole in space. Dougan stepped toward me. Not threateningly. A survival instinct to put some distance between himself and Gage.

"That's far enough," I said, halting him in the approximate position I'd been standing in the previous night. "Any closer and he'll reach down your throat and rip your heart out," I said. The hard guy cliché a nice touch I thought, inwardly amused.

"You must know Commissioner," Dougan said, finding his voice. "This only means you've just lost your family."

"About that," I said, handing him the first file on the stack, just as Gage and I had rehearsed. "Perhaps you don't personally recognize your hired help, but those were the men you had watching my family. All Phoenix Group. Two dead.

One in the hands of Interpol who had an outstanding international warrant for him."

He picked through the photographs. Mouth slightly ajar, revealing the crooked teeth he preferred to display in what he considered a charming smile.

"My family is perfectly safe by the way," I said. "Yours however," handing him the second file.

A forceful expulsion of breath escaped his thin lips. His body jerked forward as though he'd sneezed. His eyes narrowed. Their usual menace absent, instead expressing an unaccustomed incredulity. Unable to believe his own eyes.

I glanced at Gage, who'd moved to the door after retrieving the unconscious men's weapons. At least I hoped they were merely unconscious. Gage unobtrusively texted on his cell.

A tinny ringtone emanated from somewhere on Dougan's person.

"You'll want to take that call," I said. "On speaker if you don't mind."

He reached into a trouser pocket. Checked the number on the cell's display. Answered the call.

"Dad?" A tremulous female voice rose from the phone's speaker. Followed by a male voice. Guttural, hollow and harsh. As though mechanically filtered.

"Your turn. Do as you're told or she dies," the voice said.

Dougan visibly shaken. Unable to tear his gaze from the phone. His artificial tan more ash than bronze. The deep lines across his brow and at the corners of his eyes no longer distinguished and commanding, instead giving his face a haggard appearance. The lips disappeared into a thin line at his tightly closed mouth. A pang of sympathy rose within me. Quickly squelched.

"You might want to hang that up," I said instead. "You're expecting two more calls."

The call repeated twice more. A trembling female voice followed by the mechanical male voice bearing the same message.

"You have no idea who you're dealing with," Dougan sneered after the third and final call.

"You didn't strike me as a person who'd resort to clichés," I said. "Go figure. The fact is I know exactly who I'm dealing with," handing him another file. "You are James Dougan. Age sixty-two. Head of the Phoenix Group. Your hand in a lot of dirty business around the world. And speaking of business, I'm sure you'll recognize those accounts," indicating the file which he hadn't yet opened.

He peered down at the sheets in the files. Dawning recognition. The line of his mouth opened. The incredulous expression reappeared in his eyes.

"That's correct. They're yours. Personal and corporate. And you'll notice they've been accessed and drained. Hope you paid in advance for that pricey villa you're renting because you won't be able to afford it after tonight. Or the Fifth Avenue Duplex your wife currently occupies. Not to mention the Palm Beach condo you provide for your mistress. You should also know the funds were transferred to accounts and groups around the world of interest to various intelligence agencies in the United States, Britain, Europe and the Middle East. By the end of this week, they'll have torn Phoenix apart. This Phoenix isn't going to rise from the ashes. You no longer have a family, a business, or any money to return to."

"You bastard," he hissed.

"You invaded my home." My harsh bellow snapped his head back as though I'd slapped him in the face. I resisted the urge to rise from the settee and make it a physical reality.

"You threatened to murder my Family," I said, maintaining the harsh ferocity in my voice. "Call me a bastard all you want. You set this in motion. And this is the result. Not what you expected I'm sure. But exactly what you deserve."

"You still have no idea the terror that's..."

"Oh enough with the clichés man." I snapped, interrupting him.

"I know you're nothing but a messenger. A glorified errand boy. So I have a message I want you to deliver. A message for this man," I said, handing him the last file.

He opened the file. It had the desired effect. Again the sneeze like exhalation, the file almost slipping from his fingers.

"That's right. I found him. So you see, I know exactly who and what I'm dealing with. Unlike all of you when you decided to set your greedy grubby sights on my islands. You tell him that. And you'll notice the corporations listed there, and the accounts. The ones behind all the smoke and mirrors that connect directly to him. And much more I'm sure he'll wish to see for himself, including documentation of his family's activities in Nazi Germany he probably doesn't want to come to light. All of it to be handed over to the authorities in every country he does business in. Unless we can come to a mutual accommodation. Face to face."

For a fleeting moment the smug smile threatened to reassert itself.

"He will not agree to that."

"It's not your decision. You're only the messenger. You tell him this has gone beyond the level of errand boys. If he doesn't agree, he can expect his house of cards to come tumbling down, as yours did. The process has already begun. By next week he'll find some of his companies gutted. The share price of others in free fall. Investigations launched. His enemies coming out of the woodwork like cockroaches at night. The process will continue until he agrees to meet. If you fail you know what will happen to your family, and the remainder of his holdings."

Dougan's eyes squeezed shut, deepening the crinkly crow's feet at their corners. His face aged visibly. When he reopened his eyes they bore the expression of a desperate, cornered animal. Not one rearing to fight back. Instead submissive. Defeated. Gage's stage-managed presentation had pummeled Dougan like a heavyweight boxer's well timed combinations, rocking him to his core.

"Now get the hell out of my house," I commanded. "You'll have to arrange transportation back to Mustique. Unless you can pilot the boat you arrived in. These two, if they're still alive, will spend the remainder of their visit to our fair islands in Her Majesty's prison in Kingstown, charged with possession of undeclared and unlicensed firearms and ammunition, breaking and entering, threatening to cause injury, and let's not forget murder. Serious offenses carrying the death penalty here in St. Vincent and the Grenadines. Any outside interference from you or your boss, and your family pay's the price. You belong to me now."

One of the two had pulled the trigger on Whittaker, on Dougan's orders. No way to prove it unless one of them talked. But one way or the other they'd all go down for it. Dougan turned and walked toward the door Gage held open for him. Shoulders slumped, the air of haughty self-assurance nonexistent. His arrogant posture diminished. His eyes averted as he stepped past Gage's unwavering deathly stare.

"Are they alive?" I asked after Gage closed the door behind the departed Dougan. "One of them is probably Whittaker's killer."

"That's a safe bet," he said, stooping next to each man to check the carotid pulse. I'd noticed him making the same checks earlier when he'd retrieved their weapons.

"Systemic shock. They'll be comatose for a while yet. This one may develop some temporary cardiac arrhythmia issues. That one maybe a chronic kidney problem."

His cell phone still in his hand he dialed. A loud ringing indicated he'd set it to speaker mode. Jolene answered.

"What do you see?" Gage asked.

"Dougan left the house. Went directly to the boat docked at the Friendship Bay Hotel. I don't think he knows how to operate it. He's just sitting there. Looks like he's on his cell. The other two haven't come out. I take it they might be incapacitated."

"Need to get some of your guys over here. Mike's keeping these two."

"On the way" She said.

Gage collected the files scattered across the coffee table. He neatly stacked them and removed them to the guest bedroom. He was nowhere in sight when Jolene and constables from the Port Elizabeth Station arrived. I issued orders for the two men, including instructions for a doctor to examine the prisoners at the jail, not the hospital. I logged the weapons on an evidence form. The two gunmen, still unconscious, had to be carried to the police Toyota pickup.

Gage reappeared after the constables departed.

"How'd it go?" Jolene asked, delivering a chilled bottle of Heineken to Gage, a double shot of whisky for me. Another Heineken for her.

"Exactly according to plan," Gage told her. "By the way Mike, an Oscar worthy performance."

"Kinda reminded me of my undercover days," I said.

"You never told me you worked undercover Mike," Jolene said.

"My first two years with the Sheriff's Department. One of my first jobs was flying a Cessna one-eighty-two around the Keys for a drug distributor spotting marijuana and cocaine bales dumped for pickup. So you think it'll work?" I said, turning to Gage.

"You definitely sold it," he said. "And when the things you told Dougan start happening, it'll get Von Sachsen's attention. He probably won't be too concerned about the investigations. He's too well connected, and has an army of lawyers who can stall forever. But it'll be expensive and he'll be concerned by the publicity, and what it'll do to already unstable share prices. Not to mention blowing his highly protected anonymity. The sharks will start circling. But the main thing that'll get him here is you Mike. How'd a small island cop like you manage to pull this off? Have the information you have? Where'd you get it? How much more do you have? And who have you shared it with? That's what will get him here."

"Not to mention wanting to see me dead," I said.

"There's that too," Gage deadpanned.

I swallowed a mouthful of the neat whiskey. "By the way, any mention of an Elon Fredericks when you were going through Dougan's computer?"

"I'll have to double check. First time around the name wasn't on my radar. I'll also ask my guy stateside to dig deeper into him."

"I should have asked Dougan when he was here."

"You can ask him anytime you wish. You own him. But let's get some more intel on this guy before you do."

Unaware I'd been frowning, Jolene reacted to it.

"Why the face Mike?"

"I'm convinced Mackee was murdered on Fredericks's orders. Or maybe Dougan's through Fredericks. Break the only link in the chain connecting Fredericks to Dougan. Same reason they murdered Whittaker. I know it but can't prove it. And the guy who actually pulled the trigger on Mackee is probably already dead or off the island."

"Why do you think he's off the island?" Jolene asked.

"Ballistics matched the bullets and shell casings to shootings on St. Lucia and Antigua. Guy's an import. Either from the region or more likely abroad. The States, or Central or South America."

"So how do we close the cases?" Jolene asked.

"Don't know yet, but we need to. The politics surrounding Mackee's murder is too volatile for half answers and speculation. If no suspect is charged for the public to point to and blame, they'll turn to half-baked conspiracy theories. I know I have one of the people who murdered Whittaker but can't prove that either. In any case I'll make damn sure they both rot in Her Majesty's prison for a long time."

I swallowed another shot of my whisky.

"And damned if I'm going to let Fredericks get away with his part in it."

CHAPTER 26

The Coast Guard cutter returned me to its Calliaqua base early Wednesday morning. My mind at ease. I'd called my kids the night before, both unaware of the danger they'd faced and escaped, our long, newsy conversations reconnecting us. Followed by a short pleasant 'just called to say hello' to my ex. Melanie had called just before I turned in for the night. She expected to arrive on a midday flight from Barbados for an afternoon appointment at Government House. She planned to stay overnight.

My spirit soared. Enlivened by the triumph over Dougan, and the strategy we'd set in motion to end the entire nightmare. Gage continued to advise caution. The endgame the most dangerous time of any operation, he'd said. The situation still dangerous and unpredictable. Von Sachsen not to be underestimated.

I'd instructed the corporal driving the unmarked Toyota to make one quick stop enroute to the station. Elana stood waiting at the designated corner. Dressed in business attire. A black knee length sheath skirt, belted at the waist, dark stockings, and black closed toe low-heeled pumps. A burgundy blouse of silky material, ruffled collar, and half sleeves ruffled at the elbows. Her shoulder length hair straight ironed and parted in the middle, framing the high forehead and smooth contours of her chocolate brown face.

"Morning Elana," I greeted her as she settled into the seat next to me.

The driver cast curious glances at her through the rear-view mirror. More curious glances followed us through the station's hallways to my office. Most curious of all, Cecilia's, whose matronly visage transformed into a gracious smile upon our entrance, drawing the wrong conclusion.

"Good morning Commissioner," she beamed. Eyeing Elana in motherly appraisal.

"Morning Cissy," I said. "Allow me to introduce Sergeant Elana Matthews." Stunned surprise on both their faces. Cecilia's eyes shifted to professional appraisal. Elana's understandably confused.

"Another...?"

"Yes," I answered Cecilia's unfinished question. "And yes," I said to Elana. "Effective immediately you are promoted to the rank of Sergeant. Cissy, please have Sergeant Samuel report to my office as soon as he's available. Send him right in when he arrives. And I'll also need AS McKinley."

"Yes Commissioner," her gaze still focused on Elana, her smile approving and welcoming. "A pleasure to meet you Sergeant," she said to Elana before we departed for my inner office.

"Ma'am," Elana acknowledged with a polite nod.

"Have a seat Elana," I said, indicating the armchairs in the sitting area, setting my laptop briefcase on my desk before joining her.

She waited for me to sit first, smoothing the back of her skirt as she sat. Her back straight and business like in the chair designed for relaxed ease.

"As I indicated in the email," I told her, my gaze holding her expressive dark brown eyes, "Your undercover assignment has been completed. You've handed in your notice to the bank?"

"Yes Commisshunah," she said, her voice soft, lilting.

"Congratulations on a job well done," I said. "Now I have another assignment for you. In the Financial Intelligence Unit. I need you to put the intelligence you gathered during your time at the bank to use there. With your background this could be a long term assignment Elana. It's up to you. And you deserve it. I'm hoping you'll decide to remain on the force."

"Very kind sir," she said. "I have to see. But I'll complete de assignment befoh' makin' any decishun Commisshunah."

"Can't ask for more," I said.

A knock on the door interrupted us. Cecilia stuck her head in to announce Sergeant Samuel. Samuel strode into the office. Halted at the sight of Elana, a smile spreading across his face.

"You," Elana said, almost springing for the armchair.

"You know each other?" I asked, surprised, observing their interaction.

"No sir," they said in unison.

Noting my confusion Samuel explained. "I mean, I see her de other night Commissioner. De night I followed Mackee to de restaurant in Calliaqua. I saw her there. Thought it was strange for a woman like her to be by herself. And she was checking Mitchell and Mackee de whole time. So I checking her out when I glimpse de ring."

"De Ring? You know 'bout de ring?" Elana said. Then with dawning awareness, "You one of us. Dat's why you were watching me like dat?" Elana said, rising from the armchair, smiling. "I think you was just wanting to lime me. But you was following Mackee?" Her lilting inflection turning the statement into a question. "I didn't see you wearin' de ring or de medallion."

"I turned de face inside after I see yours," he said. He lifted his right hand to display the ring, which he still wore. Both smiled at each other.

"Sergeant Keston Samuel," I said, recapturing their attention. "Sergeant Elana Matthews."

His smile widened as he stepped toward her, offering his hand. Elana grasped the hand and they shook, their smiles, their gazes still locked on each other. The handshake perhaps a tad longer than necessary.

"Pleasure to finally meet you," Samuel said.

"And you," she said.

"I have something to show you both," I said. Their joined hands parted, hung at their sides. A palpable attraction filled the space between them. I pulled a file from my desk drawer. I extracted a photograph from the file.

"Constable Derrick Whittaker," I said, "posthumously promoted to Sergeant. Your colleague who died in the line of duty."

The flirtatious conviviality between them evaporated. Replaced by a funeral sobriety. Each studied the photograph at length, as though committing every detail of Whittaker's features to memory. A person they'd never met, but with whom they shared a collegial kinship.

"I've a meeting scheduled with his family later today," I said. "They'll be informed of the true nature of his work and his heroism. We'll also discuss funeral arrangements with DC Huggins. Full police honors. I'll keep you both informed."

They both nodded.

"Also, I believe we have the men responsible for his death in custody. They were arrested on Bequia last night and transferred to Kingstown prison this morning."

"They sir?" Samuel said.

"Yes. Two men. I'm not sure which of them committed the actual murder. But both were involved. The man who gave the order, an American, is being dealt with separately," I informed them, without further explanation.

They both nodded again.

"Sammy, how's that item I asked you to look into coming along?"

"Should have a report for you by end of the day Commissioner."

"Good. That'll be all for now Sammy."

"Yessir," he said, stiffening to attention and saluting. I returned the salute.

"Elana," he said turning to her, his smile charming and evocative. "I see you later," he said, his subtle inflection turning the statement into a question.

"Keston," she said, shyly receptive to the promise he'd left hanging in the air.

As he turned for the door I reached for the handset of my desk telephone.

"Cissy. Any word yet from AS Mckinley?"

"She's here waiting to see you Commissioner."

"Good. Please show her in."

The office door Samuel had exited moments before opened. Cecilia ushered Angela McKinley through the door and closed it softly behind her. McKinley halted before my desk, feet together; her posture at attention. A brisk salute.

"As you were Angela," I said, her gaze darting between Elana and me. "Assistant Superintendent Angela McKinley, Sergeant Elana Matthews," I introduced them.

"Ma'am," Elana said. Her tone formal, her posture erect if not strictly at attention.

The perplexed expression on Angela's face produced an amused smile on mine.

"Sergeants Matthews and Samuel, who you recently met, have been working undercover for the past five months," I explained. "Their identities known only to me. Elana has just completed her assignment and I've brought her in. I'm reassigning her to your unit. She has valuable intelligence your unit can use. Here is her personnel file," I said, unlocking the file drawer of my desk and retrieving the file. I handed it to Angela.

"Familiarize yourself with it here. That file does not leave this office,"

"Yes sir," she said, eyeing Elana and the unopened file in her hand.

The intercom buzzed. I picked up the handset. "Send him in," I said after listening. I turned to the women.

"Superintendent, Sergeant, Please excuse me. I need the room for a moment. You may use the conference room. And please shut the door behind you."

Two quick raps on the office door and Cecelia opened it to show in DC Huggins.

"Good Morning Reggie," I greeted him, stepping from behind my desk. "How's the family?"

"Very well t'ank you sir," his smile cheerful and earnest. "I don't know how to t'ank you Commisshunah. I don't know how you did it but..."

"No need Reggie," I interrupted him. "And how doesn't matter. The important thing is they're safe and okay."

"Yes sir," He said.

"First things first," I said indicating the sitting area. "I've brought in the other undercover. Her assignment is completed and I'm reassigning her to the FIU."

"Yes sir," he repeated. "A woman undercover?" His thick eyebrows arched upward behind the spectacles.

"Yes. I'll give you the redacted personnel file so you can officially enroll her as you did Samuel."

"Yes sir."

"Second. Last night I arrested two men on Bequia responsible for the murder of Sergeant Whittaker. They've already been transferred to Kingstown prison. Have Cecilia get you a copy of the arrest report faxed from Bequia. And notify the Public Prosecutor's office. They'll have to wait their turn for a magistrate like everyone else. No special treatment. In fact the farther back on the line they are the better."

"Understand sir," he said, a knowing smile creasing his face.

"The man who ordered the murder of Whittaker, and probably Mackee, is also the man who threatened our families. He's staying on Mustique, and as I told you yesterday, he's connected to the conspiracy against St. Vincent and the Grenadines. He's been neutralized, and being dealt with. We don't have to worry about him anymore."

"Yes sir."

"Question Reggie. Was he the only one who ever spoke to you? Did anyone else ever speak to you when you were contacted?

"Only de one man sir. But it wasn't dat many times. The first time was aftah the Mackee murder. Dat's when I received de photographs and he threatened to kill my family. He wanted to know everyting' goin' on in de investigachun. De next time was when he told me to watch you in de office yesterday."

"Okay. Dead end there then," I said mostly to myself.

"Whittaker's family is coming in this afternoon. I want you at the meeting Reggie. We'll need to discuss the funeral arrangements. I want you to handle the arrangements and take care of the family."

"Yes sir."

"That'll be all for now Reggie." I said standing. Walking him to the door I remembered. "Oh let me get you that file," I said, heading behind my desk and opening the file drawer. I handed him the sanitized file containing Elana's biographical information, her application, my signed acceptance letter.

"Don't forget to add the promotion form," I reminded him. "And ask Cecilia to get you that arrest report."

"I'll take care of it Commisshunah."

"One more thing Reggie. With both of us leaving, at some point let's have a discussion about who should sit in this chair next."

"Yes Commisshunah," he said.

After closing the door behind him I walked across the room and opened the conference room door. Angela and Elana in companionable conversation, chuckling like long time friends, conveying the impression their conversation hadn't been strictly confined to police business.

"Ladies," I said, eyeing them both.

"Impressive Commisshunah," Angela said. "Not only de Sergeant here, but dis whole undercover operation. An you right about Elana. She'll be a big help in de unit."

"Excellent," I said. "Anything else either of you need for now."

"No sir. I think we all set," Angela said.

"In that case, Elana, your paperwork and official induction is being processed. Welcome home," I said, offering my hand.

"Thank you Commisshunah," she said.

I watched them exit through the door to the outer office, both pausing at Cecilia's desk. I retrieved Elana's confidential file from the conference table and headed back to my desk. A rap on my door and Cecilia entered, a stack of telephone messages in her hand. Ostensively the reason for entering the office. But she hadn't handed them to me, and wouldn't, until she'd completed her actual purpose.

"Such a nice, charming young woman. And so brave too, working undercover like that. How many more you have out there Commissioner?"

"That's all of them Cissy," I said. There were only three in the program."

"Three? Then dere's one more."

"One of them was killed," I said. The only time I'd mentioned Whittaker's existence and murder to her. Shock registered on kindly features she allowed only me to see.

"Oh my God Commissioner. I'm so sorry."

"Thank you Cissy," I said, handing her the photograph I'd shown Samuel and Elana earlier. "His name was Derrick Whittaker. Those folks on your schedule calendar for this afternoon are his relatives. I'll tell them what his real job was, about his bravery and heroism, and make arrangements for a police funeral."

"Oh Commissioner," she said, pulling a small square handkerchief from some secret compartment on her person, a continual puzzle to me. She dabbed below her moist eyes.

"Who did this terrible thing?" she asked.

"They're in Kingstown prison as we speak," I said. "They'll get what's coming to them."

She handed me the stack of messages. "May I borrow this a while Commissioner?" she asked, holding on to the photo.

"Cissy, you..."

The cross stare she leveled at me silenced me, and forestalled any further argument.

I sat behind my desk following Cecilia's departure. Not another word spoken between us. Her customary habit in handling my phone messages was to stack them in order of priority. The first message in the stack from the Governor General's office, followed by the Prime Minister's office. Next Superintendent Bernie Rogers. At the bottom of the stack a cabinet minister, the opposition leader's office, and two members of parliament.

I buzzed Cecilia on the intercom. Asked her to get the Governor General's office on the line for me. In the meantime I dialed Bernie's extension.

"What do you have?" I asked when he answered.

"A possible descripshun of de gunman commisshunah," he said. "We finally reached de case detectives on St. Lucia and Antigua. De Antigua police t'ink dey have a descripchun of de man involved in de murder dere. Dey faxed the descripchun and we circulatin' it to de witnesses from Biabou now."

"How about immigration?" I asked.

"Already lookin' thru' de immigration records too sir. I was wonderin' if we should circulate de decripshun to de media too?"

"Let's hold off on that for the time being. We don't want to spook him into hiding if he's still on the island. But circulate it to other police forces in the region."

"Yes Commisshunah."

"Good work Bernie. Anything else?"

"I'll inform you right away if we get any results from de descripshun Commisshunah."

"Thanks Bernie," I said, and disconnected.

Cecilia buzzed the moment I'd hung up. "Governor General's office on line two Commissioner."

I pushed the button next to the blinking indicator. "Please hold for Sir Brathwaite Commissioner," a male voice requested. A moment later the deep cultured voice poured through the connection.

"Good Morning Commissioner."

"Good morning sir," I responded.

"Commissioner, I wanted to get your first hand report on the unfortunate murder of the ULP representative."

"Yes sir," I said. Assuming it'd been the reason for the earlier call, I'd mentally prepared a concise briefing designed to update him on the pertinent details, avoiding the necessity for too many questions and a prolonged telephone conversation. I included Mackee's involvement with the gang and corrupt police officers. I also included the latest development regarding a possible description of the suspect.

"My word Commissioner," he said following my recitation. "That is disturbing news indeed. I take it what you've told me is not public knowledge. I haven't seen or heard anything about it in the news, or heard anything of the like from the cabinet or parliament."

"Correct sir. We're handling it discreetly and the investigation is continuing. Not just because of the murder, but the corruption may reach higher in the government."

"Good Lord! This is more serious than I'd imagined."

"Yes Sir. And there is a connection to our other security situation. We've made a breakthrough I will need to discuss with you."

"I tell you what Commissioner. I have an afternoon tea at which that situation will be the topic of discussion. I very much think it will be advantageous if you were to join us. You are acquainted with Consul Melanie Barnes from the U.S. Embassy on Barbados?"

Acquainted. If he only knew.

"Yes sir. I am," I said.

"Then would you please join us at four this afternoon?"

CHAPTER 27

An hour before lunchtime, Cecilia entered my office to say she'd be leaving early for lunch and she'd be back late, but in time for the Whittaker Family meeting.

"Everything okay?" I asked, concerned.

"No problem Commissioner. Just a little personal matter to attend to." She exited my office without further explanation.

At three pm, I returned to the office in full dress uniform. I'd run up to Montrose during the lunch hour to change into uniform for the Governor General's meeting, immediately following the Whittaker family meeting. I hadn't planned to be in uniform to meet Whittaker's family, but as I waited, I realized it fit the occasion. Cecilia remained MIA until fifteen minutes before the Whittaker's scheduled appointment. She set out refreshments on the coffee table before escorting them into my office, where Deputy Commissioner Huggins and I waited.

A petit, elderly woman, in a simple pink dress and open toed sandals, her grey hair covered by a black tam, entered ahead of a tall younger woman. The younger woman dressed in office attire. Red skirt and red jacket over a white blouse. In one hand she held a small neon pink backpack. In the other the hand of a little girl, five or six years old, her tightly braided pigtails held by elastic hair bands, small acrylic blue marbles at the ends. The lower half of their faces, the lips, mouth, chin and jaw line, distinctly recognizable as related. Identical to Derrick Whittaker's.

I ushered them to the sitting area. Extra chairs had been brought in from the conference room. The tray on the coffee table held a large pitcher of cold lemonade and tall downturned glasses. On the side, a platter of cookies and cube sized sweet cakes.

The older women eyed Huggins and me, a mixture of nervousness and suspicion in her gaze. The little girl's eyes by contrast guiless and cheerful. Her happy smile revealed a missing front tooth as she eyed the cookies and cakes on the table.

"Please have a seat," I said. "Can I get you anything? Tea, or lemonade. How about a Ju-C for Kamecia?"

The younger woman flashed me a quick suspicious glance. How'd I know her daughter's name? The little girl nodded her head in acceptance, huge doe eyes seeking her mother's permission. Cecilia poured each of them a glass of lemonade, even though they hadn't spoken. Kamecia picked up a glass in both hands and brought it to her lips. The glass almost covered her face.

"What dis 'bout Commisshunah?" The younger woman demanded. "Poliss come to we house dis mawnin' and tell we you want see us dis aftahnoon. Den poliss come pick up me granmodder, and pick me up at me daughter school."

"Dis 'bout Derrick," the older woman said. Her posture erect. Her eyes clear, expressing a sharp intelligence. No doddering old lady behind those eyes. Her hands clasped the handles of an old, worn, white leather handbag in her lap.

"We don't have nuttin' to do wid what Derrick doin'," the younger woman said in an assertive tone.

"When was the last time you saw Derrick?" I asked, my voice gentle, leaning toward the old woman, Derrick's grand-mother, who according to Derrick's file, had raised him and his sister after the accidental death of her daughter, their mother. The father had left as a deck hand on a freighter and never returned.

"Not 'bout two months," the old woman said, her voice high pitched and strong, authoritative. "Him spendin' most a de time in de Grenadines. Den little while ago someone come round sayin' he dead. I go to de poliss but dem don't know nuttin'. And dem do nuttin' to see if me boy alive or dead. I don't see him aftah dat. And now poliss come to de house. Say de Commisshunah of poliss want see me. So mus' be true. He dead."

"I'm afraid so Mrs. Whittaker. And I'm so very sorry."

A brief flickering of her eyelids. A catch in her throat. The eyes turned inward, accessing past memories, returning quickly to the present. She straightened in her chair. Her back stiff and resolute.

"And why you have fe bring us heah to tell us dis?" said the younger woman, Derrick's sister. Her suspicious attitude undiminished.

"Dem bad man he take up wid," the old woman said, as if to herself, her gaze raised to the ceiling. No one in the room but her. "I tell him and tell him, runnin' wid dem bad man will come to no good. But he won't listen. Tellin' me is all good what him doin'. One day me will see. I tell him no good will ever come from dat."

"He was telling you the truth ma'am," I said, capturing her gaze. "Your grandson, your brother," I said to the younger woman, "Was a brave, decent man. He was a police officer, working undercover," I said, pausing to allow my words to penetrate.

The old woman's eyes alert, the sister's widening, "A…a… poliss," she stammered. "Me broddah?"

"Yes," I said. "That time he spent overseas…"

"In Tampa Florida," she said, interrupting. "Say him work on de crab boats."

"He was training with the Florida State Police," I said.

"All dis you say true Commisshunah?" the old woman asked, her enlivened eyes searching deep into mine.

"I can show you his file," I said.

"Commissioner," Cecilia said. She'd remained standing and quiet since entering the office. "If I may."

"Yes Cissy. What is it?"

She turned abruptly and headed for the office door. She disappeared into the outer office, returning after a few moments carrying a package wrapped in foil paper.

Approaching the old woman Cecilia said, "I thought you might want to have this." She unwrapped the package to reveal an enlarged framed photograph of Derrick Whittaker. The one from his file she'd taken earlier in the day. A brass engraved plaque affixed to the bottom. The black lettering read,

Derrick Whittaker, Sergeant, RSVGPF

1988 – 2012

He gave his life in service to his country

I stared at the framed photograph as the old woman gingerly accepted it from Cecilia. Her gnarled bony fingers tenderly caressed the edges, lovingly patting the portrait behind the glass, her eyes misting, but no tears.

I glanced at Cecelia. The woman a constant source of mystery and wonderment. A perfectly poignant presentation neither Huggins nor I had considered. One only a mother could.

"Can you tell us what happened Commisshunah?" The sister asked, her attitude transformed from suspicion to an appreciation of the kindness shown her grandmother.

"Not the details, I'm afraid," I said, facing her. "I can tell you he was brave to undertake an assignment he knew was dangerous. And because of him the police have put many of the bad men your grandmother mentioned in prison. I can also tell you the inscription there is true. Derrick selflessly served his country, and gave his life for it. You can all be proud of him. And the people responsible for his death are now in prison."

"Commissioner," Cecilia said softly, tapping her wristwatch when my gaze met hers.

I nodded. Glanced at my wristwatch. Three thirty.

"My apologies," I said, addressing both women again. "I have to leave for another appointment. But I also wanted to tell you, the police will be arranging Derrick's funeral. He will receive full police honors. Deputy commissioner Huggins here will go over the details with you. Anything special you require for Derrick just let him know."

I rose from my chair. Leaned over the old woman still gazing wondrously at the framed portrait of her grandson. Her head rose. Her moist eyes met mine. I leaned down toward her. Kissed her lightly on both cheeks. I shook the sister's hand. I bent to one knee before Kamecia, cupped her cherubic face in my hands and kissed her forehead.

I left them in Huggins and Cecilia's capable hands. In the outer office I turned to stare at the closed office door. The experience of meeting Derrick's family and informing them of his death still visceral. My gaze stopped cold by the office wall adjacent to the door. It had been stripped bare of the wall pictures, except for a single framed portrait. A duplicate of the one Cecilia had given Derrick's mother. Only larger. The woman never ceased to amaze.

The drive from Kingstown to Government House, nestled in a corner of the Botanic Gardens in Montrose, provided an opportunity to organize my thoughts for the impending meeting. In the distance, high stratus hung above the Grenadines, not portending any rain. Above St. Vincent, white puffy cumulus drifted slowly through a bright blue sky.

The Governor General, a neutral and unbiased arm of the government, had been privy to the conspiracy faced by St. Vincent and the Grenadines uncovered during the Jackson Taylor murder investigation. Sir Brathwaite had been the conduit for publicly disclosing the materials hidden by Jackson Taylor, and discovered by Jolene during the investigation. He was aware of many of the details, but not all. Especially details concerning Gage's very existence, let alone involvement in the investigation. Details I still needed to protect. The same applied to Melanie, also aware of many, but not all the details. And possibly details she hadn't shared with either the Governor General or me. But like the Governor General, she had no knowledge of Gage.

As usual, the Governor General's male aide met me at the main entrance, escorting me through the reception hall. Sir Brathwaite met me in the foyer outside his office.

"Good of you to come on such short notice Commissioner," he greeted me in his deep sonorous voice, a warm welcoming smile on his face. "My guest has already arrived. Shall we Commissioner?" indicating I should follow him. He fastened the middle button of his light grey summer gabardine suit. Beneath the tailored jacket, he wore a pressed white shirt and light blue silk tie.

We entered the verandah through a set of curtained double doors close to his office, requiring us to walk the length of the patio to the table where Melanie sat waiting. Her head turned to the colorful gardens, the sunlight cast an aural sheen cast on her thick silky black hair.

She turned upon hearing our approaching footsteps. Rose from her seat as we neared the table. An elegant, classy, professional vision in a lightweight charcoal grey worsted business skirt, ending at her knees, tailored to hug her figure. The white jacket tailored too, cut narrow at the waist and flared over her hips, a line of three contrasting ebony buttons securing the front. Beneath the jacket a pale turquoise shirt, open at the collar, revealing a short double strand of small white pearls around her neck, her signature accessory. Reaching for Sir Brathwaite's outstretched hand, the hiked jacket sleeve revealed a slim elegant watch face on a narrow gold band around her wrist.

"Consul Barnes, so good of you to come. I'm sure you're acquainted with our Commissioner of Police Michael Daniels," he said. "My apologies for springing another guest on you, but

Commissioner Daniels informed me he has new information pertinent to our discussion."

"No apology necessary, Sir Christopher," she said, her voice throaty smooth. "It's always a pleasure meeting Commissioner Daniels," her sparkling brown eyes a mixture of surprise and pleasure as her gaze met mine.

"Please," Sir Christopher said, indicating chairs around the table set for afternoon tea.

The unseen hovering servant materialized as though by magic the moment we settled into our seats. She poured tea into our cups, and uncovered the snack tray on the table. For this occasion, a lighter blend Earl Grey possessing a fruity citrus flavor.

"If you would Commissioner," Sir Christopher said, setting his sup into the saucer after a few initial sips, allowing Melanie and I to do the same. "Please repeat for Consul Barnes what you related to me earlier."

"We believe there is a connection between this latest murder, a local parliamentary representative killed on Monday," I said parenthetically to Melanie.

"I'm aware Commissioner," she said, her ambiguous gaze fixed on mine.

"A connection to the people behind the conspiracy," I continued. "Through another man highly placed in the Government. We believe it was a contracted killing made to look like political violence, but was in fact an attempt to eliminate the connection to this other man."

"But what use would this other man be if a different party comes to power in the upcoming election?" Sir Christopher asked.

"This man is a trusted confidant in both parties sir. He'd have the same influence no matter the ruling party."

"I take it you're unwilling to divulge the identity of this man here," Sir Christopher said, his dark eyes astutely scrutinizing me.

"Not at this time sir. He isn't aware of our interest in him as far as I know. And although I am certain of his connection to Mackee, and the foreign conspirators, so far I have no evidence to prove it."

"How then are you certain of his connection to the conspirators?"

"Through an American who has been in the Grenadines for the past month spearheading their final plans. Probably to also monitor the election and take care of any problems, such as the situation with Mackee."

Sir Christopher sat forward in his chair. Eyes bright and intense. "You've identified this person? What is being done about him?"

"He's been neutralized sir," I said, noting the flicker of lashes around Melanie's eyes.

"I was able to assembly certain information which I forwarded to the authorities in countries where this person does business, including the FBI and Special Branch. He will be occupied and distracted trying to salvage what remains of his organization," I said, hedging the truth, but I couldn't reveal the full extent of how we'd co-opted Dougan, or how we'd, that is to say Gage, had accomplished it.

"That explains the sudden change in activity," Melanie said. The Governor General and I turned our focus on her. Her glance alternated between our attentive gazes.

"You were aware of these developments?" Sir Christopher asked.

"No sir. I'm not always privy to what's taking place in the liaison offices. And I'm not sure they're completely read in to everything the Commissioner mentioned," an inquisitive stare directed on me. "However I am aware an abrupt change occurred during the weekend. The embassy no longer part of the investigative loop. Resources have been retasked to monitor a single individual on Mustique Island," closely observing my reaction as she said it.

"Sir, I'm not certain of the extent of Consul Barnes's influence in these matters," I lied, "But I'd strongly recommend no outside interference at this critical time." The prevarication served to both conceal my intimate knowledge of Melanie's relationship in the Embassy's liaison offices, and to also take her off the hook by making the request to run interference indirectly through the Governor General.

"Your reasoning Commissioner?" he said.

"This is the first, perhaps the only chance, to force the person behind all this into the open where the authorities can get at him sir," I said.

Melanie's eyes narrowed a fraction, her oblique observation of me intensified.

"How do you come to know all this Commissioner? Sir Christopher asked. "Given the U.S. and UK haven't made much progress up to now, or at least haven't been sharing it with us."

I smiled. My answer to the anticipated question already prepared.

"Those private sources you mentioned at our last tea sir," I said, a conspiratorial smile aimed at him.

The smile reciprocated, "Quite," he said.

Melanie's eyes and smile indicated a hidden amusement at this interaction.

"Were you aware Consul Barnes, these gardens were preceded only by your Bertram Garden in Philadelphia?" Sir Christopher said, changing the subject and reverting to genial host, refreshing our teacups. "It is the second oldest in the western Hemisphere, perhaps the oldest in the tropical world."

"I've read the literature Sir Christopher," she said. "And I've had the opportunity to stroll its magnificent grounds," her eyes casting a conspiratorial glance in my direction.

The conversation continued through two more cups of tea. No further mention of the business we'd been invited to discuss. Except at the end, before departing, and after I'd graciously offered a ride to Consul Barnes.

"I may count on your cooperation in this matter Consul Barnes, to take the Commissioner's request under advisement?" Sir Christopher said, his inflection turning the statement into a question.

"I will certainly do my best Sir Christopher."

Amid pleasant farewells Melanie and I departed. At the embassy house, a five-minute drive from Government House, we said our own farewells. Thirty minutes later, changed, and driving my leased Toyota Liberty, I parked in the embassy house's enclosed garage.

She'd also changed, into a short daffodil colored sundress. Unhindered by undergarments, the light fabric draped her sensual curves in an enticing manner. She greeted me carrying a low-ball glass of Jack Daniels neat. Her welcoming kiss warm, moist, and tender. Her mouth pressed mine open.

Our tongues met, tasting, entwining. An intensifying fervor grew inside us both. An immediate, ravenous hunger, which would neither be denied nor delayed, overwhelmed us, carrying away the lower half of my clothing.

She hiked the sundress's short hem above her waist. I entered her where we stood. A sharp inhalation as she accepted the hard fullness inside her. She raised her right leg onto my hip. My left arm held the raised leg, my right hand pressed against the rounded mounds of her buttocks, assisting her thrusts, establishing a rhythm with my own, the intensity growing. Gasping breaths exploded onto each other's faces. Bared teeth clicked as our mouths met. Throaty grunts escaped her open mouth as we thrust against each other. A familiar tightening in my groin as her soft smooth vaginal muscles clutched my sliding shaft. Ready to explode. A spasm seized her. Her raised leg quivered against my arm. The straight leg weakened at the knee. Her face pressed into my shoulder. Soft moaning through her open mouth. Her teeth against my skin, nipping into my flesh. I held her tight. Held her from falling as the spasms shook her, eliciting my own trembling climax.

How we'd managed to remain standing an enduring mystery. My back ached from the awkward position, and from supporting her weight. The full impact of aching muscles dulled by the euphoric endorphins flooding through me. Pushed by the heavy pounding in my chest.

"It was never like this in my marriage," she said, unburying her face from my shoulder, her eyes bright, and brown, and sparkly, staring into mine.

"Me neither," I said.

"Or even before that. Dating in college. Before I was married. God I enjoy you." A smile stretched my lips, creasing the corners of my eyes. I cupped her flushed face in my hands. Pressed my lips gently against hers.

We warmed and ate a dinner of curried chicken, rice and peas, green vegetables and salad, prepared and left by the house staff.

"So that was a pleasant surprise this afternoon," she said around a mouthful of garden salad.

"Near jumped out of my skin when he invited me. Said our 'acquaintance' would be advantageous," I said chuckling. "Saved me having to wait until this evening to see you."

"A bit circumspect in your briefing," she said, a sly attentiveness in her gaze.

"He doesn't need to know the details. At least not yet," I said.

"Ah," she said, the eyes still searching. "I'm familiar with the phrase. Does it also include me?"

"Especially you. Not because you don't need to know. But my telling you would place us both in an awkward position. I prefer our other positions better."

She laughed. A short mirthful burst of sound like a sudden sneeze.

"But it'll be resolved soon," I said in a more serious tone. "It's why I can't afford any outside interference right now. Everyone will be brought into the loop when the time comes."

"Well I can run interference as you asked. At least give you a heads up if anything risky is headed your way."

"Thanks," I said.

"Don't thank me. Thank your Governor General. I know what you did there you devious devil," a mischievous smile on her flushed face. "Are you ever going to tell me how you've managed to orchestrate all this?" her head lightly lowered to the side, eyebrows raised, wide eyes staring up at me."

"Sometime. Maybe." I said. Aware of the effect her eyes had on me. "For now it's enough to tell you I have very resourceful friends," I said.

Her eyes, still fixed on mine, reached a silent decision. Nodding, she finished the remaining morsels on her plate.

Later we sat on the upstairs verandah outside the bedroom, enjoying a companionable silence, the pale lights of Kingstown and the harbor in the distance, an evening breeze cool against the skin. The breeze also kept the mosquitoes at bay. Melanie sipped from a glass of red wine. A snifter of Amaretto for me.

"You thought about what you'll do after this?" she asked, her voice soft and uncharacteristically lilting, the slightest hint of a wistfulness I'd never heard before. The future, our future, a subject we scrupulously avoided.

"Not really. Been kindda preoccupied with everything going on."

"Moving back to the States maybe?" Again, the slight questioning tone, seeking something beyond the question asked.

"My home is here in the Grenadines," I said, turning to peer into her eyes. "Why?"

"Just wondering out loud," she said.

"About?"

Hesitation stalled the answer on the tip of her tongue.

"What do you see when you think about us?" she asked instead, prodding the four ton bull elephant in the room. A constant presence. Seldom acknowledged.

"I can't picture it," I said in blunt honesty. The door finally opened. "But I want more. I want to be with you. Fall asleep every night with you. Wake up every morning with you.

"You don't think that might ruin what we have now?"

"It's what's missing from what we have now," I said. And after a moment, "But I won't ask you to sacrifice your career. And I'm not inclined to move back to the States."

We fell silent again. The subject finally broached, if only on the surface. Whatever answers we'd find would have to wait.

Later. Long, lingering lovemaking. Unhurried. A tender tantric journey during which we savored the smell, and taste, and touch of each other. Flesh against flesh. Taking each other to the peak, pausing, climbing ever higher, pausing again. Until we arrived at the sexual summit in an orgasmic avalanche, leaving us limp and listless, and asleep in each other's embrace.

CHAPTER 28

"You're humming again," Cecilia remarked as I strode across the outer office past her desk."

"Good Morning to you too Cissy," I said.

"Pleasant evening I suppose," she said, her eyes slyly questioning, her tone sarcastic.

I ignored her, continuing toward my office. I paused to stare at the Whittaker portrait on the wall adjacent my office door.

"Cissy," I said, turning to meet her gaze. "Very sweet, and appropriate. Thank you. From all of us."

She merely nodded.

Striding to my desk my thoughts focused on my three priorities for the day. Fredericks, the Mackee investigation, Dougan and Von Sachsen. I called Gage on our secure sat line.

"Any new developments?" I asked. "I'm worried I haven't heard from Dougan or Von Sachsen yet."

"Dougan tried slithering out from under your thumb. Snuck his wife and daughters away to a ranch he owns in Colorado. The place is under heavy guard. The photos and phone calls he received after they got there dissuaded him of any notion they were out of danger. If anything having them all in one place just made it easier to get to them. We're keeping up the pressure on him. He's in panic mode. Lots of phone calls to his offices, which have been raided as we intended. Lots of calls to his lawyers. And to Von Sachsen."

"Why haven't they called?" I insisted.

"Patience Mike," Gage said, his tone calm and even. "This game is all about waiting."

"Easier said than done," I said. "Waiting isn't one of the things I do well."

"We've cloned Dougan's phone and computer. Listening to all his calls and reading his texts and emails. Von Sachsen's a much cooler customer. But he's beginning to feel the heat too. The call will come soon."

"Your guy come up with anything on Fredericks?" I asked, switching gears.

"I've emailed you what we've got so far."

Nothing further to add by either of us, we disconnected.

My morning briefings proceeded as usual. Though the routine activities of the commissions of inquiry, Carnival, and electioneering, held less of my attention and interest. The police force as an institution satisfactorily handled the day-to-day criminal offences and disturbances. My only concern the political aftermath of Mackee's murder.

"De situation still tense Commisshunah," Huggins reported. People think de Mackee murder was politically motivated. Dey want to know what de government and police doin' 'bout it. Only de Carnival competitions keepin' de situation from boilin' over. No major pahty rallies scheduled while de competitions goin' on."

"Any unusual problems there?" I asked. My interest more about volatility in the crowds.

"De junior Carnival and junior pan fest competitions are over. Official results probably out by today. De Miss Carnival beauty pageant is dis evenin'. De soca Monarch tomorrow evenin'. J'Ouvert mornin' start dis comin' Friday with de street party and Mardi Gras over de weekend."

"And the crowds?"

"Victoria Park full for most of de competitions. We have a large police presence. De usual disorderly in public from drunkenness and some fights and assaults. But no major problems."

"Good. Now how about the Whittaker funeral?"

"De service scheduled for Monday afternoon so Vincy Mas don't interfere wid it. At de Anglican Parish Church in Layou. De family is from dat side. Dey waitin' to see if his brothers and any other relatives livin' in the States can make it home for de funeral. Honor guard and band from de Old Montrose Station. We still have to choose pall bearers."

"You already have three. Me, Samuel and Matthews," I said.

"Yes sir."

"That's it for now Reggie. Thank you."

I hadn't discussed the Mackee case, or Fredericks, or Dougan. Huggins might no longer be compromised, and though he'd been acting under duress, I'd never be able to totally trust him again. Like a spouse who claimed their cheating had been a one-time mistake, it left a raw scab on my soul.

Assistant Superintendent Taylor and I discussed the ongoing political fallout of the Mackee murder, reflected mainly in the public commentary and letters in the media. As we expected, unfounded and sometimes farfetched claims of a government and police conspiracy. Angry rants against the National Democracy Party attempting to steal the election through violence. Accusations of a hit list, with Mackee among the first of more to come.

"It's turning nasty," Taylor observed. "But not too many people paying attention. After Carnival people will begin paying attention to the election. And we're not saying much to de media."

"Nothing to say at this point, "I said. "It's an ongoing investigation. But we're gonna be caught in the middle no matter what. When the news comes out about Mackee's corruption, some people will look at it as politically motivated too."

"Maybe so. But the evidence against him is strong. Sergeant Ashton and even some of the gang members have implicated him."

"Only he's not around to either confirm or deny the accusations. And we haven't been able to find any of the money to tie him to the others. What about Mitchell?"

"We've collected sufficient cause to dismiss him from the force. Besides having evidence to charge him with serious offenses, including statements from Sergeant Ashton. And of course there is the hidden cash found on his boat."

"Maybe we can use the criminal charge as leverage to get him to give us more on Mackee," I said, thinking aloud. "Maybe help us find Mackee's money."

"Yessir."

"And Colin Browne?"

"As with Mitchell our inquiries have developed sufficient cause to dismiss him. But nothing of a criminal nature to charge him."

"Nothing to connect him to Mitchell, Ashton, Mackee or the gang?"

"Nothing sir. He just looked the other way and facilitated them. No one witnessed him receiving any money or other considerations. Probably angling for a promotion after you left office."

"And the media take on all this?"

"The press is full of Carnival news sir. Nothing about Browne or Mitchell. Probably won't see anything until the dismissals become official and are announced."

"Thanks Vince. Anything else?"

"Sir how you want to handle the Whittaker funeral with the media?"

"Just a press release regarding his death in the line of duty. No details regarding the undercover assignment, his background, or anything else. I've asked the family not to discuss it with the press. I think they'll hold up. Our local press won't invade their privacy the way the U.S. media would. The funeral is scheduled for Monday. Bring me something to look over before then."

"Yes sir," he said, departing after a brisk salute.

When Sammy arrived, I'd had time to peruse Gage's email. I still hadn't seen Sammy's report. He carried a file under his arm, which I assumed contained the report he'd completed the day before.

"That the item I asked for?"

"Yes Commissioner. I finished it last evening but you weren't available and I didn't want to just leave it." He handed me the file folder.

"That's fine Sammy. Thank you. Please, have a seat," I said, indicating the sitting area.

I joined him. I opened the file, speed reading as we sat.

Elon Fredericks, age fifty two. Born Kingstown, St. Vincent and the Grenadines. Only child of Desmond and Beatrice Fredericks. Father a successful local dry goods merchant, twelve stores around SVG. Mother also successful in real estate. Desmond educated abroad in the United States. Masters Degrees in business and marketing. A two year stint with the SVG tourism board promoting SVG. Left tourism board to begin a successful business advising U.S. clients on investing in SVG, later providing financing for some development projects. Registered agent under the Aliens Holding Ordinance for foreign clients wanting to own property and businesses in SVG. Assumed management of local family businesses after father died, and mother retired and moved abroad. Extensive real estate holdings in SVG, including a residence in Cane Garden, an estate in the Richmond Park area on the Windward side, and another in Richmond Vale on the Leeward side. Also owns partnerships in the Buccament Bay and Canuoan resorts, and four other hotels. He advises government on finance and economic planning, security and foreign affairs. Married to an American, two children, boys, ages seven and ten. Spends about ten weeks total on SVG during the year. Two to three weeks at a time. Usually during Carnival and Christmas.

"Excellent work Sammy," I said, closing the file and laying it on the table. "Now I want you to follow him. But discreetly, from long range. I don't want him to even catch a whiff we're interested in him. I want to know where he goes, what he does, and who he sees. Document everything with photographs. If at any time you think he's made you, break contact immediately. And you report only to me."

"Yes sir," he said. A satisfied smile on his face. An assignment he'd been well trained for in the States.

"I'll clear it with your commander. Now get going."

"Yes sir," he repeated, offering a mild salute and heading for the door.

Gage's email had fleshed out details Sammy wouldn't have had access to or been able to obtain without tipping off Fredericks. Like Fredericks' U.S. real estate holdings, including a home in Miami and another in Brooklyn New York. Both owned by offshore corporations, which Gage listed. Or the criminal background checks which indicated no significant run-ins with U.S. law enforcement. Although he'd once been under scrutiny by the IRS. His off shore companies and tax havens eventually ruled legitimate. Still, an open question remained as to where he'd obtained the initial capital to finance foreign owned development projects in SVG. Gage had found links between three corporate entities connected to Fredericks, through which he funneled investment funds, and corporate entities controlled by Sachsen. He'd listed the corporations in his email. The connection still not amounting to direct proof against Fredericks.

I dialed Bernie Roger's extension.

"Morning Bernie," I said when he answered. "Any further developments in the Mackee case?"

"Unfortunately not Commisshunah. We had no hits wid de descripshun at immigration. If he come from off island and already left de island, he didn't do it tru' a poht' of entry. And nuttin' back from any poliss in de region we circulated de descripchun to. One t'ing though. Some of de witnesses say de sketch look like de man dey see in de van. But dey cyan be sure 'cause dey never get a good look at his face."

"Keep at it Bernie. Run down every lead. We have to find this man." I didn't mention my fear he might already be dead and buried where we might never find him.

"And Bernie, I need to borrow Sergeant Samuel for a few days."

"No problem Commisshunah."

"Thanks Bernie. Keep me posted."

Next I dialed Angela McKinley's extension.

"How's our girl doing?" I asked when she answered.

"Knows her way around finance and accounts," Angela said. "Wish I had more like her."

"I need to see her for a few minutes when you can spare her," I said.

"No problem Commisshunah. She'll be right up?"

"Thanks Angela," I said, disconnecting.

When Cecilia showed Elana in a few minutes later, I indicated the straight-backed armchair facing my desk.

"How're you fitting in?" I asked.

A shy smile parted her lips. "De work is similar Commisshunah. But I have to get used to working wid police. Dey have a real sense of duty and purpose. Not like de bank where most people had one eye on de clock all de time."

"Unfortunately it's not universal everywhere in the force. The FIU is new, they're staking out their territory. And AS McKinley is a motivated commander."

"Dat I can see sir."

"Anyway I have a little job for you," I said, getting to the point. "Here's a list of corporations and accounts I want FIU to check into. The first two at the top of the list especially. Cross reference them with the red flag list AS McKinley is already working on. I want to know which, if any, are registered with SVG offshore services, and all their transactions going back a year."

"And AS McKinley sir?"

"You may inform her of the particulars. But this list and your findings are not to be discussed within the unit. Just you, AS McKinley, and me."

"Understood Commisshunah."

I met Melanie for lunch at the Coconut Beach Hotel in Villa. Secluded. Sparsely occupied during the off season. An out of the way setting before her afternoon return flight to Barbados.

She'd arrived before me. Seated at an outdoor table close to the seawall separating the waterfront hotel from Indian Bay. The surf beat against the seawall in a deep booming bass sound. Her attire casual, tailored tan slacks, a powder blue shirred square neck short sleeve blouse, and black leather open toe, sling back flats. Her overnight garment bag and handbag draped over an empty chair.

"You okay. You seem a little tense," she said, rising to greet me, offering her cheek for the gentle kiss I planted there.

"A lot going on today," I said evasively.

"Wish we had time for me to make it go away."

I smiled. "If only wishing made it so." The sight of her stirred the longing I'd admitted to her the previous night.

A plump waitress, dressed in a canary color dress and white apron, approached to take our lunch order. Melanie selected sautéed chicken, sweet potatoes, pears and sweetened ice tea. I ordered a grilled Bonita sandwich and tall lemonade on ice.

"Sure you can't stick around another day or two?" I asked after the waitress departed.

"I really have to get back. And I want to catch up on what's been happening in the spook shop. You free for the weekend maybe?"

"Not sure. Can't make any plans with things coming to a head in the investigations."

"Just the investigations?" she asked, a sly inquiring lift of eyebrows. "You also seem a little distracted."

I smiled at her tender attentive gaze. Concealing, at least attempting to conceal, the impatient agitation within me. The wait for Dougan's damn phone call like sitting on a seat of nails, distracting me from the precious little time we had together.

"Like I said. A lot on my mind today."

"Well don't let me keep you from..."

"You're not," I interrupted. "Just my impatience showing. Waiting not my strong suit. But I'm trying not to let it spoil a single moment I have with you."

"I have a couple days free next week, including the weekend," she said. "I want to spend it with you. Maybe finish that talk we started last night," her eyes peering closely into mine.

"When a woman says we need to talk and has that look in her eyes, it usually spells trouble," I said.

"Not to worry," her smile brightening her face, her eyes crinkling at the corners and softening. "It's just that I want to spend more time with you too."

The lump forming in my throat dissolved. Replaced by a different sort of nervousness. A fluttering pulse rate and a skittish anxiety over where such a conversation might lead.

My damn cell phone rang. An undisclosed number. I swallowed hard. Goddamned hell of a time for him to call.

"I have to take this," I said, standing. My mood irretrievably altered, my eyes pleading for her understanding.

"Being together means there'll be times when I'll need to do that too. And things I won't be able to discuss with you," she said, her soft eyes expressing consummate sincerity and understanding.

My eyes beamed a silent thank you, and a silent I love you as I stepped out of earshot. As expected, Dougan's voice when I answered, announcing without preamble or greeting, another party conferencing in on the call.

"You have my attention Mr. Daniels." The voice deep and dispassionate. Cultured and confident.

"Commissioner of Police Daniels," I said into the phone. "It may not mean much to you, but it does mean I'm able to shatter your world."

The voice on the other end ignored the rebuke and threat. Wouldn't be baited.

"It is my understanding you wish to meet," he said, the voice like a winter wind on an exposed neck.

"Your understanding is correct," I said.

"And why would I wish to do that?"

"We may dispense with the dance," I said. "If you weren't prepared to meet we wouldn't be having this conversation. And I'm sure you can appreciate, as I do, the importance of looking your opponent in the eye."

"Indeed Commissioner. Shall we say in forty eight hours then?"

"Why take the time." I said. "It's to your benefit to get this over with as soon as possible."

"This isn't a negotiation Commissioner. You've made it rather difficult for me to travel openly. Arrangements need to be made."

"In two days then. After that there'll be no reason for us to meet."

An audible click disconnected the call. I stood staring at the phone. Overcome by an odd sensation, like a heavy burden falling from my shoulders. After sixteen months of a vague, unshakable, haunting anxiety initiated by an attempt on my life, followed by the murder of a friend and a visiting American, Jolene's narrow escape in New York, the collapse of a government, and near takeover of an entire nation, an end finally in sight.

"Do I need to know what that was all about," Melanie asked when I returned to the table.

Our lunch had arrived while I'd been on the phone.

"Not right now," I said. "What I can tell you is that it's more imperative than ever the spooks stay out of my yard for the next few days."

"I can't guarantee it," she said, delicately slicing her chicken into bite-sized cubes, spearing a piece on her fork and placing it in her mouth. "But as promised, I'll try to run interference, and give you a heads up if I'm unable to hold them off from coming your way. Maybe if I knew what you don't want them to see."

"No. That's too dangerous for a whole lot of reasons I can't go into right now," I said, biting into my sandwich. When I'd chewed and swallowed enough to allow me to speak again I said, "Besides, I don't want them getting any ideas which might steer them to look where I don't want them looking." A swallow of lemonade cleared my gullet.

"You still have a lot of good will capital with the FBI. Maybe they'll be willing to help."

"If I need their help I'll ask, through my contacts in New York and Washington, not the liaison office."

"You sure you know what you're doing Mike?" Concern in her voice, and in the clear brown eyes peering into mine. "Sure you're not getting in over your head on this?"

I smiled at her eyes, "I've got the best people in the world watching my back," I assured her.

As though on cue my cell phone rang again. This time I recognized the satellite access code. Gage. I accepted the call at the table.

"I was just thinking about you," I said.

"Looks like it's on," he said.

"You were right as usual," I said.

"The next call will be to set the meeting. Time and place. We'll need to talk about that. When can we get together?"

"I'll have to get back to you. I still have some things to wrap up here."

"Soon then," he said, disconnecting. As succinct as always.

Melanie ate the last bite of chicken and sweet potato remaining on her plate. She dabbed her mouth on a red cloth napkin, her eyes curious and penetrating.

"You didn't leave the table that time. So?"

"A very resourceful friend who has my back, as I was telling you. My best friend, truth be told."

"A best friend?" Her head tilting back, eyes wide beneath raised eyebrows. "You've never mentioned him before."

"No I haven't," I said, my gaze leveled at her.

"But why...?" She paused at the slight shake of my head. The curious uncertainty in her eyes replaced by a trusting acceptance.

"I can tell you trust him though."

"How in the world can you tell that?"

"The way you spoke with him, refer to him. Even though you didn't really say much at all."

"Well you're right. I trust him with my life. I'm hoping you'll get to meet him sometime soon."

"Very mysterious," she said, finishing the last of her ice tea.

"You have no idea," I said, returning her smile.

CHAPTER 29

I returned to my office after seeing Melanie off at the airport. And I'd reached a decision. The anxiety of the past year and a half replaced by an itch to get moving. For action. The final act drawing to a close. The Bogeyman, a shapeless shadowy specter haunting my dreams for so long, lured to the trap. Waiting for the weekend would tax my patience's meager reserve to its limit.

I called Gage. "Listen," I said when he answered. "This waiting is going to drive me crazy. How about we get together this evening?"

"Good. We have a lot to do if we're gonna get ahead of Von Sachsen."

"What does that mean?"

"He's probably going to wait until the last moment to give you the place and time for the meet. If he even does. He'll want to maintain control of that. We need to figure out the meeting place before he calls."

"And how do you propose doing that? Especially if he's going to travel clandestinely as he said."

"We have the advantage of knowing his destination. We work back from there. It's tracking one-o-one."

"Awright," I said. "Let's meet at my place. I'll catch the six o'clock ferry."

"How about we meet aboard Wherever. Jo promised to cook dinner. I'll pick you up at the ferry wharf."

Waiting for the workday to end challenged my self-control. I distracted myself in mundane, routine administrative tasks, while monitoring the ongoing investigations. The Mackee murder, FIU, Elon Fredericks. None of which entirely dispelled the thoughts uppermost in my brain, Godfried Wilhelm Von Sachsen. And Gage.

Tracking one-o-one for Christ's sakes. I'll bet he'd been tracking human prey most of his adult life.

The forty-minute ferry ride across the channel seemed interminable. The MV Admiral sparsely occupied for the time and day of the week. Most people were headed in the opposite direction for Kingstown, to attend Vincy Mas competitions.

Port Elizabeth quiet and tranquil as the ferry approached the dock. The Harbor's businesses closed for the day. A few dollar vans and taxis parked along the main road. Not much pickings from the handful of disembarking passengers.

Gage met me at the end of the wharf. Wherever's dinghy pulled up onto the waterfront's beach. We rode in silence across the placid harbor, skimming across the lightly lapping water past beachfront bars, restaurants, and hotels. Past the manicured landscaping of the Plantation House Hotel. We skirted the point into Tony Gibbons Bay, and the pristine crescent shaped Princess Margaret Beach. All the while, the sun hung low in an amber streaked sky, nearing its day ending slide below the horizon.

Rounding the point into Lower Bay Wherever's distinctive raked masts and sensual lines appeared in full view. No matter how many times I'd seen her, she still drew the eye, capturing my attention and provoking an admiring gaze. From her sharp bow, the gentle slope of her deck, the graceful curve of her side, to the sloped reversed transom. Her head, snug on her mooring, nodding as if in greeting when the dinghy approached.

Stepping into Wherever's salon I understood the reason for Gage's suggestion to meet on board. Not only the succulent aromas of a home cooked meal emanating from the galley, but the attention grabbing items laid out in the starboard salon, a step down from the rest of the cabin.

A variety of items lay atop the varnished mahogany coffee table. Some readily recognizable. A riflescope. The professional kind. Controls for elevation, windage, parallax, illumination, magnification, and focus. And probably a mil-dot reticle display I guessed. A spotter's scope lay next to it. A rifle stock, missing the adjustable cheek and shoulder pieces. The detached parts lay close by on the table. A long black metal cylinder, which I took to be a rifle barrel, and a much shorter cylindrical tube. A suppressor. A disassembled rifle bolt. And an empty cartridge magazine, next to a handful of loose rifle cartridges. The lethal pointed ends, partially jacketed, shined to a gleaming gloss. Forty caliber by my guess.

Other items I didn't recognize, though probably parts of the rifle assembly. And other gear which didn't appear to belong to a rifle.

"Where did you...?" unable to complete the question. My eyes riveted in disbelief on the coffee table.

"Shipment of engine parts," Gage said, stepping around me to set the dinette. "Came in yesterday."

Jolene stepped across the cabin carrying two steaming platters. Baked kingfish steaks heaped on one. Sliced roast breadfruit and lightly seared plantains on the other. Bare feet poked beneath faded blue jeans. Her waist covered by the untucked tail of a man's pale blue, short sleeved shirt. Her breasts unfettered beneath the cotton fabric. She leaned sideways to plant a greeting kiss on my cheek before setting the platters on the dinette.

"Rented a plane too," she said, in a matter-of-fact tone. "A surplus Britten-Norman Islander from SVG Air."

"A plane?" My befuddled brain attempting to assimilate it all.

"Might come in handy," he said. "Need to be prepared for any eventuality. And too many people are familiar with your Seneca. Sit," indicating a seat at the dinette. "Dinner's ready."

I loaded my plate. My appetite stimulated by the mouth-watering odors surrounding the table. Biting into the kingfish my taste buds recognized the butter, limejuice, garlic, onions, salt, hot scotch bonnet peppers, and splash of red wine in which it'd been seasoned. The baked breadfruit crispy on the outside, soft and succulent in the middle. The meal accompanied by sweet plantains, and a green salad of fresh leafy lettuce, tomatoes, sliced cucumbers, and sweet red peppers.

"Some preparation you've got going there," I said to Gage, my gaze sweeping across the coffee table. A long swallow of cold Heineken washed down my first mouthfuls. "What concerns me though is leaving the time and place, not to mention the timing, up to Von Sachsen. Sure that's a good idea?"

"Giving him the illusion of control works to our advantage," Gage said. "And his choice of meeting place might tell us how he plans to kill you."

My fork, a chunk of kingfish speared on it, froze on the way to my mouth.

"So heartwarming of you to take it so lightly," I said, laying the loaded fork on my plate.

A smile stretched his lips, hard sincere eyes held mine in an oddly reassuring gaze.

"We've got your back Mike. I won't let them harm a hair on that grey head of yours," the smile broadening, producing one of my own.

"But first we need to get ahead of him," he said.

"You said on the phone you have to backtrack him. How?"

"I know someone who can get us advance info on private aircraft and charters coming into the region. He'll disguise his identity, but the pilots still have to file an international flight plan. We need to get hold of any last minute bookings for high-end resorts. The exclusive private types. PSV, Palm Island, Buccament Bay on St. Vincent. I don't believe he'll use Mustique. It's been compromised along with Dougan. We're still monitoring Dougan's phone and computer by the way, and though Von Sachsen is being careful, Dougan might let something slip."

"I may have a way of getting that information," I said. "But then what? He'll probably use false identities. Maybe not even a name but some corporation."

"Exactly. We cross reference the lists against all the companies and corporations we've linked to him. Anyway, it's just to cover the bases. My bet is he's going for something more private. No reservations, no paper trail, no staff. A private home or estate. Secluded. Where he controls the environment. So we also need a list of foreign owned private estates fitting the bill."

"I may actually have that information already," I said. "I've had the Financial Intelligence Unit working on that, particularly if funds were funneled through off shore entities established here in St. Vincent and the Grenadines."

Jolene had finished the small portion on her plate before either Gage or I. Her enchanting eyes glanced back and forth between us as we discussed tracking the Bogeyman. Her name for the person who'd haunted our dreams for so long.

Gage stood from the dinette. He stepped across to the salon. Returning, he held two garments I'd noticed earlier draped across the settee.

"Wear this," he said, handing me what appeared to be a white undershirt. The soft material like any other tee shirt to the touch. But I knew immediately from its heft it was no ordinary shirt.

"Ballistic vest," he said. "An ultra-high density molecular material, still classified. Superior to Kevlar, Spectra, or any other material commercially available."

"You won't even know you're wearing it Mike," Jolene said, breaking her silence. "Feels more comfortable than the real thing. I wear mine a lot, even without a reason. Saved my life in New York."

"And this," Gage said, holding a full-length rain cloak with an attached hood.

"Expecting rain?" I asked.

"The material is also anti-ballistic. But it also masks body heat. You won't need to wear it. Just carry it with you. Like you're expecting rain," he grinned. "I expect Von Sachsen to have satellite support. Probably one of his own. He owns enough of them. Since I expect the meet will be at night it'll probably be scanning in infrared. He and his team will probably have some kind of tracker on them to indicate their positions. If you need to make a break for it, or hide, you put this on. You'll be invisible to his eyes overhead."

"You believe it might come to that?" I asked, concern edging into my voice.

"Missions seldom go as planned." His calm confident voice a contradiction of the unsettling statement. But my experience in law enforcement had taught me that lesson too.

"We'll plan for multiple contingencies," he continued. "Multiple points or ingress and egress; backups for the backup. The mission is to derail Sachsen's plans, while keeping ours on the tracks. We need to go over exit strategies. Over here," he said heading for the salon.

I rose from the table. Followed him. Jolene seized the opportunity to clear the vacated dinette. Bearing fresh Heinekens, she joined us on the settee.

"Back up a second," I said. "If Von Sachsen will have satellite coverage how do we overcome that advantage?"

"We have the cloaks. And we'll have our own satellite coverage," Gage said, a predatory smile creasing the lower portion of his face, not reaching the eyes.

"How in hell did you manage to get hold of a satellite?" I asked in stunned wonder, aware after the words left my mouth it'd probably be best not to ask.

"I bought time on a commercial satellite for a little geographic survey project of the Grenadines."

"My God Gage! That's gonna run into the millions."

"Not to worry. Von Sachsen's footing the bill, though he doesn't know it."

"Downright diabolical," I said, shaking my head.

"I prefer poetic," Gage said.

"We'll communicate with these," he said, picking up a closed box from the table and handing it to me.

I opened the lid, revealing four cell phones, each accompanied by a tiny glass earpiece.

"The earbuds are tuned to the bluetooth frequencies of the phone," Gage explained. "The cell phone signals will indicate our positions. Jo will be able to monitor and track us using an overlay on the sat image."

"What if they search me and take my cell phone." I asked.

"They'll probably pat you down for weapons. Let them. If you're unarmed, it'll add to their confidence. The beauty about these phones is they can be activated remotely. When you first meet them, your phone will be turned off. That way if they wand you they won't pick up any transmissions. When the phone is activated, it'll still look like it's off. As long as the phone is within a quarter mile radius of you we'll still have coms. The earbuds fit right up into your ear, virtually undetectable unless they check your ear with an otoscope. But Mike, if they try to take the cloak or your phone, or do anything you're not comfortable with, you find some excuse to walk away, reminding them of the threat hanging over Dougan's family and Von Sachsen's empire. But even then it's only a diversion."

"But with that kind of threat hanging over their heads, why would Von Sachsen risk killing me. And what do you mean by only a diversion?"

"In the first place, Von Sachsen doesn't give a shit about Dougan or his family. Dougan became expendable the moment we identified him and his connection to Von Sachsen. And second, killing you is a matter of where and when. Not if. Doing it here after the meeting is only one option. Von Sachsen wants to see your cards before making that decision. But don't underestimate him, or overlook the wild card. He may have something up his sleeve for getting out from under all this. Some sort of deal with a foreign intelligence service. Maybe even one of ours. Or maybe he's quietly pulling in his tentacles and moving his tent somewhere where no one can touch him until it's safe for him to surface again. He's not the type to forgive or forget."

I nodded. "And this diversion?"

"Part of your exit strategy," Gage said, reaching below the coffee table and handing me a dark brown leather attaché case. My gaze shifted between the case and Gage in bewildered curiosity.

"You'll be bringing him files right? Just not the ones he's expecting. We'll play it like we played Dougan. I'll prep them before the meeting. You'll carry the files in that," he said, indicating the case.

"Okay," I said. Logical enough I thought.

"The case is constructed of an explosive polymer," he said in the same impassive voice. My head swiveled to face him, my mind disbelieving my ears, my gaze boring into dispassionate eyes.

"Powerful enough to take out a medium-sized house," he said, holding my stare. Ice in his cold eyes. "It can be armed manually. Or remotely by either Jolene or me. And detonated remotely by either of us. When it's armed, it also activates a signal jammer that'll scramble any frequencies except our own. Von Sachsen will lose coms with his base, his satellite, and his men. It'll mask our signals, but won't jam them."

"Explain the explosive," I said. My voice unexpectedly low. Hard like his gaze.

"It's your exit. Maybe the only way of getting you out alive if things go south. Look Mike," he said, his voice, eyes, his entire demeanor changing from hard boiled to protective concern. "I'm not leaving anything to chance with this guy. Not where your life is concerned. I don't know his intentions or his strategy. I do know he'll set up this meet to box you in. Leave you no way out. In his shoes I'd call at the last moment, and provide transportation I control, so you'll have no idea of the destination until you get there. It leaves you without your own transportation. It's a trap Mike. And that briefcase is your only chance of springing it. That and having transportation waiting to pick you up. We'll need one more person for that job."

"I know who," I said, surrendering to Gage's logic and his prescient reading of the tactical situation. And it occurred to me, since uncovering the identities of Dougan and Von Sachsen, Gage had been thinking multiple moves ahead. Had already envisioned this scenario and prepared for it. The equipment littering the coffee table and salon ordered well in advance.

"As soon as we pinpoint the location for the meeting we'll set up your transportation and multiple routes of egress," he said. "One more thing." He picked up a small round object from the coffee table. "Button camera. Activated by the cell phone. When the phone is on, this is too. The feed is relayed through the phone. We'll have eyes and ears inside your meeting Mike. And eyes overhead. Jo will quarterback the op from Wherever."

"So this is what working with him is like," I said to Jolene. "Must have been a blast in New York."

"Watch, listen, and learn Mike. Like I did," Jolene said, a confident smile on her face. "He won't let anything happen to you." Her mesmerizing eyes, light amber in the low cabin lighting, and upward tilt of delicate eyebrows, conveyed absolute conviction.

"Now for your story," Gage said.

"What story?"

"Von Sachsen is coming here to find out how you know what you do. And who you've shared it with. He'll assume for a small island cop to have done what you have, there must be a group behind this. A group you're working for. He'll want to know who. You have to be prepared for those questions. Otherwise he'll know you're just blowing smoke. Then there's the reason for wanting to meet in the first place. The quid you're offering for his quo. He probably already assumes that's just a ruse. A lure to get him here. But he has to take the risk to determine what you know and who might be behind it. He'll be very paranoid and therefore unpredictable."

"Okay. So what's the story?"

"Not just the story. But how you tell it," Gage said, the predatory smile reappearing.

We went through it all again. Well into the night. Coffee replaced the beers. We covered as much detail as possible without knowing the actual meeting place. On that topic I had a list of tasks for the office in the morning.

"You think Carlson was working for Von Sachsen?" I asked, close to leaving.

"Don't know," Gage said. He may've been part of the group or just a hired hand. For some reason Von Sachsen needed Ramirez out of the way. Probably to keep Ramirez's territorial feud from disrupting his plans for St. Vincent and the Grenadines."

"The irony is if Carlson's hadn't tried to recruit you by shooting me," I said, "Van Sachsen might never have appeared on our radar. His entire operation is unraveling because of that one tactical decision. I think I understand now," my gaze rising to meet Jolene's, "why Carlson had to die. Gage couldn't take the chance of word getting back to Von Sachsen about us, and especially Gage." Jolene's eyebrows rose in silent acknowledgement.

"You saw this coming?" I said, switching my gaze to him, wonderment in my voice. "From way back then?"

"Something," he said.

CHAPTER 30

Gage occupied my thoughts as I lay in bed waiting for sleep. After six years he remained a mystifying enigma. And if tonight were any example, a more subtle, potent, and devastating weapon than I'd ever imagined. Possessing the strategic mind of a machine. Programmed to foresee and thwart every possible contingency and scenario. In his characteristic succinctness he'd responded modestly to my question regarding Carlson. I'd always thought he'd killed Carlson simply as an act of vengeance. But how differently would things have turned out for all of us, for St. Vincent and the Grenadines, if Gage had left him alive? No doubt in my mind Gage had sensed the Bogeyman before the rest of us.

In the morning I awoke enervated and eager to initiate my tasks. The impatient anxiety of waiting banished. I knew it wouldn't last. I'd delegate the tasks and the waiting would commence all over again.

Arriving at Central Police Station I headed directly to the Financial Investigations Unit. I tended to shy away from such unexpected appearances, my presence disrupting normal activities amid the flurry of formality.

"As you were everyone," I said as Assistant Superintendent Angela McKinley stepped from her office into the bullpen to greet me.

"Commisshunah. Good morning sir. Su'prised to see you down heah. Something special you needed sir?"

"Yes Angela. And fast," I said, indicating her office.

She followed me into the small enclosure, closing the door behind her. The louver blind hanging over the door's upper glass pane remained open. I handed her the list I'd hastily scribbled the night before and refined on the ride over from Bequia.

"Most of that information you probably already have," I said. "I need you to pull it together, collate it, fill in any missing gaps, and have it ready for me as soon as you can. This is your only priority today Angela," I emphasized.

"Yes sir, I'll get right on it" she said, studying the handwritten sheet I'd handed her.

"Can you read my scribble okay?"

Lifting her gaze from the sheet she smiled. "No problem Commisshunah."

"Thanks Angela. Call me the second it's ready."

Deputy Commissioner Huggins office my next stop. His secretary, mid thirties, pretty, dark coffee complexion, inquisitive eyes, straight broad nose and red painted lips, sprang from behind her desk as I entered Huggins' outer office.

"Is he in?"

"Yes Commisshunah. I'll just..."

"No need to announce me Cheryl" I interrupted, as she reached for the intercom on her desk. "I just need a moment."

I knocked on the heavy wood door to Huggins' office, turning the brass knob and pushing it open to his "yes?" in response to my knock.

Huggins glanced up from a file on his desk as I entered. His eyebrows rose and his eyes opened wide behind the spectacles. He sprang to attention from his chair, the back of his knees knocking it backward. He saluted.

"As you were Reggie," I said, closing the door behind me.

"Commisshunah. Good morning Sir. I was just preparin' to come up to see you for de morning briefing."

"I'm in a hurry Reggie," I said. "We'll dispense with today's briefing if there's nothing new or significant."

"Nuttin' Sir."

"Good. Then I need a favor."

He'd remained standing behind the desk as I hadn't taken a seat.

"Anyt'ing Sir. Anyt'ing," his grateful enthusiasm slightly embarrassing.

"You haven't heard what it is yet," I said.

"After what you did for me and my family Commisshunah. Anyt'ing."

"Your friend at immigration. The one who always knows in advance when a really important guest is coming for a stay in the islands."

"Yes sir," his tone less confident. Frown lines appeared on the dark forehead. "Dey not involved wid dis t'ing?"

"No. Nothing like that," I assured him.

"Dey not doin' anyt'ing illegal Commisshunah. Just facilitatin' de entry more privately. And dey discreet about who dey tell. Dey might let de papers know if it's a celebrity or such, but nuttin' illegal about that."

"Isn't what this is about," I said. "I need some of that advance information. I need to know if there's been any recent reservations like that at any of the private resorts. Or anything in the next couple of days. Big money. Would be very hush-hush. Can you reach out to your friend for me?"

"Dis havin' anyt'ing to do wid our foreign problem?"

"Yes. But that's for our ears only. And I need the information right away Reggie."

"No problem Commisshunah."

"Thanks," I said, departing his office.

Back in my office I contacted Sammy. Unaware of his tactical situation, and whether a ringing cell phone might compromise him, I sent a text message to call me as soon as convenient.

Damn waiting again, as I'd anticipated. According to the messages Cecilia handed me, I had a late morning appointment. A meeting I didn't particularly look forward to, but in this instance, it might provide a needed distraction.

The modern white four story Administration Building housing St. Vincent's government offices, stood opposite the Central Police Station, on the far side of Bay Street, right on the waterfront. I navigated the busy thoroughfare, jaywalking around rushing oncoming traffic rather than using the intersection.

Prime Minister Arturo Bacchus, expecting me, met me at the door to his office when his secretary announced me. He ushered me into the spacious corner office overlooking Kingstown Harbor. Bequia visible in the distance on the bright clear day. A large desk stood in one corner of the walnut paneled room, the national flag unfurled on a pole behind it. On the walls framed photographs of previous Prime Ministers, and the obligatory portrait of Her Majesty Queen Elizabeth, taken some forty years before. He led me to a sitting area against the far wall, next to the windows and the view.

"Have you had a chance to take in the Carnival activities Commissioner?" he asked in his bland, unassuming voice.

"No Prime Minister," I said. "I actually haven't had the time."

"Pity. Seems to get better every year."

He hadn't offered refreshments. No coffee or tea, or a cold drink. Good. I thought. This may turn out to be pleasantly short.

We didn't have the same relationship as his predecessor and I had. The man who'd appointed me to the Commissioner of Police post. A man I considered a friend. Who'd allowed himself to become ensnared in a situation resulting in his resignation, the collapse of his government, and the near takeover of the nation. To say Bacchus and I liked each other would be a stretch, but we accorded each other the respect due our respective offices.

I noted the contemplative furrows forming, disappearing and reforming on his charcoal toned forehead as he sought an opening for the topic he wished to discuss. The animated forehead merged seamlessly into a bald pate, bordered on both sides by cropped salt and pepper hair, above small, compact ears. I knew exactly what he wanted to discuss, but waited for him to broach the subject in his own time and fashion.

Intelligent in his own manner, Bacchus had been a competent, if technocratic caretaker. But he possessed neither

the political savvy of his predecessor, nor the sparkling cha-
risma of the opposition leader, who appeared a shoo-in as the
next Prime Minister.

"Commissioner, what can you tell me regarding the
current status of your investigation into MP Mackee's murder?" he asked, phrasing the question as though it caused him
physical pain.

"Nothing beyond what I've already told you Prime Minister. We haven't been able to locate the man we believe did
the shooting. We've circulated a description, but so far nothing has come of it."

"A pity to hear that," he said. "But I am more interested
in any information you may have of a political nature. I'm sure
I don't have to tell you what's being written in the papers and
said on the TV and radio."

"I'm aware Prime Minister," I said, studying his face,
peering into his eyes. Had he asked because he knew I'd been
holding back information? I hadn't informed him of Mackee's
connection to the gang, or the corrupt constables, or God
forbid, Elon Fredericks. So far we'd been able to keep a lid on
those aspects of the investigation. I wasn't about to share it.
Not even with the Prime Minister. Not this close to getting
Von Sachsen.

"Was there something specific?" I asked, studying the
dark irises as he pondered and responded to the question.

"All these rumors and stories being bandied about. I
realize it may just be electioneering, but I wonder if there is
any truth behind any of it."

"Prime Minister, it's an ongoing investigation. There's
no telling what might eventually be uncovered. But I can tell

you sir, with absolute certainty, what's been written and said in the press is utter nonsense."

"Thank you Commissioner," he said, standing. The meeting at an end. "Please keep me informed." He extended his hand.

I shook his hand and he escorted me to the door.

"And do try to enjoy at least some of the Carnival Commissioner," he said, a weak parting smile as he dismissed me.

Sweltering midday heat greeted me on the street after the air-conditioned Administration Building. Vehicular traffic raced along Bay Street. Lunchtime pedestrian traffic more congested than when I'd arrived.

I headed south toward the wharfs, deciding on a leisurely lunch and delaying my return to the office. Only more waiting awaited me there. The ambient noise, color, and bustling activity of daytime Kingstown surrounded me. Car, van and truck horns amid the thumping beat of soca and reggae music. Vociferous street vendors hawked their wares. And the excited preparations for the J'Ouvert costume parade and street 'jump up' on the weekend.

Crossing James Street an odd sensation tickled the nape of my neck. I hadn't been a patrol deputy in close to thirty years. My street skills rusty and dull. But the unmistakable sensation of being followed, palpable on the back of my neck.

I crossed Bay Street, dodging traffic and the ubiquitous wheelbarrow pushcarts. I scanned the storefront windows in front of me, checking the reflections behind me. Nothing attracted my attention. Raw nerves and paranoia from closing in on Von Sachsen? Or the stirring of a long unused instinct?

I continued walking south. Abruptly stepped into the Cobblestone Inn. As good a place as any for lunch. An ideal choice actually. The building, dating back to 1814, had been turned into a charming little hotel, the renovations recreating the original Georgian cobblestone architecture.

Its open-air third floor restaurant suited my immediate purposes. Besides a top-notch kitchen, anyone following me to the restaurant couldn't help but be seen. If they followed. They might simply wait at the ground floor bar. But the quaint architecture might also work to my advantage. I stood beneath a cobblestoned archway, covering a cobblestoned stairway, leading to the upper floors. The archway hid me from view of the front entrance.

A man entered. Tall. His build sturdy and compact. His reddish sun burnt complexion, set him apart. And his dress. Tan tropical slacks, a lime green polo shirt under a light summer jacket. A bit warm for the tropical heat. Perhaps concealing a weapon. Wary eyes casually scanned the foyer. He stepped through another archway to survey the bar.

I continued up to the roof, selected a table, and sat. My cell phone rang after the waiter departed. Sergeant Samuel.

"Afternoon Sammy," I said into the phone, my gaze glued to the restaurant's entrance.

"Commissioner, you asked for me to call sir."

"I have another special job for you. Won't be until Friday, so it shouldn't interfere with what you're doing. How's that going by the way?"

"Starting to have a dislike for stakeouts sir."

I smiled. "I need to brief you on this job for Friday. Anyway you can get away to swing by the office?" I'd hoped to arrange a meeting where I wouldn't have to pull him off Fredericks' tail. But my own tail made it risky.

"Looks like I might have a two hour window sometime dis afternoon. I'll let you know Commissioner."

"Good," I said, as the man entered the restaurant, spotted me, and walked over to the bar. I avoided gazing directly at him or in his direction, my phone conversation occupying my attention.

"I'll see you then," I said and disconnected.

In my peripheral vision the man spoke for a few seconds to the bartender, as though asking a question or making arrangements for dinner. Just another hotel guest. He turned and retreated down the stone stairway.

The waiter arrived bearing my conch roti platter and lemonade. The aroma of curried conch and potatoes appetizing. He'd also delivered a copy of the Vincentian newspaper I'd requested. I called Gage as I ate.

"I think Von Sachsen subscribes to your backups for the backups philosophy," I said when he answered. "I'm being followed."

"Not unexpected," he said in the calm nonchalant manner I suddenly found irrationally irritating. "You make him?"

"Yes. And I have a photo. I was on my cell when he showed up."

"He probably isn't alone. Von Sachsen's covering his bases. Hoping he'll learn something before the meet. You and I know it's a waste of time. But in the meantime you might have some fun leading them around."

"Yeah right." I snorted. "Listen. I may have some raw data for you by this afternoon. I'll email everything over as soon as I have it. And I'm sending you the photo of the guy tailing me."

"Good. We'll talk later," he said and disconnected.

I ate leisurely after sending the image. Confident of Gage's secure communications net. I flipped through the paper, prolonging the time when I'd have to return to the office. Maybe I should take Gage up on his suggestion. Give these guys a little walking tour of Kingstown.

Much of the paper covered Carnival news. Recent competition winners, upcoming competitions, and preparations for the big weekend. Sports coverage included articles on the inter island Hairoun cricket competition between island teams, and the Premier Division cricket championship taking place at the Arnos Vale cricket ground. Not much on politics or the upcoming election.

Except on the editorial, commentary, and letters pages in the middle section of the paper. I scanned a few. The usual political rants. One party or the other driving the country to ruin. The continuing controversy over Vincentian passports and citizenship being granted to foreigners investing in St. Vincent and the Grenadines. The money going into party coffers. I normally didn't pay much attention to the editorials, comments and letters. Much of it opinionated nonsense. I had Taylor for that chore. But it helped pass the time, and some of the letters were often amusing in their peculiar colloquial Vincentian manner. Also the Prime Minister's question had piqued my curiosity. Perhaps someone trolling too close to the truth.

I decided on a long walk back to the office. Up James to Middle Street, a narrow cobblestoned lane flanked on both sides by stores. Usually a bustling throng of street vendors and commercial activity. An ideal place to lose a tail.

Though losing the tail was not my intention. I proceeded along the narrow lane shadowed from the oppressive sun by two story buildings on either side. Its normal congestion diminished by the long Vincentian lunch break. My stride purposeful. Past the pastel red and orange Bridge House. Luncheon customers filled its outdoor dining tables. Midway along the block, between Egmont and Hillsboro Streets, close to the station, my cell phone rang. Samuel.

"Commissioner, looks like I'll have dat window to meet," he announced when I answered. "I can be dere in about half an hour."

"See you then," I said, hanging up. I'd heard engine sounds in the background during the call, the revving engine accompanying shifting gears. On the road somewhere, I concluded.

At the office Cecilia handed me a stack of messages. "AS McKinley has been asking if you're available," she said.

"If she's back from lunch tell her I'm here. And let me know the moment Sergeant Samuel arrives."

"Yes Commissioner," a fleeting smile at the mention of Samuel.

Cecilia ushered Angela McKinley into my office twenty minutes later. I'd been returning phone calls, and reading through a report left by Assistant Superintendent Taylor, when she arrived. I indicated the chairs facing my desk. She remained standing while I completed the call, saluting after I'd hung up the phone.

"At ease Angela," I said, indicating the chair again.

"What do you have," I said when she sat, meeting her steady, forthright gaze. She hadn't worked the streets for long as a constable, and had a brief stint in CID. But already she possessed the hard, penetrating, suspicious, discerning stare of a street wise cop.

She handed a file across the desk. "De information you requested Commisshunah,"

I accepted the file, opened it, scanning the pages within it. The buzzing intercom on my desk interrupted me.

"Sergeant Samuel," Cecilia announced.

"Send him right in," I said, returning my attention to Angela as the door opened. "Thank you Angela. Good job" I said.

Samuel settled into the seat Angela had vacated. His gaze expectant, anxious to hear about his new assignment. I glanced at my watch. Mentally started a countdown.

"Before we get to this other job," I said, "Status on Fredericks."

"Someting strange going on Commissioner. But I can't figure it out yet. Most time he spends at de Cane Garden home. Does most of his business from there. He and de family usually have dinner out in de evenings before attending Victoria Park for de Carnival competitions."

"What's strange about that? Who does he meet at Victoria Park?"

"Dat's not de strange part Commissioner. De only times other than the evenings he leaves the house is to go to de airport. Been there four times already to meet passengers. Dat's where he was headed again when I called you before. Seems like he meeting foreign business clients. No women or families. Only men each time. but dese men don't look like businesspersons to me Commissioner. Some hard looking men. Carry themselves like military. Something definitely off about dem."

I leaned forward in my chair, my elbows on the desk. My interest and attention sharpened by Sammy's report.

"Den de other strange part," he continued, "is where he take dem. I followed him twice now from de airport all de way out leeward to his estate in Richmond Vale. None of dese men staying in Kingstown or in any hotel. I know Mr. Fredericks business is very private, but like I said, dese men don't seem like businessmen to me."

My thoughts churned the possibilities. Could this be the break we'd been searching for? I wondered.

"You said you followed them to Richmond Vale. You're sure they didn't make you?"

"No Commissioner," he said. An assured smile on his face. "I only followed him out dere twice. Each time with a different dollar van I borrowed from a friend. I even pick up some passengers. But when he makes a pickup at de airport and I see which road he travelling, I break off, knowing where he's going. Like today. I follow him as far as Hermitage before turning back and coming here. I figure he's going to de estate same as de other times."

A thought occurred. "You were able to get photographs of the men?"

"Yes sir. Long range shots from outside de cricket stadium."

"Good work," I said. "I'm gonna need those photos."

"I figured sir" he said, reaching into his pocket and passing a postage stamp sized digital data card across the desk.

I mentally checked my countdown and glanced at my watch.

"You know where to pick him up when you leave?"

"If he keeps to de pattern he'll go directly home. Get ready for de evening. De Miss Carnival beauty pageant is dis evening."

"Okay," I said, gathering my thoughts. "Sammy, when I initiated the undercover program I explained the threat facing St. Vincent and the Grenadines. I made you all aware of the overall picture without providing details you didn't need to know at the time."

He nodded. His dark brown eyes beneath the ridged brow focused and attentive.

"I haven't explicitly said it, but I think you're smart enough to already suspect everything that's happened in the last month, Whittaker's murder, the raids, the rogue officers, Mackee, and now Fredericks, is all connected to that threat."

Nodding again, maintaining his attentive silence. His focused gaze unwavering.

"The man behind all of it will be coming here to St. Vincent tomorrow. I have a plan to put an end to his activities once and for all. I don't know yet where the meeting will take place. Although you," I said, an emphatic nod in his direction, "May have just solved that problem."

Thin eyebrows rose on the prominent brow.

"I need a vehicle and driver standing by to pick me up after the meeting." I reached under the desk for my laptop briefcase. From a side compartment I extracted a small package containing one of Gage's cell phones and ear bud.

"I don't know yet where you'll be stationed. Hopefully I'll have that information in time to brief you before the meeting. But I may only have enough time for a quick phone briefing."

"Understood sir," he said.

"We'll communicate with this," I said, handing him the equipment, quickly explaining the cell phone's operation.

I stepped to a small hanging closet concealed behind a wall panel. I pulled my Kevlar vest from the shelf above a hanging suit, an extra day uniform, and the heat-masking cloak from Gage. The tee shirt like ballistic vest from Gage I'd worn since dressing in the morning. Jolene's assessment accurate. The damn thing fit like a snug, comfortable under-shirt. Uncannily cool in the tropical heat.

"Wear this during the operation," I said, handing Samuel the Kevlar vest. "And wear a sidearm."

"Commissioner, you sure you don't need more backup than just one driver?" Concern in the dark brown eyes as a renewed appreciation of the danger penetrated his consciousness.

"I have enough backup Sammy," I said. "I just need you to do your part in this."

"Yes sir," he said, his eyes staring hard at me.

"Better get going," I said, the time on my mental countdown almost out. "We'll talk again tomorrow."

Following Sammy's departure, I turned again to the file from Angela. I flipped through the pages, and called Gage.

"I have that raw data for you," I said when he answered. "I have to scan the pages into my computer to email them."

"Good. Got some news here too. Von Sachsen's disappeared. At least according to the traffic from the intelligence services keeping an eye on him."

"Probably means he's on his way."

"You got it," Gage said. "He left a few breadcrumbs pointing to Indonesia, or Northern Africa. But we know he's headed here."

"I may have a lead on the location," I said. "A report I just received from Keston Samuel, my undercover. I've had him following Elon Fredericks. Apparently Fredericks has been picking up some hard types arriving from abroad and putting them up at his estate in Richmond Vale."

"Might be the location of the meet. Or might be for staging," Gage said. "We'll see how it meshes with the other data."

"Let me get started on scanning the file. Talk again later. Oh by the way," remembering the thing I wanted to ask him. "What's going on with Dougan? My bet is Von Sachsen didn't tell him about putting a tail on me and risking his family."

"We're still watching the family," he said. "They haven't set foot off the ranch. But every so often we contact Dougan to keep the pressure on. He's broken, and he's done. Probably knows Von Sachsen will have to get rid of him soon. But unable to do anything about it."

"Couldn't have happened to a nicer guy," I said, surprised at my own callous vindictiveness.

"You have no idea. Phoenix has been into some nasty business over the years," Gage said before disconnecting.

I'd scanned maybe half of the documents into my laptop when the intercom buzzed. Cecilia announced DC Huggins in the outer office to see me. I secured the documents, the file, and my laptop, before asking her to show him in.

"What did you get Reggie?" I asked when he'd been seated in the chair Angela and Sammy had used earlier.

"Not sure anyting useful Commisshunah," he said. "Two arrivals booked for de Grenadines dis weekend, one on PSV and one on Palm Island. But de bookings made months ago. Nuttin' for Young Island or Buccament Bay. But all have available occupancy due to de off season. Dey might take a last minute booking. I asked my friend to call me if anything come in over de next two days."

"Thanks Reggie," I said. "That's actually helpful."

"What you lookin' for Commisshunah?"

"I can't go into details right now," I said, prevaricating. "It may be nothing. Just keeping an eye out," I said.

I stood, indicating the end of the meeting. I escorted him to the door.

"Thanks again Reggie. Call me immediately if your friend hears of anything else."

"Yessir," he said, exiting the office.

I returned to my scanning chore. Completed, I formulated the email, adding the report from Huggins, and uploading the images from Samuel. I sent the email off to Gage. I perused the images taken by Sammy. As he'd said, most of them long range shots from the cricket stadium adjacent to the airport. Side on shots, many of disembarking passengers on the tarmac. A few from a different perspective. A view of the pickup area outside the terminal. Again long range, the images grainy and probably useless for facial recognition software. But Elon Fredericks readily recognizable in these shots, waiting for his passengers, the men boarding the late model Lexus he drove himself.

I formulated a mental note to request the immigration records, compare them against the images. And thinking of compare, I placed the image I'd taken at the cobblestone on the same screen as Sammy's.

My tail one of the men Fredericks had met at the airport.

CHAPTER 31

Friday evening. Miss St. Kitts and Nevis won the Miss Carnival crown. And we'd confirmed the meeting place. Elon Fredericks' Richmond Vale estate. The estate's actual ownership listed to a Vincentian offshore corporation. A corporation controlled by Von Sachsen in which Elon Fredericks owned a partnership interest.

Gage and Jolene had sailed Wherever to Indian Bay for a rendezvous after I'd ditched my tail. Wherever had the breeze on her port beam, reaching in her graceful fashion across the channel between St. Vincent and Bequia. She rose atop the crests of rolling swells, and slid into the troughs in a wash of white water.

"Looks like the Richmond Vale estate is definitely it," I said to Gage, seated on the low side of the cockpit. His eyes studied the curved bellies of Wherever's sails. "The resorts turned out to be dead ends as you thought."

"Everything fits," he said, his gaze still glued to the taut rigging. "The data crunch made the connections between the estate, the offshore corporation, and Von Sachsen."

"It's still hard to believe the extent of his holdings in St. Vincent and the Grenadines," I said, recalling the initial shock Gage's report had produced. "The bastard's been buying up the country before taking it over outright. Shit. He was this close," I said holding my thumb and forefinger a millimeter apart.

Jolene stood at the helm, making gentle adjustments on the spoked wheel. Her curls pinned against her face by the breeze.

"And you're confident about the arrival window?" I asked.

Gage turned to face me, my answer in the assured smile and confident eyes.

"The only thing fitting the bill is a Gulfstream five fifty inbound to Hewanorra on St. Lucia from the Cape Verde Islands on Saturday morning. And coincidentally, if you believe in such a thing, A hundred and five foot charter yacht departed St. Thomas in the Virgins this morning. Headed south with stops in St. Lucia, St. Vincent and Grenada. Then headed east for the Med according to crew gossip. The owner supposedly meeting it at stops along the way. It carries a helicopter on it."

"Has anyone else tracked him this way? Do we have to worry about the CIA suddenly crashing this little party?"

"They're still trying to pick up his tracks on the far side of the world. They don't know everything we know. I held back information on connections Von Sachsen thinks are still secure. Though you never know with the CIA. They're a wild card."

"I've been promised a heads up if it seems they're moving in our direction," I said.

Both heads swiveled to stare at me. Jolene the first to get it.

"Melanie Barnes," she said.

I nodded. Gage's glance switched between Jolene and me, before settling on the view to port. He nodded in silent acceptance.

"We'll wait until we're moored to go over the details," he said, "but I've mapped out three exits. The main one where your driver picks you up at the house. Two backups if things go off the rails. And you'll need to learn how to arm and disarm the case. The signals we can go over now."

"What signals?"

"If we lose coms. Technology is great only when it works. The coms are the weak link. We depend on it to activate the cells, the case, for our eye in the sky. Anything can disrupt it. Things we have no control over. A power outage or a damn solar flare. In my experience when you rely on technology the most, that's the time it decides to crap out on you. Like some kind of cosmic prank."

I laughed. "So what kind of signals."

"For one thing if we lose coms try to get them to face in my position. I'll have a scope on the room. I'll be able to read lips."

"I almost forgot about that," I said.

"Second, I don't use a laser sight, but I'll have one. Watch the chest of whoever is directly opposite you. If you see the laser dot once, use the first backup exit route. Two flashes of the laser dot you use the second backup. I'll clear your path and sweep your trail."

"How do we notify Samuel without coms?" I said.

"We try regular cell service. If that doesn't work I'll get you out. We might have to hoof it awhile until we can find a place to go to ground and figure out the coms."

"Mike, you sure you're up for all of this," Jolene asked, broaching a subject I'm sure everyone had silently contemplated, myself included.

"I'm not that old yet JJ," I said, my voice lacking the conviction of my words.

"It's not your age," she said. "You haven't been in the field or in a knock down no holds barred street fight in years."

Gage remained silent, but his gaze held mine. His scrutiny like that of a gunnery sergeant sizing up a recruit before a battle.

"I wouldn't be going ahead with this if I didn't think I was capable of seeing it through," I said, a determined strength in my voice. "We have to stop this bastard, and I'm it. End of discussion. Anyway I'm sure the tactical mastermind over here has already figured contingencies if I somehow crew the pooch."

A small tic of a smile at the corner of Gage's mouth his only acknowledgement.

"In the first place," Gage said, "getting into a hand to hand with those guys is a losing scenario. You won't stand a chance. Your best weapon is here," he said, tapping his forehead. "And I know you know how to use it. You know how to think on the fly Mike. Improvise if, and when, you have to, but just enough to get back on plan if it's still in play. If it isn't, trust your instincts and follow the protocol. Yours are better than most people I know."

For the remainder of the passage we hashed out the plan. Forwards, backwards, sideways and upside down, Wherever gliding in graceful ease across the rolling swells. In no rush. Cold beers close at hand.

We dissected and reassembled each phase of the operation. Staging, advanced positioning, communications, first contact, travelling to the location, the meeting itself, and the exit. We discussed the variables. The timing of Von Sachsen's phone call, advance positioning of his team, their countermeasures, his end game.

Wherever snug on her mooring in Lower Bay, we continued the briefing below, conversing while Gage and Jolene whipped up a quick dinner in the galley. Wherever's navigation station had been transformed into a command center containing three flat screen monitors, and keyboards connected to three laptop computers.

We ate standing up, holding our plates, studying satellite images of the Richmond Vale estate and surrounding area spread across the dinette table. Chateaubelair and Cumberland on the coast. Troumaka and Rosehall inland. The nearest bays. And the mountainous forested topography in between.

"We'll position your car and driver here," Gage said, circling a position on a topographical map about a mile from the estate. "This is the first backup exit route here." Again using the pencil. "And rendezvous here. Here's the second route, across here." His pencil drew another line on the map. "Both take you away from the closest populated areas, Richmond Vale to the North, Chateaubelair to the west. But both put you close to the main road here."

He dropped the pencil on the charts. Turned to face me.

"It's tough terrain Mike. Densely forested. And at night. I'll pre-position night gear for you. And weapons. But it's still gonna be a rough haul. On the plus side, you'll have total concealment. If our bird's eye view and coms remain on line, Jo can guide you. And I'll be behind you. We can meet up on the route if we need to. Hopefully the main exit will work and we won't need any of this."

"Well it better. I really don't need a hike through the jungle at night," I said.

"Tomorrow morning I'll do a flyby of the estate," Gage said. "Like I'm heading up for a flyover tour of Soufriere. I want close up eyes on that place and the surrounding terrain besides the sat images, and I'm counting on them not paying too much attention to an aircraft from St. Vincent and the Grenadines Air on a sightseeing flight."

We moved from the dinette to the salon. The innocuous attaché case lay on the settee.

"You just leave that thing lying around like that?" I said, an incredulous tone in my voice.

"Perfectly harmless until it's armed," he said. "Which is what you're about to learn."

Gage placed the case on the coffee table. His thumbs pushed the buttons on the lock mechanism to the side. A dull clunk as the latches released. He opened the case.

A stack of official RSVPF file folders lay inside, and a folded sheet of paper. He unfolded the sheet. Handed it to me.

"The combination," he said, closing the case. "Memorize it. Dial in the combination, release the latches," he said, demonstrating by opening the case as he had before. "Then before you do anything else, dial in one on the first digit here, and six on the last digit here, like a person trying to conceal the combination normally would. The numbers make it easy to remember. One for the first digit, six for the sixth. With me so far?"

"Got it," I said.

"With that combination set in, the release buttons can be pushed down as well as to the side. To arm the case close the lid, push the release buttons down simultaneously, and engage the latches. Once the latches snap shut the case will be armed. Two small LEDs will come on, here and here," he said pointing. I bent for a closer look, spotting the almost invisible LEDs buried in the locking mechanism.

"And Mike, set the case down flat before you arm it. It's equipped with a motion sensor. After its armed any movement of the case will trigger the explosive. As I told you the other night, the case can be armed remotely, but it's best if you make the call on the timing."

"Can't say this whole exploding briefcase thing doesn't give me an acute case of the heebie geebies."

"It's not meant to explode. It's meant to get you out of there alive," Gage said.

"Okay," I said. "Let's go over it again"

Later, satisfied I'd absorbed every molecule of Gage's plan, had made it part of my being, I glanced over at Wherever's converted nav station as I prepared to leave.

"JJ you sure you got the hang of all this stuff?"

"Oh I've been practicing every waking hour I'm not at work. And Dogpatch is a pretty good teacher.

"Dogpatch?"

"Another anonymous and mysterious friend of Gage's," she said, an amused smile on her face. "He'll be backstopping me during the op too. From wherever the hell in the world he is. And while we've been practicing, I got some really nice images of ganja crops for the Special Unit boys after all this is over."

"Actually you're not quite ready to leave yet Mike," Gage said, appearing from the aft cabin in a black neoprene swimsuit. Short sleeves and cut off at the thighs.

"Jo will run you ashore. Go up to her place and call for a taxi, or better yet a police vehicle, to pick you up there and take you home. Von Sachsen's team probably has your place in Montrose and here in Friendship Bay staked out, hoping to reacquire you at one or the other. I need to make sure you're clear until you get home. Everything we've planned gets blown if they connect us."

He stepped to the nav station and picked up a Leupold night optics scope.

"Kill the lights hon," he said, before mounting the first two steps of the companionway ladder.

Wherever's blackout curtains below had been closed during our briefing. Jolene hit the switches, one after the other, plunging the cabin into darkness. My eyes adjusted after a few moments. I heard rather than observed Gage opening the main hatch. As vision returned, I made out the lower half of his body, sitting on the top companionway step, his head and shoulders above the hatch, scanning the beach.

"Looks clear," he said after a few minutes.

He handed the scope to Jolene standing at the bottom of the companionway, before disappearing onto the deck. A slash off the port side, heard through the hull. Jolene reclosed the hatch, turned on a single light over the nav station. We waited.

When Gage called providing the all clear, Jolene and I ran the dinghy ashore. We wasted no time on the beach. We hurried to the cover of trees bordering the road. Proceeded to

the turnoff and the dark path up to her house. Gage mean-
while headed to my house in Friendship Bay.

Jolene switched on a table lamp in the living room, and
an overhead in the kitchen. The rest of the house remained
dark.

"Can I get you anything Mike? Coffee. Nightcap. Beer
for the road?"

"Nothing. Thanks JJ." I sat in the comfortable stuffed
armchair next to the couch. She joined me. Sat at the end of
the couch facing me.

"We haven't had much time alone lately, to talk," I said.
"Remember how we used to spend hours brainstorming when
you first started working for me. Making plans on how to
tackle the force?"

She smiled. "I remember."

"I miss it sometimes," I said. "Anyway what do you
think about all this?"

"What do you mean? Gage's plan? Confronting the Bogeyman? That explosive attaché case you can't take your eyes
off?"

"All of it sure, but..." hesitating to broach the subject.
I'd always considered her personal life, her relationship with
Gage, none of my business. Despite an undeniable paternalis-
tic concern. But not my place to interfere. And we seldom
discussed it.

"I guess I mean particularly Gage," I said, pushing the
door fully open.

"Hmmm, the real question," she said, smiling.

"You've changed since you've been with him, you
know," producing a slight narrowing of her eyelids, a small

crow's foot above her nose, between her eyes. Her stare on the verge of turning into a defensive glare.

"I'm not judging," I said. "I'm not saying it's good or bad. If anything I kindda like it. You seem more confident and self-assured than I've ever known you. And self-assurance was never something you lacked."

The eyes softened. The small smile returned around her lips.

"But no denying you've changed since you've been with him."

Her gaze leveled on my face. Her eyes peered deep into mine, as though probing my psyche, reaching a decision.

"Part of it, most of it really, is simply that I love him. In a way I never thought possible before I met him. Like with every molecule of my being Mike. With everything that I am," her eyes expressing the depth of her sincerity.

"The other part is a little difficult to explain. You talk about my self-assurance. He's the most self-assured person I know. And it comes from a place deep in the center of his being. Nothing manufactured about it. Combined with a calmness centered in the same place. It's who he is Mike. Like the sun is hot. You never have to question it. Put it all together, his self-assurance, his ecumenical calm, his sense of fairness, of right and wrong, his moral compass, call it what you want, he's the most evolved person I've ever met."

We gazed into each other's eyes. And perhaps for the first time, I fully understood the depth of her connection to him.

"But he's still only human Mike," she said. "He has scars. Deep physical and psychological scars. He has fears and vulnerabilities like everyone else. He's just more practiced at shielding it. But he's learning he doesn't always need to. What happened in New York really shook him. And what happened to you too. I wasn't as attuned to it then. But you getting shot really shook him too."

"What happened in New York?" I asked quietly. "We really haven't talked about it since it happened."

"You know most of it," she said. "But for a while he blamed himself."

"He saved your life," I said.

"Doesn't matter. He blamed himself that I got hurt. That it got so close. It's why he's not taking any chances on this op, especially with you in the middle of it."

"You even sound like him sometimes," I said, smiling at her. "And I mean that as a compliment."

"One of the things I learned in New York was how to be with him not just as the man I love, but also as his partner. Sometimes I think New York taught him that too. He'd been accustomed to being alone for so long. Only having to think about his own safety. I think learning to see me as a partner, able to make my own choices and take care of myself, helped him get past the blame."

Her cell phone rang. She listened. Disconnected.

It's clear all the way home. Gage doesn't see anyone watching the house. Thinks you're probably clear until you get back to Kingstown."

She called the Port Elizabeth Station. Asked if there was a patrol nearby to swing by her house and give the Commissioner a ride home.

I stepped into my dark, empty house. The distant dull roar of the surf, the scent of citrus, the branches rustling overhead in the breeze; no longer cast their magical spell.

Whether it'd been Dougan invading my personal space, or my mind's preoccupation over the past few days, the house possessed a forlorn discomfort. Something I'd have to rectify. Maybe I needed to spend more time here, a distinct likelihood in the near future. Or have guests over more often. Maybe have Melanie spend more time here. Restart the vegetable garden I'd long ago abandoned.

Something to turn it back into my happy place.

CHAPTER 32

J'Ouvert morning in full swing. The streets around Kingstown had been filling since sunrise. Steel pan music and mobile public address systems echoed through the capital, reaching the harbor, floating out across the water to greet arriving ferries before they reached the wharf.

Strange having voices in your head no one else can hear. We'd been running coms since I'd boarded the ferry in Bequia. A shake down of the equipment, and Jolene's management of it. She practiced switching the cell phones on and off, and muting the feed on individual phones. Having fun as she provided a running commentary on J'Ouvert morning celebrations across St. Vincent and the Grenadines as observed from the satellite. Funny, and at times acerbic.

I waded into the massive street party. I pushed my way through the spirited, dancing, happy crowds, making halting progress toward the Central Police Station. Conscious of the attaché case I carried as it bumped into bodies massed along the sidewalks.

Finding transportation a futile exercise. Bay Street closed to vehicular traffic. Given over to towed floats carrying elaborately constructed and colorful themed sets. Pirates of the Caribbean, Avatar, Little Mermaid, Cleopatra. Dancers costumed in the float's theme danced on top of and around the floats. The costumes as elaborate and colorful as the floats. Ponderous headdresses spouted features, wings, flowers, in bright festive rainbow colors. The lower halves of the costumes skimpy, sheer; exposing legs, stomachs, breasts.

Music blared from speakers affixed atop the tow vehicles. And from the floats of winning steel pan bands. A competing cacophony of sound meshing into a single, pulsing, sexual beat, transporting the street revelers to a bacchanalian frenzy. Dancers writhed and strutted, grinding their pelvic areas against one another. The Bum Dance, simulating anal sex, especially popular. Dancers painted all blue. Others made up to look like vampires, zombies, and devils.

I navigated the revelers stretched along Bay Street. Jolene's voice all but inaudible in my ear. A constable moved aside a barricade cordoning the police station. I entered the courtyard. The mayhem behind me. The resounding music muted by the old colonial stone walls.

Central Police Station busier than usual for a Saturday. For any day of the week. Constables on double shifts for Mardi Gras, supplemented by a large contingent called in from outlying stations and divisions, shuttled in and out of the station amid a constant parade of individuals arrested for disorderly disturbances, petty thievery, and fights. The din in the station overwhelming.

"Sounds like you're finally inside," Jolene's voice in my ear. "Quite a party going on over there."

"The last thing on my mind right now," I said. "Any word from Gage?"

"On coms," his voice said in my ear. The drone of twin engines in the background. "Just made a first pass over the estate. I'll circle Soufriere and make a second pass heading south. How you doing Jo?"

"Approaching Young Island now. Will be ready when you get here."

"Copy that. Should be landing at Arnos Vale in about fifteen minutes."

"Approaching the office JJ," I said in a low voice. "Cut me out of the feed until you need me."

Sergeant Samuel stood by Cecilia's empty desk awaiting my arrival. He stood to attention as I entered the outer office.

"As you were," I said, cutting short the salute before he had a chance to raise his hand to his brow. I strode across the outer office to my office door. Paused to glance at Whittaker's framed portrait on the wall.

Soon Derrick, I silently promised to the once lively eyes staring down at me from the image.

Samuel followed me into the office.

"What's the latest on our subject?" I asked, turning from the hidden closet where I'd placed the attaché case.

"Left home early dis morning Commissioner. Before sunrise and de start of Jewveh. Drove out leeward as usual. I figure he was heading to de estate."

I nodded. "You been checked out on the coms?"

"Yes sir. De Superintendent and I been conversing all morning."

"Good. She brief you? You know your position and your job?"

"Yes sir," he repeated. "I'll be heading out to Chateaubelair after I leave here. I have a friend live out dat way where I can get some sleep until I hear from de Superintendent."

"Sounds good Sammy. Thank you. We'll talk later."

"Yes sir. And Commissioner," he said before turning to leave, his gaze meeting mine, a compelling expression in his dark eyes.

"Good luck sir," snapping to attention, his arm raised in a crisp salute.

I smiled, returning the salute. "To you too Sammy. And thanks again."

I spent the remainder of the morning in anxious anticipation. I'd decided on the office rather than the house in Montrose because it provided more distractions. I attempted to lose myself in paperwork, but the waiting challenged the small amount of patience I'd been able to muster. The day dragged on. The continuing revelry on the streets muted by the closed windows.

Sometime in the mid-afternoon, my com came alive, startling me for an instant. I'd almost forgotten about the little bug in my ear.

"Our eye in the sky picking up a ship entering our waters from St. Lucia Chief," Jolene's voice.

"Status?" I said.

"Crisse. This thing can see right onto the deck. Every detail. No one topside though."

"And the status?" I repeated, impatience fueling my irritation.

"Don't get your knickers in a wad Chief," producing a short burst of nervous laughter. "Base established in Troumaka Bay. Watchman already ashore." Watchman, Gage's code name. I wondered who'd chosen it. Whether he'd ever used it before.

"Exit packages in place and I have eyes on the estate," his voice said in my ear. L shaped, two story building. A turret anchoring one end. Arched openings over a second floor balcony and patio entrance on the ground floor. Second floor balcony extends across the building. And the ground floor patio extends along the side. Lots of tall picture windows and open air space. Beautiful architecture actually. Great views. Richmond peak and Soufriere to the north, Couls Hill and Cumberland Bay to the south."

"Will you two quit with the commentary already," I said, exasperation rising in my voice. "Sounds like you're trying to sell me real estate for Christ sake."

Snickering sounds in my ear.

"Anyway, from the looks of how're they're setting up, it's gonna be the long shot Mike," Gage said. "I've figured the position for the best angle, but they haven't moved anyone into position yet. They could still go for a close up kill, but I think killing you is their last resort option. This is about grabbing you and forcing you to give up the information he wants. But you have the briefcase, and you have me on over-watch. You seeing anything Jo?"

"All the activity's still close to the house?" she said.

"Establishing the perimeter," Gage said.

Jolene's voice again. "Yacht's slowing. Looks like Cumberland Bay watchman."

"Got eyes on it," he said. "That's an EC 130 on the fan-tail pad. Fast. Long range. One pilot and up to seven passengers. Probably Von Sachsen's emergency exit."

"Any sightings on deck yet," I asked.

"Nothing Chief."

"Okay. Cut my feed again. Call me if anything new develops."

Undecided which was worse, the waiting, or listening to the running commentary while waiting. At least the tech stuff appeared to be working.

Later in the afternoon my cell phone rang. An unidentified blocked number. Dougan's voice when I answered. Almost unrecognizable. The wheezy, rasping, tremulous voice unlike the arrogant, self-assured voice I remembered from a few days before. Again, without preamble or greeting, he announced a third party conferencing in.

Gage had been correct. We'd broken him.

"Commissioner Daniel's," the next voice possessing the measured, confident tone Dougan once displayed.

"Cutting it pretty close," I said, ignoring the greeting. "And I hope this call is what it means. Disappointing me at this point will prove very costly for you."

"Then I will not disappoint you. Be at the corner of Lewis Street and the Leeward Highway at precisely seven p.m. Your residence is in that neighborhood I believe. A car will collect you for our meeting."

I hesitated. "Not exactly what I had in mind," I said, pretending to resist his arrangements as Gage and I had rehearsed. Don't agree too easily or quickly, Gage had cautioned. "I was thinking a more neutral location."

"Now don't you be the one to disappoint Commissioner. It is necessary for me to maintain a certain anonymity. Thanks in great part to you. I'm simply here to discuss business. To hear you out and reach a mutually beneficial solution. Besides, as you pointed out, you appear to hold an amount of leverage in this matter."

"It's to your benefit to keep that in mind," I said, acquiescing without verbally agreeing to his terms.

"Then I shall see you this evening. Until then Commissioner."

Jolene's voice in my ear after the call disconnected. "Listened in on the intercept Chief," she said. "Looks like the party's on."

"Three freaking hours. What am I supposed to do for three freaking hours?"

"Go home. Relax." Gage's voice. "You need to calm yourself for this shindig."

"I'll be calm the moment this thing gets going," I snapped. "It's the waiting that drives me up the freaking wall."

"Name of the game. Try doing it out here in the bush."

"No thank you. I don't have the patience of a rock the way you do."

"Whatever it takes Mike. Go home. Take a nap."

"You got to be kidding right?"

"I just had a terrific nap in the great Vincentian outdoors."

"Ha ha," I said.

At seven p.m. precisely, a black Mitsubishi Outlander pulled to the side of the road next to where I waited. A man, white complexion, exited from the passenger side door. Dressed all in black. A light faux leather jacket over a black tee shirt.

"Commissioner Daniels?"

"That's me," I said.

He pulled an electronic wand from beneath the black jacket. He ran it up and down my front, between my legs, under each armpit, down my back and across the cloak folded over my arm.

"Open the case please."

I did as instructed, turning the case and open lid to face him.

"Information for your boss," I said.

He ran the wand over the case and its contents. He nodded.

"And your cell phone."

I retrieved it from my trouser pocket and showed it to him. "It's turned off. But I'm keeping it," I said.

He checked the phone. Nodded again. He opened the rear passenger door and indicated I enter.

Another black clad fair-skinned man on the far side of the rear seat. Behind the driver. His vigilant gaze glued to me as I settled into the back seat, the attaché case in my lap. The driver also white, the same hard expression in his eyes as the other two.

The SUV drove onto the road, meeting a river of headlights headed in the opposite direction into Kingstown. More revelers for the street party continuing through the night and the remainder of the weekend. No one spoke. All eyes focused ahead. The man next to me cast occasional sideways glances in my direction. We crawled through Layou, its own streets alive in celebration. The driver leaned on the horn to clear a passage through the crowd.

Outside Hermitage a voice rang in my ear, "Gimme a com check chief."

"Mind if I ask where in the hell we're going?" I said.

The backseat man glanced at me. The front seat man glanced into the rear view mirror, his gaze meeting mine in the reflection. The driver's gaze glued to the winding country road. No one spoke.

"Never mind then," I said.

"Loud and clear Chief," in my ear. "Coms are good and I have your signal outside Hermitage heading north east. And we've located Von Sachsen's shooter. Watchman moving into position. Samuel's been alerted too, getting ready to move."

"Not seeing any heat signal from you Watchman, and you're under the tree cover. Invisible to eyes in the sky. Your tracker puts you twenty meters from a yellow blob at your two o'clock."

"Picking up any coms?"

"Nothing."

"Copy that. I'll get close and wait a while. See if he's using coms and has a check in procedure."

"Fifteen meters and closing. You're almost on top of him."

The voices in my ear fell silent. The Mitsubishi climbed a steep road into the island's mountainous interior. The road curved westward before descending again toward the coast.

"Show you coming up on Rosehall Chief. ETA ten minutes to the estate. Samuel in position."

"Watchman in position," said Gage's voice. "You should be picking up my heat signature now Jo. Shooter is asleep and cloaked. They're using vox activated radio com. Listening to their coms now. Hang on, vehicle arriving."

"See that too," Jolene said.

"Well how about them apples. The guest of honor has arrived. Dougan and your boy Fredericks with him Mike," Gage said.

My pulse raced on hearing Gage's words, produced by the dull rapid pounding in my chest. I forced a calming will on myself. Forced my skittering heart rate to return to normal.

"And do tell. What the hell are you doing here?" Gage's voice again.

"What's going on Watchman?" Jolene's voice.

"A face from the past. One I never thought I'd see again. I got you now you bastard." The voice in my ear unfamiliar. Still Gage, but a distinct shift in tone and timbre, possessing a deadly quality, unnerving and disturbing. It produced a discomforting knot in my gut. No time to dwell on it. Jolene's voice replaced Gage's in my ear and in my thoughts.

"Almost there Chief. Coming up on the estate any minute."

The SUV had been climbing since leaving the country road. Engulfed in a black cocoon, seemingly cut off from the rest of the world. Its headlight beams stabbed the darkness ahead, revealing massive tree trunks and dense foliage reaching toward the moving vehicle as it navigated the narrow, winding dirt drive up to the house. The Mitsubishi abruptly exited the claustrophobic darkness into a large lit clearing.

Warm amber light spilled from decorative wall fixtures along the second floor balconies, and on either side of ornate arched ground floor entrances. More lamps along the walls bordering a flagstone patio. My gaze wandered over the gorgeous open space architecture, the manicured lawn, and lush tropical landscaping. I recalled Gage's earlier description. He hadn't done it justice. The distant views he'd mentioned hidden by the night.

One escort and the driver remained at the SUV. The other led me toward the turret anchoring the far end of the building, and through decorative metal and glass double doors beneath the arch. I entered a large sitting room. Dark parquet floor polished to a gleaming gloss. Cream walls offset by lime green drapes, matching the cozy furniture and polished lemon surfaces of a bar in one corner. Potted plants placed strategically around the room provided contrasting color.

A group of men stood by the bar, their quiet conversation attracting my attention. Dougan, his withered appearance a startling contrast to the man who'd invaded my home. Dull blue eyes. Puffy bags for eyelids beneath them. The jowls at his cheeks loose and sagging. His stature physically diminished, displaying his age.

Elon Frederick. Tall. Strong build. Head shaved bald. Neatly trimmed moustache and goatee. An imposing presence in his own right. He averted his gaze, preferring to look past my shoulder.

A man I didn't know. His bland symmetrical features unremarkable except for the blunt crooked nose. Blond pine needles for hair, cropped close and barely visible against his skull. And his eyes. Blank, bloodless, devoid of emotion, or mercy. No soul behind those windows. He stared right through me, as if I wasn't a person, but an object.

His eyes shifted to my escort. An imperceptible nod. And acknowledgement. A glance toward the last man at the bar, who, following the casual silent exchange, moved toward me.

Tall. Maybe six foot two. Groomed silver hair receding from a high forehead. A thin white chevron moustache, the wings groomed on either side of his upper lip's hairless cleft. Immaculately dressed in crisp, creased white linen slacks, and a silky smooth pink oxford shirt beneath a light worsted, two button blue jacket. The peaked fold of a crimson handkerchief peeked above the jacket's breast pocket. On his feet, expensive black leather loafers.

"Commissioner Daniels," he said, "We finally meet." Blue eyes, almost hidden in the slits of baggy upper and lower lids. No eyelashes. Hard, wary, calculating eyes, studying me like a great white shark circling its next meal. He didn't offer his hand.

"A long time coming," I said.

"Can I get you a drink?" his beguiling smile practiced and disarming.

"I'd rather get down to business."

"As you wish. Shall we take our seats outside? I so rarely get out into the open air. Such a refreshing climate you have here."

Not an offer. The men moved as a group, herding me toward the patio, setting me up as the target for the long shot. Comfortable armchairs had been arranged around a low table. Two chairs. One for me, one for Von Sachsen. The other men remained standing. Dougan and Fredericks behind Von Sachsen. My escort and crooked nose had their backs against the curved turret wall.

My other escort, and the driver, nowhere to be seen. And I hadn't noticed any other men inside the house, or around the grounds. Four men had arrived in advance on St. Vincent. One may have been the shooter Gage had neutralized. The other three probably in positions on the perimeter.

"I have to say you intrigue me Commissioner," Von Sachsen said. "And I wonder how you managed to come by the information you have," an amused condescension in the predatory eyes.

"May I," I said, indicating the attaché case I'd placed on the table.

Von Sachsen's gaze shifted to crooked nose leaning casually against the wall. My escort, next to him, leaned over and whispered in his ear. A nod from crooked nose.

"Please," Von Sachsen said.

I thumbed in the six digit combination on the rotary dials. Pushed the buttons releasing the catches.

"How I obtained the information is of no concern," I said, a distraction as I thumbed in the arm code. "However," opening the lid and extracting a file. "It all began with this man," I said, opening the file. A glance toward Dougan. He'd seen this act before, and wore a pained expression on his haggard face as he recalled the experience, and wondered what might be unfolding now.

I extracted an eight by ten police crime scene glossy from the file. Handed it to Von Sachsen. Noted the movement of his moustache, produced by a fleeting twitch at the corner of his mouth. He held the photograph out in crooked nose's direction. Crooked nose stepped toward Von Sachsen and glanced at the photograph. Returning to his post, he resumed his blank eyed stare at me.

"I knew him as Robert Carlson. You probably knew him as Franz Dieter. He tried to kill me on Bequia. He paid for that mistake with his life."

I held Von Sachsen's stare. Read his reaction. His control close to being total. But his eyes betrayed him. No longer amused. The predatory stare resurfaced.

"Then there's this man," I said, handing him another photograph. Another corpse. The assassin who killed my friend Jackson Taylor, making it appear like a suicide. And who came close to killing Jolene in New York.

"And of course this man," handing him the final photograph. The so-called 'Director' who Gage had captured in New York, and renditioned to God knows where. As I handed him each photograph Von Sachsen's composure slipped a fraction more. The mouth tic more pronounced. The furrows on his forehead and creases between his eyes deepened. He lifted his head from studying the photographs. The venom in his eyes unmistakable.

If looks could kill.

CHAPTER 33

A heavy silence hung in the cool night air. The tableau strange and surreal. Surrounded by a thick tension. The men against the wall sensed the change, their stony unwavering gazes, never leaving me. Von Sachsen stared at me across the table. His cultured demeanor abandoned. Hatred poured from his cold blue eyes.

"Finally there's your errand boy over here," I said, leveling my gaze on Dougan. "How's the family by the way?" unable to resist twisting the knife. "In fact," I said, returning my attention to Von Sachsen. "It's the very people you kept sending my way who led me straight to you."

"I seriously doubt it was that simple," Von Sachsen said, regaining his voice. The arrogant condescending tone no long present. "And I doubt you managed this on your own."

"I'll admit I have some resourceful friends, but it was your continued interference in our affairs that put me on your trail. Interference I intent to end."

"I'm afraid it may not be as simple as you suppose."

"Well there's more here you've yet to see," I said indicating the files in the case. "Shall we continue?"

In fact, the files contained nothing more to use against him. Just lists of his corporations and accounts. Information, which wouldn't have the same effect as the photographs. And my photo presentation had run its course. But it had shaken him, as intended. Disrupted his once assured control over our meeting. A control he desperately needed to regain.

"I have no doubt your information is thorough Commissioner. My concern is where you obtained it. Who you are working for."

"I'm just a small island cop," I said shrugging my shoulders. "I work for the citizens of St.Vincent and the Grenadines. And my job is to put an end to your interference in their affairs."

"And how do you propose to accomplish that."

"By forcing you to leave us alone, and all this," I said, waving my hand at the files, "Will remain buried in a drawer. We'll require you to liquidate all your holdings in St. Vincent and the Grenadines of course. But we'll call the damage already done unfortunate, and go our separate ways."

His sudden laugh surprised me. The sound low and brittle, like china plates breaking on a tile floor. But a staged laugh. Another practiced affectation containing no humor. The laughter not reaching his eyes, which conveyed only contempt.

"Really Commissioner. Am I supposed to simply take your word you won't continue to use this information against me?"

"There'd be no point, would there?"

"I'm afraid I cannot simply take your word for it. I do however have a counteroffer you may be interested in."

"Such as?"

His hard stare pinned me. His eyes cold, containing a malicious gleam. Ready to show his hole card. Regain control of the situation, and me.

"Your life, and the lives of your family, in exchange for telling me who the people are helping you. I will eventually get the information, one way or the other. You may not survive it. Your family certainly won't."

"That would be your final mistake. The fact is, I can reach out and touch your family too, including your aged father in Switzerland. Just as I did your errand boy's family." My gaze drifted to Dougan behind him. "You kill me or approach my family, you'll not only lose control of this information, but your family and your empire will be destroyed."

"Perhaps it's a risk I may be willing to take. Are you?"

I returned the files to the attaché case and closed the lid, pushing the buttons downward. I held off engaging the latches. I stood from my chair, for all intents and purposes, preparing to leave.

"If your driver will take me to the nearest town. I believe this meeting is over."

"You obviously do not fully appreciate the situation Commissioner. I have no intention of allowing you to leave without first obtaining the information I seek. Look around you. You have no, how do you call it, backup. And my men are here to ensure you do not leave. Also I must advise you, I can have you shot where you stand," the inflection in his voice designed to convey his control over me.

"Then the meeting would indeed be over, and I'd die knowing you'll never be able to cause this country and its people any more harm."

His head cocked to one side. Eyebrows rose on his forehead. The thin eye slits widened, revealing surprise, and a new expression in the blue irises. A modicum of respect perhaps.

"Are you really that brave Commissioner?"

"Try me."

"Maybe I shall," he said. Victory in the slate blue eyes and wicked smile. Ready to play his trump card. He raised his left arm, his index finger performing a 'come here' motion.

Nothing happened. A perplexed frown replaced the smile.

"Was something dramatically cliché supposed to happen," I said, staring into his bewildered eyes. "Something like this perhaps," I said, raising my right hand and mimicking his finger motion.

Immediately followed by a soft thud against the turret wall. Everyone turned in time to observe the pink spray before it dissipated, leaving a red stain against the wall, and speckled red dots on my escort's face, as if he'd developed a sudden severe case of chicken pox.

Crooked nose thudded face first onto the flagstone patio. The back of his head a soft gooey red mass.

Dougan emitted a sound like a stifled scream. Fredericks, eyes bulging, mouth agape, stared down at the lifeless corpse and the red pool spreading around its shattered head. My escort the first to gather his wits. Already searching the darkness behind me. He extracted a small handheld radio from an inside jacket pocket.

"No son," I said, halting his actions. "Or you're next." Surprised at my calm, commanding tone. Surprised I could even speak. As shocked and stunned as everyone else on the patio. Inwardly I raged and cursed at Gage.

"Tango down," the calm epitaph in my ear. "Sorry about that Mike."

"Copy Watchman." A solemn sadness in Jolene's voice.

I wanted to yell and scream into the night. At Gage. This wasn't part of the plan. I hadn't agreed to an assassination, or any killing for that matter, unless they were shooting at us. My muscles clenched in the effort to control my emotions.

Von Sachsen's gaze rose from the body, meeting mine. Murderous intent in his eyes. But something else which hadn't been present before. Fear.

"You will pay for this," his voice low, harsh, like tires on a gravel driveway. The words uttered slowly, singly, with deliberate menace.

"To God maybe," I said. "Certainly not to you. And since our meeting appears to be over and you've already refused to offer me a ride, I'll just call my driver." I fished my cell phone from my trouser pocket and pretended to turn it on.

"Already on the move Chief," Jolene said in my ear. "ETA five minutes," as I feigned the phone call for my driver to collect me.

"You'll not leave this property alive. Of that I can assure you."

"I'm sure you think that's true," I said. "But here's what I know for a certainty," engaging the case's clasps. "This attaché case is actually an explosive device." I paused, allowing my words to penetrate their shocked consciousness. "A bomb powerful enough to level this entire house. I've just armed it, as you can see if you look closely, those little red indicators there," pointing at the lit LEDs.

My escort again the first to react, his gaze glued to the case.

"What type?" he said, his eyes fully alert, scrutinizing me as he waited for my response.

"A polymer," I told him, staring him straight in the eye. "The case has a motion trigger. Move it in the slightest and it detonates." I continued to address the escort, the only person on the patio possessing an immediate appreciation of their predicament. My response, and unwavering stare, convinced him it was no bluff. His facial expression and frozen posture conveyed a dawning awareness to the other men on the patio.

"It can also be remotely detonated. I'll disarm it once I'm safely away from here. But anyone attempting to stop me, follow me, or attempting to leave, can expect to end up either like that," pointing to the corpse. "Or as bits and pieces in the rubble."

I heard the crunch of tires on soft dirt. Turned to observe a Toyota RAV4 turning into the clearing, pulling up next to the Mitsubishi. Sammy behind the wheel. A sudden thought occurred. An idea half formed and out of left field. Maybe the lingering shock of sudden violent death affected my thought processes. Or the unsatisfying prospect of Von Sachsen simply walking away after the painstaking effort to get him here. Or maybe being royally pissed off at Gage. Whatever the reason, I decided to act on the thought.

I turned to face Von Sachsen. "On second thought you're coming with me," I said. "And you too Fredericks," I said turning to him.

"What you up to Mike?" Gage in my ear.

"You are both under arrest. Charged with crimes against the people of St. Vincent and the Grenadines." I had no idea if such a statute existed. I'd never heard of one. But I'd find something to hold them on.

"Mike?" Again Gage's voice. I ignored it. Jolene remained silent, off the air.

"This is preposterous" Von Sachsen exclaimed. "If you think..."

A dull splat interrupted him, shattering the arm of the chair he sat in. He sprang to his feet, eyes glued to the fluff feathery filling still billowing around the small crater created by Gage's shot.

"Get a move on Mike." Jolene broke her silence. "A perimeter guard moving toward that side of the house."

"Their coms have been down since the case armed," Gage said. "And their eye in the sky probably picked up Sammy driving in. You need to get out of there Mike."

"Both of you into the vehicle now," I commanded. "I won't say it again."

They moved. Their manner tentative. Hesitant. They glanced from the escort to me. To the darkness beyond me. But moved toward the RAV4.

"I'll disarm the case when I'm clear," I said, addressing the escort. "You'll have three hours to clean up this mess and clear out. This place will be crawling with police after that. And if I ever see any of your faces on these islands again, you'll enjoy the hospitality of Her Majesty's prison for a very long time."

He nodded.

I grabbed the cloak and fast walked to the RAV4. Opened the rear door.

"In. Move," I said, forceful shoves propelling the two men into the back seat.

"Go" I yelled at Sammy. "And give me your weapon."

He pointed to the seat. Next to him against his thigh, lay a service issued Glock 19. He'd kept the Toyota in gear, standing on the brake pedal while he'd waited. The SUV reared forward when he released the brake. He spun the wheel, heading for the dirt road hidden in the darkness beyond the clearing.

"They know something's up," Jolene's voice. "Three guards on the run, heading for the front of the house."

"He's clear," Gage said. "And I just disabled the Mitsubishi. They should stand down once the guy on the patio tells them about a shooter and the bomb. Anyone heading in this direction?"

I listened to the commentary while turned sideways facing the two men in the back seat. The Glock leveled at them for emphasis. Sammy negotiated the dark dirt road. No undue haste or risk. He hadn't been briefed on the bomb, but he'd been advised there'd be no pursuit.

"What's up Commissioner?" he asked when he'd made the turn onto the main road.

"Little change in plans Sammy. Head for the Chateaubelair Station. JJ?"

"On it. They'll be expecting you," Jolene said.

"If you think..." Von Sachsen the first to find his voice.

"Quiet." I commanded. "You're interrupting my train of thought. You'll both remain silent for the duration of this ride." His already narrow eyes closed to tiny slits.

I'd uttered the remark regarding my train of thought in passing, but in truth, I had a great deal to consider. The implications of my impulsive act uppermost in my mind. I hadn't had time to think it through before I'd acted. I needed time to sort through it now. And still angry as hell at Gage. I wanted to confront him, question him, demand an explanation. But I possessed sufficient presence of mind to hold off around the many ears in the speeding vehicle.

My stare glued to the men in the back seat as my thoughts churned. Both men dejected and bewildered. Probably wondering how this had happened. Not the outcome they'd envisioned when they awoke that morning. An outcome they'd never imagined. And undoubtedly, the adroit minds behind their downcast gazes were already contemplating the angles, engineering their way out. Their self-important arrogance intact.

A sleepy deserted atmosphere greeted me at the Chateaubelair Police Station. Despite Jolene's heads up call. A uniformed station sergeant sat on an old wood chair, his feet on a desk, reading an outdated magazine.

"Sergeant," I called.

He glanced up from the magazine, sprang to his feet when he recognized me. He stamped to attention and saluted. I purposely kept him standing at attention while I surveyed the room. The floor space cramped by too many shelve units, metal file cabinets, and battered metal desks at haphazard angles. Like a maze. A wood counter spanned the front, like in a country store.

The second story offices, usually appropriated by the Station Commander and plain-clothes units, probably in no better shape.

A large town by Vincentian standards, Chateaubelair possessed a mid-sized constabulary. It was on a short list for a new modern station, vehicles, and equipment. But prying the funding from the politicians was like pulling teeth.

"At ease Sergeant," I said, finally returning his salute. "Where is everyone? Didn't you receive a call from Superintendent Johanssen to expect me?"

"Yessah. Everyone on duty out on de street fe Carnival. I jus' radio fe a patrol car and de corporal in de back prepahin' de holdin' cell."

"We won't be here long. I need you to hold the prisoners until the Sergeant with me returns. Then two constables to transport them to Kingstown. The sergeant will follow."

"Yessah."

"Bring them in Sammy," I said, a perplexed frown on the Station Sergeant's face as I spoke into empty air.

Sammy entered the station pushing Fredericks and Von Sachsen ahead of him. "Get the corporal," I said to the sergeant. "Let's get these two locked up."

He disappeared through a door at the back of the room, reappearing a moment later, followed by a uniformed constable with corporal stripes on his sleeve. The Corporal escorted Sammy and the prisoners into the back.

"What goin' on Commisshunah? Who dese men? What de charges?"

Relieved he didn't recognize Fredericks I said, "Can't speak about the investigation right now Sergeant. But before Sergeant Samuel returns to collect them, I want the corporal stationed at that door. No one is to communicate with the prisoners. And no one gets past that door to see them. No one. Not even the station commander. Or you two will be looking for a different kind of work by Monday. Do I make myself clear Sergeant?"

"Yessah," he said, automatically stiffening to attention, his eyes bulging at the harsh threat. Or more likely increased curiosity regarding the prisoners.

I wished I'd been able to separate them. But the station probably had only two or three holding cells. And close enough they'd be able to communicate anyway. I repeated my orders and threat to the Corporal when he and Samuel returned.

Back on the road I tried Jolene. I hadn't heard her voice in my ear after escaping the estate.

"You still there JJ?" I said.

"Still here Chief. Will be till all the birds are in the nest."

"Status on Watchman?"

"Still on site. Getting ready to exfil the area."

"And the case?"

"Disarmed and harmless. Watchman says after the disarm the guards went to work on it. Knew what they were doing. Must have explosives training. They pulled it apart. Probably diffused it."

"Okay. I'm on my way to you now."

"Eye in the sky puts you ten minutes out. Dinghy's on the beach. I'll guide you to it and provide the combo when you get here"

"See you soon," I said.

Climbing aboard Wherever I experienced a flush of relief mixed with trepidation. I didn't look forward to confronting Gage. But the death on the estate's patio still rattled, and set me on edge, like a raw exposed nerve in a molar.

"What the hell was he thinking?" I lashed out at Jolene the moment I climbed below, the closest available target.

"Mike. Calm down."

"Don't tell me to calm down. You didn't have to watch that man's head explode. And don't try to lecture me either. I need a drink."

"And what about you? What's with the arrests? That wasn't part of the plan," she said. Returning from the galley she handed me a double Jack Daniels neat.

"Figured one renegade on the mission, why not two."

"Look Mike. You're upset, why not wait until morning..." her head cocked to the side. She moved to the nav station. Hit a key on one of the keyboards.

"Mike just got back. I'll come get you with the dinghy." A pause. "You sure? See you in a bit then."

"Gage is on the way. Swimming out," she said, before exiting the nav station and entering the aft stateroom by the port bulkhead door.

She returned carrying a large blue bath towel. "As I was saying Mike. Maybe you should wait until morning. We all need a good night's sleep, and time to decompress."

"I'm not sure that'll be possible until I get this off my chest JJ."

A light footstep on the deck above. She climbed the companionway steps. Disappeared through the hatch. I strained to hear their voices from above. Nothing.

She preceded him through the hatch and down the companionway. Gage climbed down into the cabin, clad all in black, the wet garments stuck against his skin. A square black backpack pinned tightly against his back by short snap buckle straps under his armpits, another strap around his torso. The backpack fitted like part of the garment.

Gage unsnapped the backpack. He handed it to Jolene. The manner in which she hefted it suggested the weight of weapons. Including I assumed, the dismantled parts of his custom sniper rifle. The thought of the rifle brushed the exposed nerve.

"What were you thinking?" I said, my anger undiminished, but tempered by the passage of time, and the relief of seeing him returned safe and unharmed. And perhaps the whisky lining my gullet and stomach.

"Goddammit Gage. You assassinated that man. Killed him in cold blood..." Eyes as hard and frigid as a glacier froze any further words in my throat.

"Damn me all you want. Judge me all you want. I've seen that bastard's handiwork up close and personal. I held the lifeless bodies of mothers, children, and infants he butchered, in my hands. I could've saved them. Their blood is on my hands too because I didn't put that rabid dog down when I had the chance. Instead I followed fucking orders. Protected the fucking mission. I don't do that anymore." His voice as harsh and cold as his eyes, damning me along with those who had stopped him the first time. "Tonight their souls may rest easier. And maybe so can mine."

He turned without another word, strode through the galley, entered the aft stateroom and closed the door behind him.

Everything in time and space stood frozen. Like an arctic wind had just swept through the cabin. It left me speechless, staring at the closed door.

Jolene stood next to me, her eyes subtly shifting color, sympathetic and understanding.

"You haven't seen the things he's seen Mike. Haven't experienced what he's experienced. Don't know the things he knows."

She kissed me lightly on the cheek. "Good night." She followed him, closing the cabin door behind her.

I lay in the comfortable bunk, listening to the soft gurgling against Wherever's hull. Waiting for sleep, which wouldn't come. Haunted by the death at the estate. The sudden, unexpected violence of it. Haunted too by the picture painted by Gage's words. My shock and anger normal reactions, I decided. Okay even. But JJ had been correct. My righteous indignation misplaced, and probably misguided. There were real live monsters in the world. And we relied on cops, and men like Gage, to go out into the cold dark night to protect us from them. Protect our lives, our principles, the luxury of righteous indignation. I hadn't walked in his shoes. I had no right to judge.

CHAPTER 34

My next conscious thought, I smell coffee. The rich aroma of Jamaican mountain roast. I shuffled on bare feet to the salon, stretching out knotted kinks in my muscles, in my stiff joints and back. Reminders of my age. I expected to see Jolene. Instead Gage stood at the galley stove, stirring a skillet. Other scents reached me, eggs, sausage, onions, potatoes.

"Sleep okay?" he asked, not glancing up. His attention focused on the sizzling skillet.

"Well enough considering. Don't remember falling asleep. The waking up part a little achy as usual. Par for the course at my age I guess."

"Yeah, tell me about it."

"You're up early."

"Been up for a while. Didn't sleep much." The somber tone in his voice stirred a pang of guilt and remorse in me.

I leaned against the bulkhead opening to the galley. "Look Gage. About last night. I owe you an apology. I overreacted."

"No worries. I don't expect you to understand."

"Fact is I do understand, precisely because I don't understand."

"Have to admit that one zipped by me. What does that mean in plain English?" He turned to face me.

"JJ said it last night. I haven't seen what you've seen. Know what you know. It's not my place to judge."

Clear brown eyes stared into mine. A piercing intensity I'd grown accustomed to. Discomforting all the same, as though he could see right into my soul.

He nodded. "Coffee's ready."

"Let me hit the head first. And then I think we need to debrief."

"What's there to debrief?"

"In case you hadn't noticed I went off plan last night too."

"I'm sure you had your reasons. And know what you're doing."

"Just the same I want your guys take on it. JJ still sleeping?"

"Yeah. Practically up the whole night talking. Makes me wish I'd had a therapist after every op when I was still working."

I smiled. Another revealing window into their remarkable relationship. Finished in the head, showered and changed, I emerged on deck. The awning had been rigged. Breakfast set out on the cockpit table. Egg and sausage omelets, hashed potatoes, slices of ripe pawpaw and coffee.

The day bright and already hot as the sun climbed higher in an azure sky. The clouds subtly shifted shape as they floated above St. Vincent's lush green peaks, and drifted across the tranquil bay. Two other vessels had joined Wherever during the night. A forty-four foot catamaran, the type used by a local bare boat charter company. And a sleek thirty-two foot sloop.

The first sips of hot coffee jump-started my brain. A sound from the companionway drew my attention. Jolene emerged through the hatch. Fresh and radiant, in cut off jean shorts and a loose oversized grey tee shirt. Damp gold streaked hair, tangled in tight curls, framed her exotic face. Her startling eyes bright green in the shaded sunlight.

"Morning sunshine," she said to no one in particular, sliding onto the cockpit seat next to Gage.

"How you doing this morning?" she asked me, discerning eyes peering into mine as she poured coffee into her mug.

"Better," I said.

"And you guys good?" Hazel eyes held mine in a probing stare over the rim of her mug as she sipped.

"No problem," I said.

"So what happened last night?" she asked.

"Damned if I know. Maybe the shock of..." Chopping off the sentence. No need to go there. "The thought of Von Sachsen just walking away..." I paused again. "Look, I haven't really sorted out what was going in my head last night. Maybe I need a session with you too," I said, smiling at her."

"We're talking now," she said, lathering dark home-made guava jelly on a slice of toast.

"What's done is done." I said, my eyes taking renewed interest in my plate as taste buds sprang awake in response to a spicy medley on my tongue.

"What'd you put in this," I asked Gage, savoring the exotic tastes as I chewed. He merely smiled.

"Anyway, my concern now is the follow up," I said. Not wishing to interrupt the delectable explosions on my palate, I shoveled more eggs and potatoes into my mouth as I spoke.

"How do we control the fallout?" I said around a mouthful. "We were always planning to arrest Fredericks either here or hand him to the FBI once we had the evidence. And give the CIA and the Brits enough to neutralize Von Sachsen. What I did last night put us ahead of our game plan. The cat will be out of the bag before we wanted it to get out. How do we control that, and hang on to these guys until we can tie them in a tight bow they can't squirm out of? They're both powerful in their own right. Fredericks has considerable local political influence. On the other hand, I now have access to his homes and his files. A fishing expedition for sure. But Vincentian law allows a bit more leeway than I'd have in the States."

Jolene nodded. Gage silent. He placed a slice of paw-paw in his mouth. Both listened in rapt attention. Strong coffee, satisfying food in my belly, verbalizing my thoughts, all helped to put the chaos swirling through my mind the night before into actionable perspective.

"Von Sachsen presents a different problem," I said. "And the risk of precipitating an international incident. Not because of his detention, or his release. But extradition. Which government is going to claim first dibs? And which has the better claim to him? And it's gonna put an international spotlight on St.Vincent we neither need nor desire right now.

"Then there's the public aspects of this thing," I continued. "If we bring charges against them it becomes a matter of public record. When Vincy Mas ends the public's attention will turn to the elections. Both parties will be going at each other tooth and nail. The recent scandals still fresh in everyone's mind. And then this. The political fallout could be seismic. And unpredictable."

"But we knew all this going in," Jolene said.

"Yes. We knew we had to figure a way to roll it out. But we hadn't gotten to that part yet. And my actions last night were premature. Right now only the Governor General knows the full extent of the conspiracy. The Prime Minister doesn't even know. And the public doesn't know.

"Maybe they shouldn't," Gage said.

"Point is how do we keep it from them now? After the arrests last night? I'm going to have a lot of explaining to do. At least it happened at the end of my tenure. Maybe that's why I acted the way I did last night. Nothing to lose."

"What the public knows and doesn't know might depend on what you charge them with," Jolene said.

"Thing is I don't know what to charge them with yet. We may get something on Fredericks. Samuel is coordinating the searches of his residences this morning. Including the Richmond Vale estate. Should be getting a report from him soon. By the way, what happened to the yacht," I asked, a swallow of coffee washing down the last delicious mouthful.

I'd directed the question at Jolene. Gage answered instead. "No sign of it. Cumberland Bay empty when I checked the satellite this morning. It's gone from Vincentian waters. But the team from the estate will report their master's arrest. You may have less time than you think."

"I'm not deluding myself I can hold these guys for long," I said. "I have at least until tomorrow to charge them. Maybe longer. Tomorrow is the earliest they can see a magistrate. And the magistrates' calendars are full. But they have the juice to get pushed to the top. Or get a quick appearance. And like you said, the diplomatic wrangling, at least for Von Sachsen, will probably start sooner than later. In the meantime, they'll both have a chance to experience the accommodations of Her Majesty's prison. No segregation. No special treatment. They're gonna love that," I said, a wicked smirk on my face.

"I need to get an edited partial of the button cam video stateside," Gage said. "Close the book on Botha. I've got a couple of back channels I could use. But I've used them before and I don't want to raise any red flags. Anyway it'd be best coming from you guys. This was your operation. We should also send any photos we have of the other guys at the estate. At least get them on a watch list. They did a pretty thorough job cleaning the site. Probably done it before."

"That's the other thing," I said, turning to Gage. "How do I explain that? And may I ask what that was all about? Why you had to kill him?"

"You won't need to explain," he said. The harsh glacial tone of the night before absent. His demons at rest. Probably Jolene's handiwork. The eyes staring back at me soft, sympathetic. "No one will want to go near it. They'll probably want to pin a medal on you in a secret oval office ceremony."

"Who was he?" I asked.

"Name's Botha. South African. A sanctioned target by at least three governments I know of. Got on our radar about fifteen years ago when he orchestrated a massacre of a Chadian village. Two hundred thirty men, women and children. Made it look like rebel militia. Turns out a certain corporation wanted the land the village stood on. Specifically the natural gas and minerals beneath it. Perhaps now we know who was behind it. Had him in my sights once. I'd been tracking him for days when I got called off. Ordered to abort the mission. And he just kept on killing. Lives that might've been saved if I'd just taken the shot when I had the chance." A hardness returned in his eyes, and his voice acquired a distant quality as though his words evoked a painful memory.

"Gage," Jolene said softly to him. Her hand rested lightly on his arm.

"Point is there're task forces on at least three continents on the lookout for Botha," he said, his equanimity restored. "Now they can close the book on him. One less evil son of a bitch in the world."

"We could send the video through Forde at the FBI," Jolene suggested.

"Or Melanie," I said. "That reminds me. I'll have to brief the Governor General before any of this becomes public."

"What about the Prime Minister?" Jolene asked.

"I'll discuss it with Sir Christopher. It may be best the Prime Minister and parliament hear it from him."

Breakfast consumed, Jolene stood to clear the table when my cell phone rang.

"It's Sammy," I said, checking the display after pulling the phone from my trouser pocket.

"Morning Sammy. Got anything for me?"

"How 'bout a early Christmas present. Or birthday. When's your birthday Commissioner?" His cheerful exhilaration evident over the phone.

"I like the sound of that. What'd you find?" I asked after placing the phone on the cockpit table and activating its speaker mode.

"Well we still sorting through de stuff from de house in Cane Garden. Had an office he used there. FIU can probably make better sense of it. And we got a computer and some flash drives. Nothing from Richmond Vale. Looks like he didn't keep any personal or business records at de estate."

"All sounds pretty good Sammy but I don't see a Christmas or birthday present in any of that."

"I savin' dat for last Commissioner," as my imagination conjured a satisfied grin on his face.

"I was just finishing at Cane Garden when I get a call from de team up by Richland Park. They found a man staying at de estate. At first they thought he's de caretaker, or maybe a laborer on de farm. But one of de officers recognized him." A pause.

I leaned toward the phone. "Okay Sammy, you can tell a good story," my amused tone also containing a hint of exasperation. "You've got me in suspense. Now get to the punch line."

"He fit de description of de man who shot Glenford Mackee."

Stunned silence in the cockpit. Jolene's eyebrows arched upward, her mouth slightly ajar. A playful grin stretched Gage's lips and mouth.

"Commissioner?" the voice rising from the cockpit table filled the silence.

"Sammy, you're sure?"

"Yes sir. And Commissioner," again a pause. "Dey recovered de gun."

"Where are you?"

"Heading up to Richland now. I called Assistant Superintendent Rogers. He's meeting me there."

"Listen Sammy. Take charge of the prisoner and the weapon when you get there. So far you're the only one who knows of the Elon Fredericks connection and his arrest. You'll have to bring the AS up to speed. He can reach me on my cell with any questions. And Sammy, my orders are nobody questions him until I do. In the meantime run his prints through RSS."

"Yes sir."

"Well whaddayou know," I said, disconnecting the call, staring at the silent phone. "Looks like our hand against Mr. Fredericks just got stronger. Look guys, with this new development I gotta get moving. Gage can you get the video ready? I'm gonna need it before I leave. Maybe two copies," I said, retrieving my cell phone and dialing a new number.

"Sure," he said, pushing himself up from the soft cockpit cushions.

"Hey," I said, my voice low and breathy, eliciting a raised eyebrow from Jolene. She finished clearing the table, glanced at me, a parting coquettish smile before disappearing down the hatch.

"You sound good," Melanie said. "Things must be going well."

"Better than expected. One of the reasons I'm calling. Besides just wanting to hear your voice."

Her soft chuckle audible through the phone. "And the other reason."

"I have something for your spook shop. An unexpected development at a recent meeting. I've got a video they'll be interested in."

"What do you need me to do?"

"I'm sending you the video. You need to get it distributed as soon as possible. Also there've been developments in our security situation you need to know. I'm trying to see the Governor General this afternoon."

"Nothing you can't tell me now?"

"Too much to tell and I'm pressed for time. But it's pretty much over."

"Are you serious?" Her voice raised in surprise. "How?"

"I've got a lot to tell you. You mentioned you had a few days off. Think you could get over here this evening? Or tomorrow? I'll fly you over and back if necessary."

"Let me see. Send me the video. We'll take it from there."

"See you soon," I said, disconnecting.

"How we doing Gage?" I said stepping from the companionway to Wherever's nav station. The electronics we'd used during the operation since disappeared.

"Just about done," he said.

"Good. I have a small window to see the GG. Gonna be tight getting to Kingstown, send this, and get back to Montrose."

"Send it from here," he said.

"I don't have my laptop. This has to look like it came from my email account right?"

"I have my laptop," Jolene said from the salon. "It has my official police account."

Sir Christopher Brathwaite met me on the verandah of Government House's residence wing. Dressed in casual clothing. Dark grey slacks and white Guayabera shirt.

"Thank you for seeing me on such short notice sir," I said, shaking his hand.

"I gather it is quite urgent," his deep baritone polite and cultured as always.

"Yes sir. There's been a breakthrough in our security situation you need to be aware of before it becomes public."

"Please Commissioner, have a seat," indicating cushioned wicker armchairs around a round table on the verandah. The table shaded by a large green umbrella opened above it.

A long, heavy silence hung between us following my recital of the previous night's events, including the arrest of Von Sachsen, Fredericks, and the suspect in Mackee's murder.

"My word Commissioner. How much more can the country take?" he sighed, breaking the silence.

"Yes sir," I said in genuine empathy. "But the conspiracy has been stopped. The concern now is managing the fallout."

"I agree. The local political element will eventually work itself out after much chest thumping and ballyhooing, especially if it's managed as a strictly criminal matter. The international aspect concerns me though."

"I've taken the liberty of informing Consul Barnes at the U.S. Embassy of the situation, without providing too much detail."

A frown crossed his face. His intelligent eyes scrutinized mine."

"Was that wise Commissioner?"

"We're familiar with her, and she with us. We have a good working relationship. I believe she's someone we won't have a problem dealing with as far as U.S interests are concerned. You might want to reach out to the British High Commissioner sir, give him a similar heads up."

He nodded his head in agreement. "Yes. Yes. I take your point."

"Also sir, I will of course take your advice on the matter, but I believe informing the Prime Minister and parliament might best be accomplished by you, as we did in disclosing Jackson Taylor's information."

"You may be correct again Commissioner. I'll take it under advisement." Glancing at his watch. "If there's nothing else Commissioner, I'm already late for another engagement. You've given me a great deal to think about."

"Nothing more at this point sir. We've gathered a great deal of material from Fredericks's residences we still have to go through. And we'll proceed as with any other criminal investigation and prosecution."

"Thank you Commissioner," he said, standing, offering his hand. "Please keep me informed."

The next stop my office. A briefing for my unit commanders. Hoping they'd be gathered by the time I arrived. Samuel and Rogers had been supervising the Richland estate search, and had to transport the prisoner to the Central Police Station for booking. Other unit commanders had the day off. Probably out enjoying the final day of Mardi Gras. Except Superintendent Milton Byron, Commander of the Southern Division, which included Kingstown, who had his hands full overseeing Mardi Gras and supervising the still crowded, bustling station. I excluded Commanders whose divisions were not actively involved in the investigations. A routine status report would be forwarded to the Western and Eastern Division Commanders, in whose areas the crimes and arrests had taken place. Navigating Kingstown's clogged streets may also have delayed them. Passage through the streets still difficult and time consuming as Vincy Mas built to his climatic conclusion.

I was surprised to find all the commanders I'd summoned assembled in the outer office. Also pleasantly surprised by their casual attire. I was unaccustomed to seeing them out of uniform. Superintendent Byron alone attired in the daily greys. Their quiet conversation ceased as I entered my outer office. They stood at attention at my approach, saluting in unison like cadets on parade.

"As you were everyone," I said, hastily returning the salute.

I led them toward the conference room door. Held it open as they filed in. They stood around the long rectangular table waiting for me to sit. For the moment, I preferred standing.

"Please sit," I said, indicating the chairs.

A noisy shuffling of chairs and the scraping of wood furniture on the wood floor filled the small, enclosed room, as they settled into seats around the table. insufficient seating for everyone, the junior officers stood against the wall. My gaze settled for a moment on each of them as I glanced around the room. Superintendent Milton Byron of Southern Division, Superintendent Basil Hughes of RSS, Assistant Superintendent Bernard Rogers of Major Crime and the Rapid Response Unit, a satisfied grin on his face. We hadn't officially announced his replacement at Major Crime yet. Assistant Superintendent Keith Manley of the Special Services Unit. Assistant Superintendent Leroy Phillips of narcotics, Lieutenant Commander David Pompey of the Coast Guard, and Assistant Superintendent Angela McKinley of the Financial Intelligence Unit. Next to me at the head of the table stood Deputy Commissioner Huggins. Sergeant Samuel stood against the wall on my right.

All eyes stared at me in curious anticipation. A sad expression on some, expecting a different kind of announcement. Angela McKinley's eyes alert and attentive. Huggins' expression serious and contemplative.

"First let me thank all of you for coming in on a day off on such short notice," I said. "Secondly, anything you hear discussed in the next few minutes must remain within this room. That is a direct order not to discuss anything you hear today with spouses, girlfriends, boyfriends, family, or even among yourselves unless you're directly involved in the case."

I paused. My gaze continued around the table, lingering a few moments on each face. Their expressions now uniformly attentive.

"You are all aware we've been investigating some high profile cases lately," I said. "And of course you're also aware of the recent scandals in the country. The resulting resignations, cabinet reshuffles, various commissions of inquiry, and the call for early elections.

"What isn't public knowledge is all of these events, including the Mackee murder, and the murder of undercover Police Sergeant Derrick Whittaker." Mention of a murdered undercover officer produced perplexed expressions on a few of the faces around the table. "Also the rogue police officers within the RRU, and come to think about it, the attempt on my life sixteen months ago and the murder of Jackson Taylor, are all connected to a foreign conspiracy aimed at taking control of St. Vincent and the Grenadines."

A rush of discordant noises followed my announcement. Furniture scrapped the floor as postures shifted in the chairs. Voices were raised in astonished exclamation. Breaths expelled by nervous thoracic spasms. Shocked and bewildered expressions on the faces around the room.

"Besides myself, only the Deputy Commissioner, Superintendent Johanssen, and Sergeant Samuel here, were aware of this conspiracy. In fact, I initiated the undercover program and recruited Sergeant Samuel and two other undercover officers in response to the conspiracy. Outside the force only the Governor General knows about this conspiracy. And only he, I, and Superintendent Johanssen are aware of the details."

"De Superintendent sir?" The question from Milton Byron.

"Yes," I said in a sharp tone. Byron among the few of a vanishing breed on the force still encumbered by a patriarchal chauvinism toward female officers. "Superintendent Johanssen was the first to discover the conspiracy from information she developed during her investigation of my shooting. And she uncovered the full extent of the conspiracy during her investigation of Jackson Taylor's murder." My disapproving stare leveled at him.

"What you sayin' Commisshunah? Dis some foreign country? We lookin' at foreign invasion heah or what?" The concern voiced by Lieutenant Commander David Pompey. His Coast Guard the first line of defense against any such invasion.

"No. More subtle and insidious David. It's a global corporate conglomerate, controlled by one man, a family actually. For the past three years they've been pouring money into St. Vincent and the Grenadines through development projects and extensive land purchases, corrupting local politicians, businessmen, policemen, and undermining our financial institutions. It's taken us almost a year to identify the person behind this, which we only did in the past two weeks. Once we'd identified this individual, I set in motion a plan to lure him here to St. Vincent. Last night Sergeant Samuel and I arrested him, along with Mister Elon Fredericks, his agent on St. Vincent."

Renewed noise around the room. The name Elon Fredericks repeated in hushed, shocked disbelief.

"It's my belief Elon Fredericks arranged the murder of Glenford Mackee to protect Fredericks' connection to the conspiracy."

This time stunned silence. No scraping of chairs, or vocal exclamations. The shock of the latest bombshell registered as widened eyes and silent gaping mouths.

"Now listen up people," I said, pausing to gather their full attention again. "Because of these two arrests we can expect a shitstorm headed our way. An international shitstorm at that. Already forming I have no doubt. I seriously doubt I'll be able to hold this man on St. Vincent for long. And his involvement is so far removed from the actual crimes, it makes charging and prosecuting him virtually impossible. Even if we had the evidence against him, other countries will have claims on him. It's gonna be a diplomatic dogfight."

"Fredericks on the other hand is a Vincentian national we can hold and prosecute. We can connect him financially to the conspiracy." My gaze steadied on Angela. "We also collected records from his residences which FIU will go through for further evidence. And this morning during a search of Fredericks' Richland Park estate, we found and arrested the suspect wanted in connection with the Glenford Mackee murder. We also recovered the gun used in the murder. I want Fredericks for murder too people. Our best chance is to flip the gunman. So I need the strongest case we can build against this guy."

I turned to Bernie Rogers, sitting three chairs down from me.

"Bernie bring us up to date on the prisoner."

"We find tree different passpoh'ts in his possession Commisshunah. One American wid de name Carl Vincent. A St. Lucia passpoh't in de name Vincent Tully. And a Antigua passpoht in de name Vincent Smalls. We don't know his real identity or nationality yet. We send his prints off to RSS."

"Broaden the search to the FBI and DEA," I said. "What about the gun?"

"We already know de gun match a murder on St. Lucia and one on Antigua. We already received de case files from dose investigachuns. We conductin' ballistic tests on de gun now, but we already know it de same caliber, and we feel sure we goin' get a match."

"We need to connect that gun to him," I said. "Start a trace. See if you can track the movements of the gun. And we also need to put it in his hands. Probably won't be able to get residue off him after all this time, but check all the clothing you found where he was staying. Depending on how the clothing was handled we may get something from it, if we're lucky. You've been using the RSS forensic resources?"

"Yes Commisshunah. Dey been consultin' on evidence collection since we start de investigachun. De labs been runnin' de forensic tests for us. Especially de trace evidence from the van. We've already eliminated some of dat from de owner and some odder passengers. What leave must be from de gunman."

"Good. We put him in that van too and we'll have a pretty strong case."

"Yes Commisshunah," the satisfied grin reappearing.

"That's it then guys. With the arrests last night, St. Vincent and the Grenadines is clear of this thing. We just dodged a one-fifty-five howitzer shell aimed at us. I wanted you all to know the facts now that the situation is contained, and before the shitstorm hits and wild stories start circulating in the media. And let me repeat, nothing you've heard here today leaves this room. Certain aspects of these cases will soon become public knowledge. You'll be free to comment on those once they do. But given the circumstances its best if you keep what you know to yourselves, and refer all media inquiries to AS Taylor. You're dismissed."

Renewed rustling and scraping of furniture as they pushed back their chairs and stood from the table. I delayed Commander David Pompey's departure to arrange a ride across to Bequia after the next and final item on my agenda. A visit to the murder suspect.

The prisoner sat on the hard stone floor of the dingy malodorous holding cell rouge RRU officer Devon Weekes had occupied earlier. I studied him as the constable attending the jail opened the cell door. Medium height. Fit physique. The muscles of his arms well toned and defined. Dark coffee complexion. Hair cropped short against his scalp. Long oval face, broad straight nose. Wide mouth surrounded by a moustache continuing down the sides to a short goatee on his round chin.

"I want something from you," I said, addressing him across the six by six cell. "And fortunately I have something to trade you probably want very much to keep."

He remained in his seated position as I addressed him. Legs crossed in front of him on the floor. His gaze rose to meet mine. The wide spaced eyes dull and blank, not acknowledging my presence, seeing right past me in a thousand yard stare. He maintained his silence.

"That's assuming of course you're just a hired professional who was unlucky enough to get caught, and not a true believer, willing to martyr yourself for a cause."

The eyes still unfocused he said "Me ain't no terrorist." The voice soft and muted, as if heard from a distance.

"Of course not. But are you willing to hang for someone else?"

"Whey de hell you talkin' 'bout?" A defiant tone crept into the soft voice.

"We're going to hang you Vincent, or whatever your name is. You know that's the sentence for a premeditated murder. And the man you murdered was a politician. A representative in the parliament. We have witnesses who put you at the scene. We have the gun. We have the van. We have forensic evidence connecting you to the gun and the van. So you're going to hang by the neck until dead," I said. "But even before that the man who hired you will probably hire someone else to kill you in prison. Happens all the time. Either way you're dead."

Another silence. But my words registered, evident from his eyes darting left and right, still not focusing on me, but assessing everthing I'd said.

"So what dis ting' you have fe trade?" So he had heard me.

"Your life," I said, pausing to allow it to register. "All you have to do is give up the man who hired you. We'll keep you here instead of putting you in the Kingstown prison while your case is in the courts. We'll protect you. So you decide if you want to live or die. But you have to decide soon. Or I can't help you."

I signaled the attendant. The blank eyes finally focused on me as I exited the cell.

As I stepped into the station courtyard my cell phone rang. "Some wasp's nest you stirred up," Melanie said when I answered.

"Nothing compared to what comes next," I said.

"What's that supposed to mean?"

"Shitstorm's coming. And I'm going to need you. Sir Christopher and I agreed you're the U.S. face we want to deal with on this. And I need to brief you so you can get ahead of the storm."

"Well after the ruckus your video kicked up here the ambassador wants me in St. Vincent ASAP. They've got me on a charter this evening."

"Great. Means you can switch the destination to J.F. Mitchell on Bequia."

"Sure that's a good idea?"

"It's where I'll be if you want an ASAP briefing."

Her soft laughter carried over the phone.

"I'll call you when I arrive," I said.

"No need. I'll be there to meet you."

"How'll you know....?"

"I'm the Commissioner of Police remember. I'll see you later," disconnecting the call.

Sammy waited for me in the courtyard. I'd asked him to drive me to Calliaqua. During the drive I wanted to run through the arrangements for Whittaker's funeral the next day. We were both pallbearers, and he'd be my ride from the airport.

CHAPTER 35

The house acquired an entirely new aspect when Melanie walked through the door. I'd met her at the Bequia airport in Paget Farm, timing my arrival by the exchanges between the pilot and tower controller heard over my VHF scanner.

I placed her bags, as in plural, intended for more than an overnight stay, in the master bedroom. Returning to the living room I observed her exploring the room. Her eyes examined the décor, the furniture, my books, my memorabilia, lightly running her fingers along the objects as she walked by them. Having her in the house like a fresh coat of bright colors on the walls.

"Finally," I said. "I've wanted you to see this place for so long. For us to be here together."

"It's absolutely charming," she said. "And so you."

We stepped onto the verandah. The evening soft and cool. A breeze rustled the branches atop tall coconut trees along Friendship Bay's beach. We sat next to each other on the cushioned wicker loveseat, savoring the sights, sounds, and smells of the tropical evening. The sky awash in stars. A new crescent moon cast a pale light over the landscape.

408 Michael W Smart

"I'm going to tell you the whole story," I said, breeching the companionable silence. "Information Langley probably hasn't shared with the embassy."

Her gaze followed me as I retrieved a file from the living room, switched on the verandah light, and returned to the seat next to her.

"Remember last week all of a sudden the priority at the embassy changed?"

"Yeah. They began focusing on Mustique."

"That's because besides the searches being done by Langley and the FBI, I had a very resourceful friend of mine searching too."

"This friend..."

"I'll get to that later," I said, interrupting her. "Collating what he had and information I'd been gathering in our Financial Intelligence Unit, led us to this man," I said, handing her a photograph of Dougan from the file.

"His name is James Dougan. Head of a global private security firm called The Phoenix Group. Really a private army. He'd been staying on Mustique.

"That's why the sudden focus on Mustique," she said.

"Yes. This man Dougan ordered the murder of an undercover officer I had working in the Southern Grenadines. He probably also ordered the murder of Glenford Mackee, arranged by their mole here on St. Vincent. The mole hired a guy to commit the murder. We arrested the gunman this morning."

"Nice work."

"It gets better. Dougan led us to this man," handing her a photograph of Von Sachsen. "Godfried Wilhelm Von Sachsen, head of a global conglomerate, and the man behind the conspiracy."

"My God Mike."

"I sent this information to my contacts in the FBI and the CIA. That's when all hell broke loose, and when the spook shop in Barbados got new orders to focus on Mustique. Intelligence services on three continents were suddenly interested in Von Sachsen. But then he disappeared. What Langley didn't know was he slipped everyone's net to come here. For a meeting with me. I'd coerced him into the meeting through Dougan."

"But how'd you get a man like Dougan to flip."

"The details aren't relevant. Suffice it to say I managed to compromise Dougan. Anyway, Von Sachsen gets here yesterday evening, figuring he's going to neutralize me. The guy in the video was part of his security detail, along with some other hard types. But things quickly go off the rails for Von Sachsen. Before anyone knows what's happening this guy gets shot, and I hightail it out of there with Von Sachsen and his mole on St. Vincent. A man named Elon Fredericks. A highly connected local financier and advisor to both political parties. I arrested them last night. I have both of them locked up in Kingstown Prison. Definitely not the six star accommodations they're accustomed to."

Lively light brown eyes swimming in artful amusement gazed at me. A shrewd smile parted her lips, defining her lovely cheekbones.

"Very nice story Mike. But I don't buy half of that crap. I'm pretty sure you've left out some important chunks you're not telling me."

"You got the highlight reel," I said. "Tell me about this guy who was killed," I asked in a quick segue.

The smile remained. Her astute gaze continued to study me. Her head cocked to the side, slanting the straight silky black bangs across her forehead.

"His name was Karl Botha. Known as Botha the butcher. An Afrikaner. Operated mostly on the African continent. Got his start in the South African Bureau of State Security and its successor the National Intelligence Service during Apartheid. Went freelance after the collapse of Apartheid. Then he dropped out of sight. But not his special brand of killing. Had a reputation for leveling and clearing villages, usually by slaughtering every living soul in the village. Been causing headaches in the State Department for years in African conflict zones where we'd tried to get the opposing sides talking. On the top of America's most wanted list. Whispers of a classified Presidential Finding. A sanctioned kill on sight order. That's the highlight reel," she said, a mischievous smile playing around her lips.

"I have a funeral tomorrow afternoon." I said. "The murdered undercover officer I told you about."

"Mike, I'm so sorry," laying her hand on mine, imparting a gentle, comforting squeeze.

"Make yourself at home," I said. "You can work from here. I think the shit's gonna hit the fan sooner than later. Some of Von Sachsen's men got off the island on a yacht he arrived on. They'll have reported his arrest by now."

"Evenin' Commisshunah." The call from the road at the back of the house.

I stepped to the corner of the verandah. Peered out into the yard.

"Come around front," I shouted. Turning to Melanie, "Dinner's here," I said. "And with it, the end of any more shop talk."

Two tall girls, their slim teenaged figures fully formed, approached from the side of the house. Each carried two cloth covered wicker baskets. They paused at the foot of the stone steps to the verandah.

"Here or inside," I said to Melanie.

"Here's fine," she said, a mysterious smile on her face I couldn't define.

"Evening Darcy. Vilma," I said to the girls.

"Evenin' Commisshunah. Miss," they said. Shy smiles and curious glances directed at Melanie.

"Set it out here please," I said to the girls, indicating a low rectangular wicker table.

"Yes Commisshunah," Darcy said, uncovering their baskets and setting out a dinner for two on the table.

When the girls departed, generous tips in their pockets, Melanie and I pulled armchairs close to the table.

"Delivery. How extraordinary," she said, the amused mischievous smile still in place.

"I'm the Commissioner of Police," I said. "I make extraordinary happen."

"I don't doubt it for a moment," Melanie said. "As in that story you just told. But as you said, no more shop talk. I'm starving, and it smells delicious."

"Curried chicken, rice and peas, local dasheen, plantains and sweet potatoes. One sec." I said, darting into the house. I returned carrying lit sandalwood scented citronella candles for the table. I doused the overhead light on the verandah. I also carried two wine glasses for the chilled Sauvignon Blanc I'd ordered to accompany the meal.

We ate in companionable silence, sitting back in the comfortable armchairs, our plates on our laps. Melanie gazed out over the coconut trees lining the beach, into the open bay. The moon's silver glow danced across gentle rollers moving across the white capped surface. The deep bass boom of the surf reached us, drumming against the shore in rhythmic regularity.

"I definitely see the appeal of this place," she said. "Must be such a respite from the noise and bustle of Kingstown."

"I fell in love with this place the first time I set eyes on it," I said. "Used to rent a place right over there in La Pompe when I first started coming to Bequia. That house right on the point," I said, pointing with my fork. "But I liked the seclusion of this place. At the time, most of these other houses weren't here. No hotel. Just trees and bush, and that wonderful windward breeze."

I glanced at her. The elongated soulful eyes reflected the candle's flickering flame. Its light danced across the strong mature face, its mix of ethnic features, and the lustrous black hair and bangs.

"I'm hoping you'll spend more time here," I said, delicately broaching the subject.

"Hmmm," laying her plate on the table. She picked up her wine glass by the stem and sipped. "That would mean bringing our little secret into the open." her eyes searched mine in the dim glow of the candlelight.

"That's the point," I said. "I'm ready for that next step."

"To be honest, so am I. But Mike..."

"Baby steps," I said. "One thing at a time. I want to be able to spend more time with you, like this, out in the open. Doesn't mean we have to make a general announcement, or write it across our foreheads," I said.

She laughed. "Still doesn't change the reasons why we kept this on the down low in the first place. If my superiors decide our relationship puts me in a compromised position, I could be taken off this assignment. Recalled home."

"I won't be the Commissioner of Police for much longer," I said.

"It's the reason I'm even willing to consider this," she said. "And there're other assignments in the embassy which might benefit from my local experience. Actually I've been thinking about it a lot lately," her eyes peering into mine, searching, acknowledging a sentiment I'd hope to see in them.

"Speaking of steps, I have a couple of friends I want you to meet." Her eyes grew wide. The sensuously curved eyebrows rose to meet the tips of her bangs.

"From baby steps to a giant leap," she smiled.

"Still baby steps. Actually you've already met Jolene. I want you to meet the man she's with. My best friend I told you about. We can have dinner together tomorrow evening. But before I ask them, I need you to make me a promise." I gazed into her eyes, assured of my trust in her, despite what I knew, or suspected, about her. Her real position in the Embassy. She unaware of my suspicion. Or perhaps she was. Both of us circumspect in the information we shared given our official positions. Perhaps that was about to change as well.

"I need you to promise me you'll not mention my friend, or speak of him to anyone. In fact as far as anyone else is concerned, he doesn't exist."

"Now I'm intrigued," she said.

"I'm trusting you with a life Melanie. The life of a man I trust with mine. Who's saved mine on more than one occasion. And Jolene's too. I need that promise before I can ask if he's willing to meet you," I said, still searching her eyes as I spoke. I noted the slight skeptical narrowing, the aroused curiosity. And in the end, a reciprocal loving trust she had never verbalized.

"And you have it, of course Mike. I promise."

Like a fantasy made real, we lay naked together in bed. My bed. In my house. Her gentle kisses and caressing fingers awakened my desire. The soft gentle stroking of her hand produced a throbbing erection. She climbed atop me. Guided me to the warm velvet opening between her thighs. Her breath hot on my cheek as I slid inside her. She gasped as she rocked back and forth, building a rhythm, inflaming our raw desire. Its intensity increased as her slow writhing dance morphed into a rodeo, Melanie riding atop a bucking bull. Her curved breasts swung like loose wild pendulums, brushing my face. My upward thrusts met hers. Squeaking bed sounds amidst animalistic grunting. Until a sudden shuddering release consumed us both. She collapsed into my arms. Both of us drenched in the sweat of our exertion.

I spent Monday morning in my office reading updates on the investigations and reports on the Mardi Gras. A perfunctory exercise. My thoughts occupied elsewhere, particularly Whittaker's funeral that afternoon. Across St.Vincent and the Grenadines only two fatalities during the weekend celebration. One accidental, one due to violence. The usual arrests for petty offenses. All in all Vincy Mas had proceeded without significant incident. The police presence had ensured a joyous, peaceful celebration.

I returned home to Bequia just before sunset. When I arrived, Melanie had been pacing the verandah, a cell phone pressed to her ear. Her conversation intense, but quiet, not loud enough to overhear beyond the verandah. She completed her call, turned to greet me. Bright oval sympathetic eyes peered into mine.

"How'd it go?"

"Wonderful service. Police honors, complete with rifle salute and folded flag presented to his grandmother. God I hate funerals."

"You knew him well?"

"Well enough. All three of them. I selected them. Mentored them during their training overseas. I was the piece of home they'd left behind. The thing that anchored them here when they could've easily opted for a life in the States, like so many of their family and countrymen. Yeah, I knew them well. Maybe too well."

"That's never a bad thing Mike. Despite the pain of loss."

I leaned in to kiss her. A short soft hello and thank you. But she prolonged it, her soft tender lips comforting. She released me as the tension eased from my shoulders and arms.

"What was that about?" I said, referring to the phone still clutched in her hand.

"The shitstorm you've been expecting," she said. "It's gathering. Somehow von Sachsen got the Swiss involved."

"His father lives there," I informed her. "As did his grandfather after the war. The family has Swiss citizenship."

"Well the Swiss are representing Von Sachsen. Their embassies in Britain and the States are already making inquiries. Fortunately both governments were able to assure the Swiss they were already involved in the situation and had diplomatic representatives on the ground. I called the Ambassador this morning to report I'd been briefed on the situation, and that the Governor General and Commissioner of Police had requested me to represent U.S. interests. He agreed. Sir Christopher had called the British High Commissioner and briefed him last night."

"What did the Swiss have to say?" I asked.

"Not much right now. You and Sir Christopher allowed us and the Brits to get ahead of this thing. The fact we're already looking into it came off well with the Swiss, nullifying the usual diplomatic posturing you get with these sorts of situations. At any rate, you have some time. The Swiss representative arrives tomorrow, and figure a day or more to hash out an arrangement."

"Let me get out of this damn uniform," I said. "We can relax. Enjoy the sunset. Get ready for Dinner. Jolene's having us over to her house. Less public, she figures," a bemused smile on my face as I turned for the door.

The sun below the horizon, a star studded canopy above, we walked hand in hand from Friendship toward Lower Bay. I paused at a turn in the steep road above Lower Bay. I drew her close.

"This is my friend's favorite spot on the island," I said, gazing out at the panoramic sweep of Admiralty Bay, and the three smaller concave shaped bays within it. Soft pale moonlight frolicked across the tranquil water.

"That's his schooner moored in the bay. Wherever."

"It's gorgeous."

"That she is. But don't let him hear you call Wherever 'it'. He's uncharacteristically sentimental about her."

We continued down the steep rut filled road into Lower Bay. Past newly erected rental homes. Past De Reef's open-air restaurant on the beach, and into the village of simpler, one room wood structures. We headed in the direction of Moon Hole, a private community and wildlife preserve on Bequia's narrow western tip. Known for the quirky architecture of its homes constructed into the natural volcanic substrate of the Island, using native stone, hardwoods, and whalebone.

I steered Melanie off the road at Jolene's cutoff. We climbed the steep path marked by flat stones ascending like steps. The night air perfumed by frangipani, lilac, and jasmine plants bordering the path. Jolene's favored scents.

We emerged into the open, sloping front lawn. Large fruit trees cast moonlit shadows across the yard. The diffused glow of shaded lanterns illuminated the front verandah furnished in comfortable relaxing wicker armchairs. One of Gage's hammocks slung across a corner.

"Ahoy," I called, stepping onto the verandah, Melanie alongside. Soft jazz emanated from within.

"In here," Jolene's voice acknowledged my hail.

We stepped into the warm lighting of shaded table lamps spaced around the room. Jolene busy setting the dining table on a section of the room raised a step above the living room. Gage busy at the stove, a kitchen towel thrown casually across his right shoulder.

Jolene glanced up from the table, her eyes greeting us. She breezed across the floor toward us. Bare feet beneath a red floral thigh length sheath sundress. The thin fabric draped the curved figure beneath. The color accented her smooth mocha complexion.

"Consul Barnes," she said, taking Melanie's hand. Her bright liquid green eyes friendly, inviting. Her smile welcoming. "So happy to have you guys here."

"My pleasure," Melanie said. "And please, I won't call you Superintendent Johanssen if you don't call me Consul Barnes."

"Melanie, right?" still smiling at her. "What can I get you to drink?"

I left the ladies to themselves, joining Gage in the kitchen. The scents emanating from his concoctions produced a flow of gastric juices and a gurgling in the pit of my stomach.

"What're you making?"

"A special chicken dish in a chutney sauce. A blend of Lebanese and Caribbean cuisines for a special occasion. Creamed potatoes and herbed mushrooms on the side."

"Jesus. Where'd you learn to make that?"

"I know how to cook a lot of different cuisines Mike. Especially places where I've spent some time. A hobby to pass the time."

"I should know better than to ask already. Come, let me introduce you."

"Give me a sec here," he said, adjusting the flame on the stove, wiping his hand on the kitchen towel, and following me across the room.

"Melanie," I said, as we approached her and Jolene discussing a framed Ansel Adams Yellowstone landscape hanging on the wall.

Melanie turned. Her gaze met mine before shifting to Gage. A flicker of surprise in the perceptive, discerning eyes studying him.

"This is my very best friend Nicholas Gage. But he prefers just Gage. Gage, my very special friend Melanie Barnes."

They studied each other for what seemed an interminable moment. Jolene followed the exchange as nervously as I did. A smile creased Gage's lips, growing wider, exuding a discernible, tangible charm. He offered his hand. When Melanie accepted it, he raised her hand to his mouth. A light touch of his lips brushed the back of her hand. His head in a slight bow, his eyes still locked on hers.

"A genuine pleasure to meet you," he said, his incandescent smile washing over her.

The first time I'd seen Melanie blush. "Same here," she said, recovering after Gage released her hand. "So you are the best friend I've heard nothing about until last week?"

"Don't take it personally. He only mentioned his 'special' friend a couple of weeks ago."

She studied Gage a few moments longer, before turning to face me, wearing the undefinable smile I'd noticed the evening before.

"I understand now," she said.

CHAPTER 36

An army of people toiled at clearing and cleaning the streets, collecting and loading piles of trash and debris remaining from the day before. The task requiring days, performed by store owners, street vendors, members of the Public Works Department, garbage haulers, even low risk prisoners in bright orange jumpsuits under the watchful gaze of uniformed prison guards and police constables. Mechanized street sweepers unavailable in St. Vincent's inventory, anything close at hand was put to use sweeping and shoveling, including hand brooms, palm fronds, whisker brooms, tree branches, rakes, shovels, whatever. In any case, many of Kingstown's streets too narrow for mechanized sweepers and payloaders.

I observed the laborious activity from the rear passenger windows of the passing SUV. Melanie silent beside me studying briefing notes, professional and businesslike in a dark grey pinstriped business pantsuit and crisp ivory silk shirt. Her signature strand of pearls adorned her elegant neck. She was headed to Government House to meet the Governor General, and a Permanent Secretary from the Foreign Ministry, in preparation for the Swiss Representative's arrival.

She glanced up from her notes as the RAV4 pulled into the police courtyard.

"I'll call you if we have any questions or need anything," she said, our eyes conveying the parting kiss our lips couldn't.

Cecilia greeted me with a benevolent smile rather than her usual stern visage. "Good morning Commissioner."

"Morning Cissy," I said, continuing on to my office, turning to find her on my heels.

"The papers and radio and TV been calling all morning," she reported, following me into the office. "I've been referring those calls to Assistant Superintendent Taylor's office. The PM wants you to call as soon as you get in. And Assistant Superintendent McKinley has been waiting to speak with you. The Director of Public Prosecutions also wishes you to call him back."

"Let Mckinley know I'm in. And I need to see Assistant Superintendent Rogers too if he's available. The Prime Minister can wait. Get me the DPP first."

"Yes Commissioner. Such a lovely service yesterday," she commented, surprising me by her continued presence. "You did right by him, Commissioner."

"Thanks Cissy," I said. "That means a lot."

"And this thing with Elon Fredericks. Lord have mercy. Arrested and in prison. What this world coming to? You can't tell good from bad anymore."

"Greed Cissy," I said. "And hubris. The oldest motives in the world."

"And one of the seven deadly sins," She said, stepping to my desk, lifting the phone and dialing.

Cecilia not the type to engage in idle gossip or speak behind a person's back, finding it a loathsome practice. Nor was she in the habit of lingering in my office. We hadn't seen much of each other the day before, except at the funeral, and hadn't had a chance to discuss the momentous developments of the past Sunday. Now her comments, her inquiring confused stare, a lingering state of shock, indicated an apparent need for a comforting presence. A phenomenon probably being repeated across the country. And more shocks to come.

"Yes," she said into the phone. "This is the Commissioner of Police's office returning your call. The Commissioner just arrived and is available. Thank you. Please hold for the Commissioner."

"The DPP's office Commissioner," handing me the phone and exiting the office, closing the door softly behind her.

"What a thing, Commissioner," Prosecutor Chambers' deep gravelly voice rasped over the phone line.

"Happens when privileged individuals think they're above the law Wes," I said.

"You have the particulars ready to file? 'Cause he goin' pull every string at his disposal to get a quick hearing before a magistrate."

"We're still investigating and processing the evidence. Inspector Viera began the paperwork yesterday. I haven't seen the particulars yet, but we'll be charging Fredericks in the serious offenses court. Murder, conspiracy to murder, solicitation for the purpose of murder, and threatening a police officer with murder. Soon as it's ready I'll have Viera hand deliver it himself. There may be other financial offenses to add later."

"God Almighty in heaven Commissioner. I'll need those particulars right away."

I buzzed Cecilia. "Cissy, track down Police Prosecutor Inspector Viera. I need to see him right away."

"Yes Commissioner, and AS McKinley is here for you."

"Show her in,"

Angela Mckinley entered the office, her uniform crisp and fresher than her appearance. Her expression worn and tired. Noticeable bags beneath her eyes as she drew to attention and saluted.

"As you were Angela," I said returning the salute. "Have you had any sleep?"

"Been heah most of de time sir," she said.

"Do I need to order you to get some rest?"

Her dark brown eyes held me in a determined stare. "If only people know what you done to save dem and dis country..." Unable to complete the sentence. Her gaze broke away to glance about the room at nothing in particular.

"I'll rest when dis finished sir," she said, her gaze returning to meet mine.

"What do you have?" I said, the words almost choking on the pride and gratitude welling within me.

She handed me a file. "We have evidence to charge Mr. Fredericks with serious financial offenses Commisshunah, including instances of fraud, circumvention of the Aliens Holding Ordinance, money laundering, and corruption of public officials."

"These are the particulars?" I asked, opening the file and flipping through the completed forms.

"Yes Commisshunah.

"Thank you Angela. Now please get some rest. We've got him. It's over."

"Yes Commisshunah," she said, saluting. Executing a sharp about face, she headed for the door.

The constable on jail duty opened the heavy iron door to Clifford Parsons' cell. The name associated with his fingerprints on file at the DEA. He'd been arrested on drug charges in New York a number of years before, following a raid on a West Indian gang. He'd also been implicated in the death of a rival gang member, but there'd been insufficient evidence to charge him. He'd learned his trade and made his bones in New York, returning to the Caribbean where he'd hire out as freelance muscle. His initial connection to Fredericks not yet established.

Bernie Rogers had not returned to the station, but Cecilia had tracked him down by phone. He briefed me on the fingerprints hit. Still awaiting results of forensic tests on Parsons' clothing from labs in Barbados. The ballistics tests, performed locally, confirmed the gun used to kill Mackee was the gun found on Parsons when he'd been arrested.

Parsons had changed into the one-piece orange prison jumpsuit. He appeared rested and well fed when I entered the cell.

"Time's up Clifford," I said, his eyes opening in surprise at the name I used.

"What? You forget we have your fingerprints now. Why is it in this age of fingerprints, DNA, forensic science, computers, and instant communications, you guys still think you can commit a crime, run, hide, and the police won't catch you. So what happened with you? How come you didn't leave St. Vincent right after shooting Mr. Mackee?"

Dark doleful eyes stared back at me. The thousand-yard stare replaced by a calculating defensiveness. The cunning desperation of a trapped animal.

"What 'bout dis deal?" he said.

"That goes away when I walk out the door," I said. "After that you're a walking dead man."

"What you goin' charge me wid? And what goin' be de sentence?"

"That's up to the prosecutor and magistrate. If you forego a trial, plead guilty, and give evidence against the man who hired you, the charge might be reduced, and you won't get the death penalty. They might even allow you to serve your sentence somewhere else. Maybe Barbados."

His eyes shifted right and left as though examining the grime caked walls of the cell. His gaze fell to the floor. When he raised his head, I read his decision in the dull dispirited eyes before he spoke.

We moved to an interrogation room. No larger than his cell. Audio recording equipment had been set up on a worn, paint chipped metal table. A video camera on a tripod recorded from a corner of the room. Police Prosecutor Inspector Viera observed through a one-way mirror from an adjoining room.

Parsons gave up everything. Including Fredericks. Their association dated back to Parsons' days in New York. Fredericks had hired him for odd jobs over the years. As security during clandestine meetings. A currier to transport cash. Intimidation of business rivals. How and when Fredericks had contacted him and hired him on retainer, arranging transport to St. Vincent to be available during some delicate business deals he had going on. How he'd been contacted for the Mackee hit. A week after the raids. And the night of my first encounter with Dougan.

I repeated the question I'd asked in the cell about why he hadn't fled the island.

"Somet'ing must be happen to de usual network, cause Fredericks tell me he have to mek new arrangements to get me off de island. But I don't hear from him. And when I finally contact him, he vex. Somet'ing else must be happen 'cause he say somet'ing he must tek care of first dat more important. And anyway he might need me to do annoder job. More money. Plenty money."

When did he tell you this? I asked.

"A week ago. Last Wednesday." After my second encounter with Dougan, I thought. The day after I'd turned him.

"He say just a few more days and de job be done. He tell me to stay at de estate. Nobody find me dey. Den poliss raid de place."

In my office, Inspector Viera and I completed the particulars required to file charges against Fredericks, listing the evidence gathered so far against him, including Parson's statement.

"I'm confident we have enough evidence to convince de Chief Magistrate to call for a preliminary inquiry Commisshunah. And an indictment following the PI," Viera said.

"And no bail." I said. "Argue for remand in custody. Mr. Fredericks is charged with serious offenses and with his resources considered a flight risk."

While Viera hand delivered the particulars on Fredericks to the public prosecutor's office, I spent the next few hours reviewing the particulars charging Von Sachsen, Dougan, and the two Dougan thugs still in custody in Kingstown prison. Under no illusions Von Sachsen or Dougan would ever see the inside of a Kingstown courtroom. The particulars on Dougan noted he'd already fled the country. I had no doubt he'd be arrested in some other jurisdiction. If he survived that long.

My objective was to secure indictments and arrest warrants should either Von Sachsen or Dougan ever set foot in St. Vincent and the Grenadines again. Cecilia faxed copies of the particulars to the Foreign Ministry and Governor General's office.

Melanie and I spent the night at the Montrose embassy house. Our conversation dominated by her meetings and the preparations for the Swiss envoy's arrival in the morning. We fell asleep in the warm comfort of each other's arms.

In the morning, I dropped Melanie at Government House before heading to Kingstown. Public Prosecutor Chambers called just before lunch to report Fredericks, as expected, had used his influence to obtain an early appearance before the Chief Magistrate. Scheduled for the afternoon in the serious offenses court. He'd also retained Kingstown's premier defense attorney."

By day's end when I departed the office, no decision had been reached. Fredericks entered a 'not guilty' plea, as expected. The Chief Magistrate granted a request by Fredericks's attorney for a postponement. But rejected the argument for bail, remanding Frederick to custody in the Kingstown prison.

When I arrived at Government House to collect Melanie, Sir Christopher's aide rushed to the vehicle, informing me the Governor General wished a word. Sir Christopher met us

in a hallway outside the conference room, our arrival interrupting a quiet conversation between him and Melanie.

"If I might have a private moment, Consul," Sir Christopher said to Melanie.

"Certainly sir," casting a curious glance in my direction.

The aide escorted Melanie toward the front of the
building. Sir Christopher turned to a closed door off the
hallway, opened it. He gestured for me to enter. The room a
smaller receiving area. Elegant dark wood furniture polished
to a glossy sheen. Green Satin drapes framed large windows
offering views of the magnificent gardens.

"Commissioner," he began, "As we expected Von Sachsen will be leaving with the Swiss Consul. There's nothing
more St. Vincent and the Grenadines can do to hold him. And
we're of the opinion we don't need the headache anyway. The
other nations involved will of course continue to press their
claims with the Swiss. He's been declared a persona-non-grata
subject to arrest if he ever returns to St. Vincent and the
Grenadines. He will be released from Her Majesty's prison
this afternoon, scheduled to leave the country tomorrow. But
that is not the matter I wished to discuss with you."

He drew himself to his full height, his eyes bright and
compelling, holding me in his stare. "No matter the outcome
of the elections, you will be asked to stay on as Commissioner
of Police. Usually we stay out of these decisions of the elected
government, but in this case, we will let it be known you are
Her Majesty's preferred and only choice. We will make the
necessary arrangements."

His words hit me like a wave knocking me off my feet,
cart wheeling me upside down, forcing me to hold my breath,
and fight my way to the surface.

"Sir, I'm not sure…"

"I understand Commissioner," raising an arm to silence my stuttering response. "Of course the decision is entirely up to you. God knows you deserve a rest after all this. This country owes you a debt of gratitude they may never know. Over the last few months their faith and trust in our institutions have been shaken to the very foundations. It will be the over-riding priority of the next government to renew that faith and trust. Your police force, as an institution, and you in particular Commissioner, represent the most valuable tool we have in accomplishing that task."

His voice, his words, continued to penetrate my consciousness. But as if from for some far off distant place. My attention focused instead on the implications this unexpected turn might mean for my future. Particularly a future with Melanie.

"Politicians come and go Commissioner," the disembodied voice continued. "But as far as the security of this country is concerned, you have Her Majesty's complete confidence, gratitude, and trust. We need you for just a bit longer. Will you at least consider it Commissioner?"

Melanie perceptively aware of my distraction during the drive to the airport. She needed to report in person to the Ambassador. She planned to return to Bequia for the weekend. I hadn't mentioned the Governor General's conversation. Still undecided. I needed time to think the whole thing through.

Still nowhere close to a decision on Thursday. The day Von Sachsen departed St. Vincent in the company of the Swiss envoy on a chartered flight to St. Lucia, where his private jet still waited.

Or on Friday. I contemplated the office I'd spent the last ten years occupying. The parade of mentored, trusted colleagues. The battles fought and victories won. The tremendous progress we'd made. My thoughts stirred ambivalent emotions, presenting pros and cons to consider. I was eager to return home to Bequia, where I'd be able to talk through my dilemma with the two people closest to me. Anticipating Melanie's return later in the evening. I'd asked Jolene and Gage to meet me at the house before Melanie arrived.

Preparing to depart the office, my cell phone rang. An anxious moment when I heard Melanie's voice. I feared something had arisen to cancel our weekend.

Instead, "Just got some news I thought you should hear right away. Von Sachsen's disappeared," she said.

"What do you mean disappeared?"

"As in vanished. Gone. Perhaps dead."

"What the hell happened?"

"They were on their way to Europe in Von Sachsen's private Gulfstream. Somewhere over the Atlantic the pilots reported a mechanical problem and diverted to the Azores. While the aircraft was being checked out and the Swiss Envoy was in the terminal, the aircraft took off without the envoy. Last radar contact had it heading toward the South Atlantic, over the Cape Verdes. The pilots requested a revised flight plan to an island in the South China Sea. But the flight never made it there, or anywhere else anyone can find. An international search was launched. Still continuing. Only thing they've come up with so far was a faint HF radio call, more static than anything, which may have been a Mayday. Occurred around seventeen hundred Zulu. That'd be about an hour after the flight departed the Azores."

"And no trace of the plane since then," I asked in shocked amazement.

"None. Zilch."

"What do your guys think happened?"

"No one knows. But there're two prevailing theories. One, the plane went down in the South Atlantic. There were two converging storms along the flight path. Add to that what they believe is a Mayday call and there's reason to believe the plane may have gone down. They're searching the area. The more skeptical are subscribing to the second theory. That Von Sachsen orchestrated the whole thing so he could disappear. Fake his own death, disappear, and after a while everyone stops looking for him. He can't go back to Switzerland by the way. The Swiss are so pissed at him for leaving them with egg on their faces they might end up revoking his citizenship. The proponents of theory two point to the fact close to a billion dollars disappeared from a number of Von Sachsen's accounts around the same time he did."

"Disappeared?" A distressing itch surfaced in the forefront of my thoughts.

"They were tracking wire transfers from his accounts when a few ended up in firewalled accounts. By the time they contacted the banks involved the funds had been converted to bearer bonds and vanished. Anyway, I'll fax over a report. We still set for the weekend?" abruptly changing the subject.

I still hadn't told her about the Governor General's offer. I wanted to make a decision before telling her.

"You bet," I said. "Can't wait to have you back on Bequia."

"Me either. I'll call you if I get anything new. If not, I'll see you later."

The nagging itch in my brain acquired shape and form as I disconnected the call.

Gage!

An uncharacteristic calm settled over me when Gage and Jolene arrived at the house later that evening. I hadn't been angry, I realized, the emotion more akin to an unsettling disturbance. Tempered by a promise to myself to reserve judgment. To allow Gage the benefit of the doubt. Not that I had any doubt he'd somehow engineered the whole thing, but that he had a motive I'd be able to justify and abide. Even so, cold-blooded assassination didn't sit well with me. The second in less than a week. I needed to hear him admit it. And I needed to know why.

"I can't help but suspect this is your doing," I said, throwing the faxed report onto the coffee table. "Actually I'm pretty sure of it."

"What the hell are you talking about Mike? Jolene said. She picked up the report and scanned the pages. She turned to Gage, her eyes wide, her expression amused.

"You didn't," a spontaneous peal of laughter burst from her, shaking her entire body.

"And you," I exclaimed. More ferocity in my voice than I'd expected or intended. Incredulous at her sudden laughter. The sound appalling to my ears. "You I'm beginning to think I don't understand at all. You think this is funny? I want to know if this is your handiwork," I said turning on Gage. "And I want to know why."

Gage sat unconcerned in the armchair. Bland blameless brown eyes stared back at me.

"Calm down Mike," Jolene said, rising to stand next to me. Her hand a gentle pressure on my arm.

"How can you ask me to calm down?" staring into her eyes. "How can you be calm with this? Another man is dead. Assassinated in cold blood. Was this your plan all along?" An accusatory stare leveled at Gage. "Get him here so you could kill him. And what about the pilots on that plane? What about them? How do you justify that?" My agitation increasing.

I paused. Inhaled deeply. A calming breath. I didn't want to lose control and turn the conversation to useless recriminations, remembering why I'd asked them over in the first place.

"This isn't just about Gage," I said in a calmer voice. Jolene's perceptive eyes accurately discerned a different frustration vexing me.

"Mike. What's going on? What's wrong?"

"I just didn't need this distraction right now," I said, peering into the green pools of her eyes. "The Governor General asked me to stay on as Commissioner of Police. Says it's the preference of Her Majesty's Government, so accommodations will be made no matter who the next Prime Minister is."

"What? Mike, that's great news," her face lighting up in genuine pride and affection.

"Except for the past few weeks I've been mentally preparing to step down," I pleaded. "Convinced myself I was done and made decisions, took actions, based on that inevitability. Including my relationship with Melanie. Staying on as Commissioner will continue to place a barrier in our relationship. We'd been hoping to get past that after I was no longer Commissioner."

"What did Sir Christopher say?" she asked.

"A very convincing 'the country needs you' pitch. The hard sell. He's a better salesman and politician than anyone

Michael W Smart

gives him credit for. I've been wrestling with this thing all week and still can't decide what to do. And Melanie's arriving tonight. It's why I asked you to meet me here. You're the only two people I can talk to about it. And then this," I said pointing at the report, the strident tone resurfacing.

"Listen Mike. Have a seat," Jolene said, steering me toward the settee and pushing me down onto it. "One drink coming up," she said, heading toward the cabinet holding the liquor.

She returned holding a double shot of Jack Daniels neat. She handed me the drink and sat on the settee next to me.

"First things first," she said, lifting the report from the table. "Let me tell you what this is." Her gaze turned to Gage. "Stop me if I get anything wrong," she said. A conspiratorial smirk his only response.

"I don't know the details," Jolene said, her attention returning to me. "They don't really matter. What matters is, Von Sachsen is alive and whole and experiencing the less than luxurious accommodations he's accustomed to in some horrid prison. Probably in a country he perpetrated crimes against, where he'll spend the rest of his life in anonymous obscurity."

My eyes a blank stare, her words not registering initially. Dawning awareness as I noticed the twinkling amusement and shifting colors in hers, my incredulous mind attempting to visualize the image her words conveyed.

"I haven't read the report," she continued. "But I'd guess a sizable amount of Von Sachsen's money also disappeared," her eyebrows raised in a questioning tilt. "Am I right?"

I nodded.

"The money will find its way into a very special, very anonymous, widows and orphans fund," her fingers forming mock quotation marks around the words widows and orphans. She glanced at Gage. Gage's gaze steady on her, a subtle, loving, appreciative admiration in his eyes. His non-descript smirk firmly in place.

"Mike the money will be used to help people victimized by Von Sachsen," Jolene said, her gaze refocused on me. "And the best part," a Cheshire cat grin widening her eyes and lifting the smooth brown skin over her cheekbones. "The next time you take an overseas flight with your best bud here, who for all practical purposes owns his own private airline, it'll be in a very fancy.....what was it again?" She flipped the first two to three pages of the report. "Yeah here it is, a very fancy Gulfstream five-fifty flown by a tall white haired guy named Monk."

I turned to Gage. "You didn't?" I said, an unexpected, spontaneous smile blossoming across my face, producing another peal of laughter from Jolene beside me.

The smirking son-of-a-bitch winked at me.

About the author

A native New Yorker, Michael W. Smart spent eight years sailing around the Eastern Caribbean. Deadeye is the second novel novel in the Bequia Mysteries, which draws on his intimate knowledge of the islands, its people, and his sailing adventures in the Caribbean.

Thank you for reading my book. If you enjoyed it please take a moment to leave a review where you purchased it and spread the word to your friends. Thank you. Fair winds and following seas.

Experience the Bequia Mysteries in pictures

Visit the Bequia Mysteries Website

http://www.bequiamysteries com

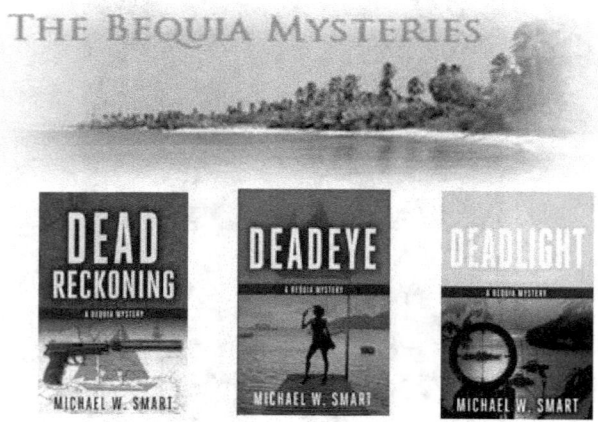

Subscribe to my newsletter and be among the first to receive news and updates on upcoming Bequia Mystery titles and all my other novels

A glossary of nautical and aviation terms used in the Bequia Mysteries

Abeam - A relative bearing perpendicular to the sides of a vessel or off the wingtip of an aircraft.

Abeam the Runway – Indicates the runway is directly perpendicular to the right or left side of the aircraft.

Aboard - On or in a vessel or aircraft.

Adrift - Afloat and unattached in any way to the shore or seabed, but not under way. Also refers to any gear not fastened down or put away properly.

Aft - Towards the stern (rear) of a vessel or aircraft.

Aground - Resting on or touching the sea bottom (usually involuntarily).

Ahead - Forward of a vessel's bow or aircraft's nose.

Ahoy - A shout to draw attention. Term used to hail another vessel.

Air Data Computer (ADC) – An instrument which displays information on the surrounding atmosphere and the aircraft's flight through it, such as pressure altitude, outside air temperature, airspeed, and aircraft attitude.

Aileron – A control surface attached to the outer trailing edge of an aircraft's wings allowing the aircraft to bank.

Alee - To leeward. Referring to the lee side (away from the wind) of a vessel.

Aloft- In the rigging of a sailing ship. Above the ship's uppermost solid structure; overhead or high above. An aircraft at altitude. High altitude winds.

Alongside - By the side of a vessel or pier.

Amidships (or midships) – At the middle of a vessel.

Anchor – A metal hook or plough-like object designed to dig into the seabed and hold a vessel in place. Attached to the vessel by a line or chain. A sea anchor is used to prevent or slow a vessel's drift at sea.

Anchor/Mooring buoy- A small floating buoy secured by a line to an anchor or mooring to indicate position of the anchor or mooring.

Anchor Chain - Chain connecting the vessel to the anchor. (See Ground Tackle)

Anchor Light – A white light displayed by a vessel at anchor usually from the tallest masthead. Anchor Rode - The anchor line, rope or cable connecting the anchor chain to the vessel. (See Ground Tackle)

Anchor Watch – An electronic instrument (GPS) or crewmen assigned to monitor the ship while anchored or moored, to ensure the anchor is holding and the vessel is not drifting. Most marine GPS units have an Anchor Watch Alarm capability.

Anchorage - A suitable area for a vessel to anchor. A harbor or port.

Anchors Aweigh – An anchor pulled clear of the bottom.

Aport - To port. Referring to the port (left) side of the vessel.

Apparent Wind - The combination of the true wind and the headwind caused by a vessel's forward motion.

Approach Charts – An aviation chart displaying instrument approach information such as holding fixes and procedures, approach and missed approach procedures, in addition to the plan and profile views of various instrument procedures. Other information on approach charts include obstacle location and clearance height; navigational aid frequencies and identifiers; transition altitudes and levels; airfield elevation; approach, tower, ground and ATIS radio frequencies; the location of outer, middle and inner markers; approach fixes and missed approach points; minimum safe descent altitudes; final approach course; decision height/altitude, and other airport information.

Approach Control – Air traffic controllers assigned to the approach segment of a given airport who provide directional guidance (vectors) to the final approach course.

Approach Segments - The parts of an instrument approach to an airport: arrival, initial approach, intermediate approach, final approach and missed approach segments.

Area traffic Control Center – Air traffic controllers responsible for large areas of enroute airspace, as opposed to approach, departure, tower and ground controllers.

Ashore - On the beach, shore, or land, as opposed to being aboard or on board).

Astarboard – Referring to the starboard (right) side of the vessel.

Astern – Referring to the stern (rear) of a vessel.

ATIS (Automated Terminal Information Service) - A continuous broadcast of recorded airport information updated hourly including active runways, arrival and departure procedures in use, weather, radio frequencies and other safety information.

ATR - A twin-engine turboprop regional transport aircraft used by many regional airlines in the Eastern Caribbean.

Attitude - An aircraft's position in flight relative to the three axes: pitch, roll and yaw.

Auto-flight System (AFS) - The combination of autopilot, autothrottle /autothrust, flight director, and autoland systems used to control flight through an aircraft's Flight Management System (FMS)

Autoland - An autopilot function which enables a "hands-off" automatic landing.

Autopilot (AP) - An automated computerized system which enables an aircraft to pilot itself.

Autothrottle (ATHR) - A computerized engine power control system enabling an aircraft to automatically adjust its power settings in different flight configurations.

Backstays - Lines or cables from the stern of a vessel to the masthead to support the masts. Part of the vessel's standing rigging.

Backtrack – To taxi on a runway in the opposite direction used for landing or takeoff.

Bank - A large area of elevated sea floor. The angle at which an aircraft is inclined about its longitudinal axis, used mostly during a turn.

Bareboat Charter – To hire or charter a vessel without a crew or provisions.

Base Leg - Part of the standard airport circuit an aircraft completes when landing. The aircraft parallels the runway on a downwind leg and turns to a base leg perpendicular to the runway before turning to the final landing leg. Referred to as "turning base".

Beam - The width of a vessel at the widest point, or a point alongside the vessel at the midpoint of its length (abeam).

Beam Ends - The sides of a vessel. "On her beam ends" may mean the vessel is literally on its side and possibly about to capsize. More often the phrase means the vessel is listing 45 degrees or more.

Beam Reach – A point of sail with the wind directly over the vessel's beam.

Bear down or bear away - Turn away from the wind. Also fall off.

Beat or Beating - Sailing as close as possible in the direction from which the wind is blowing.

Becalmed – A sailing vessel unable to sail due to lack of wind.

Belay - To secure a line around a fitting, cleat or belaying pin. Belaying Pins - Short movable iron bars or hard wood to which running rigging may be secured.

Berth (navigation) – Safe distance to be kept by a vessel from another vessel or an obstruction, hence the phrase, "to give a wide berth."

Berth (sleeping) - A bed or sleeping accommodation on a vessel.

Berth (vessel) - A dock, slip, or mooring area provided for vessels to tie up or moor.

Bilge - The compartment at the bottom of a vessel's interior hull. The lowest area of a vessel's interior.

Bimini Top - Canvas top covering the cockpit of a vessel, usually supported by a metal frame.

Binnacle - The stand on which the vessel's compass is mounted.

Bitt or Bitts - A post or posts mounted on the vessel's bow for fastening ropes or cables.

Bitter End - The last part or loose end of a rope, cable or chain.

Block - A pulley or set of pulleys.

Boarding Ladder - A portable flight of steps down a vessel's side or over the stern.

Boat-hook - A pole with a hook on the end, used to reach into the water to catch buoys or other floating objects.

Bobstay – A cable or chain which supports the bowsprit from below, counteracting the upward pull of the forestay.

Bollard - A stout vertical pillar on a dock or pier around which dock lines are made fast.

Booby hatch - A sliding hatch or cover.

Boom – A spar to which the foot (bottom) of a sail is attached.

Boom vang - A line which applies downward tension on a boom, countering the upward tension of the sail. The boom vang anchors the boom and allows control of the sail shape.

Boomkin (Bumpkin) - A spar, similar to a bowsprit, but projecting from the stern to extend the backstay or mizzen sheets.

Boot Stripe (Boot Top) - A painted stripe along a vessel's hull at the design waterline.

Bow - The front of a vessel.

Bowline - A type of knot, producing a strong loop of a fixed size.

Bowsprit - A spar projecting from the bow used to extend the forestay forward allowing the headsail to be set further forward.

Brightwork - Exposed varnished wood or polished metal on a vessel.

Britten Norman Islander – A twin engine light utility aircraft manufactured by the Britten-Norman company in the UK in the 1960's and still used by some regional airlines in the Caribbean for its STOL characteristics.

Broach - When a sailing vessel is forced by wind, sea, or too much sail into a sudden sharp turn which may lead to a capsize. The sudden change in direction is called broaching-to.

Broad Reach – A point of sail with the wind between the beam and stern, or 'on the quarter'.

Broken (BKN): A meteorological terms indicating cloud cover between 50% and 90% of the sky.

Bugs (Speed, Heading, Altitude) - Small plastic markers on analog instruments, or dials for digital displays, which are set at critical airspeeds, altitudes or headings during takeoff, climb and descent. When autopilot is engaged it automatically pursues the bug setting.

Bulkhead - An upright, watertight, load-bearing wall within the hull of a vessel or separating compartments on an aircraft.

Bulwark - The extension of the vessel's side above deck level.

Buoy - A floating object of defined shape and color used as an aid to navigation. A floating object indicating the position of an anchor or mooring.

Burgee - A small flag, typically triangular, flown from the masthead to indicate yacht-club membership.

Cabin - An enclosed room inside a vessel or aircraft.

Cabin Altitude (Pressure) - the artificially maintained atmospheric pressure inside an aircraft during high altitude flight, approximately 6,000- 8,000 feet inside the cabin.

Cabin Sole - The cabin floor, also referred to as an interior or lower deck.

Cable - A thick rope or bundle of spun wire.

Calibrated Airspeed (CAS) - The indicated airspeed (IAS) of an aircraft corrected for airspeed instrument errors.

Call-out – Verbal readout of flight data by a co-pilot or automated synthetic voice.

Capsize - When a vessel lists too far and rolls over, exposing the keel, often resulting in sinking.

Cardinal Points - Refers to the four main points of the compass: north, south, east and west.

Careening - Tilting a ship on its side, usually when beached, to clean or repair the hull below the water line.

CAT III Conditions - When visibility is very poor and aircraft require ILS automation for take-off and landing.

CAT IIIC - The crew, aircraft and airport are qualified and equipped to land in CAT III Conditions of 0 feet longitudinal visibility and a Decision Height of 0 feet.

Catamaran - A vessel with two hulls.

CAVOK - Ceiling and Visibility OK, spoken by pilots as "CAV-O-KAY".

Chafing - Wear on a line or sail caused by constant rubbing against another surface.

Chafing Gear - Material applied to a line or spar to prevent or reduce chafing.

Chain Locker - A space in the forward part of the ship containing the anchor chain and rode, typically behind the bow in front of the foremost bulkhead.

Checklist - A series of checks which are performed and confirmed during specific phases of a flight.

Chine - The angle formed where the sides and bottom of a vessel join. Soft chine is when the two surfaces join at a shallow angle, and hard chine is when they join at a steep angle.

Chocks - Rubber or wooden blocks placed against an aircraft's tires to prevent the aircraft from rolling while parked.

Circuit Breaker - An electrical safety device on vessels and aircraft which opens a circuit in case of current overload. On vessels the CB panel is located with or in close proximity to the main electrical panel. In large jet aircraft circuit breakers are located on the cockpit overhead panel, and at the bottom of the instrument panel on smaller aircraft like Mike Daniel's Piper Seneca.

Clean Up- To retract an aircraft's flaps, gear, slats and other exterior devices which may affect aerodynamics and speed.

Clew - The forward corner of a sail attached to the deck or forward end of a boom.

Close Aboard - In close proximity to another vessel.

Close-hauled – A vessel sailing as close to the wind as possible, referred to as beating.

Close Reach – A point of sail with the wind between the bow and beam.

Clear (CLR) – A meteorological term indicating a clear sky with no clouds.

Clearance (Cleared) - Authorization from air traffic control to proceed as requested or instructed.

Coach- roof – A cabin roof higher than the main deck.

Coaming - The edge of a hatch, cockpit or skylight raised above the deck to keep out water.

Cockpit - The area on deck containing helm and other vessel controls. Compartment from which a pilot operates an aircraft.

Companionway - A ladder leading from an entrance hatch to cabins below deck.

Compass – Navigational instrument indicating the direction of the vessel in relation to the Earth's geographical or magnetic poles.

Control Tower - An air traffic control facility located at an airport.

Controlled Airspace - Airspace of defined dimensions within which air traffic control is exercised and mandatory for aircraft flying through it.

Crabbing - Flying with drift due to crosswind.

Crossfeed - A valve which allows an aircraft's engines to obtain fuel from any of the available fuel tanks. A crossfeed also allows transfer of fuel from one tank to another.

Crosswind - A wind blowing at an angle to an aircraft's flight path, not necessarily perpendicular, which is a direct crosswind.

Dash 8 - A twin engine turboprop regional transport aircraft manufactured by De Havilland Canada (now Bombardier).

Davit – A paired set of cranes used to hoist, lower and hold a dinghy in place, usually affixed to the stern of a sailing vessel.

Dead Ahead - Directly ahead in front of the vessel.

Dead In The Water - Not moving; used only when a vessel is afloat and neither tied up nor anchored.

Dead Reckoning – To navigate without the aid of precision instruments or celestial observation where current position is estimated based on time and distance travelled from a know fix.

Deadeye - A wood block with holes (but no pulleys) which is spliced to a shroud. Used to adjust the tension in the standing rigging of a sailing vessel by lacing a lanyard from the deck through the holes. Performs the same job as a turnbuckle.

Deadlight - A strong shutter fitted over a porthole or other opening and closed in bad weather.

Deadrise - The design angle between the keel and vertical rise of the hull as measured from the horizontal.

Deadwood – The structural reinforcement of the aft portion of a vessel's hull between the keel and sternpost.

Decision Altitude (DA) - The altitude at which a pilot must decide to land or go around.

Decision Height (DH) - The height above the ground as displayed on a radio altimeter at which a pilot must decide to land or go around.

Deck - The top surface of a vessel. An interior floor below the top deck (See Cabin sole).

Deck Hand - A person (crew) performing tasks which aid in sailing and maintenance of the vessel.

Decks Awash – When the deck of a vessel is partially or wholly submerged.

Dinghy - A small inflatable or rigid hull boat carried or towed as a transport tender for the vessel. May be rowed, powered by an outboard motor, and some types can be rigged for sailing.

Displacement – The volume (weight) of water displaced by a vessel's immersed hull. Exactly equivalent to the vessel's weight.

Displacement hull - A hull designed to travel through the water, rather than planning over it.

Distance Measuring Equipment (DME) - A radio transmitter located on the ground which provides distance information for aircraft. Though still used its been mostly replaced by GPS.

Dock – A pier or wharf which a vessel can tie up to. Also maneuvering a vessel against a pier or wharf to tie up.

Dockyard - A facility where ships or boats are built and repaired. Dockyard is usually associated with vessel mainten-ance and repairs, while shipyard is usually associated with vessel construction.

Dodger - A hood with a clear plastic section to prevent wind and spray from entering the cockpit. Functions like a windshield.

Double Ender – A boat with its stern shaped like the bow enabling it to move forward or backward equally well.

Downwind Leg – Part of the standard airport circuit an aircraft completes when landing. On the downwind leg the aircraft parallels the runway before turning onto the base leg perpendicular to the runway.

Draft -The depth of a vessel's keel below the waterline.

EGT (Exhaust Gas Temperature) - Indicated by a gauge in the cockpit. EGT is a principal engine performance parameter monitored during flight.

Elevator – A part of an aircraft's horizontal tail section which controls pitch.

Empennage - the tail section of an aircraft, consisting of the fin, tailplane or elevator, and the part of the fuselage to which they are attached.

Endurance - The time an aircraft can fly without refueling.

Engine Room – The space containing the vessel's engine, batteries and other machinery like a generator.

Engine Run-up - Operating an aircraft's engine on the ground over its full power range. Usually conducted following repair and prior to takeoff.

Ensign - The principal flag or banner flown at a vessel's stern to indicate its nationality.

ETOPS (Extended Twin Operations) - The term for long distance twin-engine operation over the ocean, desert or arctic regions where there is no suitable airport within 60 minutes of flight in case of an emergency. Referred to by pilots as "Engines Turning Or Passengers Swimming".

Fairlead - A ring, hook or other device used to keep a line or chain running in the correct direction or to prevent it chafing or fouling.

Fall- The part of the tackle or line a crewman hauls on.

Fall Off - To steer away from the direction of the wind. Also to bear away, bear off or put the head down. The opposite of pointing up or heading up.

Fast – Secure, as in tied or held securely.

Fathom – A unit of length equal to 6 feet (1.8 m). Particularly used to measure depth.

Feet Per Minute (FPM) - A unit of measurement indicating an aircraft's rate of climb or descent.

Fender - An air or foam filled bumper used to protect the sides of a vessel from rubbing against a dock or another vessel tied alongside. Used tires are most often used on locally owned boats in the Grenadines.

Fetch - The distance across water the wind or waves have traveled. Also to reach a navigational mark without having to tack.

Final Approach Fix (FAF) – A navigational reference point from which an aircraft begins its final approach to an airport. The beginning of the final approach segment.

Final Leg (On Final) – Part of the standard airport circuit an aircraft completes when landing. The aircraft turns onto the final leg inbound for landing from the base leg, referred to as "turning final" or "on final".

Fitting-out – The interior construction of a vessel after the hull has been completed and launched.

Fix - A radio transmitted beacon or GPS coordinates indicating an aircraft is in a specified position, either an enroute waypoint, or a point from which to begin an initial approach (IAF) or final approach (FAF).

Fixed Base Operator (FBO) - An airport operator serving General Aviation aircraft.

Flare – A nose-up pitch movement to slow an aircraft just prior to touchdown.

Flight Deck - Compartment from which the crew operates an aircraft. Also cockpit, flight compartment, or control cabin.

Flight Plan - Specified information relating to the whole or portion of an intended flight.

Flight Management System (FMS) – An onboard computerized system using preprogrammed route data and flight instrument data to interface with an aircraft's Automatic Flight Control System (AFCS) and Electronic Flight Instrument System (EFIS) allowing automated flight.

Fluke - The wedge-shaped part of an anchor's arms which dig into the sea bottom.

Following Sea – Waves or tide moving in the same direction as the vessel.

Foot – The lower edge of a sail. The bottom of a mast.

Fore/forward - Towards the bow (front) of the vessel.

Forecastle – The area (usually a cabin or locker) at the forward end of the vessel just aft of the bow.

Forefoot - The lower part of the stem (bow) of the vessel.

Foresail - The headsail on a sloop. The sail directly ahead of the mainsail on a schooner.

Forestays – Lines or cables from the bow or bowsprit of the vessel to the masthead to support the mast. Part of the vessel's 'standing' rigging.

Frame - A transverse structural member which provides the hull's shape and strength.

Freeboard - The height of a ship's hull measured from the waterline to the highest gunwale.

Furl - To roll or gather a sail against its mast or spar.

Fuselage - The main body of an aircraft excluding wings, tail, landing gear, etc.

G-IV – A twin engine jet aircraft designed and built by Gulfstream Aerospace for private and business use.

G-V – Larger and improved version of the G-IV with a longer range.

Gaff – On a Gaff rigged vessel the upper spars (a short boom) which hoists and stretches the upper edge of the four sided Gaff sail.

Gaff Rigged – A vessel rigged to use a four-sided fore-and-aft sail with the sail's upper edge supported by a spar or gaff which extends aft from the mast.

Galley - The kitchen on a vessel or aircraft.

Gear - The landing and ground operation apparatus on an aircraft, including the wheels, tires, struts and other mechanisms connected to them.

General Aviation Pilot - A pilot who flies for pleasure, business or hire.

General Aviation Terminal – Airport terminal serving private, business and leisure aircraft.

Genoa (Genny or Jib) - A large triangular sail flown at the front of the vessel from the forestay. Referred to as the pulling sail since it functions in the same manner as an airplane wing.

Gibe or Gybe - To change from one tack to the other by turning a sailing vessel's stern rather than its bow through the wind. Also known by the historical term 'wearing' or 'to wear'.

Glareshield – A cockpit panel above the main instrument panels and below the windshield in an aircraft to protect the instruments and prevent reflected glare.

Glide Path - The flight path of an aircraft during landing approach to a runway.

Glideslope - A cockpit instrument depicting an aircraft's glide path during an instrument landing.

Global Positioning System (GPS)- A satellite based navigation system providing continuous worldwide coverage of position and time on the ground, at sea, and in the air.

Global Navigation Satellite System (GNSS) - A GPS based instrument Landing System which combines satellite and local data to provide accurate navigational positioning for landing.

Go-around - Pulling up and flying to a hold position or reentering the airport traffic pattern after discontinuing an approach to landing.

Grounding - When a vessel while afloat touches the seabed or goes 'aground'. A vessel hard aground is stuck in the sea floor.

Ground effect - the increased lift an aircraft's wings generate close to the ground. When landing ground effect may cause the aircraft to 'float' and delay touchdown. On takeoff ground effect allows level flight just above the ground in order to accelerate to a safe climb airspeed. Especially useful when taking off from a short runway.

Ground Tackle - All the parts of the anchor system including the anchor, anchor chain, anchor rode and shackles.

Gunwale – The top edge of the hull or Bulwark.

Halyard - A line used to raise a sail. Also refers to any line used to raise any object aloft, like a flag, pennant or spar.

Hangar – Building for garaging aircraft on the ground.

Hank - A fastener attached to the luff of the headsail which then attaches the headsail to the forestay. The hanks slides along the forestay as the headsail is raised.

Hatch - An opening or entrance in a vessel's deck providing access to the vessel's interior. The cover or door to the opening is also called a hatch.

Hauling Wind - Pointing the vessel in the direction of the wind.

Hawsepipe, Hawsehole or Hawse – A shaft or hole in the side of a vessel's bow, bulwark or stern through which the anchor chain or dock lines pass.

Haze - Fine dust particles causing the sky to appear unclear and reducing visibility.

Head - The forwardmost or uppermost part of a vessel. The forwardmost or uppermost part of any individual part of the vessel, e.g., the masthead, beakhead, stemhead, etc. The top corner of a triangular sail. The toilet on a vessel.

Heading – The direction in which a vessel is sailing or an aircraft is flying as indicated on a magnetic or electronic compass, and distinct from the directional track of the vessel or aircraft.

Header - A change in wind direction which forces the helmsman to steer further away from the current course or requiring a tack. The opposite of a lift.

Headsail - Any sail flown in front of the most forward mast. Usually attached to the forestay.

Head Sea – A sea in which the waves are directly opposing the forward progress of the vessel.

Headwind - A wind blowing in a direction opposite to an aircraft's flight path and affecting the aircraft's speed over the ground (SOG). The opposite of a tailwind.

Heave - A vessel's up-and-down (pitching) motion in a seaway.

Heel/Heeling - The lean of a sailing vessel onto its side caused by the wind's force on the sails. Also measured by the angle the deck is tilted sideways from horizontal.

Helm – The Vessel's steering mechanism connecting the wheel in the cockpit to the rudder.

High Frequency (HF) – Radio frequencies in the 3 to 30 MHz range used for aeronautical and marine communication beyond VHF (Very High Frequency) range. HF is not affected by the line of sight limitations of VHF, but are susceptible to atmospheric conditions including ionization by solar flares.

High Intensity Runway Lighting (HIRL) - Airport runway lighting where the brightness can be adjusted by the Tower depending on atmospheric conditions and time of day.

Hitch - A knot used to tie a rope or line to a fixed object.

Hold - An interior space in a vessel used for storing cargo. A circular flight pattern around a specified fix flown by an aircraft waiting to descend and land (Holding Pattern).

Horizontal stabilizer – The horizontal tail section of an aircraft's empennage which articulates up and down to control the aircraft's pitch. Also referred to as the tailplane or elevator. It can be trimmed by a control in the cockpit to reduce the aerodynamic pressure on the tail which the pilot feels as resistance on the control yolk.

Hounds - Attachments on the masts for connecting stays and shrouds and to support topmasts.

Hull - The shell and framework of the flotation part of a vessel.

Hypoxia - An inadequate amount of oxygen reaching the brain which occurs in an unpressurized aircraft cabin above 10,000 feet, requiring the use of supplemental oxygen.

Indicated Airspeed (IAS) - The relative speed of an aircraft through the surrounding air as displayed on an airspeed indicator in the cockpit.

Inertial Navigation System (INS) - A self-contained computerized navigation system using laser gyroscopes and accelerometers to sense an aircraft's movement and velocity around all three axis and calculate its precise position without external references.

In Irons - When the bow of a sailboat is pointed directly into the wind and the vessel is unable to maneuver.

Initial Approach Fix (IAF) - The point from which the initial segment of an ILS approach begins.

Iron wind/Iron Jenny – Using a sailing vessel's engine.

Instrument Approach Procedure (IAP) - The procedure for a specified ILS approach at an airport.

Instrument Landing System (ILS) - A system using radio signals to guide an aircraft down to the runway in poor weather conditions. The system depicts a Localizer for horizontal guidance and a Glide Sloop for vertical guidance on cockpit instruments.

Instrument Meteorological Conditions (IMC) - Weather conditions (cloud, fog, rain etc.) making it impossible to fly by outside visual references (VMC). The pilot has to fly solely by reference to the aircraft's instruments (IFR).

Jenny (Genoa or Jib) - A triangular headsail flown at the front of the vessel.

Jeppesen Charts – Aviation charts manufactured by the Jeppesen Sanderson Company used by pilots worldwide.

Jib (Genoa) - A triangular headsail flown at the front of the vessel.

Keel - The central structural foundation of a vessel's hull. The vessel's 'backbone'.

Ketch - A two-masted sailboat with the aft mast (the mizzen) shorter than the main mast and stepped (mounted) closer to the stern.

Knot - A unit of speed: 1 nautical mile (1.8520 km; 1.1508 mi) per hour.

Landing Distance Available (LDA) - The actual length of runway which can be used for landing and roll-out.

Lanyard - A rope or line which ties something off or from which something is suspended.

Lay – The direction (relative bearing) of a designated mark in relation to a vessel's course.

Lazarette - A small stowage locker on deck, usually toward the aft end of a vessel. Also seat lockers in the cockpit.

Leading Edge - The forward edge of an aircraft's wing, engine blades, tail fin and stabilizers.

Lee - The side of a vessel or island away from the wind.

Lee Shore - A shore downwind (to the lee) of a vessel. A vessel which cannot sail well to windward risks being blown onto a lee shore and grounded or smashed against a rocky coast.

Leech - The aft or trailing edge of a sail. The leeward edge of a spinnaker.

Leeward - In the opposite direction from which the wind is blowing.

Leeway - The amount a vessel is blown sideways by the wind.

Length Overall (LOA) - The maximum length of a vessel's hull measured parallel to the waterline, including any over-hanging ends which extend beyond the bow and stern. In sailing vessels this might include the bowsprit, boomkin, or stern swim platform.

Liferaft - An inflatable, covered raft, used in the event of a vessel being abandoned.

Lift – A change in wind direction enabling a close hauled sailboat to steer up from its current course to a more favorable one. The opposite of a header.

Line - The nautical term for the cordage or ropes used on a vessel. A line may have a specific name specifying its use, such as main or jib halyards, or main and jib sheets.

Luff - The forward edge of a sail.

Luffing - When a sailing vessel is steered too close to the wind causing insufficiently filled sails to flap. The luff of the sail begins to flap first.

Mach Number – Commonly used to express a jet aircraft's airspeed, measured as a ratio to the speed of sound.

Main Deck - The uppermost continuous deck extending from bow to stern.

Mainmast - The tallest mast on the vessel on which the mainsail is hoisted.

Mainsheet (See Sheets) – A tackle line attacked to the main boom used to controls the trim of the mainsail by controlling the angle of the boom. The downward tension on this line also affects the shape of the mainsail, sometimes aided by a boom vang.

Making Way - A vessel moving under its own power.

Marconi Rig – A fore-and-aft sail rig using triangular sails, as opposed to square rigged or gaff rigged. Also call the Bermuda Rig.

Marlinspike - A tool used in rope work such as unlaying rope for splicing, untying knots, or forming a makeshift handle.

Mast - A vertical pole on a sailing vessel which supports sails.

Maximum Landing Weight - The weight at which specific aircraft can land without risking structural damage.

Maximum Takeoff Weight - The weight at which specific aircraft can take off without risking takeoff and climb performance.

METAR - A weather report from an airport or other ground weather station used by pilots during flight planning, enroute, and approaching the destination.

Minimum Approach Speed - The minimum speed at which a specific aircraft can safely maintain flight in the approach to landing configuration (flaps, slats and gear extended).

Minimum Descent Altitude (MDA) - The altitude in the terminal area (around an airport) below which no aircraft must descend unless it is on its approach path. At some airports the MDA may be different in different directions depending on terrain.

Missed Approach - When a aircraft aborts its landing approach usually due to low visibility or a runway obstacle and performs a go around.

Nautical Mile - A unit of distance corresponding to one minute of arc of latitude. 1,852 meters; approximately 6,076 feet; 1.1508 mile.

Navigation Display (ND) - In an aircraft cockpit equipped with LCD panel screens navigational data is digitally displayed on a screen in front of the pilot next to the Primary Flight Display (PFD) screen.

Navigation Lights – Required on marine vessels and aircraft to avoid collision by indicating position, relative angle and direction of travel. The location and type of lighting is specified by international law to include lights visible on both sides of a vessel or aircraft - red on the port side or wingtip, green on the starboard side or wingtip; and a white light visible from the rear of the vessel or aircraft. Aircraft also use high intensity flashing or rotating strobe lights.

NOTAM (Notice to Airmen) - A printout providing information regarding changes to aeronautical facilities, services, procedures or hazards used during flight planning.

Outhaul - A line used to tension the foot of a sail along the boom.

Outer Marker – A radio beacon used for ILS approaches positioned 4 to 7 miles from the runway threshold and aligned with the runway centerline. The outermost of three beacons including a middle marker and inner marker.

Painter - A rope attached to the bow of a dinghy used for towing or tethering the dinghy.

Phosphorescence – A bright blue-green luminosity in a vessel's wake seen at night, caused by the bioluminescence of marine organisms disturbed by the vessel's passage.

Pilot Flying (PF) - The pilot actually doing the hands-on flying of the aircraft at a given moment.

Pilot In Command - The pilot in command of the aircraft, not necessarily the pilot flying.

Pilot Report (PIREP) – Updates of weather or other flight conditions provided by pilots when they encounter them enroute or during approach and landing.

Pitch - A vessel's motion in a seaway in which the bow and stern rise and fall repetitively (See heave). The nose up or down attitude of an aircraft in flight.

Plane - To skim over the water at high speed rather than push through it.

Point Up - To change the direction of a sailboat so it is heading more upwind. To steer toward windward. Also called heading up. The opposite of falling off.

Points Of Sail - The course sailed in relation to wind direction. Close hauled (sailing as close into the wind as possible); Close reach (wind between the bow and beam); Beam reach (wind on the beam and the vessel perpendicular to the wind); Broad reach (wind on the quarter between the beam and stern); Running, sailing downwind with the wind behind.

Port - The left side of a vessel or aircraft when facing forward.

Port Tack – Sailing with the wind blowing from the port side of the vessel. Must give way to vessels on starboard tack.

Porthole or port - An opening or window in a vessel's side for admitting light and air, fitted with thick glass, and often a hinged metal cover.

Precision Approach Path Indicator (PAPI) - A series of flashing lights leading to the runway threshold providing pilots with a visual approach reference.

Radio Management Panel (RMP) - A control panel located on the center pedestal between the two pilot seats where the pilots tune and manage the aircraft's communications radios including VHF, HF and satellite up and down links. On smaller general aviation aircraft like Mike Daniels'

Piper Seneca the radios are usually located in the center of the instrument panel.

Reaching – Any point of sail from about 60° to about 160° off the wind including close reaching, beam reaching and broad reaching.

Reefing - Temporarily reducing sail area in strong or gusty wind conditions by reducing the amount of exposed sail. Mainsails usually have reef points constructed into them.

Regatta - A series of sailboat races.

Rigging - The system of masts and lines on ships and sailing vessels.

Rode - The anchor line, rope or cable connecting the anchor chain to the vessel. Also Anchor Rode.

Roll - A vessel's motion in a seaway in which it rolls from side to side about the fore-aft/longitudinal axis. An aircraft in a bank about its longitudinal axis.

Rollout - An aircraft's ground roll along the runway after landing. A return to level flight after banking.

Rudder - A steering device attached at or near the aft end of a vessel controlled by a tiller or wheel. On an aircraft the rudder is attached to the trailing edge of the vertical tailfin and controlled by foot pedals in the cockpit.

Run Up – An engine test at full power prior to takeoff.

Running Before The Wind or Running – Sailing with the wind behind the vessel. (See Points of sail).

Running rigging – The lines and tackles used to manipulate sails, spars, etc. in order to control the movement of as sailing vessel.

Runway - The paved surface of an airport designed for aircraft take-offs and landings. Runways are designated by the compass direction in which they are aligned.

Runway Edge Lighting - White lights, usually on stalks, on both sides of the runway.

Sail – A dacron or nylon fabric (formally canvas) designed and arranged so it causes the wind to drive a sailing vessel along. Sails are attached and manipulated by a combination of masts, spars (booms), and ropes (running rigging).

Sampson Post- A strong vertical post near the bow of a vessel used to support a vessel's anchor windlass and the heel (back end) of a vessel's bowsprit.

Scattered (SCT) - A meteorological terms indicating clouds distributed irregularly in the sky.

Schooner - A type of sailing vessel characterized by two or more masts with the mainmast being the tallest.

Scuppers - Openings in a vessel's bulwarks to allow seawater to drain from the deck.

Seacock - A valve fitted through the vessel's hull.

Sea Shanty – Song about sailors or the sea.

Shackle - A metal U-shaped device secured with a clevis pin or bolt across the opening used to connect rigging to an object or one piece of rigging to another.

Sheer - The curve of a vessel's sides.

Sheet - A rope attached to a boom or clew of a sail used to control the sail's trim.

Shoal - Shallow water.

Shrouds - Ropes or cables which hold and support a mast from the sides. Part of a sailing vessel's standing rigging.

Sloop – A sailing vessel with a single mast for a mainsail and headsail.

Solo – The first flight of a student pilot unaccompanied by an instructor, usually confined to the traffic pattern.

Speed Over Ground (SOG)- Speed of a vessel over the ground irrespective of its speed through the water. The speed of an aircraft over the ground irrespective of its airspeed. A vessel's speed over the ground is affected by tidal currents, while an aircraft's speed over the ground is affected by head-winds, crosswinds and tailwinds.

Speed Through The Water (STW) - Speed of a vessel through the water as measured by a speedometer log attached to the hull below the waterline. While STW indicates a vessel's performance, SOG is the relevant measure used for navigation.

Spar (Boom) – A wood or aluminum pole used to support rigging and sails.

Spinnaker – A large light fabric sail hoisted in front of the vessel when sailing downwind.

Spreader - A short spar positioned on both sides of a mast to deflect (spread) the shrouds allowing greater support of the mast.

Stall – A sailing vessel in irons. The position of an aircraft's wings relative to the surrounding air (angle of attack) at which lift is no longer generated.

Stanchion - Vertical posts spaced along a deck's edge to support a bulwark, rail or lifelines.

Standing Rigging – The combination of stays, shrouds, attachments and tensioners used to support masts and spars.

Starboard - The right side of a vessel or aircraft when facing forward.

Starboard tack - When sailing with the wind coming from the starboard side of the vessel. Has right of way over boats on port tack.

Stay – A line or cable running forward (forestay) and aft (backstay) from a mast to the hull to support the mast.

Staysail – A small triangular sail behind the jib or headsail attached to an inner forestay (between the head forestay and mast). On large vessels the foot of the staysail is usually attached to a staysail boom.

Steerage - The helm's effect on the vessel's steering.

Steerageway - The minimum speed at which a vessel will answer the helm, below which the vessel cannot be steered.

Stem (Stempost)– The upward extension of a vessel's keel at the forward end of the vessel, to which the bow is attached.

Stern (Sternpost) – The upward extension of a vessel's keel at the rear end of the vessel, to which the transom is attached.

Stick Shaker - An aircraft's stall warning system which when triggered by angle of attack sensors causes the stick or control column to vibrate. In small aircraft like Mike Daniels' Piper Seneca a stall warning horn sounds.

STOL – Short takeoff and landing.

Stow - To store or to put away personal effects, tackle, gear or cargo.

Straight-in - Approaching an airport's runway without executing any legs of the airport's traffic pattern. Also referred to as a long final.

Squawk - An identifier code which identifies transponder equipped aircraft on ATC radar screens.

Squawk Sheet - A list of maintenance items to be performed on an aircraft indicated in the aircraft's logbook.

Standard Pressure Setting - The 29.92 inch Hg altimeter setting universally used above the 29,000 feet transition level.

Superstructure - The parts of the vessel which project above the main deck not including masts.

Tacking – Turning the vessel's bow through the wind to bring the wind onto the opposite side of the vessel. Such a zig-zagging course is necessary to sail a vessel toward a mark in the direction from which the wind is blowing.

Tackle – The combination of rope passed through a pulley (block) or set of pulleys to provide mechanical leverage for hoisting, lowering or applying tension. (See also Ground Tackle).

Tailwind - Wind blowing in the same direction as the aircraft's direction of travel. The opposite of headwind.

Take-off Roll - The process of accelerating down the runway in order to take off.

Tarmac – Commonly used to refer to an airport's paved surfaces including runways, taxiways, terminal and other parking ramps. Short for tarmacadam, the name of the surfacing material.

Taxiway - Paved roadways for aircraft to move about an airport. Indicated by blue lights along the sides and named for letters of the alphabet pronounced phonetically.

Tell-tale (Tell-tail) - A light piece of string, yarn, or plastic attached to a stay or a shroud to indicate the apparent wind direction. Also sometimes attached to the body and/or leech of a sail to indicate air flow over the sail's surface.

Terminal Aerodrome Forecasts (TAFs) – Weather information similar to METARs but providing forecast information for an airport. Used by pilots during flight planning.

Terminal Control Area (TCA) – Controlled airspace around an airport used for departures and arrivals.

Threshold - The beginning of a runway usually marked by broad white stripes.

Thrust - The propulsive force generated by an aircraft engine; the other three forces which act on an aircraft are lift, weight and drag. The force generated by wind on a vessel's sails.

Thwart - A bench seat across the width of an open boat, like a dinghy.

Topping Lift – A line attached from the masthead to the aft end of a boom to control the boom angle and therefore the shape of the sail.

Topsides - The part of the hull between the waterline and the deck.

Touch and Go - A pilot training exercise in which pilots practice approaches and touch downs on a runway without rolling to a stop, instead taking off again for another circuit in the traffic pattern. This 'touch and go' or 'circuit and bump' is repeated several time in a single practice session.

Touchdown Speed - The airspeed at which the aircraft makes contact with the ground on landing.

Touchdown Target – A point on the runway a pilot aims for during the landing approach.

To Weather - The side of a vessel exposed to the wind. Turning toward the wind.

Track – The actual directional path (course) of a vessel or aircraft due to the effects of leeway, tidal currents or crosswinds.

Transom – The aft (rear) section at the stern of a vessel. May be vertical, or raked (sloped). Traffic Advisory – An air traffic control message advising a pilot of the presence of traffic in their vicinity. An advisory does not require pilot action but allows the pilot to visually locate and observe the traffic.

Traffic Pattern - A predefined flight circuit of the runway intended for landing consisting of downwind, base and final legs.

Trailing Edge - The rear edge of a wing, stabilizer or propeller blade on an aircraft. A sail's leech.

Transponder - A radio which transmits a coded response to identify aircraft on ATC radar. A mode C transponder also provides the aircraft's altitude.

Trim - Adjustments made to sails in relation to wind direction to maximize their efficiency. Adjustment of an aircraft's control surfaces to minimize control pressure on the yolk.

Turbo-Prop – an aircraft with propellers driven by turbine (jet) engines.

Underway - A vessel moving under control that is neither anchored, moored, tied up, aground nor adrift.

Vertical Speed Indicator (VSI) – A cockpit instrument which displays an aircraft's vertical speed, (rate of climb or descent) in feet per minute.

VHF- A marine and aviation radio using the very high frequency band.

Visual Approach Slope Indicator (VASI) – A system of 3 lights at the side of a runway which provide a visual descent/glide sloop when landing.

Visual Flight Rules (VFR) – Flight by visual references outside the aircraft in visual meteorological conditions (VMC). As opposed to Instrument Flight Rules (IFR) when flying by instruments in instrument meteorological conditions (IMC).

VOR – A ground based omnidirectional radio transmitter used for aircraft navigation. The intersection of two VOR radials provides the aircraft's position.

Wake – The trail behind a vessel caused by its passage through the water. The turbulent downdraft caused by the passage of a large aircraft through the air. Also referred to as wake turbulence or wake vortex.

Walkaround – An external inspection and check of an aircraft prior to flight.

Weatherly - A vessel which is easily sailed and maneuvered and makes little leeway when sailing to windward.

Weather helm – The tendency of a sailing vessel's bow to swing to windward.

Weigh Anchor – To pull up an anchor prior to sailing.

Weight and Balance – A document recording an aircraft manufacturer's approved weight distribution and center of gravity (CG) for that type aircraft. Required to be kept aboard the aircraft at all times. A pilot calculates weight and centre of gravity when loading the aircraft to ensure it meets the aircraft's weight and balance parameters. An overweight and out of CG aircraft may not get off the ground, and even if it does, it may be impossible to handle in the air.

Whaleboat (Bequia) – A narrow open boat pointed at both ends (double-ended) enabling it to move forwards or backwards equally well.

Whaler (Bequia) – A fisherman specializing in catching whales.

Wick Static Discharger - Located on the trailing edges of an aircraft's wings to discharge static electrical built up in the airframe during flight.

Winds Aloft – Forecasts of winds at altitudes above 3,000 feet. Upper level wind forecasts provide information on winds up to 39,000 feet for the polar jet streams and at higher altitudes for the subtropical jet streams.

Windward - In the direction the wind is blowing from.

Wing on Wing- A method of sailing downwind with the mainsail extended on one side and the Genoa extended on the opposite side.

Yaw – The tendency of a vessel's bow to swing off course in a seaway. The turn of an aircraft's nose left or right due to rudder input. The adverse tendency of an aircraft's nose to swing left or right, controlled by rudder input or a yaw damper.

Yoke – The control wheel and column in an aircraft cockpit.

Zulu – Used in marine and aviation radiotelephony for Universal Coordinated Time (UTC), also Greenwich Mean Time (GMT).